DEADLY RESPECT

Xizor almost felt sorry for the bounty hunter. Pity was not an emotion Xizor had ever experienced. Whether he was operating on behalf of Emperor Palpatine or secretly advancing the Black Sun's criminal agenda, Xizor manipulated all who came into his reach with the same non-emotion he'd display for pieces on a gaming board. They were to be positioned and used as necessity dictated, sacrificed, and discarded when strategy required.

Still, thought Xizor, *an entity such as Boba Fett . . .*

The bounty hunter merited his respect, at least. To look into that helmet's concealing visor was to meet a gaze as ruthless and unsentimental as his own. *He'll fight to survive. And he'll fight well. . . .*

But that was part of the trap that had already seized hold of Boba Fett. The cruel irony—and one that Xizor savored—was that Fett was now doomed by his own fierce nature. *All that had kept him alive before, in so many deadly situations, would now bring about his destruction.*

STAR WARS®

THE BOUNTY HUNTER WARS

BOOK ONE

THE MANDALORIAN ARMOR

K. W. Jeter

BANTAM BOOKS

LONDON • NEW YORK • TORONTO • SYDNEY • AUCKLAND

STAR WARS:
THE MANDALORIAN ARMOR
A BANTAM BOOK : 0 553 50601 3

Published in Great Britain in 1998 by Bantam Books, a division of
Transworld Publishers

3 5 7 9 10 8 6 4

Bantam Books are published by Transworld Publishers,
61–63 Uxbridge Road, London W5 5SA,
a division of The Random House Group Ltd,
in Australia by Random House Australia (Pty) Ltd,
20 Alfred Street, Milsons Point, Sydney, NSW 2061, Australia,
in New Zealand by Random House New Zealand Ltd,
18 Poland Road, Glenfield, Auckland 10, New Zealand
and in South Africa by Random House (Pty) Ltd,
Endulini, 5a Jubilee Road, Parktown 2193, South Africa.

Printed and bound in Great Britain by
Cox & Wyman Ltd, Reading, Berkshire.

**To Lori Foster, Lexy House
and Shelby House**

THE BOUNTY HUNTER WARS

B O O K   O N E

The
Mandalorian Armor

1

The live ones are worth more than the dead ones.

That was the general rule of digital appendage for bounty hunters. Dengar hardly had to remind himself of it as he scanned the bleak and eye-stinging bright wastes of the Dune Sea. Right now he'd spotted a lot more dead things than living, which all added up to a big zero for his own credit accounts. *I'd have done better,* he told himself, *getting off this miserable planet.* Tatooine had never been any luckier for him than it'd been for any other sentient creature. Some worlds were like that.

His luck wasn't as bad as some others' had been—Dengar had to admit that. Especially when, as his plastoid-sheathed boots had trudged up another sloping flank of sand, a gloved fist had seized on his ankle, toppling him heavily onto his shoulder.

"What the—" His surprised outcry vanished echoless across the dunes as he rolled onto his back, scrabbling his blaster from its holster. He held his fire, seeing now just what it was that had grabbed on to him. His fall had pulled a hand and arm free from the drifting sands that formed the shallow grave for one of Jabba the Hutt's personal corps of bodyguards. Some reflex wired into the dead warrior's battle-glove had snapped the dead hand tight as a womp-rat trap.

Dengar reholstered his blaster, then sat up and began peeling the fingers away from his boot. "You should've stayed out of it," he said aloud. The Dune Sea's scouring wind revealed the corpse's empty eye sockets. "Like I did." Getting into other creatures' fights was always a bad idea. A whole batch of the galaxy's toughest mercenaries, bounty hunters included, had gone down with the wreckage of Jabba the Hutt's sail barge. If they'd been as smart as they'd been tough, Dengar himself wouldn't have been out here right now, searching for their weapons and military gear and any other salvageable debris.

He got his boot free and stood up. "Better luck next time," he told the dead man.

His advice was too late to do that one any good. In his own memory bank, Dengar filed away the image of the corpse, with its clawing fingers and mouth full of sand, as further proof of what he'd already known: *The guy who comes along after the battle's over is the one who cleans up.*

In more ways than one. He stood at the top of the dune, shielding his eyes from the glare of Tatooine's double suns, and scanned across the wide declivity in front of him. The forms of other warriors and bodyguards, sprawled across the rocky wastes or half-buried like the one left a few meters behind, showed that he'd found the still and silent epicenter of all that fatal action he had so wisely avoided.

More evidence: Bits and pieces of debris, the wreckage of the repulsorlift sail barge that had served as Jabba's floating throne room, lay scattered across the farther dunes. Scraps of the canopy that had shaded Jabba's massive bulk from the midday suns now fluttered in the scalding breezes, blaster fire and the impact of the crash having torn the expensive Sorderian weftfabric to rags. Dengar could see a few more of Jabba's bodyguards, facedown on the hot sand, their weapons stolen by scavenging Jawas. They wouldn't be fighting anymore to protect their boss's wobbling bulk. Even in this desiccating heat, Dengar could smell the sickly aftermath of death. It wasn't unfamiliar to him—he'd been working as a bounty hunter and general-purpose mercenary long enough to get used to it—but the other scent he'd hoped to catch, that of profit, was still missing. He started down the slope of the dune toward the distant wreckage.

There was no sign of Jabba's corpse, once Dengar reached the spot. That didn't surprise him as he used a broken-shanked scythe-staff to poke around the rubble. Soon after the battle, he'd seen a Huttese transport lifting into the sky; that'd been what had guided him to this remote spot. The ship undoubtedly had had Jabba's body aboard. Hutts might be greedy, credit-hungry slugs—a trait Dengar actually admired in them—but they did have a certain feeling toward the members of their own species. Kill one, he knew, and you were in deep nerf waste. It wasn't sentimentality on the part of the other Hutts, so much as a wound to their notorious megalomania, mixed with a practical self-interest.

So much for Luke Skywalker and the rest of them, thought Dengar as the point of the staff revealed sticky and distasteful evidence of Jabba's death. As if that little band of Rebels didn't have enough trouble, with the whole Empire gunning for them; now they'd have the late Jabba's extended clan after them as well. Dengar shook his head—he would've thought that Skywalker and his pal Han Solo would have, at the least, an appreciation of the Hutt capacity for bearing grudges.

Even without Jabba's obese form rotting under the thermal weight of the suns, the debris zone stank. Dengar lifted a length of chain, the broken metal at its end twisted by blaster fire. The last time he'd seen this hand-forged tether, back at Jabba's palace, it'd been fastened to an iron collar around Princess Leia Organa's neck. Now the links were crusted with the dried exudations from Jabba's slobbering mouth. *The Hutt must've died hard,* thought Dengar, dropping the chain. *A lot to kill there.* He'd gotten an account of the fight from a couple of surviving bodyguards that had managed to drag themselves back to the palace. When Dengar had left, to come out here to the Dune Sea wastes, most of the remaining thugs and louts were busily smashing open the casks of off-planet claret in the cool, dank cellars beneath the palace, and getting obliterated in a orgy of relief and self-pity at no longer being in Jabba the Hutt's employ.

"Yeah, you're free, too." Dengar picked up an unsmashed foodpot that the toe of his boot had uncovered. The still-living delicacy inside, one of Jabba's favorite trufflites, scrabbled against the ceramic lid embossed with the distinctive oval seal of Fhnark & Co., Exotic Foodstuffs—WE CATER TO THE GALAXY'S DEGENERATE APPETITES. "For what it's worth." His own tastes didn't run to the likes of the pot's spidery, gel-mired contents; he hooked a gloved finger in the lid's airhole and pried it open. The nutrient gases hissed out; they had sustained the delicacy's freshness, all the way from whatever distant planet had spawned it. "See how long you last out there." The trufflite dropped to the sand, scrabbled over Dengar's boot, and vanished over the nearest dune. He imagined some Tusken Raider finding the little appetizer out there and being completely perplexed by it.

One substantial piece of wreckage remained, too big for the Jawas to have carted away. The hardened durasteel keelbeam of the sail barge, blackened by explosions that had destroyed the rest of the craft, rose at an angle from where the stern end was buried beneath a fall of rocks. Dengar scrabbled aboard the curved metal, nearly a meter in width, and climbed the rest of the way up to where the barge's bow had been, and now only the exposed beam was left, tilted into the cloudless sky. He wrapped one arm around the end, then with his other hand unslung the electrobinoculars from his belt and brought them up to his eyes. The rangefinder numbers skittered at the bottom of his field of vision as he scanned across the horizon.

This was a pointless trip, Dengar thought disgustedly. He leaned out farther from the keelbeam, still examining the wasteland through the 'binocs. His bounty-hunting career had never been such a raging success that he'd been able to refrain from any other kind of scrabbling hustle that chanced to come his way. It was a hard trade for a human to get ahead in, considering the number of other species in the galaxy that worked in it, all of them uglier and tougher; droids, too. So a little bit of scavenger work was nothing he was unused to. The best would've been if he had found any survivors out here that could either pay him for their rescue or that he could ransom off to whatever connections they might have. The late Jabba's court had been opulent—and lucrative—enough to attract more than the usual lowlifes that one encountered on Tatooine.

But the bunch of rubble Dengar had found out here—the few scattered and pawed-over bits of the sail barge and the smaller skiffs that'd hovered alongside as outriders, the dead bodyguards and warriors—wasn't worth two lead ingots to him. Anything of value was already trundling away in the Jawas' slow, tank-treaded sandcrawlers, leaving nothing but bones and worthless scrap behind.

Might as well just stay here, he thought. *And wait.* He'd sent his bride-to-be, Manaroo, aloft in his ship, the *Punishing One,* to do a high-altitude reconnaissance of the area. Soon enough she'd be finished with the task, and would come back to fetch him.

The knot of frustration in Dengar's gut was instantly replaced with surprise as the keelbeam suddenly tilted almost vertical. The strap of the electrobinoculars cut across his throat as they flew away from his eyes. He held on with both hands as the beam pitched skyward, as though it were on a storm-tossed ocean of water rather than sand.

Charred metal scraped tight against the ammo pouches on his chest as the keelbeam rotated. As the beam twisted about, Dengar could see the surrounding dunes heaving in a slow, seismic counterpoint to the wrecked barge's motion, cliff faces of rock and sand shearing away and tumbling downward, slower clouds of dust stacking across the suns' smoldering faces.

At the center of the dunes, the slope grew deeper, like a funnel with a black hole at its center. Another shudder ran beneath the planet's surface, and the keelbeam rolled almost sideways, nearly dislodging Dengar from his grasp upon it. His feet swung out from beneath him; Dengar looked down, past his own boots, and saw that the hole at the bottom of the sand funnel was lined with teeth.

Jaws clenched, Dengar muttered an obscenity from his homeworld. *You gnurling idiot*—he cursed his own stupidity, getting himself stuck here in the middle of the air, with no escape route. He hadn't considered what his presence might awaken, and how hungry it would be.

The Great Pit of Carkoon gaped wider, sand and rubble swirling around the blind, all-devouring Sarlacc creature at the center of the vortex. A sour stench hit Dengar like a wind hotter than any that crossed the desert's reaches.

A glance around him revealed to Dengar that the keelbeam had slid partway down the funnel, then snagged on a solid rock outcropping. He turned his face against his shoulder as the sail barge's scattered debris rained past him, the larger pieces hitting the Pit's sloping sides and pitching end over end into the Sarlacc's gaping maw. The keelbeam gave a sudden lurch in Dengar's sweating grasp as the end below him shattered part of the outcropping. Suddenly the beam swayed backward, leaving him dangling precariously, only a couple of meters from the Sarlacc's throat.

A pumping kick enabled him to get first one, then the other of his boot soles up onto the beam. He squatted into a deep knee bend on the narrow metal surface, then jumped, fingertips clawing for the funnel's edge above him. His belly hit the slope; sand slid maddeningly under his hands as he thrashed and kicked, struggling toward the bright and empty sky. With a gasp of effort, Dengar managed to get his chest across the shifting edge of the funnel, then scrabble the rest of his body over and tumble down the other side.

Too bad for the Jawas—that was all that Dengar could think of as he wrapped his arms around himself and waited for the animate disturbance in Tatooine's crust to subside. There might have been something of worth brought to the surface; but unless the little scroungers wanted to dive down the Sarlacc's throat to get it, that load of valuable salvage was lost to them now.

The Dune Sea grew silent again. Dengar let a minute pass, measured by his heartbeat gradually slowing to normal, then scrambled to his feet. The Sarlacc had most likely pulled its head back underground and was busy digesting the bits of wreckage it'd just been fed, or trying to. He figured that would give him time enough to get a safe distance away, if he hurried. Brushing sand from his gear, Dengar started trudging up the slope of the nearest dune.

Three dunes later he stopped to catch his breath. To his amazement, he saw that the scraps of debris, the barely distinguishable pieces of Jabba the Hutt's sail barge, still filled the center of the pit. The truth dawned on him. *It's dead,* thought Dengar. Something—or someone—had managed to kill the Sarlacc. The rotting stench had been from the creature's own torn-apart flesh, visible beneath the wreckage.

Now the sense of life, however malignant, beneath the desert's surface was extinguished. Only bits of wreckage, no longer recognizable as to form and function, and a few facedown bodies lay scattered around the empty zone.

The stink from the slope-sided hole motivated Dengar in the opposite direction, toward Jabba's palace. This was as good a time as any for him to verify the rumors about what the palace had become since the death of the Hutt. The orgiastic celebration of

Jabba's liberated underlings had been just beginning, the last time Dengar had been inside the forbidding, windowless pile. If the palace was empty now—reports differed on that score—then the thick walls of the interior chambers would give him a safe place to hang out while night and its attendant hazards took possession of the Dune Sea, and he waited for Manaroo's return. His own private hideout, which he'd previously carved into a desert ridge of stone and stocked with supplies, would have done the same—but at the palace, there might be some remnants of Jabba's court, like the Hutt's majordomo, Bib Fortuna, and others who would be looking for ways to profit by the employer's death. *Great minds think alike,* Dengar noted wryly. *Or at least the greedy ones do.*

He gave the area one more scan, sweeping the horizon with the electrobinoculars. One of the suns had already begun to set, pushing his own shadow ahead across the wasteland. He was just about to power off the 'binocs when he spotted something nearly fifty meters away. *That one looks like he took the worst of it*—another corpse lay on a stretch of rough gravel. Faceup; Dengar could make out the front of a narrow-apertured helmet. That was about all of the corpse's gear that was intact. The rest of the dead man's gear looked as if it hadn't been burned away so much as dissolved, some kind of acid bath reducing uniform and armaments to rags and corroded, pitted shapes of useless metal and plastoid. Dengar thumbwheeled the 'binocs into closer focus, trying to figure out what could've happened to create that kind of lethal effect.

Wait a minute. The sprawled form filled the electrobinoculars' lenses. *Maybe not exactly lethal,* Dengar corrected himself. He could see the figure's chest moving, a slight rise and fall, right on the edge of survival. The half-naked combatant, whoever it might be, was still alive. Or at least for the time being.

Now, *that* was worth checking out. Dengar slung the 'binocs back onto his equipment belt. If only to satisfy his own curiosity—the distant figure looked as if he'd discovered a whole new way of getting killed. As a bounty hunter and general purveyor of violence, Dengar felt a professional interest in the matter.

He glanced over his shoulder and saw his own ship, the *Punishing One,* descending a few kilometers away, its landing gear extended. His bride-to-be, Manaroo, was at the ship's controls. *Good,* thought Dengar. He'd be able to use her help, now that he had determined that there would be no immediate danger to her. He didn't mind risking his own life, but hers was another matter.

Balancing himself with one hand held back against the slope of the dune, Dengar worked his way toward the humanoid-shaped mystery he'd spotted. He hoped the other man would still be alive by the time he got there.

This way of dying's not so bad. . . .

Somewhere, past a jumble of disjointed thoughts and images, the oleaginous voice of Jabba the Hutt could be heard in memory, promising a new definition of pain, one that would last thousands of years, excruciating and never-ending.

The fat slug had been correct about that, to a degree; the dying man had to admit it. Or was he already dead?—he couldn't tell. This fate, the infinitely slow etching away, molecule by molecule, of epidermis and nerve endings, had been intended for someone else. It struck the dying man as no more unjust than all the rest of the universe's workings that he should suffer it instead.

Or have suffered it. Because the Hutt seemed to have been misinformed about how long the dissolution and torment would last. A few seconds had been more than adequate for pain's new meaning to have become clear, as the enfolding darkness's acids had seeped through uniform and armament, touching skin like the fire of a thousand commingled suns. And those few seconds, and the minutes and hours—days, years?—that followed had indeed seemed to stretch out to eternity. . . .

But they had ended. That pain, beyond anything he had ever endured or inflicted, had come to a stop, replaced by the simpler and duller ebbing away of life force. By comparison, that was a comfort like drifting asleep on pillows of satin filled with downy feathers. Even the blindness, the perfect acidic night, had been broken by a muted dawn. The dying man still could not see, but he could sense, through the T-shaped visor of his helmet and the wet rags swaddling him, the unmistakable photonic warmth of suns against his face and the eroded skin of his chest. *Perhaps,* the dying man thought, *it reached up into the sky and swallowed them, too.* The giant mouth, when he'd fallen down its ranks of razor teeth, had seemed that big.

But now he felt gravel and sand beneath his spine, and his own blood miring him to the ground. That had to be some kind of a tactile hallucination. He had no gods to thank, but was grateful anyway for the blessings of madness. . . .

The light on his face dimmed; the differential in temperature was enough that he could just make out the blurred edges of shadow falling upon him. He wondered what new vision his agony-fractured brain was about to conjure up. There were others, he knew, here in the belly of the beast; he had seen them fall and be swallowed up. *A little company*, the dying man decided. He might as well hallucinate voices, from those about to be digested; it would help pass the long endless hours before his own body's atoms floated free from one another.

One of the voices he heard was his own. "Help. . . ."

"What happened?"

He could almost have laughed, if any twitch of his raw muscles hadn't hurt so much, pushing him toward unconscious oblivion. Shouldn't hallucinations know these things?

"Sarlacc . . . swallowed me." The words seemed to come of their own volition. "I killed it . . . blew it up. . . ."

He heard another voice, a female's. "He's dying."

The man's voice spoke again, in hushed tones. "Manaroo—do you know who this is?"

"I don't care. Help me get him inside." The female's shadow fell across him.

Suddenly he felt himself rising, dirt and grit falling from his mangled form. The next sensation was that of being thrown across someone's broad shoulder, an arm encircling his waist to steady him. A sense of shame filled the dying man. There had been so many times when he had faced his own extinction—painful or otherwise—the contemplation of his death, and the dismissal of it as being of no concern, had given him strength. And now some weak part of him had summoned up this pitiful fantasy of rescue. *Better to die,* he thought, *than to fear dying.*

"Hang on," came the hallucinated voice. "I'll get you someplace safe."

The man called Boba Fett felt the jostle of the other's footsteps, the motion of being carried across the stony ground. For a moment his vision cleared, the blindness dissipating enough that he could see his own hand flopping limp and disjointed, leaving a trail of spattered blood on the sand. . . .

That was when he knew that what he saw and felt was real. And that he was still alive.

2

A small object, moving by its own power through the cold expanses between the stars, had finally breached a planet's sensory perimeter. Kuat of Kuat had felt the hyperspace messenger pod's approach even before his own corporate security chief came to tell him that it had been intercepted. He had a fine-tuned awareness of machines, from the smallest nano-sporoids to constructions capable of annihilating worlds. It was a family trait, something encoded deep within the Kuat blood for generations.

"Excuse me, Technician"—an obsequious voice came from behind him—"but you asked to be notified as the outer comm units picked up any traces. Of your . . . package."

Kuat of Kuat turned away from the great domed viewport and its vistas of emptiness studded with light. Far beyond the expanded orbit of the planet that bore the name identical to his, the hazy arm of one of the galaxy's more aesthetically pleasing spiral nebulae was about to rise into sight. He tried not to miss things like that; they served to remind him that the universe and all its interconnected workings was, in its essence, a machine like other machines. Even its constituent atoms, beyond the confusion of uncertainty principles and observer effects, ticked like ancient, primitive chrono gears. *And finer things than that,* Kuat of Kuat told himself, not for the first time. *Such as men's spirits.* Those were machines as well, however ineffable their substance.

"Very well." He stroked the silky fur of the felinx cradled in his arms; the animal made a deep, barely audible sound of contentment as his long, precise fingers found a specific zone behind the triangular ears. "That's just what I've been expecting." Machines, even the ones built in the Kuat Drive Yards, did not always function as intended; there were random variables that sometimes deposited metaphorical sand in the gears. It was a pleasure—frequent, but still undiminished—when things did work according to plan. "Has there been any readout on the contents?"

"Not yet." Fenald, the security chief, was dressed in the standard Kuat Drive Yards worksuit, devoid of any emblem of rank except for the variable-dispersion blaster slung conspicuously at his hip. "There's a full crew working on it, but"—a wry smile lifted a corner of his mouth—"the encryption codes are rather tight."

"They're meant to be." Kuat of Kuat would not be disappointed if the KDY employees weren't able to crack them; he had designed and implemented them himself. Setting Security's info-analysis division to work on them was a mere test, to see how well he'd done. "I don't care for anyone else reading my mail."

"Of course not." A slight nod in acknowledgment; despite the importance of Kuat Drive Yards as the elite and most powerful contractor of engineering and construction services to the Empire, the formalities of KDY headquarters were minimal, and had been for generations. Pomp and show and courtly flourishes were for those who didn't understand where true power came from. Fenald gestured toward the viewport, its hexagonal strutwork curving three times higher than his boss's imposing two-meter height. "I doubt if anyone has."

The felinx purred louder in Kuat of Kuat's arms; he'd found the exact spot wired into its pleasure centers. Born that way; a good amount of the minimal brain mass in the animal's excessively narrow skull— a trait of its inbred species—he'd had to replace with biosimulation circuits, to keep it from bumping into walls and gnawing raw the flesh beneath its fur. His fingertips felt the edge of the cut into the animal's skull as he stroked it. Transmuted even this far into a true machine, the animal was much more satisfactory, and—in ways Kuat of Kuat appreciated—even more beautiful.

A single bell note sounded in the spacious office suite of KDY's hereditary CEO. Kuat of Kuat turned back to gaze at the viewport's limitless vista as his security chief leaned the side of his head against the small transponder embedded in his palm. The felinx had closed its eyes in ecstasy; it didn't see the rising edge of the far-distant nebula, like luminous smoke against black.

"They're bringing it in now," said Fenald.

"Excellent." Outside, in vacuum, an ion engine streaked fiery red, moving past the seemingly chaotic maze of construction platforms and grav-dock bays at a navigable sublight speed. The small utility shuttle, with its precious cargo aboard, was heading for the core of KDY's industrial complex. Perhaps a quarter of a standard time part before the shuttle arrived; Kuat of Kuat glanced over his shoulder at the other man. "You don't need to wait." He smiled. "I'll take care of it myself."

Security chiefs were paid to be curious about everything that happened within their sphere of operations. "As you please, Technician." The words were spoken with a stiffened spine and a nod just bordering on curtness. He was also paid to obey orders. "Let me know if there's anything else you require, in regard to this matter."

The felinx protested as Kuat of Kuat bent down, depositing it on the intricately tessellated floor. Tail demandingly erect, the creature rubbed itself against a trouser leg cut of the same utilitarian dark green as all the other work uniforms worn by KDY employees. The concerns of the most powerful beings in the galaxy—perhaps the most powerful beyond Emperor Palpatine's inner circle—didn't matter to the animal. A heat source and continued stroking were the limits of its desires.

As Kuat of Kuat straightened back up, the office suite's doors slid shut behind the departing chief of security. The felinx bumped its head more insistently against his shin. "Not now," Kuat told it. "I've got work to do."

Persistence was a trait he admired; he couldn't be angry at the animal when it jumped up on his workbench. He let it march back and forth, level with his chest, as he assembled the necessary tools. Only when the pilot of the shuttle team, whose flight he had spotted from the viewport, entered and placed an elongated silver ovoid on the bench, then withdrew from his presence, did Kuat of Kuat shoo the animal away.

A pair of hovering worklights drew closer, erasing all shadow, as he leaned over the mirror-finished torpedo. This messenger pod was not just wired with, but actually built of, self-destruct modules, to prevent unauthorized access—or access by anyone except Kuat of Kuat himself. And even that was intended to be difficult; if he erred now, KDY would have a new hereditary owner and chief designer.

Held between thumb and forefinger, an identity probe bit almost painlessly into his flesh, drawing samples of fluid and tissue. The microcircuitry inside the slender needlelike device ran through its programming, matching both genetic information and the automutating radioactive tracers that had been injected into his bloodstream. The probe gave no sign, audible or visible, whether everything checked out. The only indication would be when he held the inoxide tip to the messenger pod; if his charred remains weren't embedded in the wall behind him, then all was as it should be.

The probe tip clicked against the curved, reflective surface. No explosion resulted, except for the slight one of his held breath being released.

A hairline fissure opened along the side of the pod. The work went faster now as Kuat of Kuat pried open the silvery ovoid, dismantling the pieces of its shell in a precise order. A misstep, a segment taken out of turn, would also result in a fatal explosion, but he wasn't concerned about that happening. The only place where the proper sequence had been put down was in his memory, but no more accurate record could be imagined. When he admired machines, he admired himself.

The one on the workbench functioned just as perfectly: the last of the encasing shell separated into its component parts and fell away from the core. "You've come a long way, little one." He laid a tender, possessive hand on the holoprojector unit that had been revealed. "Just what do you have to tell me?"

A fading heat radiated into Kuat of Kuat's palm. The messenger pod's energy cell was an accelerated-decay module, producing enough power for a onetime jump in and out of hyperspace. The navigational coordinates were hardwired; a matter of a few days ago it'd left the distant world of Tatooine. It could have reached the Kuat Drive Yards headquarters even sooner if a randomizing sublight process hadn't been programmed, to evade detection. Kuat of Kuat's own security men weren't the only ones watching the perimeter. A matter of business: paranoia was one of the operating costs that came with being of service to the Emperor.

Hands sheathed in insulated gloves, Kuat of Kuat lifted out the holoprojector. A standard playback unit, similar to ones found throughout the galaxy, but with tweaks and modifications far beyond the ordinary. Palpatine himself couldn't get this kind of detail in communications with his various underlings. *But then . . . he doesn't need it,* Kuat of Kuat reminded himself. *Not the way I do.* The Emperor could always get what he wanted through fear and death. In the engineering business, one had to be a little more careful, not to eliminate one's market.

"Go away," he said to the felinx winding between his ankles. "You won't like this."

The felinx didn't heed the warning. When Kuat of Kuat used the rest of his precise tools to complete the circuits inside the holoprojector, the images and sounds of another great room were laid over the office suite. The oppressive darkness generated by the recording and its chaos of noises, from the rattling of subsurface chains to cruel cross-species laughter, brought the silken fur straight up along the animal's spine; it hissed at what it saw, particularly the holoform of one grossly elephantine individual with tiny hands and immense, greedy eyes. When that image's lipless mouth opened to emit wetly glottal laughter, the felinx scrambled to safety beneath the farthest corner of the workbench.

Kuat of Kuat used the magnetically fastened tip of the probe to freeze the playback; the cacophony was replaced by silence as he glanced over his shoulder and saw the court of Jabba the Hutt rendered motionless. He turned away from the bench and walked into the center of the hologram. The forms were insubstantial as ghosts—he could have passed his hand through any one of the sycophants and hangers-on surrounding the Hutt's thronelike hover platform—but detailed in such perfection that he could almost smell the sweat and rank odors of decay rising from the grates in the synthesized floors.

"You're dead, aren't you?" With a thin smile, he brought his face close to the stilled image of Jabba the Hutt. "That's such a shame. I hate to lose a good customer." Over the years Jabba had commissioned several large orders, lethal equipment for his thugs and hirelings from KDY's personal armaments division, plus elaborate palace furnishings and a superbly appointed sail barge, with military retrofits, from one of the Kuat subsidiaries devoted to luxury vessels. There had been extras thrown in that Jabba had known nothing about: hidden recording devices that had captured nearly everything that took place in the palace on Tatooine and aboard the floating barge. *A good contractor,* thought Kuat of Kuat, *knows his accounts. Better than they even know themselves.*

Word of the Hutt's death had already seeped through the galaxy, gladdening many, setting off an acquisitive scramble among others. Of all of his species, Jabba had been the most active—if that word could be applied to something so obese and slow—and with the farthest reach in his shady enterprises. *They're already at each other's throats*—the late Hutt's associates, including Jabba's own supposedly grieving relations, struggling for control of his intricate and criminal legacy. That would be good for business; Kuat of Kuat already had appointments scheduled with some of the worst and most ambitious of the lot. New plans always called for new weapons.

The notion of throats mordantly amused him. What he'd already heard about Jabba the Hutt's death was confirmed by the holographic image. One of Jabba's ineffectual little hands held a length of chain, its other end fastened to a collar around the neck of a human form; standing at the edge of the re-created platform, Kuat of Kuat appraised with a connoisseur's eye the revealed attractiveness of Princess Leia Organa. His own wealth and power had brought many varieties of feminine beauty through his private quarters, even from the highest ranks of the nobility. The princess, however . . .

He made a mental note to seek this woman's acquaintance, if he ever had the opportunity. If it happened, he wouldn't be such an idiot as to leave something as simple and deadly as an iron chain lying about. "Never hand your enemy"—Kuat of Kuat spoke aloud to the dead Hutt's image—"the means by which she can kill you."

Jabba's death was a minor concern at the moment, though. Even the presence of Leia Organa at the late Hutt's court was, at this moment, of no great significance to Kuat. There were others that he sought, faces to be found in the past. He returned to his workbench and, with a few delicate adjustments to the playback unit, ran the recording back toward its beginning, before Leia Organa had ever entered Jabba's palace, disguised as an Ubese bounty hunter with captured Wookiee in tow. *That should do it,* thought Kuat as he glanced over his shoulder; he lifted the probe's tip from the device, freezing the image once again.

Stepping past Jabba's thronelike platform, Kuat of Kuat looked around the hologram of the Hutt's court. The assembled faces were a rogues' gallery of interstellar villainy, ranging from petty theft to murder—and beyond. Hutts tended to attract these types, the way small fur-bearing animals attracted fleas. Though in a certain sense, it was a symbiotic rather than parasitic relationship: At home in his palace, Jabba had been able to look around himself and at least see sentient creatures whose morals were on a par with, or even below, his own.

Kuat of Kuat walked slowly through the re-created court, looking for one face in particular. Not even a face, but a mask. He paused before the frozen image of Jabba's majordomo, a glittering-eyed, evilly smiling Twi'lek named Bib Fortuna. The males of the planet Ryloth, even with all the extra cognitive abilities packed into the heavy, tapering appendages hanging from their bare skulls onto their shoulders, had no capacity for generating wealth and no courage to steal it, even though they were nearly as avaricious as Hutts. This particular one had tried to worm his way into the Kuat Drive Yards' corporate bureaucracy, before a noteworthy display of untrustworthiness had gotten him booted from the headquarters on the planet Kuat. Hutts, however, had more of a taste for flattery and tail kissing; Kuat of Kuat wasn't surprised that Fortuna had wound up in Jabba's palace.

He didn't spot what he was looking for until he raised his eyes toward the holographic court's encircling gallery. *There he is,* thought Kuat of Kuat. The distinctive helmeted visage of Boba Fett, the galaxy's most feared bounty hunter, gazed down at the mingled courtiers below like a totem of some planet's primordial deity, contemplating a justice colder than the spaces between the stars. Arrayed along Fett's arms and slung at his back were his working tools, the wrist lasers and miniaturized flamethrower, and all the other weapons that were as precise in his hands as the tiny probes were in Kuat of Kuat's. The helmet, with its dark T-shaped visor, hid the bounty hunter's eyes and the measured calculations going on behind them.

Satisfied for the moment, Kuat of Kuat walked back to the edge of the hologram. Even being in a three-dimensional simulation of Jabba's court, with its miasma of avarice and bad hygiene, brought a twinge of nausea to his gut. Better to watch from the outside of the hologram, from the pristine and mathematic angles of his own office. At the workbench, he adjusted the probe's angle in the holoprojector's circuits. Without even glancing over his shoulder, he could sense Jabba's image and the others in the Hutt's dimly lit court restored to motion, acting out their parts in this little segment of the past.

Another adjustment muted the audio portion of the playback; Kuat of Kuat didn't need to hear Jabba's slobbering voice and the cruel laughter of his sycophants to discern what was happening. Another Twi'lek, a female—on Ryloth, the females were nowhere as repulsive as their male counterparts—had become the source for Jabba's amusement. A pretty slave, a pantalooned dancing girl with her distinctive Twi'lek head appendages decorated to resemble an ancient court jester's cap of bells—but her childlike appeal and grace wasn't enough to satisfy her master's appetites. A look of apprehension, close to panic, had moved across her face as she had sat decorously at one side of the court, as though she'd had a prescient glimpse of her fate. Which was being played out again as the image of Jabba the Hutt, wattled bulk jiggling and eyes widening with delight, reeled in the chain fastened to the Twi'lek dancing girl's iron collar, dragging her toward the thronelike platform. The poor girl must have seen the same thing happen to others before her; beautiful creatures had been a disposable commodity for Jabba.

Just as Kuat of Kuat expected, the next few moments of the playback showed the trapdoor sliding open in front of Jabba's platform. The dancing girl's fall snapped the links of the chain; the court's motley denizens clustered around the grates, straining to watch her death at the claws and teeth of the rancor, Jabba's favorite pet, in the darkness below. The nausea returned to Kuat of Kuat's stomach, sharpened to disgust. *A waste,* he thought. The dancing girl had been beautiful enough to be useful to someone; the destruction of such a pretty device angered him more than anything else.

He'd seen enough, at least at this level of detail. If the fat slug was as dead as had been reported, he now didn't regret the loss of trade. There'd be others, moving up the ranks of the Huttese species' galaxy-wide hierarchy. Kuat of Kuat reached over and froze the playback, the better to scan the images for the one in whom he had the most interest.

And who was no longer there in the hologram. The helmeted visage of the bounty hunter was missing from where Kuat of Kuat had spotted it before, up on the gallery overlooking the central area of Jabba's court. Kuat of Kuat stepped away from the workbench and across the nearest edge of the hologram, looking up toward the simulation of the rough-domed ceiling, then around to the openings of low, tunnellike passages branching off to other parts of the palace. The image of Boba Fett was nowhere to be seen.

Kuat of Kuat ran the recording unit back to the point where the bounty hunter, face hidden behind the visored mask of his uniform, could be seen watching the court below him. This time, he didn't let himself be distracted by the fate of the Twi'lek dancing girl; starting up the playback again, he saw where Boba Fett had slipped unnoticed from the gallery and out of the court, even before Jabba had started pulling on the chain and dragging the girl over the trapdoor.

Interesting. Kuat of Kuat let the holographic recording play on. *Our friend,* he thought, *had another agenda.* Not surprising; Boba Fett had not reached the top of the bounty-hunter trade without building up a network of business interests and contacts, some of them—if not most—completely unaware of each other. Jabba the Hutt might have been stupid enough to believe that by paying Fett a generous retainer, he had thereby secured the bounty hunter's exclusive services. If so, that indicated how much Jabba had been slipping, making the kind of mistakes that had led to his death.

Always a mistake to completely trust a bounty hunter. Kuat of Kuat didn't commit mistakes like that.

Kuat ran the hologram playback forward. There was no sign of Boba Fett until much farther on in the recording. He spotted the bounty hunter's image then, snapping a blaster rifle up into firing position as the disguised Leia Organa held up an activated thermal detonator and demanded payment for the captive Wookiee she had brought. That potentially lethal confrontation had ended with the Hutt's guttural laughter and admiration for his resourceful opponent; the bounty for Chewbacca had been paid and Boba Fett had lowered his weapon.

So he did return there, mused Kuat as he watched the hologram. Whatever mysterious appointments Boba Fett might have kept in Jabba's palace, they hadn't prevented him from attending to his duties as the Hutt's freelance bodyguard. It was a safe assumption that the reports gathered by Kuat's corporate intelligence division were accurate: they had described Jabba's death, out on his sail barge, hovering at the edge of the Great Pit of Carkoon in Tatooine's Dune Sea, and had mentioned Boba Fett being there at the struggle.

More than that, the reports had also described Boba Fett's death. What Kuat of Kuat wanted was proof of that. Operating without that proof was like building a machine with a critical component left untested. *A machine,* he thought, *that could kill its master if it broke down.* Someone like Boba Fett had a disquieting habit of survival; Kuat of Kuat would have to see the bounty hunter's death before he would believe it.

He looked at the pieces of the messenger pod and its curved, reflective casing scattered on the workbench. The next pod to drop out of hyperspace and penetrate the planet Kuat's atmosphere would very likely carry the necessary information inside it. All the units had been designed to carry only partial segments of what had been recorded at Jabba's palace

and aboard the Hutt's sail barge. There was less like-
lihood that way of any of KDY's powerful enemies
intercepting the units and, if they managed to get
past the security procedures, figuring out Kuat of
Kuat's own concerns.

One last thing to do with this message: He
reached into the device and extracted the micro-
probe. The breaking of the circuit initiated the self-
destruct program; the metal grew white-hot, twisting
in upon itself as it was consumed. From underneath
the bench, the felinx fled in terror, streaking toward
the office suite's farthest recesses. A few more seconds passed, then the holoprojector and its contents
had been reduced to blackened slag on the workbench's surface, cooling into a single indecipherable
hieroglyph.

The contents of the message, that had come so
far to reach him, was safely locked away in Kuat of
Kuat's memory. When proof of Boba Fett's death
came, he might allow himself to forget the smallest
particle of information. *When it's safe,* Kuat of Kuat
had already decided. *Not until then.*

And if that proof didn't come . . . he would
have to make other plans. Plans that would include
more than one death as part of their internal workings. Meshing gears often had cruelly sharp teeth.

He turned away from the workbench and walked
slowly through the empty spaces of the office suite,
looking for the felinx. So that he could pick it up and
cradle it in his arms, and soothe it of the fright it had
received.

3

It took some doing, but she found him. For the second time.

The girl crouched behind one of the Dune Sea's rocky outcroppings as she watched the barely noticeable hole dug into the barren ground below. The twin suns bled into the horizon, the chill Tatooine night already unfolding across the sands. Around her bare shoulders, she pulled tighter a salvaged scrap of sail-barge canopy—blackened by fire and explosion along one ragged edge, stiff with dried blood along another. The delicate fabrics with which her body had been adorned in Jabba's palace were little protection against the cold. A shiver touched her flesh as she continued to watch and wait.

She'd known that the bounty hunter, the one called Dengar, would have some hiding place away from Jabba the Hutt's palace. *What used to be his palace,* she corrected herself. The monstrous slug was dead now, that had held the end of her chain and the chains of the other dancers. But when Jabba had been alive, most of the thugs and bodyguards in his employ had had little warrens out in the rocky wastes, where they could seal themselves in for a few hours' sleep, safe from being murdered by each other—or by their boss. Jabba's court hadn't been easy to survive in; she knew that better than anyone. *But it's not me who died,* she thought with a bitter satisfaction. *Jabba got what he deserved.*

In the dimming light, she put away her brooding, the little vengeful spark that kept her warm inside. She'd spotted, down below, the approaching figures for which she'd been waiting.

Two medic droids trundled across the sand; their parallel tracks headed toward the warren hole in the rocky wasteland. They were probably refugees from Jabba's palace, just as she was; all of the medic droids there had been modified with wheels in place of the original stumpy legs so they could get around in the desert terrain. Neelah watched them for a few seconds more, then eased out of her hiding place and carefully worked her way down the farther side of the dune, where the droids wouldn't be able to see her.

"Hold it right there." She caught the droids just as they were transmitting the security code that would unseal the subsurface warren; a row of numbers, softly glowing red, showed on the panel embedded in the magnetically reinforced durasteel. "Don't move. I promise I won't hurt you—but don't move."

"Are you frightened?" The taller of the two medical droids, a basic MD5 general-practitioner model, scanned her against the hole's rough circle of evening sky. "Your pulse is quite elevated for a standard humanoid form. Plus"—a tiny grid irised open on the droid's dark-enameled head, drawing in an air sample—"your perspiration contains significant levels of hormones indicating an emotionally agitated state."

"Shut up. I also want you to do that." Rocks slid loose beneath her as she scrambled down toward the droids. "Just shut up."

"Did you hear that?" The taller droid swiveled its multilensed gaze toward its companion, a white-banded MD3 pharmaceutical model. "She's telling us to be quiet."

"Rudeness." Dust sifted from the shorter one as it tucked its syringes and dispensing appendages closer to itself. "Foresight of difficulties."

"Great—" Anger spurred her heart even faster. "Then you can't say you didn't know this was coming." She grabbed a vital-signs monitor sticking out antennalike from the taller one's head and slammed the droid against the dirt wall of the warren entrance, hard enough to send the lights dancing across its front display panel. Another pull in the opposite direction sent it crashing into the other droid; that one squealed as it toppled over, exposing the wheeled traction devices below the lower rim of its cylindrical body. "*Now*, how about shutting up?"

"It seems like a very good idea." The taller droid retreated, flattening itself against the unopened security hatch.

She gulped down a deep breath, trying through sheer willpower to slow down her heartbeat and still the trembling in her hands. Few violent acts had been required in her life—as far as she knew; she had no memories of any life before finding herself at Jabba's palace—and even as something as minor as banging a little sense into the medical droids' heads was enough to dizzy her. *Get used to it,* she sternly told herself. The realization had already come to her that a lot more scary things were going to happen. That was all right; at least she was alive. Others in her position hadn't been so fortunate. The memory was still vivid inside her, of seeing the other dancing girl falling into the pit beneath Jabba's palace. That memory ended with screams, and the slavering growls of Jabba's pet rancor.

"Excuse me, your ladyship . . ."

That puzzled her. Neither Jabba the Hutt nor any of the others at his court had ever called her anything like that.

"But you require medical attention." The taller droid kept its speech mechanism at minimal volume. A handlike examination module, with a fiber-optic light source mounted at the wrist, reached tentatively toward her face. "That's a very bad wound. . . ."

She slapped away the droid's hand, before it could touch the edges of the jagged line running down one side of her face. "It'll heal."

"With a scar." The taller droid shone the beam of its handlight lower, down to where the wound, the physical memory of a Gamorrean pikestaff, ended below her throat. "We could do something about that. To make it better."

"Why bother?" Other memories, nearly as unpleasant as those from the pit, flooded her thoughts. Whatever her life might have been before, the time in Jabba's palace had been enough to convince her that beauty was a dangerous thing to possess. It'd been just enough to entice Jabba's sticky hands—and the hands of those underlings who had been his current favorites—but not enough to protect her when the Hutt grew bored with her charms. "I can do without it," she said bitterly.

"Anger," noted the other medical droid. Needlessly—the scent of negative emotion was almost palpable in the warren hole's entrance. "Treatment inadvisability."

"I remember seeing you." The taller droid's low, soothing voice continued. "At Jabba's palace." The handlight beam moved across her face. "You were part of the entertainment."

"I was—" She glanced over her shoulder toward the warren's darkening entrance, to make sure no one was approaching, then turned back toward the droids. "But not now."

"Oh?" An inquiring gaze seemed to move behind the droid's optic receptors. "Then what are you?"

"I . . . I don't know. . . ."

"Name," spoke the shorter of the two droids. "Designation."

"They called me . . . Jabba called me Neelah." She frowned. Something—the absence of memory, rather than anything she could actually recall—told her that wasn't right. *That name's a lie,* she thought. "But . . . that's what they called me. . . ."

"There's worse names." Voice brightening, the taller droid tried to comfort her. "Consider my own subidentity coding—" Its complicated hand pointed to a data readout on the front of its dark metallic body. "SHΣ1-B. Most sentient creatures can't even pronounce it. This one's luckier."

"1e-XE." The shorter droid extruded a pill-dispensing module and gently tapped the back of her hand with it. "Acquaintance; pleasure."

They're working on me, thought Neelah. She knew enough about medical droids—from where?—to be aware of the soothing effects they were designed to provoke in their patients. Anesthetic radiation; she could feel a low-level electromagnetic field locking into sync with the neurons inside her head, drawing out the lulling endorphins. . . .

"Knock it off," she growled. She shook her head, snapping herself free of the droids' influence. "I don't need that, either. Not now." Neelah drew one hand back in a small but effective fist. "If I have to whack you again, I will."

Like extinguishing a torch, the field abruptly cut out. "As you wish," said SH∑1-B. "We're only trying to help."

"You can do that by telling me where he is." The wound across her face stung once more, but she ignored it.

"Who?"

She nodded toward the security hatch. "The bounty hunter. The one whose hiding place this is."

"Dengar?" One of SH∑1-B's metallic hands pointed toward the warren opening behind her. "He's back at Jabba's palace."

"Supplies," noted 1e-XE. "Various."

"That's right." SH∑1-B opened a small cargo pod bolted to the side of its body. "He sent us back here with what we required. As you see—antibiotics, metabolic accelerators, sterile gel dressings—"

"Fine." Neelah interrupted the droid's inventory of its contents. "But Dengar—he's still back at the palace?"

SH∑1-B's head unit gave a nod. "He said he wanted to find one of Jabba's caches of off-planet edibles. That might take some time, though—the palace has been very badly looted by the Hutt's former employees."

"Mess." 1e-XE rotated the top dome of its cylinder back and forth. "Disgust."

There wasn't time to consider her decision. "Open the hatch," said Neelah, pointing to the magnetically sealed disk, the coded digits still blinking in its readout panel. "I want to go inside."

"Dengar told us not to let—" The taller of the two droids caught the look in Neelah's eyes. "All right, all right; I'm opening it."

The tunnel on the other side of the hatch descended at close to a forty-five-degree angle. Heading down it, with the droids clunking behind her, Neelah felt a claustrophobic panic crawling along her spine. The darkness and the close, scarcely ventilated air felt like the tunnel through which she'd crawled to escape from Jabba's palace. After what had happened to her poor friend Oola, any risk had seemed preferable to winding up as rancor food.

Though her own death had almost found her, before she had gotten away. The scything blade of a Gamorrean perimeter guard's pikestaff had slashed the raw-edged wound on her face. She'd left the blade buried halfway through the guard's throat; Jabba had always made the mistake of hiring thugs who were bigger than they were fast. She'd only felt fear afterward, as she'd stepped over the widening pool of blood, then ran into the desert.

In this dimly lit space, she was finally able to stand upright in a central chamber. "Where's the other one?" She glanced over her shoulder at the two medical droids as they emerged from the tunnel and clicked back into their normal positions. "The one you're taking care of?"

"Dengar told us—" SHΣ1-B's voice snapped silent. "Over here," it said grudgingly. The taller droid led Neelah past disorganized stacks of weapons and ammunition modules, mixed with the discarded wrappings of autothermal field-ration containers. "It's not really suitable—this patient should've been medevac'd to a hospital immediately—but we've done the best we can. . . ."

Neelah tuned out the droid's words. At the low, rounded entrance to the side chamber, she halted and peered inside. "Is he . . . is he awake?" A dim glow filled the space; a black cable ran from a shielded worklight to a fuel-cell power generator in the middle of the main chamber's clutter. "Can he see me?"

"Not with what we gave him." SH∑1-B stood just behind her. "I prescribed a five-percent obliviane solution from 1e-XE's anesthetic stocks. On a constant basis, too; the patient's injuries are unusually severe. That was one of the reasons we had to go back to the palace, to try and find more. But if we didn't, the pain from this kind of trauma could go into a feedback loop and completely burn out the patient's central nervous system."

She stepped into the chamber, ducking under the doorway. An improvised bed, polyfoam stuffed inside flexible freight sheathing, left only a small space between the unconscious man and the medical droids' intravenous units and monitoring equipment. She squeezed past the humming machines, dials, and tiny screens ticking with slow pulses of light, and stood looking down at someone whose face she had never seen before.

One of her hands reached to touch him, but stopped a few centimeters away from his brow. *He looks worse than I do,* thought Neelah. The man's flesh looked as raw as it had when she'd found him the first time, out in the desert; the skin that he had lost in the Sarlacc's digestive tract was replaced now with a transparent membrane, linked to tubes trickling fluids from the wall of machines alongside the bed. "What's this?" She touched the clear substance; it felt cold and slick.

"Sterile nutrient casing." SH∑1-B reached out and made a slight adjustment to one of the equipment controls. "It's what we normally use on severe burn victims, when there has been major epidermal loss. When we were in the service of the late Jabba the Hutt, we saw and treated a lot of burns."

"Explosions," said 1e-XE.

"Just so." SH∑1-B lifted part of its carapace in an approximation of a humanoid shrug. "The kind of persons who worked for Jabba—the *rougher* sort of his employees—they were always blowing themselves up, one way or another."

"Turnover. High rate."

"That's true; there were always some we just couldn't put back together. But 1e-XE did get rather skilled at burn-treatment protocols. This individual's somatic trauma, however, is a little different." SH∑1-B scanned over the unconscious figure. "No one, as far as can be recalled from our memory banks, has ever survived even temporary ingestion by a Sarlacc. So we're doing the best we can, with what we've got."

Neelah glanced over at the medical droid. "Is he going to live?"

"Hard to tell. An exact prognosis for this patient is difficult to make, due to both the severity and the unusual nature of his injuries. It's not just the epidermal loss; 1e-XE and I have determined that there was also exposure to unknown toxins while he was in the Sarlacc's gut. We've attempted to counteract the effects of those substances, but the results are uncertain. If we had access to records of other such humanoid-Sarlacc encounters, the probability of his survival could be calculated. But we don't. Though just on a personal basis"—SH∑1-B's voice lowered, a simulation of confidentiality—"I'm surprised that this individual is still alive at all. Something else must be keeping him going. Something inside him."

The droid's words puzzled her. "Like what?"

"I don't know," replied SH∑1-B. "Some things

are not a matter of medical knowledge. Not the kind I have, at any rate."

She looked back at the figure on the bed. Even like this, with his mere human face exposed and unconscious beneath the machines' care, his presence brought a chilling unease around her own heart. *There's something*, thought Neelah, *between us*. Some invisible connection, that she had caught the tiniest glimpse of back in Jabba's palace. When she had looked up to the gallery and she had seen this man, unmistakable even when masked; seen him and felt the touch of fear. Not because of what she'd remembered at that moment, but because of what she couldn't remember. If this man stood somewhere in her past, he stood in shadows, stretching back farther and deeper than any mere rancor pit.

"What about Dengar?" With another effort of will, Neelah brought herself back to the present. "Why's he doing this? Taking care of him?"

"I have no idea." SHΣ1-B's optic receptors gazed at her blankly. "He didn't tell us, when he came to the palace and found us. And frankly, that's not a matter of concern to us."

"Unimportance," said 1e-XE.

"We're programmed to provide medical care. After Jabba the Hutt's death, we were just glad to be provided with an opportunity to do that."

That left the other bounty hunter's agenda as a mystery to her. She'd taken a chance when she left this one out on the desert sands, where Dengar would find him. She'd been horrified by the extent of his injuries; there would have been no way she could have taken care of the rawly bleeding man. In Jabba's palace, she had seen enough to be aware of the enmity, the professional rivalry and personal hatred, that existed among all bounty hunters—but then, this one would have been no more dead if Dengar had found him, then gone ahead and stood on his throat until he'd stopped moving. Instead, a certain strange sense of relief had stirred in her as she'd crouched behind an outcropping and had witnessed Dengar examining the injured man. That same inexplicable emotion had risen when she'd followed the medical droids to this hiding place and had found the man still alive. . . .

There wasn't time to ponder what that meant. *You've been here long enough,* she warned herself. Whatever Dengar's motives might be for keeping his rival alive, he might not be so charitably inclined toward her. Bounty hunters were secretive creatures; they had to be, in their trade. Dengar might not be happy to find that someone else was aware of not only his hiding place, but what—and who—was inside it.

"I'm going to leave now," Neelah told the droids. "You carry on with your work. This man must stay alive—do you understand that?"

"We'll do our best. That's what we were created for."

"And—you're not to tell Dengar anything about me. About my being here at all."

"But he might ask," said SHΣ1-B. "Whether somebody had been here or not. We're programmed to be truthful."

"Let's put it this way." Neelah leaned her scarred face closer to the droid's optics. "If you tell Dengar about me, I'll come back here and take you apart, and I'll scatter your pieces all across the Dune Sea. Both of you. And then you won't be able to do your jobs, will you?"

SHΣ1-B appeared to mull over her statement for

only a few seconds. "That certainly overrides the truthfulness programming."

"Silence," interjected 1e-XE hastily. "Completeness."

"Good." She glanced around the chamber to see if she'd left any telltale sign of her visit. Against the base of the rough-surfaced wall was something she hadn't spotted before. She stepped closer to it and saw that it was a pile of rags, the tattered shreds that she'd found still clinging, wet with the Sarlacc's digestive fluids, to the injured man's torso. On top of the pile was another object, not rags but metal, etched by its time in the beast's gut, but still recognizable. Neelah leaned down and picked up the helmet with its unmistakably narrow, T-shaped visor.

That was what she had seen before. In Jabba's palace—the helmet's mask was a cruel, implacable face in itself, the gaze hidden inside as sharp as any cutting blade. Neelah grasped the helmet in both hands, holding it before her, like a skull or part of a dead machine. Even empty, it looked back at her in silence—and she was afraid.

Boba Fett . . .

The name sounded in her thoughts, though not spoken by her. That was what he'd been called. She knew that much; she'd heard the name whispered, by those who'd both hated and dreaded him.

"You'd better go now." The medical droid's voice broke into her thoughts. "It won't be long before Dengar returns."

Her hands trembled as she set the helmet back down on the pile of rags. At the chamber's entrance, she stopped and looked back at the figure on the bed. A thread of something almost like pity crept into the knot of fear inside her.

She turned and hurried away, toward the slanting tunnel that would lead her to the more comforting darkness outside.

There had been voices. He'd heard them, from somewhere on the other side of a blind sea.

He supposed, in a still-functioning area of his brain, that that was part of dying. In a cortical nexus lying under the weight of pain and blurry not-pain, the remains of his mind and spirit picked over the few scraps of sensory data that impinged upon the living corpse that his body had become. They were like messages from another world, frustratingly incomplete and mysterious.

Of all the voices he'd heard, only one had been a woman's. Not the same one as before, which he could remember being addressed as Manaroo; he had still been lying out on the desert, vomited up by the Sarlacc, when he had heard that one.

But that had been the past; now he heard another woman's voice. That was the one that tormented him, that made the sleep of his dying a place where memories rose out of the darkness.

His eyelids had fluttered open, or had tried to; they were mired in some pliable substance clinging tightly to his face. As weak as he was, the stuff bound him as tightly as Han Solo had been in the block of carbonite he'd delivered to Jabba the Hutt. But he'd managed to raise his eyelids just enough, a fraction of a centimeter, that he'd been able to catch an unfocused glimpse of the female. She had been there in Jabba's palace, a simple dancing girl—but he knew she was something more than that. Much more. Jabba had called her . . . Neelah. That was it; he could remember that much. But that wasn't her real name. Her real name . . .

Fragments of memory touched, then drifted apart, as the effort of vision took him back beneath the lightless weight pressing upon him.

There, he dreamed without sleeping, died yet still lived.

And remembered.

4

"Stick with me," Bossk told the new Guild member. "And I'll show you how it's done."

He could feel the other's rising anger, like the radiation from a reactor-core meltdown. That was exactly the response he wanted, that his comments were designed to evoke. There wasn't the tiniest segment of a standard time cycle that Bossk wasn't angry to some degree. He even slept angry, the way all Trandoshans did, dreaming of their razor fangs locked on the throats of their reptilian species' ancient enemies. Rage and blood lust were good things in the Trandoshan galaxy-view. That was how things got done.

"You needn't act wise and superior with me." The close-range audio unit built into Zuckuss's breathing apparatus had enough bandwidth to let his irritation sound through. "I've collected nearly as many bounties as you have. Your family connections are the only reason for your rank in the Guild."

Bossk displayed an ugly, lipless smile toward the

partner he'd been assigned. The urge to reach over and pull the other's head off, air hoses and comlink wires dangling like the tendrils of swamp weed surrounding the birth pits back on Trandosha, was almost irresistible. *Maybe later*, Bossk told himself, *when this job's over*.

He pointed a talon down the corridor in front of them. Both he and Zuckuss had their spines flat against the wall of a side passage; from behind sealed doors some twenty meters away, the brittle music of a jizz-wailer band sounded, mixed with the high-pitched babble of the casino's customers blowing their credits on rows of rigged jubilee wheels. Gambling held no attraction for Bossk; he preferred surer things. Another sentient creature's death was the best, especially if there was profit involved. Sometimes, though—as with this job—the quarry had to be taken alive, if there was going to be any payoff. That complicated things.

"The thermal charges are already in place." The point of Bossk's claw indicated a pair of tiny bumps on the doors of the casino's main accounting office. A chameleonoid visual sheath on the charges' casings prevented the security optics from detecting them. "When I blow them, I want you straight through those doors. Don't bother scanning for guards, just dive in—"

"Why me?" Zuckuss turned his large-eyed gaze toward him. "Why don't you do that bit?"

"Because," said Bossk, grating out an unconvincing show of patience, "I'll be covering you from behind." He held up his blaster rifle, its stock and grip controls modified for his talons, large even by Trandoshan standards. "I'll draw off any fire while you're securing the counting room. It's a standard two-prong attack, straight out of the Guild manual for this kind of situation."

"Oh." Leaning his head out from the passage, Zuckuss studied the doors. "That makes sense . . . I suppose. . . ."

Idiot, thought Bossk. The actual reason was that the first one into the room was more likely to get sliced into bleeding pieces by the guards' tight-focus lasers. *Better you than me*—especially since his partner's death would mean he'd get to keep all of the bounty for himself, or at least the part that was left after the Guild took its share.

"Let's go." He shoved Zuckuss out ahead of himself, at the same time as he hit the trigger device mounted on the sleeve of his stalking gear. The faint sounds of music and frenetic pleasure were drowned out by the bass-heavy rumble of the thermal charges ripping open the sealed doors.

Bossk planted himself in the middle of the corridor, clawed feet spread wide, blaster rifle raised to his slit-pupiled eye. One talon squeezed onto the rifle's trigger stud in anticipation; the cold heart in his chest sped up with excitement as he peered through the coiling smoke. . . .

No fire came from beyond the ripped, heat-distorted metal.

"Zuckuss!" He shouted into the comlink mike mounted near the leathery scales of his throat. "What's going on?"

A moment passed before the other bounty hunter's reply came. "Well," said Zuckuss's voice, "the good news is that we don't have to worry about the guards. . . ."

Bossk charged down the corridor, rifle clutched in both sets of talons, and into the casino's accounting room. Or what was left of it: the smoke from the thermal charges' explosion had lifted enough that the scattered taliputer and vidlink terminals could be seen. Along with the bodies of a half-dozen casino guards—each one had had a laser hole drilled through the chest plate of his uniform with impressive accuracy. *And speed,* Bossk managed to note. None of the guards had even managed to get his weapon unslung and up into firing position; whoever had taken them out had done so in a matter of seconds.

"Look," said Zuckuss. He bent down and touched the hole in one guard's chest plate. "I'm getting a thermal reading here. The plastoid hasn't cooled—they were all lasered while we were still standing out in the corridor!" The bounty hunter stood and pointed to the room's far wall. A jagged hole, big enough for Bossk himself to have walked through without stooping, revealed the stacked cylinders of the power converters behind the main casino building. "Somebody beat us to it—"

"That's impossible," snapped Bossk. "That wall's monocrystal-chained; we'd have heard any blast powerful enough to get through it. Unless . . ." A sudden suspicion hit him; he glanced over his shoulder to the opposite wall. A sonic dissipator, the dials on its silvery ovoid surface trembling at the overload point, hung overhead by its automatically extruded gripfeet. The indicators slowly backed away from their red zones as the impact of the wall-breaching explosion was converted into a harmless sibilant whisper.

The rage inside Bossk leaped up, as though it could blow out another hole, even bigger and hotter. *That crossbred spawn of a . . .* The curse died between his gritting fangs. There was only one bounty hunter who used that kind of sophisticated—and expensive—equipment. Either it had been smuggled into the counting room somehow, or—more likely—an access hole just big enough for the device had been drilled through the wall, followed by the explosive charge itself when the dissipator had been activated to soak up the noise.

There was no point in looking around for the quarry for whom he and Zuckuss had come here. Bossk gripped the edge of the hole torn in the casino's exterior and scanned the planet's pockmarked horizon. In the distance, the infuriatingly familiar shape of a high-speed interstellar craft lifted into the deepening violet of the sky. The ship's engines trailed fire as it headed off-world.

"Come on!" Bossk grabbed Zuckuss by one arm and pulled him toward the gap in the wall. Shrieking alarms sounded from the corridor, triggered by the charges that had taken out the doors; it would only be a few seconds more before guards from other sections of the casino got here. He slung his rifle behind his shoulder and prepared to jump.

"But—" Zuckuss drew back. "But we must be ten meters up! At least!"

"So?" He growled at his partner. "Can you think of a quicker way out of here?"

A few seconds later he and Zuckuss were scrambling to their feet. The urge to murder filled Bossk again as Zuckuss groaned in pain.

"I think I broke something. . . ."

As laser shots from the casino guards above sizzled the ground, melting the planet's silicate-heavy ground into patches of glass, he started running, aware that Zuckuss was right behind him.

They caught up with their adversary out beyond the planet's atmosphere.

Bossk jammed the point of his talon down on the

comm button as Zuckuss, beside him in the navigator's seat of the *Hound's Tooth*, fussed with a broken connector to one of his air hoses. "Shut off your engines," he barked into the link. There was no need for formalities; in this remote zone of the starways, no other ship was within hailing range. "You have merchandise onboard that belongs to us. Specifically, one sentient individual by the designation of Nil Posondum, formerly employed by the Trans-Galactic Gaming Enterprises Corporation—"

"Your property?" A cold, uninflected voice sounded from the speaker mounted above the *Hound*'s controls. "And why would this said individual—*if* he were aboard my ship—why would he belong to you?"

"Maybe," whispered Zuckuss, "we shouldn't get this barve angry. He can be a tough customer."

"Shut up." Bossk pressed the comm button again. "By authority of the Bounty Hunters Guild. That's what makes him ours. Hand him over now, and you won't get into trouble."

"That's very amusing." No emotion, amused or otherwise, was discernible in the other's words. "But you seem to be laboring under a severe misapprehension."

"Yeah?" Bossk glared at the *Hound*'s forward viewport. The other ship showed no sign of cutting its speed. "What am I mistaken about?"

"I'm not restricted by the authority of your so-called Bounty Hunters Guild. I answer to a higher law."

"Which is?"

"Mine." The temperature of the scattered atoms between the ships couldn't have been closer to absolute zero. "Specifically, what's mine I keep. Until I get paid for it."

Bossk's words grated through his fangs. "Look, you conniving, diseased *gnathgrg*—"

The comm indicator blinked off, the connection broken by the other ship.

"There he goes." Zuckuss gazed up at the viewport.

The flaring trails from the engines of the *Slave I,* the transport of the galaxy's most ruthlessly efficient bounty hunter, blurred and disappeared into hyperspace. Cold and mocking stars filled the sector where it had been.

Bossk's slit pupils narrowed as he glared at empty space. The other ship, and its pilot and his captured prize, might be gone—but the seething fury in Bossk's scaled breast wasn't.

The figure in the cage cowered back from the bars as Boba Fett approached.

"There's no need for that." The *Slave I*'s minimal galley had ejected a tray of some nondescript edible substance, a lumpish gray gel that was unappetizing but adequate for a standard humanoid lifeform. Fett placed the tray on the metal-grated flooring and pushed it through an opening in the cage with the toe of his boot. "I'm not being paid to hurt you. Therefore you won't be hurt."

"And if you were being paid to do that?" The former head accountant for the Trans-Galactic Gaming Enterprises Corporation gazed sulkily from the holding pen, the only one presently occupied aboard the *Slave I.* "What then?"

"You'd be in a world of pain." Boba Fett pointed to the tray; a little of its glistening contents had slopped onto the pen's floor. "As merchandise, you are more valuable alive than dead. In fact, you would be worthless to me as a corpse. To deliver you unharmed—relatively so—is the primary requirement for collecting the bounty that was posted on you. If you try starving yourself, you will be force-fed. I'm not known for being gentle about that sort of thing. If you were to be so foolish as to try to injure yourself in any other manner, you'll find yourself in restraints considerably less comfortable than your present situation."

The accountant named Nil Posondum looked around the bare cage. A thin pale hand gripped one of the bars. "I'd hardly call this comfortable."

"It can get worse." The shoulders of Boba Fett's armored combat gear lifted in a shrug. "My ship is built for speed, not luxury accommodations." He'd left the *Slave I*'s controls set on autopilot; a small datapad clipped to his forearm monitored the craft's uninterrupted course through hyperspace. "You should take what pleasure you can from your time here. Things won't be any better for you where you're going."

In fact, Boba Fett knew they would be much worse for the accountant. Posondum had made the grievous error of shifting allegiances, changing jobs in an industry where loyalty was prized—and disloyalty punished. Worse, the accountant had been keeping the financial records for a chain of illicit *skefta* dens in the Outer Rim Territories that were controlled by a Huttese syndicate. Hutts tended to view their employees as possessions—one of the reasons that Boba Fett had always kept a freelancer's independent relationship with his frequent client Jabba. The accountant Posondum hadn't been so smart; he'd been even stupider when he'd gone over to his former employers' competition with a cortical datasplint loaded with the Hutts' odds-rigging systems and gray-market transfer shuffles. Hutts were even more secretive than possessive; Boba Fett had sometimes wondered if they grew so huge by greedily ingesting everything that came into reach of their little hands and huge mouths, and letting nothing go. Not even one frightened accountant with a computer-enhanced brain full of numbers.

"Why don't you just kill me now?" Posondum hunkered on the floor of the cage, his back against its bars. He'd tasted the tray and pushed it away in disgust. "You'd do a quicker job of it than the Hutts will."

"Likely so." He felt no pity for the man, who'd brought his troubles upon himself. *You hang out with Hutts,* he thought, *you'd better be careful not to get rolled over on.* "But as I said. I do what I get paid for. No more, no less."

"You'd do anything for credits, wouldn't you?"

Boba Fett could see his own reflection, doubled in the small mirrors of the accountant's resentfully burning eyes. The image he saw was of a full helmet, battered and discolored, yet completely functional; his face was concealed by the narrow, T-shaped visor. His combat gear bristled with armaments, from shin to wrist; the tapered nose of a directional rocket protruded from behind one shoulder. A walking arsenal, a humanoid figure built out of machines. The lethal kind.

The reflected image nodded slowly. "That's right," said Boba Fett. "I do the things I'm good at, and for which I get paid the best." He glanced down at the data readout. "It's nothing personal."

"Then we could make a deal." Posondum looked up hopefully at his captor. "Couldn't we?"

"What kind of deal?"

"What do you think?" The accountant stood up

and gripped the bars nearest to Fett. "You like getting paid—I know the kind of outrageous fees you charge for your services—and I like remaining alive. I'm probably as fond of that as you are of credits."

Boba Fett let his masked gaze rest upon the other's sweating face. "You should have considered how precious your life is to you *before* you incurred the wrath of the Hutts. It's a little late for regrets now."

"But it's not too late for you to make some credits. More credits than the Hutts can pay you." Posondum pressed his face into the bars, as though he could somehow squeeze out between them through the sheer force of his desperation. "You let me go and I'll make it worth your while."

"I doubt it," said Fett coldly. "The Hutts pay excellent bounties. That's why I like taking on their jobs."

"And why do you think they want to get me back so badly?" Posondum's knuckles turned white and bloodless as his fists tightened. "Just for the old ledgers I've got stowed away inside my head? Or just so the competition won't find out a few little trade secrets?"

"It's not my business as to why my clients desire certain things. Things such as yourself." A small indicator light pulsed on his wrist-mounted data readout; he'd have to return to the *Slave I*'s controls soon. "I'm just pleased that they do want them. And that they'll pay."

"Just like I will." Posondum lowered his voice, though there was no one to overhear. "I took more than information when I left the Hutts. I took credits—a lot of 'em."

"That was foolish of you." Fett knew how tight the Huttese were with credits; it was a characteristic of their species. There had been times when he'd needed to take extreme measures to get paid for the completion of a job, even when the terms had been agreed upon beforehand. So to steal from a Hutt, and to think that one could get away with it, was the height of idiocy.

"Maybe so—but there was so *much* of it. And I thought I could get away, that I could hide. And my new bosses would protect me. . . ."

"They did the best they could." Boba Fett shrugged. "It just wasn't good enough. It never is, when I'm involved."

"Look, I'll give you the credits. All of them." Posondum trembled with the fervor of his plea. "Every credit I stole from the Hutts—it's all yours. Just let me go."

"And just where are these credits?"

Posondum drew back from the cage's bars. "They're hidden."

"I could very easily find out the location." Fett kept his voice as level and emotionless as before. "The extracting of useful information is a specialty of mine."

"It's memory-encrypted," said the accountant. "Below the conscious level. And with a trauma sensor implanted." He pointed to a small scar just above his left ear. "You try to dig the info out of me, it'll trip and wipe the cortical segment clean. Then nobody will ever find where I put the credits."

"There's ways around those things." Boba Fett had seen them before. "Bypasses and shunts—they're not pleasant. But they work." He supposed the Hutts were already preparing a deep neurosurgical dissection room for Posondum upon his return. "It doesn't matter to me, though. Since I'm not making a deal with you, anyway."

"But why not?" The accountant had reached one of his skinny arms through the bars, trying to grab hold of Boba Fett's sleeve. "It's a fortune—it's more than the Hutts have offered you—"

"It very well might be." He had stepped away from the cage, back to the unadorned and functional metal treads that would return him to the *Slave I*'s cockpit. "You might be as good a thief as you are a number cruncher. And if you're going to steal even one credit from a Hutt, you might as well steal a billion. The consequences are the same. But even if you do have that kind of credits hidden away, I'm not interested in them. Or not interested enough. I have my reputation to think of."

"Your . . ." Posondum gaped at him in amazement and dismay. "Your *what*?"

"The Hutts and all my other clients—they pay me the kind of bounties they do because of one thing. I deliver. Once I've caught my prey, nothing stops me from bringing it in. *Nothing*. If I take on a job, I complete it. And everyone in the galaxy knows that."

"But . . . but I've heard of other bounty hunt- ers . . . who'll cut a deal. . . ."

"Other bounty hunters may conduct their busi- ness as they please." Fett barely managed to keep from his voice the contempt with which he held the so-called Bounty Hunters Guild's members. That kind of shortsighted greed was one of the reasons he had no desire to associate himself with the Guild. "They have their standards . . . and I have mine." One of his gloved hands grasped the ladder's side rail; he looked back over his shoulder at the cage. "And I've got the merchandise, and they don't. There's a connection."

Posondum's knees visibly weakened, his hands sliding down the bars as he sank limply toward the cage's floor. Whatever glint of hope had been in his face was now extinguished.

"I suggest you go ahead and eat." Boba Fett nodded his helmet toward the tray and its congealed contents. "You'll need to keep up your strength."

He didn't wait for an answer. He climbed up from the ship's holding pens and back toward its waiting controls.

5

"Here he comes." Lookout had spotted the approaching ship. That was its job. "I can see him."

"Of course you can," said Kud'ar Mub'at. "That's a good node." With the tip of one multijointed, chitinous leg, the assembler stroked the little semicreature's head. The exterior-observation node was one of the more simpleminded subassemblies scurrying about the web. Kud'ar Mub'at had let just about enough cerebral tissue develop inside so that it could focus its immense light-gathering lens on the surrounding stars and anything that moved among them. "Tell Calculator just what you saw."

The necessary data zapped along the web's tangled neurons. Another subassembly, with useless vestigial legs and a softly fragile shell encasing its specific-function cortex, mulled over what it had received, converting raw visuals to useful numbers. "Thyip thyoud arrive . . ." Calculator's tiny lisping mouth moved beneath the wobbling lump of neural matter. "In leth thyan thuh-ree thtandard time part-th."

"I know who it is!" Identifier scrambled up onto Kud'ar Mub'at's shoulder—if arachnoids could be said to have shoulders—and excitedly chattered into its earhole. The little database subassembly had listened in to what Lookout had told Calculator. "I know, I know! It's the *Slave I!* Positive identification made—"

"Of course it is." With another leg, Kud'ar Mub'at plucked Identifier from its body—the childlike subassemblies would swarm all over it, if it let them—and set the node down on one of the web's structural strands. "Now just settle down, little one."

"Boba Fett must be aboard!" Identifier, with its own miniature versions of its parent's stiff-spined legs, skittered back and forth on the taut silken fiber. "Boba Fett!" The subassembly had no particular liking for the bounty hunter; it just got excited over any visitors to the web. "It's Boba Fett's ship!"

Kud'ar Mub'at sighed wearily, someplace deep inside his near-spherical abdomen. His own mannerisms were slow and somewhat languid, or as much so as the latter term could be applied to a chitin-encased arachnoid. The constant chatter of Identifier annoyed him on occasion. *Perhaps,* mused Kud'ar Mub'at, *I should reabsorb that node. And design and develop another one. A quieter one.* But right now the problem wasn't so much that of raw materials—Kud'ar Mub'at could always extrude more subassembly fiber—as of time. Time lag, to be precise; even a node as relatively uncomplicated as that took hundreds of time units to develop to an operational standard. With as much business as Kud'ar Mub'at was handling right now, it couldn't afford to be without a functioning identifier.

Maybe later, thought the assembler as it hung suspended in a nexus of the web's thicker strands. *When this business with Boba Fett is over.* Kud'ar Mub'at figured that its credit accounts would be fat enough then, so that it could afford to take a little time off. It would have to talk to Balancesheet about that.

"Go tell Docker and the Handler twins." Kud'ar Mub'at gave the little chore to Identifier, rather than just plugging back into the web's communication neurons. "Tell them to get ready for company."

The little subassembly jumped and scurried away, down the dark, fibrous corridors to the web's distant landing snare. *That'll keep it out of my leg hairs for a while,* thought Kud'ar Mub'at. It gently moved Lookout aside and applied one of its own compound eyes to the view hole, scanning the stars for any visible indication of his enemy and business associate.

He'd long ago decided that this was the worst part of the job. *I'd rather hang out with the Hutts,* thought Boba Fett. And that was saying something: Huttese palaces, like the one Jabba the Hutt kept on Tatooine, were sinkholes of gratuitous depravity. Every time he'd been in one, either delivering a captive or collecting a bounty in person, he'd felt as though he had been slogging through a sewer filled with the galaxy's offal and waste. The careless ease with which someone like Jabba could dispose of an underling—Boba Fett had heard of the pet rancor creature that Jabba kept beneath his palace, but hadn't yet seen it—always irritated him. Why kill when there was no profit involved? A waste of time, credits, and flesh. But even a Hutt's palace was more to Fett's liking than Kud'ar Mub'at's web.

The tapering cylinder floated in the *Slave I*'s viewport, gradually growing closer. It didn't even look like a constructed artifact, as much as it resembled some accidental conglomeration of glue and wire, strung together with a Corellian scavenge rat's idiot thrift. As Fett's ship approached, and Kud'ar Mub'at's web blotted out more of the stars in the viewport, various bits of machinery could be seen, sharper-edged than the clotted fibers in which they were embedded. Boba Fett had been dealing with the arachnoid assembler long enough to know that it couldn't resist a bargain, no matter what kind of worthless junk was involved; portions of the web were a museum of defunct interstellar transports and other dead castoffs. Even Jawas pursued their trade in junk and used droids as a way of turning a profit; Kud'ar Mub'at apparently just liked accumulating stuff, incorporating it into the space-drifting home the assembler had spun out from its own guts.

Though it wasn't all just junk, Boba Fett knew; that was merely what Kud'ar Mub'at let show on the surface of the web, perhaps as a matter of protective camouflage. Not everyone had done as well in their encounters with the assembler as he had; the few times that Fett had actually gone into the web, he'd spotted some not inconsiderable treasures, bits and pieces that the less fortunate had been obliged to leave behind, to discharge their debts to Kud'ar Mub'at. It would probably be better to leave one's skin behind than try to cheat the spidery entity.

Faint greenish lights showed in a rough circle, indicating the docking section of the web. One of Kud'ar Mub'at's subassemblies—Signaler was what it was called, if Fett remembered correctly—was a phosphorescent herpetoid node, long enough to encircle one end of the web with its glowing, snakelike form. Kud'ar Mub'at had let enough intelligence develop in the node so that it could blink out a simple directional landing pattern for any ship making a rendezvous with the web. Another group of subassemblies, arrayed just inside the pulsing circle, were devoid of even that much brainpower; they could sense the proximity of a spacecraft and, like the tentacles of a Threndrian snareflower, grab hold and bring it in tight and secure to the web's entry port. Boba Fett loathed the idiot appendages, with their flexing vacuum-resistant scales like rust-pitted armor plate. He'd told Kud'ar Mub'at before, that if he ever found any scraps from the tentacles still clinging to the *Slave I* after he'd left the web, he'd turn around and pluck the nodes one by one from the web with a short-range tractor beam. That'd be a painful process for Kud'ar Mub'at; every piece of the living web was connected to the assembler by a skein of neurofibers.

He cut the *Slave I*'s approach engines, leaving the craft with enough momentum to keep it on a slow and steady course toward the web's dock. Inside the ring of light, the tips of the grappling nodes had already begun to ease into position as the subassemblies woke from their dreaming half sleep.

"Ah, my dear Fett." A high-pitched voice greeted him as he clambered down from the docking port into the narrow confines of the web's interior. "How truly a delight it is to see you once more. After how horribly such a long time it has been—"

"Stow it." Boba Fett looked up and saw by the top of his helmet one of Kud'ar Mub'at's mobile vocal appendages, a subassembly that was little more than a rudimentary mouth tethered by a glistening cord. This one must have been just recently extruded by the assembler, the neural silk was still white and unmarked by the web's centuries of accumulated filth. "I'm here for business, not conversation."

The little voice box scurried along the tunnel's

fibrous ceiling, a pair of tiny claws reeling in its connecting line as it kept pace with Fett. "Ah, that is truly indeed the bounty hunter of my long acquaintance, so bold and vivid he is in my remembering! How sadly long I have been without the pleasure of your succinct and charming wit."

Fett made no reply as he clambered through the tunnel, its interwoven tissues yielding beneath the weight of his boots. Wherever his thick gloves grabbed hold, ripples of firing synapses sparked in fading concentric circles, as though from a stone dropped in an ocean filled with phosphorescent plankton. A few light nodes, the smaller brethren of Signaler on the web's exterior, glowed before him and dropped back into darkness after he had passed by. Fett supposed that when Kud'ar Mub'at had no visitor, the web remained unlit. The assembler required no light to move around inside an artifact constructed of its own spun-out cortex.

"There you are in your entirety!" The same voice, like sheet metal being torn in half, sounded from in front of Boba Fett as he ducked beneath a ridge of hardened silk. "I knew you'd return, crowned with the eminence of success." The words were louder, coming from Kud'ar Mub'at's own mouth rather than the little voice-box node. "And of undeniable punctuality you are as well, indeed."

Boba Fett stepped into the web's central chamber, a space large enough for him to stand upright in. It was more than a matter of simile that it seemed to Fett as though he had walked into the center of the assembler's brain. That was the reality of Kud'ar Mub'at's nest and body, an interconnected unity, one and the same thing. *It lives inside its armor,* thought Fett, *as I live inside mine.*

"I returned here when I said I would." Fett

turned his masked gaze upon the assembler. "It was a simple enough job."

"Ah, for one of your exceedingly multifarious talents, yes, I imagine it was." Kud'ar Mub'at's compound eyes focused on his visitor. One of its jointed, spike-haired forelegs inscribed a graceful acknowledging gesture in the chamber's thick air. "No complications, I take it?"

"The usual." He folded his arms across the front of his battle-gear. "There were a couple of other bounty hunters who were hoping to nab him before I did."

"Ooh." The eyes, like dark black cabochons, glittered with anticipation. "And you took care of them?"

"I didn't have to." Fett knew how much the assembler enjoyed war stories, the more violence-filled the better. He didn't feel like indulging the arachnoid creature's taste. "They were just the usual feckless types that the Bounty Hunters Guild sends out. It's easier to walk around a pile of nerf dung than step right into it."

"How very droll! You amuse me greatly!" Kud'ar Mub'at reached up to the chamber's ceiling with several of its hind legs, lifting itself up from where it had been resting its pale abdomen. "It is a savory bonus of our relationship that I am privileged to hear your scintillating repartee." The bed node wheezed as it reinflated its cushiony pneumatic bladders. Kud'ar Mub'at worked his way across the chamber's ceiling, finally dangling its mandibled face directly in front of the bounty hunter. "Have we not more than a mere business relationship, my dear Fett? Please say yes. Say that we are friends, you and I."

"Friends," said Boba Fett coldly, "are a liability

in my trade." He drew the visor of his helmet back from the assembler's glittering eyes and V-shaped smile. "I'm not here to amuse you. Pay me the bounty you're holding in escrow, I'll hand the merchandise over to you, and I'll go."

"Until the next time." Kud'ar Mub'at turned its head, regarding him with another set of gemlike eyes. "Which cannot be anytime too soon, for my preference."

Maybe it's this part of the job, Boba Fett thought to himself, *that's the worst.* Tracking someone down, pursuing him the width of the galaxy, capturing, transporting, killing anyone who had to be killed in order to get the job done—those things were all cold pleasures, to be savored as tests and confirmations of his own skills. Dealing with any of the clients, whether it was a matter of direct negotiation such as with the Empire's Lord Vader or a sleaze mountain such as Jabba the Hutt, or a third-party negotiation with a middle entity such as Kud'ar Mub'at, was more repellent than satisfying. It always turned out to be the same thing, every time. *They never want to pay up,* brooded Fett. *They always want the merchandise; they just never want to part with their credits in exchange.* With Hutts, it was always an emotional issue, at least at the start. Their megalomaniacal rages at any perceived sign of disloyalty led them to post huge, eye-popping bounties; later, when they had simmered down a bit, the Hutts' natural cold-blooded greed kicked in and they tried to take the prices down. The members of the so-called Bounty Hunters Guild would accept a fraction of an original bounty, sometimes as low as ten percent. That was one of the reasons that Boba Fett despised them: he had never taken a credit less than the agreed-upon sum, and had no intention of starting.

"I have other business to take care of," said Boba Fett. That was true. The galaxy was wide, with lots of dark nooks and crannies, remote worlds and even entire planetary systems that could serve as hiding places. And there were always those entities with reasons to hide, either to save their epidermis from Emperor Palpatine's coruscating wrath or to clutch in their sweating hands the meager piles of credits they had managed to pry out of Jabba's coffers. Even with as much "business" as Boba Fett handled, there were still plenty of scraps left for the Guild to dole out to its members, the small stuff that he couldn't be bothered with. But the longer that Kud'ar Mub'at needlessly detained him here, cackling and wheezing at him inside the tangled corridors of its own expanded brain, the greater the chance that some hustling Guild member would be able to snatch some prize bounty away from him. That notion would have infuriated Fett, if any such word of passion could have been applied to the coldly unfeeling logic that dictated his actions. As it was, he let his masked gaze rest upon Kud'ar Mub'at's insectile face like the sharp point of a bladed weapon. "Pay me, and I won't detain you from your own . . . *business*."

Everyone in the galaxy knew what Kud'ar Mub'at's business was. There was no other entity among the stars quite like the notorious assembler. If there were other members of its species on some distant planet, covered with skeins and nets of their extruded neural silk, that world hadn't been discovered yet. Perhaps Kud'ar Mub'at was the only existing assembler; Fett had heard rumors, dating back to a time before he'd become the galaxy's most-feared bounty hunter, of Kud'ar Mub'at's predecessor, another assembler of whom Kud'ar Mub'at itself had been a node, a semi-independent creature like the ones that scuttled around this web, dragging their neurofiber tethers behind them. That parent assembler had made the mistake of letting one of its offspring become a little too developed and independent, and had paid the price: death and ingestion by the web's new owner, the usurper Kud'ar Mub'at. *The assembler is dead,* thought Boba Fett with distaste, *long live the assembler.* Even Hutts, with their monstrous appetites and vicious family rivalries, drew the line at actually eating one of their own clan that they might have beaten out for control of some typically shady enterprise.

With the web, drifting through interstellar space, and its contents had come the assembler's business. *Some* entity had to act as the universe's go-between and intermediary, especially among all the worlds' criminal elements and those who did business with criminals. If there had ever been a time when there had been honor among thieves, it was long over in this galaxy. Boba Fett had never cheated any of his clients, though he had been forced to kill quite a few. If everybody had held to his standards of business morality, there wouldn't have been any need for an operator like Kud'ar Mub'at. As it was, the assembler took a justifiable percentage for the services he provided, the setting up of deals between murderously inclined entities, the holding in escrow of bounty payments, the transfer of captives to those who had put up the credits for them. The Bounty Hunters Guild worked almost all their jobs through Kud'ar Mub'at; Boba Fett used the assembler when that was the client's preference and the percentage was raked off from the other side and not his own.

"But my highly esteemed Fett—" As Kud'ar Mub'at dangled from the web's ceiling, it rubbed its tiniest and most agile forelimbs together. "It is not entirely a matter of such highly enjoyable socialization that causes me to desire the extending of your visit to my abode. You speak of your own business, which you are naturally in such a haste to attend to. Very well; let us speak of business together. You know me—" The assembler's compound eyes twinkled. "I'm as delightedly happy to talk about that as any other subject. And right now your business and mine once again coincide. Is that not a pleasing happenstance?"

Boba Fett studied the assembler's narrow face, looking for any clue that would reveal the creature's true intentions, always hidden beneath its oily chatter. "What business are you talking about?" Usually, any news of a bounty being posted was caught directly by the *Slave I*'s programmed comm scanners. "A private job?"

"Ah, you are so astute." The assembler's forelimbs made little scraping noises, like thin and cheap plastoid shells. "Little wonder that you are such a success in your chosen field of endeavor. Yes, my dear Fett, a very private job indeed."

That interested Fett. Of all the things that Kud'ar Mub'at could have said, that caught his attention more than any other. Private jobs were the cream of the bounty-hunter trade. There were times when clients, for reasons of their own, wanted some fugitive entity caught and delivered with a maximum of discretion. Posting a bounty galaxy-wide effectively eliminated any chance of maintaining secrecy; for the client to get what it wanted, arrangements would have to be made with one particular bounty hunter. More often than not, that would be Boba Fett himself; over the decades he'd built up a reputation for confidentiality as well as effectiveness.

"Who's the client?" It wasn't essential for Boba

Fett to know, though it sometimes made the job easier. If it was all being arranged through Kud'ar Mub'at, the client's desire for secrecy might be absolute, without even the hunter knowing who was putting up the bounty. "Is it one of the Hutts?"

"Not this time." Kud'ar Mub'at displayed his approximation of a smile again. "You and I have done so much business for Jabba and his brethren lately. After I turn over our little friend Posondum to them, I would not be greatly surprised if they decided to tighten their purse strings for a while. No, no; don't say a word—" The forelimbs waved about. "You don't need to remind me that I can hardly deliver anything to anybody until you've been paid. Balancesheet!" The assembler's screech rang down the length of the web. "Get in here! Immediately!"

Kud'ar Mub'at's accountant node carefully picked its way along the fibers and entered the central chamber. Of all of the subassemblies, this was the one that Boba Fett had always found most to his liking—and not just because it was the one that actually handed over the bounties that its parent would be holding in escrow. The crablike Balancesheet, as Kud'ar Mub'at had named its extruded creation, had a laconic, no-nonsense approach to its duties that Fett found similar to his own. He would be sorry—or as much so as he ever was—when Kud'ar Mub'at would determine that the little accountant node had developed as much intelligence as could be allowed. Balancesheet, like other nodes before it, would be eaten by its parent before there was any danger of independence and mutiny of the kind that had made Kud'ar Mub'at master of the assembler web.

"Boba Fett, current account; balance due . . ." The accountant node maneuvered its pliable shell close to his shoulder, extending its eyestalks parallel to the chamber's floor as it made an ID scan of the bounty hunter's distinctive helmet. "Just a moment, please."

"Take your time," said Fett. "Accuracy is a virtue."

Balancesheet said nothing, but a brief flicker in its gaze acknowledged that it and Boba Fett were kindred entities, in spirit if not species.

"Previous balance zero." Balancesheet had finished its show of calculation. "Due upon delivery of one humanoid, designation Nil Posondum, client being the Huttese business front Trans-Zone Development and Exploitation Consortium, the sum of twelve thousand five hundred credits." The accountant node swiveled its eyestalks toward its parent. "Our fee has already been paid by the Hutts. The entire bounty being held is now payable to Boba Fett."

"But of course," crooned Kud'ar Mub'at softly. "Who would deny it?"

The eyestalks turned back toward Fett. "And the individual Nil Posondum is in a living and desirable condition, certain nonessential injuries excepted, as per standard bounty-hunting practice?"

Boba Fett raised his wrist-mounted comm unit to the front of his helmet. A tiny red spark indicated that the link to *Slave I's* cockpit controls was unbroken. "Open inspection port Gamma Eight." That port allowed visual access to the cages in his ship's cargo hold. "Perimeter defenses on standby."

A moment later Balancesheet looked over at its parent. "Designated merchandise appears to be in good condition." The announcement was more for Boba Fett's hearing than the assembler's; the sensory data from the remote optical node had traveled down the neural network linking Kud'ar Mub'at with the accountant and all the other subassemblies in the web. "Initiating transfer."

That was the kind of thing that would get the little accountant eaten; it hadn't waited for Kud'ar Mub'at's order. Boba Fett supposed that the next time he came to the web, a newly extruded node would be maintaining Kud'ar Mub'at's intricate finances.

"I most sincerely hope that you enjoy the well-earned possession of those credits." Kud'ar Mub'at watched as Fett tucked the amount-sealed credit packet into one of his gear's carrying pouches. Balancesheet had made the payment and picked its way over to another section of the chamber. "I often wonder—" The assembler extended its smiling face toward him. "Just what is it that you *do* with all the credits you get paid? Granted, you have considerable expenditures, to keep going such a level of operation. The equipment, the intelligence sources, all of those things. But you make so much more than that; I know you do." A few of Kud'ar Mub'at's eyes peered more closely at him. "But what do you spend it on?"

One of Boba Fett's rare flashes of anger rose inside him. "That's none of your business." *Slave I* had signaled that the captive had been removed from the cargo hold and into one of the web's dismal subchambers; all ports had been resealed. The temptation to stalk out of this place, to get back into his ship and tear himself into the cold, clean depths of space, was almost overwhelming. "Let's talk about the business that you and I do have with each other."

"Ah, yes! Most certainly!" Kud'ar Mub'at flexed its main limbs, causing its segmented torso to bob up and down in front of its visitor. "It's not really the usual sort of thing you do; it's not a matter of tracking down someone and delivering them, all wrapped up in a neat little package. But you're *so* versatile— aren't you?—that I'm sure it's something you can handle with your characteristic dispatch."

Fett's suspicions were always aroused when a job was described as being out of the ordinary. That usually meant that the danger to him would be greater, or that getting paid would be more difficult, or both. Jabba the Hutt was always coming up with numbers like that, where Fett was expected to risk his life on some flaky errand. "I asked you before," he growled. "Who's the client?"

"There isn't one." Kud'ar Mub'at seemed delighted to make that announcement. "Or at least, not in the usual sense. I'm not acting on behalf of a third party. This job would be for *me*."

The suspicions heightened. Kud'ar Mub'at had always been the perfect intermediary, keeping his role scrupulously separate from his clients' interests. That go-between function was valued so highly that even the most ruthless connivers such as Jabba had never tried to cheat the assembler. It was hard to imagine who could have incurred Kud'ar Mub'at's enmity, to the point of the assembler requiring Fett's lethal skills.

At the same time, though—Boba Fett's calculations clicked over inside his helmeted skull—there was no doubt that Kud'ar Mub'at could pay for whatever it wanted. Fett wasn't in the habit of questioning his various employers' desires—but just delivering them. Not every job required a living piece of merchandise; leaving a dead body on the blood-soaked soil of a remote planet was also within his range of expertise.

"So just what is it that you want me to do for you?"

Kud'ar Mub'at pointed one of its jointed fore-limbs toward him. "Tell me first—or tell me *again*—what you think of the Guild. You know; the Bounty Hunters Guild."

"I don't," said Fett. He gave a slight shrug. "It's not worth thinking about. If any of its members were at all proficient, they wouldn't be in it. An organization like that is for the weak and harmless, who think that by combining their forces they might become deadly. They're wrong."

"Harsh words, my dear Fett! Harsh words, indeed! There are some accomplished hunters in the Guild, with achievements nearly equaling your own. The Guild has been headed for many years now by the Trandoshan Cradossk; he was a legend among the stars when you were first starting out."

"So he was." Fett nodded once. "And now he is old and feeble, if still cunning. His offspring Bossk was one of those who got in my way as I was capturing Nil Posondum. If the son were one tenth the bounty hunter that the father had been, I might have some competition. But he's not, and I don't. The Bounty Hunters Guild's glory days are long in the past."

"Ah, my dear Fett, I see that your opinions have not changed." Kud'ar Mub'at shook its dust-speckled head. "You wield them like something that you've taken from that arsenal you carry on your back. I'll have to make it very much worth your while, expensively thus, to entice you into accepting this little job of mine."

Fett kept his helmet's featureless gaze on the assembler. "Which is?"

"It's really very simple." Kud'ar Mub'at clicked the points of his forelimbs together. "I want you to *join* the Bounty Hunters Guild."

The assembler's compound eyes were not the only ones watching him. Boba Fett could sense the tiny crablike accountant and all the rest of the web's interconnected nodes, their overlapping vision feeding into the central cortex of their master and parent. They were all watching—and waiting for his answer.

"You're right about one thing," said Boba Fett.

Kud'ar Mub'at's eyes glittered even more brightly. "Yes? What's that?"

His suspicions hadn't gone away; if anything, they were even sharper and harder. *The simple jobs,* he said to himself. *Those are the ones you get killed on.*

"This job of yours . . ."

"Yes?" The tethered subassemblies crept closer to Kud'ar Mub'at, as though the web itself were narrowing tighter.

Boba Fett gave a slow nod of his helmet. "It'll cost you."

6

From a small viewport embedded in a wall of tangled fibers, a slit-pupiled eye of deep violet hue watched the bright trail of an interstellar craft, dwindling among the wide-flung stars. A moment later the engine flare blinked out of sight, as the *Slave I* leaped into hyperspace and was gone.

"Your Excellency—" One of Kud'ar Mub'at's household nodes hesitated, then skittered closer and tugged at the hem of the ornate, heavy robes brushing the observation chamber's matted floor. "Your presence is now desired by your host."

Prince Xizor turned away from the viewport. His cold reptilian glance took in the trembling subassembly. Perhaps, if he were to crush it beneath the sole of his boot, a shock of pain would flash along the web's neurofibers, straight into Kud'ar Mub'at's chitinous skull. It would be an experiment worth making; he had an interest in whatever might produce fear inside any of the galaxy's inhabitants. *Someday,* Xizor told himself. *But not right now.* "Tell your master," he said in a smooth, unthreatening voice, "that I'll be there directly."

When he entered the web's main chamber, he saw that Kud'ar Mub'at had settled its globular abdomen back into its padded nest. "Ah, my highly esteemed Xizor!" It used the same obsequious voice that he had overheard it lavishing on the departed bounty hunter. "I so very much hope that you weren't uncomfortable in that wretched space! Great is my mortification, my embarrassment that I should offer such—"

"It was more than adequate," said Xizor. "Don't fret yourself about it." He folded his heavily corded forearms across his chest. "I'm not always surrounded by the luxuries of the Emperor's court. Sometimes . . ." He let the corner of his mouth lift in a partial smile. "Sometimes my accommodations—and my companions—are of a rougher sort."

"Ah." Kud'ar Mub'at nodded quickly. "Just so."

The assembler knew better than to speak anything aloud of what his noble guest had just referred to. Even the two words "Black Sun," in as private a place as this, were forbidden. To make silence a general rule was to ensure that no one would discover the other side of Xizor's double existence. In one universe, he was Emperor Palpatine's loyal servant; in that universe's shadowed twin, he was the leader of a criminal organization whose reach, if not power, was as galaxy spanning as the Empire's.

"He took the job." Xizor said the words as a statement of fact, not a question.

"Yes, of course he did." Kud'ar Mub'at fussed nervously with the pneumatic bladders of his nest. "Boba Fett is a reasonable entity. In his way. Very businesslike; I find that to be of the utmost charm in him."

"When you use the word 'businesslike,' " noted Xizor, "you mean . . . 'can be bought.' "

"What other possible definition is there?" As Kud'ar Mub'at gazed at him, the assembler's eyes filled with innocence. "My so dear Xizor—we're all businessmen. We can *all* be bought."

"Speak for yourself." The partial smile on his face turned into a full sneer. "I prefer to be the one who's doing the buying."

"Ah, and so happy am I to be one of those whose services you have purchased." Kud'ar Mub'at settled itself more comfortably into its nest. "I hope this grand scheme of yours, of which I am so small yet hopefully an essential part, will turn out exactly as you, in your ineffable wisdom, wish it to."

"It will," said Xizor, "if you perform the rest of your role as well as you did with hoodwinking Boba Fett."

"You flatter me." Kud'ar Mub'at bowed its head low. "My thespic abilities are regrettably crude, but perhaps they sufficed in this instance."

The assembler had had to be no more than its usual conniving self to set the trap in which the bounty hunter was already ensnared. One of the nodes in the central chamber was a simple auditory unit, a tympanic membrane with legs, tied like all the rest of the nodes into the web's expanded nervous system. From his hiding place, Prince Xizor had been able to listen in, another one of Kud'ar Mub'at's attached offspring whispering into his ear all the words passing between the assembler and Boba Fett. The web surrounding them wasn't the only one that Kud'ar Mub'at could spin. Fett was not aware of it yet, but strands too fine to be detected were already tangling about his boots, drawing him into a trap without escape.

Xizor almost felt sorry for the bounty hunter. The reptilian Falleen species was even more cold-blooded than Trandoshans such as the aging Cradossk and his rage-driven offspring Bossk; pity was not an emotion that Xizor had ever experienced. Whether he was operating on behalf of Emperor Palpatine or secretly advancing the Black Sun's criminal agenda, Xizor manipulated all who came into his reach with the same nonemotion he'd display for pieces on a gaming board. They were to be positioned and used as necessity dictated, sacrificed and discarded when strategy required. *Still,* thought Xizor, *an entity such as Boba Fett . . .* The bounty hunter merited his respect, at least. To look into that helmet's concealing visor was to meet a gaze as ruthless and unsentimental as his own. *He'll fight to survive. And he'll fight well. . . .*

But that was part of the trap that had already seized hold of Boba Fett. The cruel irony—and one that Xizor savored—was that Fett was now doomed by his own fierce nature. All that had kept him alive before, in so many deadly situations, would now bring about his destruction.

Too bad, thought Prince Xizor to himself. In another game, a piece as powerful as that would have had it uses. Only a master player would dare a strategic sacrifice such as this. To lose, however necessarily, such an efficient hunter and killer was his only regret.

"Pardon my admittedly clumsy intrusion." Kud'ar Mub'at's high-pitched voice broke into his musing. "But there are some other tiny, almost insignificant matters to be taken care of. To ensure the complete success of your endeavors, which are as always of such brilliance and—"

"Of course." Xizor regarded the assembler sitting in its animate nest. "You want to be paid."

"Only for the sake of keeping our records straight. A mere formality." With an upraised forelimb, Kud'ar Mub'at directed his accountant node toward the prince. "I'm sure one of your keen perception understands."

"All too well." He watched as the subassembly named Balancesheet picked its way toward him. Nothing happened with Kud'ar Mub'at except on a pay-as-you-go basis. "We've done business together enough times for me to remember without prompting."

A few moments later, when the transfer of credits had been completed, Balancesheet swiveled its eyestalks toward its parent. "The prince's account is once again current, with no outstanding sums due. Per your existing agreement, final payment will be made upon a satisfactory resolution of the Bounty Hunters Guild situation." Balancesheet gave a small nod to Xizor and returned to its perch on the central chamber's wall.

"Affairs are going well," said Xizor. "So far." He had already summoned his ship, the *Virago*, from inside the detection shadow of one of the moons of the nearest planetary system. "I'll be watching to make sure they continue that way."

"But of course." Waving all its sticklike forelimbs, Kud'ar Mub'at dispatched a scuttling flock of nodes to ready the web's docking area. Boba Fett's *Slave I* had departed only a little while before, leaving behind a captive in the darkest subchamber. "You have nothing to fear in that regard." Xizor knew that as soon as he was gone, Kud'ar Mub'at would be in contact with the Hutts, to hand over the bounty hunter's merchandise and collect its middle-entity fee. "All will be well. . . ."

The screech of the assembler's words followed Prince Xizor as he stalked down the tunnel toward the docking area. He'd already decided that as soon as he got back to the Emperor's court, he'd spend a few soothing hours listening to the dulcet croon of his own personal troupe of Falleen altos, to flush any residue of that drilling and defiling voice from his ears.

"What a fool." Kud'ar Mub'at muttered the words with a grim satisfaction. Right at this moment the designation could apply to either of two entities. Both Prince Xizor and Boba Fett were somewhere in hyperspace, speeding toward their destinies; the bounty hunter to a rendezvous with the despised Bounty Hunters Guild, Xizor to the Empire's dark corridors of power. Neither one of them suspected what they had gotten themselves into, the finer web in which they were already enmeshed. *They don't know,* thought Kud'ar Mub'at. That was how it preferred things. *I spin the traps, then pull them in.*

It reached out with one of its smallest forelimbs and stroked the shell of its accountant node. "Soon," said Kud'ar Mub'at. "Soon there will be a great many credits for you to tally up and keep track of." As far as Kud'ar Mub'at was concerned, true power equaled riches, something that one could rake delicate claws across. Only maniacs like Palpatine and his grim lieutenant Lord Vader valued the trembling, bootlicking fear of a galaxy of underlings. That was the kind of power that Prince Xizor wanted as well; his criminal associates in Black Sun were no doubt unaware of their leader's long-range intent. They might not ever find out, either. Some traps were woven for their prey to die in.

"Very well." Balancesheet tapped its own tiny claws together, as though the numbers involved could be counted that simply. "Your accounts are all in good order."

Something in the node's bland response troubled Kud'ar Mub'at. It had extruded this particular sub-assembly some time ago, and had developed it into one of the web's most valuable components. *Flesh of my flesh,* mused Kud'ar Mub'at, *silk of my silk.* And a part of its brain as well: Kud'ar Mub'at could look into Balancesheet's compound eyes and see a calculating replica of itself. Had the node discovered the joys of greed yet? That was the important question. *I must watch for that,* decided the assembler. Greed was a higher sense, perhaps the most important of all. When Kud'ar Mub'at perceived that in the little tethered node, it would be time for death and re-ingestion. Kud'ar Mub'at didn't want to wind up as its own parent had so long ago, a meal for rebellious offspring.

It watched as Balancesheet picked its way into some darker recess of the web. *I hope that won't be for a while yet,* thought Kud'ar Mub'at. Its interconnected business affairs were at a crucial point; much inconvenience would be suffered if it didn't have a fully functioning accountant on claw.

Kud'ar Mub'at decided to think about that later. It closed its several pairs of eyes and happily contemplated all that would soon be added to the web's coffers.

After every job came the cleanup. The *Slave I* was a working vessel, not some pleasure schooner fitted out for languorous cruising between the stars. Even so, Boba Fett preferred keeping the craft as neatly functional as possible. Minor dings and scrapes to the exterior hull were war badges, emblems of encounters that he had survived and someone else hadn't. But future survival might depend on his being able to lay his armor-gloved hand on one of the *Slave I*'s weapon-systems remotes in a split second, without the firing buttons or data readout being obscured by dirt or dried blood.

Besides, thought Boba Fett grimly, *I can't stand the smell.* He squeezed his fist tighter, a soapy antiseptic wash trickling into the bucket set on the floor of the cargo area. There was something nauseating about the humanoid scent of fear that seeped into the very metal of the cages. Of all the sensory data he had ever experienced, from the acrid steam of the Andoan swamp islands to the blinding creation-swirl of the Vinnax system's countervacuum, those molecules signaling panic and desperation were what Fett found to be the most alien. Whatever minute subcutaneous organ produced fear sweat, it was missing in him. Not because he had been born without it—no sentient creature was—but because he had forced it into nonexistence, excised it from his mind with the razor-sharp scalpel of his will. The ancient Mandalorian warriors, whose lethal battle-gear he wore, had been just as coldly ruthless, according to the legends that were still told and retold in whispers throughout the galaxy. Long ago, when he had first gazed upon one of their empty helmets, a relic of an extinguished terror, he had seen in its narrow, unreadable gaze an image of his own future, of the death-bringing entity he would become.

Less than human, mused Boba Fett as he swabbed down the bars that his most recent captive had been held behind. That was what fear did, that was the transformation it wrought in those who let it spring up in their spirits. The thing in the cage, which had carried the name of Nil Posondum, had been some kind of talking, fruitlessly bargaining animal by the time Fett had transferred it to Kud'ar Mub'at's web. Fear of death, and the pain that Hutts enjoyed producing in the targets of their vengeance, had swallowed up all the human parts inside the little accountant.

An odd notion moved in Boba Fett's thoughts, one that he'd turned over and examined like a precious Gerinian star-stone many times before. *Perhaps . . . I became more human than human.* Not by adding anything to himself, but through a process of reduction, of stripping away the flawed and rotten parts of his species. The antiseptic rag in his glove slid over one of the cold-forged bars, leaving no microbe behind. The ancient Mandalorian warriors had had their secrets, which had died with them. *And I have mine.*

Fett dipped the rag in the bucket again. He could have left these chores to one of *Slave I*'s maintenance droids, but he preferred doing it himself. It gave him time to think, of just such matters as this.

The soapy liquid trickled from the battle-gear's elbow as Fett checked the forearm-mounted datascreen patched into the *Slave I*'s cockpit. Rendezvous with the Bounty Hunters Guild's forward base was not far off. He was ready for that—he was never *not* ready, for anything that might happen—but he would still regret the termination of this little slice of nontime, the lull and peace that came between jobs. Other sentient creatures were allowed to enjoy a longer rest, the ultimate peace that came with death. Sometimes he envied them.

He unlocked the empty cage and stepped inside. The fear scent was already diminished, barely detectable through the mask's filters. Posondum hadn't left much of a mess, for which he was grateful; some merchandise let their panic devolve them well past the point of maintaining control of their bodily functions.

The floor of the cage was scratched, though. Bright metallic lines glinted through the darker layer of plastoid beneath Boba Fett's boot soles. He wondered what could have caused that. He was always careful to take any hard, sharp objects away from the merchandise, with which they might damage themselves. Some captives preferred suicide to the attentions they were scheduled to receive from those who had put up the bounties for them.

Fett glanced over to the corner of the *Slave I*'s cargo area, where he had tossed the food tray. None of the gray slop had been touched by Nil Posondum, but one of the tray's corners had been bent into a dull-pointed angle. Just enough to scrape out the markings on the cage's floor—the accountant must have been working on it right up until Kud'ar Mub'at's subassemblies had crept in through the access portal. The spiderlike minions had looped restraining silk around him, then carried him from one prison to another. He might have had time enough to finish whatever message he'd wanted to leave behind.

But there wasn't time now to read it. A red light pulsed on the data readout, alerting him that a return to the craft's piloting area was necessary. The jump out of hyperspace couldn't be accomplished by means of a remote; the *Slave I*'s maneuvering thrusters were too finely gauged, set for zero lag time, in case any of Fett's many enemies and rivals might be waiting for his appearance. And right now he would be sailing straight into the nest of all those who bore him a grudge. He supposed that lizard-faced bumbler Bossk would already have returned to Guild headquarters, licking his wounds and complaining to his spawn-sire Cradossk about the impossible assignment he'd been given. What Bossk wouldn't mention would be *why* it had been impossible, and just who had beaten him to the goods. Cradossk was a wilier old reptile, though—Boba Fett even had a grudging respect for the head of the Bounty Hunters Guild, from some long-ago encounters with him—and would know just what the score was with his feckless underlings.

The Mandalorian battle-gear had a built-in optical recorder, its tiny lens mounted at one corner of the helmet's visor. Boba Fett leaned over the scratches left by the captive accountant, not even bothering with an effort to decipher them. A second later he had scanned the marks and inserted them into the helmet's long-term data-storage unit. He could deal with them later, if he grew curious about what pathetic epitaph the accountant might have devised for himself. Maudlin self-pity held little interest for Boba Fett. Right now an additional beeping tone was sounding in sync with the red dot; *Slave I,* his only true companion, demanded his attention.

He left the bucket of cold, dirty water on the cage's floor. If it spilled and slopped across the plastoid-clad metal, if the feet of all the captives to come scuffed out the scratched message, whatever it was, there would be no great loss. Memory was like that: the leavings of the dead, best forgotten and erased after payment for their sweat-damp carcasses was made. The moment when his hand was about to seize the neck of the merchandise was the only time that mattered. Readiness was all.

Boba Fett climbed the ladder to the interstellar craft's cockpit, his own boots ringing on the treads.

The new job that he had taken on, this scheme of the assembler Kud'ar Mub'at, was about to commence. Soon there would be more payments to add to his account. . . .

And more deaths to be forgotten.

7

"I want to see him." The female had a gaze as sharp and cold as a bladed weapon. "And to talk to him."

Dengar could barely recognize her. He remembered her from Jabba's palace; she had been one of the obese Hutt's troupe of dancing girls. Jabba had liked pretty things, regarding them as exquisite delicacies for his senses, like the wriggling food he'd stuffed down his capacious gullet. And just as with those squirming tidbits, Jabba had savored the death of the young and beautiful. The pet rancor, in its bone-lined cavern beneath the palace, had merely been an extension of Jabba's appetites. Dengar had witnessed one of the other dancing girls, a frightened little Twi'lek named Oola, being ripped apart by the claws of the beast. That had been before Luke Skywalker had killed the rancor, followed sometime later by its owner's death. *No great loss,* thought Dengar. *With either one of them.*

"Why?" Leaning against the rocky wall of his hiding place's main chamber, he kept a safe distance from the female. "He's not exactly a brilliant conversationalist at the moment."

Her name was Neelah; she had told him that much when he had caught her sneaking down the sloping tunnel from the surface. He had gotten the drop on her, catching her off guard from behind a stack of empty supply crates. With her throat in the crook of his arm, as Dengar's other hand had painfully bent her wrist up toward her shoulder blades, she'd answered a few questions for him. And then she had caught him in the shin with a hard, fast back kick, followed by a knee to the groin that had sent a small constellation of stars to the top of his skull.

"That's personal." They were in a standoff now, glaring at each other from across the cramped space. "I have my own business with him."

What business would an ex–dancing girl have with a bounty hunter? Especially one as close to death as Boba Fett was right now. *Maybe,* mused Dengar, *she thinks she can get a discount from him, since he's so messed up.* Though who would she want him to track down?

He glanced over to the doorway of the hiding place's other chamber. "What condition is our guest in today?"

The taller medical droid tilted its head unit to study the display of vital signs mounted on its own cylindrical body. "The patient's condition is stable," announced SHΣ1-B. "The prognosis is unchanged from its previous trauma-scan indices of point zero zero twelve."

"Which means?"

"He's dying."

That was another question: Why couldn't these fnarling droids just say what they meant? He'd had to bang this one around until the solenoids had rattled inside its carapace just to get it to speak this much of a plain Basic.

"Wounds," added SHΣ1-B's shorter companion. "Severity." 1e-XE gave a slow back-and-forth rotation of its top dome. "Not-goodness."

"Whatever." Dengar was looking forward to being rid of this irritating pair. That would come with either Boba Fett's death—or his recovery. Which was looking increasingly less likely.

"If that's the case," said Neelah, "then you're wasting my time. I need to talk to him right now."

"Well, that's sweet of you." Arms folded across his chest, Dengar nodded as he regarded her. "You're not really concerned with whether some bounty hunter pitches it or not. You just want to pump him for some kind of information. Right?"

She made no reply, but Dengar could tell that his words had struck home. The look the female gave him was even more murderous than before. A lot had changed since she'd been one of Jabba's fetching playthings; even in this little time the harsh winds of Tatooine's Dune Sea had scoured her flesh leaner and tauter, the heat of the double suns darkening her skin. What had been soft, nubile flesh, revealed by gossamer silks, was now concealed by the coarse, bloodstained trousers and sleeveless jacket that she must have scavenged from the corpse of one of Jabba's bodyguards; a thick leather belt, its attached holster empty, cinched the uniform tight to her waist and hunger-carved belly.

Starving, thought Dengar. She had to be; the Dune Sea didn't exactly abound with protein sources. "Here—" Keeping an eye on her, Dengar reached into one of the crates and dug out a bar of compressed military rations, salvage from an Imperial scoutship that had crash-landed years before. He tossed the bar to the female. "You look like you need it."

Appetite widened her eyes, showing their deep violet color. Her fingers quickly tore open the thin metallic wrappings; she raised the slab, already softening as it absorbed what moisture it could from the air, to her mouth, but stopped herself before taking a bite.

"Go ahead," said Dengar. "I'm not in the habit of poisoning people." He reached behind himself to one of the niches concealed in the chamber's stones. "If I wanted to get rid of you"—his fist came out with a blaster in it; he raised the weapon and pointed it at Neelah's forehead—"I could do it easier than that."

Her gaze fastened on the blaster, as though its muzzle were doing the talking.

"Good," said Dengar. His groin still ached from the blow he'd received. "*Now* I think we understand each other."

A few seconds passed, then the female nodded slowly. She took a bite of the rations bar, chewed and swallowed.

"I must inform you," came SHΣ1-B's voice from the subchamber doorway. "That any further casualties will have a deleterious impact on our ability to perform our functions in a manner consistent with an appropriate level of therapeutic practice."

Dengar swiveled the blaster toward the droid. "If there's any more 'casualties' around here, I'll be sweeping them up with a magnet. Got me?"

SHΣ1-B leaned back, bumping against his companion. "Understanding," said 1e-XE, speaking for both of them. "Completeness."

"That's nice. Go take care of your patient," said Dengar, slipping the blaster inside his own belt. He glanced back over at Neelah. "You enjoying that?"

She had virtually inhaled the rations bar. Her

pale fingernails plucked out a few last crumbs from the wrappings.

"Give me some answers," said Dengar, "and you can have another one."

She crumpled the foil into a shining ball inside her small fist.

I'm getting soft, thought Dengar. There had been a time when he wouldn't have bothered asking questions. He wouldn't have lowered the blaster, either, until there had been a corpse lying in front of him, with a hole burned through its brain. That was what letting himself fall in love—not with this female, but with his betrothed, Manaroo—had done for him. That was always a fatal mistake for a bounty hunter. Somebody like Boba Fett survived at this game for as long as he had by stripping those useless emotions out of his heart. To look at Fett, even when he was unconscious on the pallet in the other chamber, was to look at a weapon, an assault rifle fully primed and charged for maximum destruction. Peel away that Mandalorian battle armor of his, and something equally hard and deadly was found beneath. And that, Dengar knew, was the difference—one of them, at least—between himself and the galaxy's most feared bounty hunter. There was still something human inside Dengar, despite his having worked the bounty-hunter trade, with all its spirit-eroding capabilities. That was the part that had looked upon Manaroo, and had decided, despite all the rest of his scrabbling, callused nature, to twine his fate with hers. Manaroo had asked him to marry her, and he had said yes; that human part had wanted to stay human, like a dwindling flame that struggles to keep from being snuffed out. He didn't want to wind up like Boba Fett, a killing machine with a blind, unfathomable mask for a face.

It was that human part that had also decided to send Manaroo away, once she had helped him get Boba Fett into this hiding place. Their separation from each other would continue at least until this business with Boba Fett was over. Dengar knew the risks in getting involved with someone who had as many grudge-bearing enemies as Fett; there were plenty of diehards from the old Bounty Hunters Guild who had good reason to hate his guts. If they found out that Boba Fett was still alive, they'd be swooping down on Tatooine en masse to finish him off. *And me,* Dengar had told himself. That hot-tempered Trandoshan Bossk would naturally assume that anyone befriending his longtime rival Boba Fett was an enemy to be killed with quick dispatch. This little hiding place would get filled up with corpses pretty quickly.

Risks meant profits, though, in the bounty-hunter trade. And profits were what Dengar needed if he was going to have any chance of paying off the massive debt load he was carrying and then have any kind of life with Manaroo. He wanted out of this game, and the only way to accomplish that was to keep on playing it, for at least a few more rounds. And the best way to do that, he'd decided, was with a partner like Boba Fett. *And that's what he offered me*—when Dengar had discovered him, half-digested by the gullet of the Sarlacc, lying in the suns-baked wasteland, Fett had had enough remaining strength to speak, but not to protect himself. Dengar could have put him out of his misery right then and there, but had stayed his hand when Fett had spoken of a partnership between the two of them. The only card he'd had left to play . . .

And a good one. *We could clean up,* Dengar had

decided. *Him and me.* A real good team. It all depended on just one thing.

Whether Fett had been lying to him.

He could have been just playing for time. Time enough for his wounds to heal, and for him to get his act back together. Dengar had been mulling it over ever since he had carried Fett down here. There was no history of Boba Fett ever working with a partner before; he had always been a lone operator. Why should he want a partnership now? What there was a history of was playing it fast and loose with the truth. In that, Boba Fett was no different from any other bounty hunter; it was that kind of a business. Fett was just better at it, was all. What had happened to the Bounty Hunters Guild was proof of that.

Things might be different, Dengar knew, when Boba Fett got his strength back. Fett might not want to repay Dengar with a partnership, for all that he'd done to keep him alive and safe. Dengar's reward might be a blaster charge right into his chest, leaving a scorched hole big enough to put a humanoid's fist through. Fett's obsession with secrecy was notorious in all the scummy dives and watering holes across the galaxy; his past was largely unknown, and was likely to stay that way, given how those who poked into his affairs had a way of turning up dead. That was the real reason Dengar had sent Manaroo away. It was one thing for him to risk Fett's lethal treachery; he didn't want the female he loved to wind up facing a blaster muzzle.

"So what did you want to know?"

Dengar pulled himself back from his grim meditations to the hard-eyed female regarding him from the other side of the chamber.

"Same thing I wanted to know before." He nodded toward the entrance to the subchamber. "What's your connection with Boba Fett?"

Neelah shook her head. "I don't know."

"Oh, *that's* a good one." Dengar gave a quick, derisive laugh. "You come sneaking in here—not exactly the smartest thing to do—and you don't even know why."

"That's what I came here to find out. That's why I wanted to talk to him." Neelah glanced toward the subchamber, then back toward Dengar. "That's why I left him where you would be sure to find him—"

"Wait a minute," said Dengar. "*You* left him?"

She nodded. "I found him before you did. But I knew there was nothing I could do for him, not with what the Sarlacc had done. He needed medical attention—more than anything I could do. I took a chance that you'd take care of him. That you'd keep him alive."

"And why's that so important to you? He's a bounty hunter, and you were a dancing girl in Jabba's palace." Dengar peered more closely at her. "What's he got to do with you?"

"I told you before—" Neelah's voice rose to a fierce shout. "*I don't know!* I just know that there is a connection—some kind of connection—between the two of us. I knew that back when I first saw him. In the palace, in Jabba's court. When that fat slug had poor Oola killed . . . when she was tugging against the chain, and the trapdoor in front of the throne was opening . . ." Both of Neelah's fists were trembling and white-knuckled. "All of the other girls were watching from the passageway . . . and there was nothing any of us could do. . . ."

"There never is," said Dengar. He could taste his own bitterness in his mouth. "That's how things happen in this universe."

She wasn't here in this chamber with him; she was lost in her own memory. "And then we could hear her screaming . . . and I couldn't look anymore. That was when I saw him. Just standing there at the side of the court . . . and watching. . . ."

"Bounty hunters," said Dengar dryly, "make it a habit to stay out of other creatures' business. Unless they're paid to do something about it."

"And when the screaming was over, and Jabba and the others were still laughing . . . he was still there. Just as before. And still watching." Neelah closed her eyes for a moment as a shudder ran through her slight body. "And then . . . the strangest thing . . . he turned and looked at *me*. Right into my eyes." Her voice filled with both fear and wonder. "All the way across Jabba's court . . . and it was like there was nobody else there at all. That was how it felt. And that was when I knew. That there was something between the two of us." She refocused her gaze on Dengar. " 'Connection' isn't the right word. It's something else. Something from the past. I even knew his name, without asking anyone else." Neelah slowly shook her head. "But that was all I knew."

"All right." The story intrigued Dengar. A matter of practical interest as well: If this female meant something to Boba Fett, then knowing just what it was might give him an additional bargaining chip. "You said it was something from the past. *Your* past?"

She nodded.

"Well, that's a start. But nothing you can remember, I take it?"

Another nod.

"So how did you wind up at Jabba's palace?"

"I don't know that, either." Neelah's fists uncurled, empty and trembling. "I don't know how I got there. All I remember is Oola . . . and the other girls. They helped me. They showed me . . ." Her voice ebbed softer. "What I was to do . . ."

Her memory had been wiped; Dengar recognized the signs. The confusion and welling fear, and the little bits and pieces, scraps of another existence, leaking through. No wipe was ever complete; memory was stored in too many places throughout the humanoid brain. To go after every bit, eradicating them all, would probably be fatal, a reduction beyond basic life-maintenance processes. There were easier, and less expensive, ways of killing a sentient being. *So someone*, thought Dengar, *wanted her alive*. Fett?

"What about your name?" Dengar nodded toward her. " 'Neelah'—was that something you remembered?"

"No; Jabba called me that. I don't know why. But I knew . . ." Her brow furrowed with concentration. "I knew it wasn't my real name. My true name. Somebody took that from me . . . and I couldn't get it back. No matter how hard I tried . . ."

What she told Dengar coincided with his own suspicions. Neelah was a slave name—it didn't fit her. The aristocratic bearing she possessed was too obvious, even in the ill-fitting, scavenged outfit she wore now. She wouldn't be alive now—the Dune Sea's loping predators would be cracking her bones—if there weren't some tough fighting spirit inside her. Things would have gone differently if Jabba had tried to throw her, instead of the other girl, Oola, to his pet rancor. It would've been Neelah rather than Princess Leia wrapping the chain around

Jabba's immense throat and choking the life out of him.

Dengar had more suspicions, which he didn't feel like voicing right at the moment. *Fett must've done it.* The other bounty hunter must've brought her to Jabba's palace; he'd probably also been the one who'd performed the memory wipe on her. The big question was why. Dengar couldn't believe it had been done on Jabba's orders; the Hutt had enjoyed young and beautiful objects, but he'd also been too tight with his credits to have commissioned the kidnapping of the daughter of one of the galaxy's noble houses. The only reason Leia Organa had wound up on the end of one of Jabba's chains was that she had come into Jabba's lair of her own accord, seeking to rescue the carbonite-encased Han Solo. A captured noblewoman, with a blanked-out memory, wasn't exactly the same kind of a bargain.

So Fett must have been working for someone else while he had ostensibly been in Jabba's employ. That wouldn't have been unusual; Dengar knew from his own experience that bounty hunters nearly always had more than one gig going on at a time, with no particular loyalty to any creature whose payroll they might be on. Or—the other possibility—Boba Fett might have had his own reasons for wiping the memory of this female, whoever she really was, and bringing her to Jabba's palace, disguised as a simple dancing girl.

The puzzle rotated inside Dengar's mind. Maybe Fett had been stashing her away, in some place where she wouldn't be likely to be found. That was one of the sleazier bounty-hunter tricks: finding someone with a price on his or her or its head, then keeping the merchandise hidden until the price for it was raised higher. Dengar had never done it, and he hadn't heard of Boba Fett doing it, either. Fett didn't have to; he already commanded astronomical prices for his services.

"Is there anything else you remember?" Dengar rubbed the coarse stubble on his chin as he studied the female. "Even the littlest thing."

"No—" Neelah shook her head. "There's nothing. It's all gone. Except . . ."

"Except what?"

"Another name. I mean . . . another name besides *his*." She tilted her head to one side, as though trying to catch the whisper of a distant voice. "I think it's a name that belongs to a man."

"Yeah?" Dengar unfolded his arms and hooked his thumbs into his belt. "What's the name?"

"Nil something. Wait a minute." She rubbed the corner of her brow. "Now I remember . . . it was Nil Posondum. Or something like that." Neelah's expression turned hopeful. "Is that somebody important? Somebody I should know about?"

Dengar shook his head. "Never heard of anybody like that."

"Still . . ." Neelah looked a little crestfallen. "It's something to go on."

"Maybe." He had his doubts about whether it was anything useful. He had even bigger doubts about Neelah herself. *Or whatever her real name is,* thought Dengar. Keeping one's contacts primed for information was an essential part of the bounty-hunter trade; he had been in and out of Mos Eisley and other scumholes on a regular basis, listening and asking the right questions, and he hadn't heard anything fitting her description. If anybody was looking for her, they were doing it on the quiet. That might make getting paid for finding her somewhat difficult.

Or else—another possibility rose in Dengar's

thoughts—*somebody doesn't want her to be found.*
Boba Fett might have been working for someone
who had wanted this Neelah to be disposed of,
maybe in some way that left her still alive. What
better way than to strip out her memory and stick
her on a backwater planet like Tatooine? Though
how long she would've stayed alive in Jabba's palace
was debatable, given the Hutt's murderous amusements. Whoever had sent her there couldn't have
been too concerned about her survival. Then why
not just kill her quick and fast, for whatever reasons
they had, rather than leave her where any number of
the galaxy's hustling scoundrels, the criminal dregs
that had found employment with Jabba, might have
spotted her?

His brain felt weighted down with all these questions stacking up on top of each other. Mysteries and
skulduggery were what one dealt with in the bounty-
hunter trade; all this reminded Dengar of why he had
wanted to get out of it. *There must be an easier way
to make a living.*

Or a safer one. Now he had two potential bombs
on his hands, either one of which could result in a
quick death for him, if he was lucky, or a messy one,
if his luck ran true to form. It hadn't been bad
enough getting involved with Boba Fett's fortunes;
now he had to deal with the enigmatic Neelah as
well. She was a loose laser cannon by herself—if
she'd had a blaster, Dengar supposed he would've
been crisped by now—plus there were those unseen
figures from her past, who'd put her here. They
might not be too happy about her turning up again.
If they were the kind of people who hired Boba Fett
to do their dirty work for them, they wouldn't be
likely to have too many scruples about eliminating
everyone hooked up with her.

None of it looked good. Which had its own up-side: *The more risk,* Dengar reminded himself, *the more profit.* That, more than anything in the so-called Hunter's Creed, was what governed the actions of bounty hunters, from Boba Fett down to himself. If there was a chance of being partners with Fett, and reaping the rewards from that, he would have to ramp up his courage to a new level.

"All right," said Dengar aloud. He unfolded his arms and pointed to the female on the other side of the hiding place's main chamber. "Let's work out an arrangement, you and me. Stipulation number one: Don't try to kill me. If we're going to get anything accomplished around here, that's a basic requirement."

Neelah appeared to think it over, then nodded. "Okay."

"And if you try, I'm going to make sure it's *your* corpse that gets thrown out of here. Got me?"

She nodded again, with just a trace of impatience.

"Number two: I'm in charge here. I'm running the show—"

Neelah's anger flared. "Wait a minute—"

"Shut up," said Dengar. "It's for your own good. And it's just for the time being. You get back to wherever you came from, you get your real name and everything that comes with it returned to you, then you can do whatever you want. But right now you don't even know who you are, you don't know who might be gunning for you, you don't know *anything* about what the galaxy's like once you get off this little rock heap's surface. Even if you could find some way out of here without my help, you might poke your nose into some place like Mos Eisley and get your whole head detached from your neck. There's plenty of types who'd do that for you, even *without* knowing who you might be."

His lecture had a visible effect on her. "Very well," said Neelah sullenly. "You're in charge. For now."

The things I put up with, thought Dengar to himself. It was all for Manaroo's sake; he had to keep that in mind. On the other side of all this, there was her, and a life together with the female he loved. *If I get that far.*

"I'm glad we understand each other." Dengar pointed to a larger, open niche at the farthest end of the chamber. "You might as well make yourself comfortable down here. I don't want you wandering around topside. There's food and supplies; anything else you need, just let me know. I'll have those two medical droids give you a quick scan, to make sure you're all right. Tatooine's got some nasty bugs you can pick up."

Neelah looked straight back at him. "What about Boba Fett? That's why I came here."

"That's number three. You don't see him, you don't talk to him, you don't have anything to do with him, unless I'm right there with you."

"Why?"

"Like I told you before. For your own good." Dengar indicated the subchamber with a tilt of his head. "That guy's one dangerous barve. If there's some kind of connection between you and him, it might not be one that's to your benefit. When he's got his strength back, he might kill you just as easily as look at you. And you won't be asking any more questions then, believe me."

The message seemed to sink in. "All right," said Neelah. "Whatever you say."

There was more that he hadn't said. His precautions weren't just for her sake. *I don't want the two of them conspiring against me,* thought Dengar. Even before Boba Fett got his full strength back, that razor-sharp mind of his would be working and scheming away. Fett would be fully capable of making his own deals with Neelah that she wouldn't be able to resist falling in with. A bounty hunter didn't get the drop on people just with weapons that someone could see and feel burning through one's gut; the history of what Boba Fett had pulled off with the old Bounty Hunters Guild indicated that he was a master at ensnaring sentient creatures in subtler traps. *Though you wind up just as dead,* thought Dengar, *either way.* And if Boba Fett had been lying and playing for time, back when Dengar had found him out there in the Dune Sea's wastes, the quickest way to dissolve any partnership would be to use Neelah as his cat's-paw.

Now I've got two that I've got to watch out for. That was another reason Dengar had wanted the female down here, rather than wandering around on the surface. He had his hands full as it was; he didn't need anyone else hooking up with Neelah, for whatever agenda they might have.

She might as well have read his thoughts. A thin smile appeared as Neelah regarded him. "You trust me?"

"Of course not." On that point, Dengar could afford to be honest with her. "I don't trust anyone." That was almost true; there was always Manaroo. But that was something different. "Nobody survives in this business by going around trusting creatures. Let's just say that I've got an idea of what to expect from you now. And if you're smart enough to play along with me, maybe you'll get what you want."

Neelah signaled her understanding with a quick nod. "I still want to see him."

"That's easy enough," said Dengar. "But if you were planning on having any kind of talk with Fett, I don't think that's going to happen anytime real soon. He's still unconscious."

"Just as well." The thin smile faded from Neelah's face. "I changed my mind about that part. For now. I've begun to see the wisdom of your cautious attitude. Maybe it's better if he doesn't know about me. That I found him out in the Dune Sea, and that I'm here, waiting. As you pointed out . . . whatever our connection is, it might not be exactly safe for me."

"Suit yourself." Dengar's caution went up a notch. *She's a fast learner,* he thought. All the more reason to be careful. "Come on." He pushed himself away from the wall of the main chamber. "Let's go pay our guest of honor a visit."

The tall medical droid's appendages raised in warning as Dengar and Neelah entered the sub-chamber. "Please observe the necessary hygienic protocols." The chart of vital signs scrolled down the display on SHΣ1-B's cylindrical torso. "The patient's condition remains very critical—"

"Yeah, right." Dengar pushed the droid aside, away from the pallet in the center of the space. "This barve's survived worse things than your attentions. If you haven't managed to kill him, then nothing will."

Neelah stepped close to the side of the pallet and looked down at the unconscious form. "That's him?" She sounded almost disappointed. "That's Boba Fett?"

"No—" From the pile of gear in the sub-chamber's corner, Dengar picked up a battered helmet, etched with the digestive fluids of the Sarlacc's gullet. He turned the helmet's narrow-visored gaze toward Neelah. "*This* is Boba Fett."

She shrank back from the empty helmet, a sudden fear showing in her widened eyes. One hand tentatively reached out to touch the pitted metal, then jerked back as though scorched. She slowly nodded. "That's what I saw." Her voice was a barely audible whisper. "And I knew . . . I knew it was him. . . ."

"That's how everybody knows him." Dengar turned the helmet's blank visage toward himself. He could guess how the female felt; a little apprehensive chill ran down his own spine. "All through the galaxy." He nodded toward the figure on the pallet. "Not very many creatures have seen him like that. Or if they have, they didn't live to tell about it."

For a moment the only sound in the subchamber was the clicking and sighing of the cardiopulmonary assists that the medical droids had set in place. Then Neelah turned a somber gaze toward Dengar. "I did," she said quietly.

Dengar was unable to make a reply. The dark spaces in her eyes, and what might lie beyond them, unnerved him as much as the empty helmet. He turned away, to set it back down on the rest of Boba Fett's gear.

"Remember," said Neelah. "Don't tell him. Don't tell him anything about me."

By the time Dengar turned back around, the female had slipped out of the subchamber. He was alone with the other bounty hunter. The presence of the medical droids barely registered on Dengar's senses.

He stood looking down at Boba Fett for a while longer. The little trace of fear hadn't gone away; it was still there, inching along his spine. Even unconscious, this man was enough to spook ordinary creatures.

There's too much past, thought Dengar. Inside Boba Fett's skull; a whole galaxy full of it. Who could tell what was going on in there as he slept and dreamed his dark dreams?

8

He couldn't believe his good luck.

"I've got him this time," said Bossk. He had upgraded both the firepower and the tracking abilities of the *Hound's Tooth* since his last unfortunate encounter with Boba Fett. The other bounty hunter snatching the accountant Nil Posondum away from him had been the final irritant underneath his scales; he had sworn to himself that if he ever got the chance, he would put his rival out of commission for good. *And nothing will do that,* thought Bossk, savoring the words, *like blowing Fett to atoms.* "When I get done, there won't be enough of him left to find without an electron microscope."

Beside him, Zuckuss leaned the hoses of his face mask toward the cockpit's target-acquisition screen. "I don't know. . . ."

"What, you can't tell that it's Boba Fett approaching? Are you blind?" Bossk rapped a claw against the screen, hard enough to leave a permanent mark amid the glowing vector lines. "Of course it's him! There's all the identification data on the *Slave I*." A tiny column of numbers scrolled down from the triangular icon swiftly moving across the screen. "That's his ship, so he's aboard it."

"Oh, it's Boba Fett, all right." Zuckuss nodded slowly. "There's no doubt about that. I'm just not sure if you should—what's the phrase you always use?—'blow him away' right now."

Bossk angrily glared at the shorter bounty hunter. "When's there going to be a better time?"

"Well, maybe when he's not traveling under an assurance of safe passage from your father." Zuckuss sounded even more doubtful and nervous. The breath in his air tubes rasped quicker and louder. "Boba Fett already contacted the Guild council—you know that—and Cradossk and the others gave him their word that he could dock at the perimeter station without anyone taking a shot at him."

"They gave him *their* word." The slits in Bossk's eyes narrowed. "They didn't give him mine."

"Still . . ."

You little insect, thought Bossk. When he inherited the leadership of the Bounty Hunters Guild—he had already killed, as was Trandoshan custom, all of his father Cradossk's younger spawn—he intended to review the requirements for membership. A certain amount of guts, he figured, should be a prerequisite. Which meant that this sniveling partner that had been foisted on him would be out the air lock like the gnawed bones of yesterday's lunch.

"Maybe," whined Zuckuss, "you should think about this a little more. . . ."

"Thinking takes too long." Bossk's claws moved across the control of the *Hound*'s weapons systems. "Action gets things done."

"Your father isn't going to like this."

"That remains to be seen." The same blood ran in his and the old reptilian's veins; he had the comfort of knowing that his spawn-father was just as mean and vicious as himself. "For all you know, this is exactly what he and the rest of the Guild council are expecting me to do."

"Destroy another bounty hunter without warning?" Incredulity pitched Zuckuss's voice higher. "That's hardly in line with the Hunter's Creed!"

Bossk always felt a simmering impatience when someone mentioned the Creed to him. "Boba Fett has violated the Creed enough times," he growled, "that he deserves no protection from it."

"But he's never been bound by the Creed! He's never been a member of the Guild!"

"Spare me your tedious legal analysis." Bossk had locked the concentric rings of the tracker sight onto the distant craft. "If Boba Fett wants to lodge a complaint against me, he'll have to do it from the other side of the grave. If enough of him can be scraped up to put into one."

He ignored the rest of Zuckuss's tiresome fretting. His index claw hit the main fire button, and a quick rumble rolled through the *Hound*'s frame. On the screen, a brilliant white tracer shot toward the icon representing Boba Fett's ship.

"Got him!" The shot must have caught Fett completely by surprise; he'd taken no evasive action at all. *What a fool,* thought Bossk with contempt. *That's what you get for trusting other bounty hunters.* The advantage of being considered lowlife scum by most of the galaxy's inhabitants was that maintaining one's reputation was never an issue. "You know," said Bossk, "I'm almost disappointed. . . ."

"Why?" Zuckuss turned his large-lensed gaze away from the screen. "Because he didn't put up more of a fight?"

"No." Bossk peered at the red numbers that had

flashed on. "Because there's anything left of him."
He clawed in the command for a damage assessment
on the laser cannon's most recent target, then studied
the result. "That ship of Fett's had some serious armor on it. It's still holding together." The glowing
triangle had stopped in the middle of the screen, but
hadn't disappeared. To have taken that kind of a hit,
enough to punch a hole through the main deck of an
Imperial battle cruiser, and still be in one piece, however badly damaged, was amazing. It didn't corre-
spond with the velocities that the *Slave I*'s engines—
high-thrust but low-mass-capable units from Mandal
Motors—could attain. Like most bounty hunters,
Boba Fett had always prized speed and maneuver-
ability over protection. Right now, though, Bossk
didn't have time to puzzle over the discrepancy.
"Let's go finish him off."

The distinctive half-rounded shape of the *Slave I*
filled the viewports as Bossk piloted his own craft
toward it. He kept his claws on the controls for the
emergency reverse thrusters in case Boba Fett, like
the devious scoundrel he was known to be, was lying
low inside the other ship, waiting for his own chance
to take a shot at his attacker.

"Looks like a clean kill to me." Zuckuss pointed
to the cockpit's forward viewport. "Right through
the center and out the other side. There *couldn't* be
anyone left alive on that ship."

"I'll believe that," said Bossk, "when I see Boba
Fett's charred corpse." He started moving the
Hound's Tooth in toward the drifting wreckage.
"I'm going inside."

"Well, if you need that kind of proof . . ."
Zuckuss gave a shrug. "I suppose you'll have to."

He didn't even glance over at Zuckuss. "You're
going, too."

"Oh."

They managed to establish a transfer connection between the *Hound's Tooth* and what was left of the *Slave I*. No atmosphere support was needed; enough of the *Slave I*'s systems were still operating to have sealed off the central interior sections.

"Something's wrong," said Zuckuss as he looked about the *Slave I*'s empty hold.

"Something's always wrong, as far as you're concerned." This time, though, Bossk wondered whether his partner might be right. A sense of unease crawled across his scales; he drew his blaster and slowly scanned across the open hatchways.

Zuckuss reached over and poked a gloved finger at one of the bulkheads. The thin material wobbled back and forth; another poke, and Zuckuss's finger went right through it.

"It's a decoy." Zuckuss gave a few more exploratory proddings to the hold's confines, with similar results. "That's why there's nothing here—it's just a shell!" He turned toward Bossk. "No wonder your shot went right through. There's no real mass to have taken the hit. It's like shooting through flimsiplast."

Rage boiled up inside Bossk, nearly blinding him. "That slimy . . ." Words failed him. He stomped toward the dummy ship's aft section, shoulders smashing apart the sides of the flimsy hatches.

"This is why we got a positive identification." Zuckuss had followed behind, into what would have been the cockpit if they had been aboard a real ship. He pointed to a beacon transmitter mounted to one of the space's curved walls. "Look—you can see that it's been programmed with the *Slave I*'s ID profile." Zuckuss nodded in admiration. "Setting up something like this takes a lot of work; you have to force through overrides almost down to the subatomic level. And then to build it back up with the false data . . ." He stepped back from the unit. "Fett must have had this decoy already prepared, just keeping it for sometime when he'd need it." Even behind Zuckuss's face mask, there was a hint of amusement as he glanced over at Bossk. "Like when he might be heading into some territory where creatures might have a grudge against him."

"I'll kill him." The words seethed out through Bossk's clenched fangs. "I swear it. I'll find him and I'll kill him so hard . . ."

"Chances are pretty good, I'd say, that Fett's already slipped by us. We're wasting our time here." Zuckuss peered at another device, a cylinder of black metal studded with biosensors. "Now, this is interesting. I wouldn't have expected something like this aboard a simple decoy vessel."

Bossk knew his partner had more of an interest in technological matters; right now all that moved inside his own head were grim fantasies of cracking bone and spurting blood. He didn't even bother to look around, but kept on brooding at the mocking stars visible through the port. "What is it?"

"Offhand . . . I'd say it's a bomb. . . ."

"You fool!" Bossk whirled on his clawed heel, in time to see a row of lights flash into fiery life along the cylinder's casing. The device emitted a faint hum, already gaining in pitch and volume. "We've triggered it! The thing's going to blow!"

He dived for the false cockpit's hatchway; a fraction of a second later Zuckuss landed on top of him. Both bounty hunters scrambled to their feet. Through the hatch, Bossk could see the bomb detach itself from its mountings on the flimsy bulkhead; with slow, ominous grace, the bomb's miniaturized antigrav repulsors swiveled it about, bringing the scrutiny of its blind gaze toward them.

"Get out of my way!" Bossk shoved his partner aside and sprinted for the transfer port fastened to the decoy ship's central hold. He could hear Zuckuss right behind him as he furiously grappled his way through the tube's flexing pleats and back aboard the *Hound's Tooth*.

The first explosion ripped the transfer away from both ships, sending ragged strips of plastex spiraling across the *Hound*'s midsection viewports. With his stomach across the back of the pilot's chair, Bossk slapped at the hull integrity controls, sealing off his own ship before any significant amount of air could escape.

"We . . . we should be okay now. . . ." Panting, Zuckuss supported himself against the cockpit's naviputer displays. "That wasn't . . . much of a bomb. . . ."

There wasn't even time for Bossk to tell the other bounty hunter not to be an idiot. The second explosion, larger than the first, struck the *Hound's Tooth*. Roiling thermic fire filled the viewports as the impact of Bossk's spine with the bulkhead above stunned him into barely conscious silence. Blood swirled across the scales of his face as the ship's artificial-gravity generators struggled to catch up with its end-over-end tumbling. Bossk smashed his fist against as many of the thruster controls as he could reach; the resulting force had him digging a hold into the pilot's chair to keep from being flung through the open hatchway behind him.

A stern-mounted scanner showed the bomb, smaller now but even deadlier, trailing in the erratic wake of the *Hound's Tooth*. "It's . . . it's locked onto us. . . ." Zuckuss clawed his way up beside

Bossk. He pointed to the screen above the controls. "Here it comes. . . ."

Bossk knew how incremental-sequence bombs functioned. *The first two charges work you over,* he told himself. *The third one kills you.* His voice grated in his throat: "Not . . . this time . . ."

He hit the rest of the thrusters, at the same time throwing the *Hound* into a suicide arc. Stars blurred across the viewport as the angle of the ship's turn deepened. A deep basso groan sounded as increasing vectors tore in different directions across the hull. Sharper cracking noises signaled the navigation modules ripping away from the exterior.

The third and final explosion completed the partial disassembly of the *Hound's Tooth*. Bossk's desperate maneuver had put enough distance between the ship and the bomb; the hull shook with the impact but remained intact. Zuckuss was knocked onto his face mask by the bulkhead deforming behind him, the blast's force warping the section from concave to convex. The pilot's chair broke in two, sending Bossk sprawling across the cockpit's floor, claws holding the padded back of the seat tight against his chest. A rain of sparks, bursting out of the access ports, sizzled across both bounty hunters.

A few seconds later silence filled the *Hound's Tooth*. The smell of burning circuitry hung acrid in the air, mixed with the steam of the ship's automatic fire-dousing units. A few last sparks stung Zuckuss, and he slapped at them with his heavily gloved hands.

"We'll be here awhile." Bossk didn't need to do a preliminary damage assessment on the *Hound* to know that. Until the navigation modules were rigged back into some kind of operating order, he and Zuckuss were stuck in this remote sector of space. If

Trandoshans had any capacity for the emotion of gratitude, he would have been glad that the sequential bomb hadn't torn the *Hound's Tooth* into bits. He and Zuckuss would have been dead instead of merely adrift. As it was, he just felt a deep irritation over how much work it was going to take to put his ship back together again, with the tools and probes that were now undoubtedly scattered all over the engineering lockers.

"Look there—" Zuckuss pointed to the one viewport still functioning, set at an angle from the *Hound's* midsection.

Sitting in the middle of the cockpit floor, Bossk looked over his shoulder at the screen. A fiery course of light, with a too-familiar shape at its head, shot across the field of stars.

"That's the *Slave I*," said Zuckuss. Unnecessarily—any fool would have known that much. "The real ship."

"Of course it is, you idiot." If Bossk had had a wrench in his claws, he would have been torn between throwing it at his partner or at the screen, as though he could somehow hit Boba Fett's ship with it. "That was the whole point, with the decoy and the bomb." The *Slave I* was already dwindling away, heading for the perimeter station of the Bounty Hunters Guild. "Fett knew somebody would be waiting for him."

"Apparently so." Zuckuss gave a slow nod of his head. "Somebody like him . . . he's got a lot of enemies."

"He doesn't have any fewer now." Bossk glared at the empty screen. *You made one mistake,* he told the vanished Boba Fett. *You should've used a bigger bomb.* One that would have killed instead of merely humiliated. Bossk—and his hunger for revenge—was still alive.

Another quick burst of sparks shot from behind the screen. A knot of tangled circuits, welded together and emitting smoke, dangled bobbing from one of the overhead panels. The image of the stars blanked out and was gone.

"Come on," said Bossk. He stood up, then reached down to pull Zuckuss to his feet. "We've got work to do."

9

Everything was settled by the time Cradossk's son finally showed up.

Boba Fett could tell that the younger Trandoshan was not in a good mood as he strode into the council chamber of the Bounty Hunters Guild. Failed assassination attempts often had that effect on sentient creatures. There really was nothing worse than making the decision to kill someone else, and then not being able to bring it off. *All the emotions associated with violence,* mused Fett. He had never experienced them, himself, but knew that others did. *And none of the benefits.* It was sad, really.

The council's long, crescent-shaped table had been set for a celebratory banquet. One of Cradossk's scurrying servants had set a crystalline goblet, the mingled shades of cobalt and amethyst within revealing the expense of the vintage it contained, in front of Boba Fett. He had touched the dark liquid with a gloved fingertip, just enough to send a few ripples across its surface. Etiquette demanded that much; anything less, and the old reptilian sprawled next to him would have been offended. If other sentient creatures wished to deal in hollow symbols rather than reality, it made no difference to

Fett. Cradossk and all the other Guild elders could befuddle themselves with strong drink, if they wished; this goblet's contents would remain untasted.

He watched as the tall, arched doors of the council chamber were shoved open, the gilded and gem-encrusted panels flying to either side as Bossk stormed in. Servants bearing flagons and laden platters scattered in all directions; anger-ridden Trandoshans were notoriously rough on the hired help.

"Ah, my son and heir!" Cradossk was already well on the way to inebriation. His age-blunted fangs were mottled with wine stains, and his yellow-slitted eyes gazed with blurry affection at his spawn. "I was hoping you'd be here for the festivities." More wine slopped down Cradossk's scaled arm and from his elbow as he lifted his own goblet high. "We'll tell the musicians to strike up the old songs, the ones our spawn-fathers knew, and we'll do the lizard dance all around the courtyard—"

The goblet went clattering across the chamber's terrazzo floor, the wine a ragged pennant on the inlaid tiles, as Bossk knocked it from his sire's hand with one swing of his clawed hand. Across the high-ceilinged space of the chamber, hung with the empty combat gear and other trophies taken off the Guild's long-ago enemies, silence fell. The collective gaze of the council members turned toward their chief and his enraged offspring.

"Your manners," said Cradossk softly, "are severely lacking. As usual."

Boba Fett had had enough experience with Trandoshans over the years to know what a bad sign it was when their voices went low and ominous like that. When they shouted and snarled, they were ready to kill. When they whispered, they were ready to kill *everything*. He carefully shifted away from Cradossk's side so as not to be in the way if the old reptilian decided to leap over the table and tear out his only son's throat.

"As is your understanding." Bossk spoke with a cold control, through which his anger still managed to appear. "What kind of brain-withered old fool shares wine with his enemy?" He flung a gesture toward Boba Fett. "Have you forgotten so much, has every day faded from your memory, that the Guild's history is a blank slate to you? This man has made fools of us more times than we can count." Bossk turned to either side, making sure that everyone in the chamber could hear his words. "You all know who it is that sits with you now. He's taken the credits out of our pockets and the food out of our mouths." He looked back at his sire. "If you weren't drunk"—Bossk's voice sounded like dry gravel scraping across rusted metal—"you'd take what's fallen into your grasp and sink your teeth into Boba Fett's heart."

"I wasn't drunk when he arrived here." Cradossk's response was both mild and somewhat amused. "But I intend to get very drunk—and *very* happy—now that we've all had a chance to listen to Fett. What he came here to say has pleased me a great deal." He raised his goblet and took a long draft that left wet lines trickling down the sides of his throat, then slammed the goblet down. "That's one of the differences between him . . . and *you*."

Barely suppressed laughter ran along the arms of the crescent table. Without turning his head, Boba Fett could see the other council members and their lackeys whispering back and forth, their sardonic glances taking in the young bounty hunter standing before them. *Be sure you know who your friends are,* he wanted to warn Bossk. *This lot will carve you up anytime it suits them.*

"What're you talking about?" Bossk gripped the edge of the table in his claws and leaned toward his father. "What's this sneaking scum told you?"

"Boba Fett has made us an offer." From an ornately enameled tray held behind him, Cradossk plucked another empty goblet, holding it out to be filled by one of the other attendants. He held the wine out toward his son. "A very good one; that's why we're celebrating." Cradossk's mottled smile widened. "As you should be."

"Offer?" Bossk didn't take the goblet from the older Trandoshan. "What kind of offer?"

"The kind that only a fool would refuse. The kind of offer that solves a great many problems. For all of us."

Confusion showed in Bossk's gaze as he looked over at Boba Fett, then back to his father. "I don't understand. . . ."

"Of course you don't." Boba Fett spoke this time, leaning back against the leatherwork of the chair that had been given him. "There's so *much* you don't understand." He might as well start working Bossk into an irrational fury now as later. "That's why your father is still head of the Bounty Hunters Guild. You have a lot of wisdom to acquire before you'll have your chance."

"Explain it to him." With a single crooked claw, Cradossk motioned one of the other council members over. "I tire so easily nowadays. . . ."

"Then take a nap, old man." Bossk turned angrily toward the robed figure that had approached. "Spit it out."

"So simple, is it not?" The watery pupils at the

ends of the council member's eyestalks regarded Bossk with kindly forbearance. "And so indicative— yes?—of both your father's and our guest's foresight. Though Boba Fett is not to be called our guest anymore, is he?"

"All I know," growled Bossk, "is what *I* call him."

"Perhaps so, but should you not call him 'brother' now?"

Those words struck Bossk speechless.

"For is that not what Boba Fett has offered the Guild?" The council member folded his hooked, mantislike forearms together. "To be one of us? Our brother and fellow hunter—has he not offered to join his not inconsiderable forces and cunning with ours, and thus become a member of the august Bounty Hunters Guild?"

"Damn straight he has." Cradossk drained his goblet and slammed it back down on the table. "Let's hear it for him."

"It's true." Another one of the Guild's younger bounty hunters had sidled up to Bossk's elbow; Fett remembered this one's name as Zuckuss. "I just heard about it outside." The shorter bounty hunter pointed a thumb toward the chamber's tall doors. "That's what the word is—that Boba Fett has asked for membership in the Guild."

"That's impossible!" Bossk's claws tightened into fists, as though he were about to swing on either his partner or the elder from the council, or both. "Why would he do something like that?"

Fett regarded the reptilian with no show of emotion. "I have my reasons."

"I bet you do. . . ."

"And are they not good reasons?" The elder swiveled its eyestalks toward Bossk. "Should not all propositions make such excellent sense? For all of us—do we not gain the benefit of the esteemed Boba Fett's skills? Known throughout the galaxy!" A saw-edged forelimb gestured toward Fett on the other side of the table. "And does not he acquire thereby the many advantages that come with membership in our Guild? The warmth of our regard, the comradely fellowship, the excellent weapons maintenance facili-ties, the medical benefits—that alone is not to be lightly considered in our hazardous line of work."

"He's lying to you!" Bossk looked across the faces of the other council members. His straining fists rose alongside his head, nearly knocking over the smaller Zuckuss. "Can't you see that? It's some plan of his—like all his other plans—"

"What you don't see," said Boba Fett, "is how the times have changed. The galaxy is not as it was, when your father was as newly hatched as you. The fields upon which we pursue our quarry are shrink-ing, just as the strength of Emperor Palpatine in-creases." He could see the council members around the crescent nodding their acknowledgment of his wisdom. "The Bounty Hunters Guild must change as well, or face its extinction. And so must I change my ways as well."

"The old days," murmured Cradossk, slumped down and gazing wistfully into his empty goblet. "The old days are gone. . . ."

"Anyone with eyes and a brain can tell that the bounty-hunting trade is being squeezed into a tighter and tighter corner." Some of the words Fett used were straight from what Kud'ar Mub'at, back at its web drifting in space, had told him. They were true enough, or at least to the point where they would be believed by these fools on the Guild council. "Not just by the Empire; there are others. Black Sun . . ."

He merely had to mention the name of the criminal organization for that point to be made. The whispers turned into guarded silence. "Bounty hunters such as ourselves have always operated on both sides of the law, as need be; that's the nature of the game. But when both sides turn against us, then we must band together to survive. There's no room for an independent agent such as myself. We either join forces, you and I, or we go our separate ways. And await our separate destruction."

A strange, raw ache tightened Boba Fett's throat. It had been a long time since he had spoken that many words all at one go. He didn't live by making speeches, but by performing deeds: the more danger, the greater the profit. But the job he'd accepted from Kud'ar Mub'at was, in some sense, a job like any other. *Whatever it takes,* thought Fett. If it required getting a bunch of aging, dull-fanged mercenaries like Cradossk and the rest of the Bounty Hunters Guild council to swallow a well-oiled line, then so be it. If anything, it was just proof that words could trap and kill as well as any other weapon.

"Should you not thank Boba Fett?" The elder standing near Bossk made a sweeping gesture with his serrated forearm. "For your sake, has he not repeated what he already has so eloquently stated to us?"

"And you fell for it." Bossk sneered at all the council members, his father included. "You don't have the guts to fight him, so you'd rather believe that he's on your side now."

Boba Fett raised his inner estimation of the Trandoshan bounty hunter. *He's going to be trouble,* thought Fett. *Not just another dumb carnivore.* If the time ever did come when Bossk inherited the leadership of the Bounty Hunters Guild, it might in fact become serious competition for him. But right now Bossk's smarts and his fierce temper were weapons to be turned against him and the others.

"You'll see, my little one." Cradossk roused himself into an approximation of sobriety. "If I didn't love you the way I do, I'd have your scaly hide peeled off and tanned into a wall hanging for our new member's quarters." He extended a wobbling claw toward Bossk. "But because I want there to be something someday for my spawn to possess and lead, the way I lead the Guild now—and because I'm not dead yet, so there's still time for you to gain both some manners and some knowledge of how the galaxy works—that's why I'm not *asking* you to be brothers with Boba Fett. I'm *telling* you to do it."

"Very well." The slits in Bossk's eyes narrowed into apertures a honed razor might have cut. "As you wish. Maybe there is something I can learn from an . . . *old* one like you." He smiled the ugly smile characteristic of his species. "After all—you murdered your way to control of the Guild. I have but to wait, and it's mine."

"Is not patience a virtue, even among the assassins?"

Bossk pushed the other council member aside, knocking him against the smaller figure of Zuckuss. The Trandoshan stepped up to the crescent-shaped table, directly in front of Boba Fett. One clawed hand grasped the goblet by its stem. "To your health." Bossk drained the contents, then threw the goblet against the wall behind; it clanged like a bell, then rolled clattering across the hard stone tiles of the floor. "However long it lasts."

"I suppose"—Fett returned the other's gaze—"it'll last long enough."

Dark wine seeped around Bossk's fangs as he

leaned toward Fett. "You might fool the others," he whispered, "but you're not fooling me. I don't know what your game is—but I don't worry about you knowing mine." His voice dropped lower and more guttural as he brought his snout almost against the visor of Fett's helmet. "I'll be a brother to you, all right. And I know how, believe me. I had brothers when I was spawned. And you know what?" Bossk's breath smelled of wine and blood. "I ate them."

He turned and strode away, toward the council chamber's doors. One of Bossk's clawed feet connected with the empty goblet he had thrown, sending it skittering against the wall like a tiny droid whose circuits had been scooped out. The other bounty hunter, Zuckuss, glanced around at the watching faces, then ran after Bossk.

Sitting next to Boba Fett, Cradossk heaved a sigh. "Don't judge us too harshly, my friend." Cradossk took the flagon from the tray being held near him and refilled his own goblet. He knocked that back and filled it again. "Sometimes our get-togethers go a *little* better than this. . . ."

10

"You've been a long time away," said the Emperor. The ancient, withered head slowly nodded. "Many are the stars you travel among."

"All my journeying is in your service." Prince Xizor inclined his head, a courtly signal of submission. The dark serpent of his topknot brushed across his shoulder. "And to the glory of the Empire."

"Well spoken, as always." Emperor Palpatine swiveled his throne toward another section of the immense room. "Whatever else might be said of him, you must agree that the prince has a way with words. Don't you think so, Vader?"

Xizor turned toward the hologram of the dark-caped figure—an intimidatingly life-sized image, transmitted from the *Devastator*, Lord Vader's personal flagship. *Don't try it on this one*, Xizor warned himself. He had witnessed too many examples of what happened to those whose words caused the Dark Lord of the Sith to lose patience. The Emperor might be keeping him on a short leash. *But one long enough*, thought Xizor, *to reach my throat*.

"Your judgment, my lord, exceeds mine." Vader kept his own words as diplomatically inscrutable as the mask that concealed his face. "You know best where to place your trust."

"Sometimes, Vader, I think you'd prefer it if I trusted no one but you." The Emperor put his fingertips together. Behind him, framed in the towering windows of the throne room, the curved arms of the galaxy extended, like shoals of gems in an ink-black sea. Below the stars, the towers and massive shapes of Imperial City rolled like the crests of a frozen sea across the hidden surface of Coruscant, a monument in durasteel to both the ambition and the grasp of Palpatine. "I see into so many creatures' hearts, and all I find there is fear. Which is as it should be." The deep-set eyes contemplated the empty cage formed by his hands, as though envisioning the worlds bound by the Empire's power. "But when I look into yours, Vader, I see . . . something else." Like a hooded mendicant rather than the ruler of worlds, Emperor Palpatine peered through the angles of his fingers. "Something almost like . . . desire."

Prince Xizor managed to keep his own smile from showing. *Desire* among the Falleen, his species, meant only one thing. His cruel beauty, the sharply chiseled planes of his face, and his regal bearing, combined with a pheromone-rich musk that evaded all conscious senses, were what put a female of any world under his command. *Humanoid* female, of a type pleasing to his own sense of aesthetics; if the members of the more repulsive of the galaxy's species were similarly affected, that was not something he had yet felt the need to put to the test.

"It is only the desire to serve you," said Lord Vader. "And the Empire."

"Of course; what else could it be?" Palpatine smiled indulgently, an effect no less intimidating than any other expression that moved across his age-creased face. "But I am surrounded by those who wish to serve me. Xizor, for one—" The Emperor's hand gestured toward him. "He says all the same things as you do. If you are closer to what's left of my heart, Vader, if for the moment I place more trust in you than I do in others, it's because of something beyond words."

"Actions," said Xizor with cold hauteur, "indicate more than words. Judge my loyalty by what I achieve for the Empire."

"And what is that?" Vader's image turned the force of his penetrating gaze upon Xizor. "You scurry about on your mysterious, self-appointed errands, your rounds of those whose devotion to our cause is somewhat *less* than ideal. Fear motivates many creatures, but there are still those who believe their meager cunning can line their pockets. Criminals, conspirators, thieves, and builders of their own little empires—you know too many of those types, Xizor. I sometimes wonder what their attraction is for you."

Standing against Vader—even in this insubstantial form—was like facing radiation hard enough to strip flesh from bone. Not for the first time Xizor felt an invisible hand settle around his throat. His own willpower kept the breath sliding in and out of his lungs. But if Vader were to unleash his complete wrath, the force of will might not be enough. Xizor had seen others, the highest-ranking officers in the Empire's forces, clutching their throats and gasping for air, writhing like a Dantooinian garfish caught on a barbed trawling line. Perhaps wisely, Vader tended to avoid such displays in front of the Emperor; why tempt the old man into showing how much greater was his own mastery of the Force that penetrated and bound the galaxy together?

"There is no attraction for me, Lord Vader." As always before, he wondered just how much Vader knew. How much he might suspect, and how much he could prove. Vader's disdain for the galaxy's less reputable schemers and thugs was well known; he dealt with such as bounty hunters only on rare occasions. *Which is to my benefit,* thought Xizor. For Vader and the Imperial high command, criminals and mercenaries were all vermin that would be swept away, and soon if their latest plans went as expected. *So that kind is left to me*—he had built his own shadow empire, that of the Black Sun, out of exactly such rejected dregs. If the Emperor and Vader didn't want to dirty their hands, then he had no such tender scruples. "I do what I must," said Xizor, not untruthfully. The fact that he was still standing here, in Emperor Palpatine's private sanctuary, and not cut down by the Emperor's or Vader's swift wrath, indicated that Black Sun still operated in the eclipse of its secrecy. *For now,* thought Xizor. He turned toward the Emperor. "This sacrifice," he lied, "I also make on your behalf. Judge as well, those who think it beneath them."

"Excellent." The Emperor displayed a cold smile. "If you had no other value to me, Xizor, I would still require your presence, just for the . . . *stimulating* effect you have on Lord Vader."

He already hates my entrails, thought Xizor as he glanced over at the black-robed figure. Nothing had been lost in this exchange.

"But you still haven't answered my questions." The Emperor leaned forward, his sharp gaze fastening on Xizor. "I summoned you here for a reason. Let us set aside, for the time being, all this fractious comparison between your loyalty and that of Lord

Vader. You say you have been busy on my behalf. . . ."

"On yours, my lord, and the Empire's."

"One and the same thing, Xizor. As all the worlds shall soon know." The Emperor settled back in the throne. "Very well. Your doings are not something which you have discussed with either Lord Vader or myself. Either you have shown commendable initiative—or foolhardy rashness." Any trace of amusement had drained out of the Emperor's voice. "Now is your chance to convince me that the former is the case."

He had known that this time would come. It was one thing to go out and set one's schemes in motion—that was the easy part—but it was another to come back here and defend those schemes when one's life or death depended upon eloquence. *And,* thought Xizor, *lying eloquence, at that.*

"As great as your empire is, my lord, it is still at peril." The combined gaze of Vader and the Emperor made him feel as transparent as glass, as though their mastery over the Force enabled them to look straight into the essence he kept so carefully shielded. "Great are your powers, but they are still not enough to achieve all that you want."

"You say nothing new." Contempt showed in the Emperor's eyes. "That is the same thing that my admirals tell me. They are not believers, as Lord Vader is; they doubt the existence of any power that they cannot unleash with the push of a button. They doubt, even when they've had the edifying experience of feeling the Force crushing the life out of them. Doubt weakens and makes fools out of such creatures." An unwavering hand raised and pointed toward Xizor. "You're not such a fool, are you?"

Xizor bowed his head. "I do not doubt, my lord."

"That's why I'm still listening to you." The Emperor's hand lowered and stroked the arm of the throne. "My patience is such, however, that I listen to the Imperial admirals as well, fools that they are. Even fools say wise things, from time to time. And that is why I gave permission for their great project, the construction of what they called the Death Star—"

"You should have listened to me," said Vader. The rush of his breath sounded louder and angrier. "The Rebellion was growing even then, and the admirals wasted your time on such folly. I told them that the Death Star, when it was completed, would be a machine and nothing more. Its power would be nothing compared to that which you already possess." Vader's voice darkened in tone, indicating the depths of his annihilating temper. "And I was proved right, was I not, my lord?"

"Indeed you were, Vader." The Emperor gave a single nod. "But even in the wretchedness of their folly, my admirals were still right about one thing. Their little minds are made of the same unenlightened stuff as are the minds of most of the galaxy's inhabitants. They see things the same way—and other things are invisible to them. The Jedi Knights are no longer; they were the only ones, other than ourselves, who could see the Force for what it is. These lesser creatures are blind to that which moves the stars in all the worlds' skies and the blood in the veins of those below. They need something they *can* see—that was what my admirals hoped to give them with the Death Star. Its power—such as it was—lay within the comprehension of all the lesser creatures; it would have evoked the fear and obedience that the subtleties of the Force would take a great deal longer to achieve. You were right that it was a machine and nothing more. But still a useful machine. A tool. When all that is required is a hammer, it is folly to turn the universe's primal energy to such mundane purposes."

Darth Vader stood unmoved by the Emperor's words. "I trust that you will remember one thing. A hammer can be broken, as can any other tool. The Death Star was destroyed. But the Force is eternal."

"I won't forget, Vader. But for now, all such simple tools are the concern of my admirals. Let them occupy themselves with building better ones, if they can. We have already distracted ourselves from our purpose here." The Emperor turned back toward Prince Xizor. "You say the Empire is at risk. You tell me nothing new. I am aware of the threat presented by the Rebel Alliance—a threat that will be extinguished in due time. But the level of your concern, Xizor, is what I find surprising. It sounds like doubt to me, no matter what you say to the contrary. And doubt should be eliminated at the source."

"Not doubt, but the truth." The edges of Xizor's own intricately stitched robes trailed across his boots as he folded his arms across his chest. "You cannot vanquish the Alliance without creating new threats to your authority. As your power increases and becomes closer to absolute, so does an unavoidable hazard. A hazard that is woven into the very fiber of the Empire."

"He speaks nonsense, my lord."

"Nonsense to those who cannot see." Xizor gazed from the corner of his eye at the black-garbed figure standing next to him. "Perhaps Lord Vader is blinded by the Force. After all, his mastery of it is not equal to your own."

The invisible hand Xizor felt at his throat suddenly tightened, as hard and constricting as an iron band. Even Vader's mere image had the power to kill. Xizor's chin was thrust backward, the vision in his eyes filled with trapped blood.

"Leave him be, Vader." The Emperor's voice came from somewhere beyond that darkening red cloud. "I'm intrigued by what he has to say. I want to hear the rest. Before I make my decision."

The hand let go, and breath flooded back into Xizor's lungs. He had kept his arms folded throughout the brief ordeal, determined not to claw at his throat the way he had seen Vader's other, weaker victims do. *But I won't forget,* brooded Xizor. The other's touch, invisible or not, was an affront to the haughty pride that was characteristic of all Falleens. The day would come when all such offenses would be paid for.

"I speak better," said Xizor, "when the Emperor keeps a tight leash on his underlings." His voice rasped in his throat; when he swallowed, he tasted his own blood. "But the quality of those who serve my lord is exactly that on which I need to speak." His slit-pupiled gaze took in Vader and the Emperor. "You have both spoken of the fools who serve the Empire; necessary fools, but fools nonetheless. Do you think the situation is going to get any better, especially now that the Rebellion courts all those with an independent streak to their natures?"

A sneer sounded in Vader's voice. "They seal their fates with their 'independent' natures, as you describe them. The Rebels will be crushed."

"Undoubtedly so," said Xizor. "But that day of triumph is delayed by the Emperor's own power. That seems a riddle, but it is one that can be solved by those with eyes to see."

"Go on." The Emperor gestured toward Xizor. "You have my full attention. Make sure you use it well."

He had prepared for this moment; the words were already chosen. He had only to speak them. And then await the outcome of his gamble.

"As I said: The problem is with those who serve you." Xizor pointed to the high transparisteel windows behind the throne, with their vista of limitless stars. "On all the worlds that are within your grasp, those who resist your power will be crushed; Lord Vader speaks the truth about that. But what does that leave you? Fools such as the Imperial admirals; fools who cannot even recognize the existence of the Force. If they are not fools before they enter your service, they become so soon after. How can it be otherwise? Your power annihilates their will, their capacity to judge and make decisions, their ability to operate on their own. Not everyone in the galaxy has a nature as strong as mine or Lord Vader's."

"This is true," said Emperor Palpatine. "And it is not a matter that has gone unnoticed by me. I see those who have gone over to the side of the Rebellion, and I recognize their strengths. It is a cruel waste to destroy them, no matter how necessary that might be." His voice dropped, low and musing. "How much better it would be if they could be brought over to our side. . . ."

Xizor concealed a shiver of disgust. As far-reaching as his own ambitions were, they paled by comparison to Palpatine's. There was something in the withered figure that didn't want just to control the galaxy's sentient creatures, but to consume them the way a greedy Hutt swallowed its wriggling food. *The small and weak ones will go first,* thought Xizor. *And then someday it'll be the turn of Vader and me.* That would be the reward for their loyalty. To be consumed last . . .

Survival as well as ambition had dictated the creation of Black Sun. The Rebels were brave idiots to openly oppose the Emperor's might; for himself, Xizor had already decided that an existence in the shadows, the darkness in which criminals always wrapped themselves, was preferable to the Empire's insatiable appetite.

"There are those," said Xizor, "who would prefer death rather than serve the Empire."

Palpatine gave a small shrug. "So be it."

"But in the meantime you must deal with those whom you do command. And many of those are—let us be realistic about this, my lord—not of the first caliber. Some were born fools, others achieved idiocy through their own efforts, but many of the rest simply had their minds and spirits obliterated by your power." Xizor unfolded his arms so he could spread his hands apart, palms outward. "Fear is an effective motivator, but it is also a corrosive one. It has an effect inside those who suffer it—"

"Are you one of those, Xizor?"

He shook his head. "Since I do not fear death, I do not fear that which might cause it. I fear your disapproval, my lord." Another lie. "If your displeasure is sufficient cause for my death, then I will have earned that fate."

"You haven't displeased me," said the Emperor. "Yet. Continue."

"Not many of your servants, my lord, would risk your anger by telling you what you need to know. If some call me rash"—he glanced over at Vader—"you nevertheless might come to value my excess of courage. For this is the truth: That which makes you powerful, that makes sentient creatures into tools in your hands, is the same thing that makes those tools weak and ineffective. It is an unavoidable concomitant of great power. There are those that I command, though not at a scale comparable to you, and I can see it in their eyes. And if you wish to crush the Rebellion, you will need the strongest possible forces at your call. I have contacts, spies that I have planted within the Alliance, and they have informed me of both the Rebels' plans and their determination to achieve them. They'll stop at nothing to achieve your overthrow; that's how insane their hunger for freedom is." He understood how the Rebels felt; if he hadn't cast his lot in with Black Sun, he could easily have joined the Alliance. "You will win, of course, my lord; power such as yours always wins. But not without cunning, and not without the services of your underlings. And that's where the problem lies. The more overwhelming the control that you establish over your empire, and as more and more of the universe's sentient creatures come under your dominion, the more you risk losing the very elements you need to complete your galaxy-wide hegemony and defend it from the small but growing forces of the Rebellion."

Lord Vader spoke up. "At one time I would have said that such words were nonsense, if not close to treason. However, I'm forced to admit that Prince Xizor may speak truth. I would not have had the difficulties that I've experienced with the Imperial high command if their brains were not addled with cowardice. But then, if your admirals were wiser creatures, the Death Star would not have been destroyed so easily."

"Precisely so." Things were going better than Xizor had hoped; to have Vader agree with him about anything was a surprise. "The Empire, by its very nature, destroys that which it needs to grow and survive. Take the Imperial stormtroopers, for example; you have trained them to obey, to fight, and to die in the service of the Empire . . . but not to think. The same holds true with practically everyone else throughout the Empire's chain of command, right up to the topmost ranks; most of your underlings, my lord, lack any creative spark, any capability of deep analysis or real cunning; that's all been beaten out of them, crushed by your power. But the fledgling elements of the Rebellion *do* possess those characteristics; that's why they're in the Rebellion. Foolish they may be, to the point of being suicidal; nevertheless, their rebellious nature is exactly that which makes them a threat to the Empire."

The Emperor nodded, mulling over Xizor's words. "You're very eloquent on this matter. I don't have to worry about *you* showing initiative, do I?" Palpatine raised his head, showing his unpleasant smile. "So what would you have me do about my servants? Perhaps I should just be . . . *kinder* to them. Would that work?" Sarcasm turned his voice darker and uglier. "Or else I should just throw away the power I hold over them. But then, what power would I have left?"

"It's not a matter of throwing away power, my lord. Even as they are, your servants have their uses. A hammer doesn't need a mind or a spirit to fulfill the purpose of he who holds it. Your admirals obey your orders; that is sufficient for them. The Imperial stormtroopers are tools for creating the desired level of terror on your subject planets; they would be less terrifying if they were capable of thought. But they are like machines, right to the core that no longer exists in them; set upon their course, they obey and die and kill, with no possibility of swaying them from their orders, by appeal to reason or emotion. That is how it should be; that is how these servants are most useful to you and to the Empire's glory." With a nod of his head, Xizor indicated the stars slowly wheeling behind the throne. "Nothing is achieved by throwing away those tools, my lord, however limited their uses may be. But what you must find are *other* tools, ones that are not within the absolute grasp of your power."

"I think," said the Emperor, "that I already have such tools, and such servants. Standing here in front of me."

"Just so." Lord Vader's image regarded Xizor for a moment, then turned again toward the Emperor. "And you must decide whether such a tool's usefulness is greater or less than the danger it represents to the Empire."

Back to where we were before, thought Xizor. If Vader had appeared to agree with him, it had been only for a moment. And only for the purpose of driving another wedge between the Emperor and any of Vader's rivals for influence. *Someday he and I will come to grips with each other.* With grim determination, Xizor looked forward to that confrontation with Darth Vader. *And then we'll settle things, once and for all.*

The Emperor spoke up. "When that happens," Palpatine said coolly, "it will be a judgment laid upon you as well, Lord Vader."

"Let your judgment be on our accomplishments, my lord." Xizor's gesture took in both himself and Vader. "And on our service to you. But as I said, the Empire requires other servants and tools. And those cannot be such as your stormtroopers and admirals, or even such as Lord Vader and myself. To destroy the Rebellion, to crush once and for all the resistance that has grown against your power, you must employ those who have sworn no loyalty to you."

"I think, Prince Xizor, that you may be increasing the dangers to the Empire rather than lessening them."

"Then I have yet to make my meaning clear to you, my lord. Extraordinary times require extraordinary measures. The day will come when the Rebellion is no more, when your grasp of all the galaxy's worlds will be final and never-ending. Then you will have no need of servants and tools with minds of their own. You may, perhaps, have no need of me. But that is no concern of mine; my fate is nothing compared to the glory of the Empire. But that time is not yet here. In this time you must take into your hand the most dangerous tools. If a vibroblade's edge is sharp enough to cut both ways, then he who uses it must be careful. But the only thing more dangerous than picking it up is the failure to do so."

"You've thought this over a great deal, Prince Xizor." The Emperor's cold, deep-set eyes studied him. "I can hear in your words the sound of well-polished gears meshing together. You seek to convince me. Very well; you have. To some degree. But what I haven't heard from you is what these sharp-edged tools are, that I should bend to my purposes."

"That answer is very simple," said Xizor. "The tools you need are those individuals known as the *bounty hunters*."

Vader's words broke in, deeper and even more contempt-filled. "We have gone here from folly to madness. What the prince seeks to convince you of is nonsense. We waste our time even contemplating it. While Prince Xizor amuses himself with these idiotic notions, the Rebellion marshals its forces and conspires against the Empire."

"Your antipathy to the prince's suggestion seems somewhat extreme, Lord Vader." Beneath the unadorned hood, the Emperor's head tilted to one side. "Have you not employed bounty hunters yourself from time to time? You have even spoken to me of one, that rather enigmatic individual named Boba Fett. He's been a bounty hunter for long enough to have gained a reputation nearly as fear-inspiring as your own."

"A bounty hunter has his uses," said Vader stiffly. "The prince is correct about that. But they are limited. If I've given a few of your credits to any of them, Boba Fett included, it was because they were willing to do those jobs dirty enough to match their own mercenary natures. Bounty hunters come from the sewers of the galaxy; they find it agreeable to troll through various criminal dens, sinkholes of depravity that can be found on any number of planets, and locate those whose greed rather than misplaced idealism has brought them into contact with the Rebellion. Scum seeks out other scum; even our Imperial stormtroopers are incapable of anything but the most rudimentary searches through places like that."

"Exactly," said Xizor. "Even if those were the only uses that bounty hunters had, they would still be of irreplaceable value to the Empire. But they have more than that. Lord Vader uses the word 'mercenary'; he speaks perhaps more tellingly than he realizes." He could sense, even through the dark lenses of Vader's mask, the angry reaction his words provoked. "A bounty hunter is just that: a mercenary. Boba Fett and the others like him will do anything for credits. It is greed and not fear that drives them, and that alone marks them as different from your admirals and stormtroopers, my lord. Violence is a commodity for the bounty hunters, not merely the result of following orders. Creatures such as those that serve in the Empire's military forces are blind to the deaths and terror they create; they do as much as they are told to, and then they stop, like children's toys whose power sources have run down. Bounty hunters, on the other hand, seek to maximize the return from their efforts; they have an entrepreneurial attitude rarely found, if ever, among your followers."

"Though it is found often enough," said Vader, "among the galaxy's criminal classes."

The suspicion struck Xizor once again, about just how much Vader knew. Or could prove. The difference between those conditions might be what kept Vader silent. *For now,* thought Xizor.

"If you are referring to such creatures as the Hutts, you are correct." Xizor pointed to the windows full of stars. "And there are others besides them, working away, building up their own little empires and spheres of influence. They'll be dealt with, eventually. The only reasons we should not eliminate them right now is that the Rebellion is a more pressing concern, and the Hutts and their ilk provide an environment for the bounty hunters to flourish in. And that is to our advantage. Criminals such as the infamous Jabba keep the members of the Bounty Hunters Guild fed on a regular basis so that they're available for our purposes whenever we need them; independent operators such as Boba Fett find a way to survive, and even prosper, no matter what. Since bounty hunters deliver their services to the highest bidder, the Empire can always get the best ones to take care of our dirty work, as Lord Vader would call it. And right now there is a great deal of dirty work that must be dealt with."

"Sewers," grated Vader, "and the vermin that live in them are better dealt with by draining rather than lying down in them."

"The Rebellion doesn't have the same sort of scruples that you do, Lord Vader." Xizor regarded the black-robed figure through narrowed eyes. "And that is why the Rebellion is a growing danger to us. The Rebels' desperation leads them to places that the Imperial stormtroopers and all our spies and informers are incapable of entering—or if they do go in there, they don't come back out except as corpses. The creatures that live in those shadows may be scum, but they are clever scum, for the most part. The Rebellion can deal with them, but the Empire can't. We need intermediaries that are just as clever and ruthless, and the only ones that fit the requirements are the bounty hunters."

"Your bickering does not interest me." The Emperor's voice was like the lash of a whip, pulling both Vader's and Xizor's attention toward the throne. Palpatine's hard gaze shifted toward Xizor. "Even if what you say is true—even if, Xizor, you have convinced me that your words contain any wisdom—there are still problems with the course you recommend. True, I prefer terror and fear to any other means of ensuring obedience to my commands; fear obliterates sentient creatures' essences, and that is always a worthwhile result. But I have no absolute aversion to buying the services the Empire requires, whether from bounty hunters or anyone else. Perhaps Boba Fett and the others have no spirits to be eradicated; if there is still something within them that can be driven by greed, then I can use that. But you still have not convinced me that these bounty hunters are the efficient tools you say they are."

"My lord, I speak only of—"

"Silence." The Emperor grasped the throne's arms and leaned forward, gaze boring into the slit pupils of Xizor's eyes. "There is little that I do not know of in this galaxy. I know more than you can imagine, Xizor; remember that. And I know a great deal about Boba Fett and the others, the ones who belong to the Bounty Hunters Guild. Before you ever came to my court, I was aware of Fett; not everything that you regard as a mystery about him is a secret to me. He wears the armor of the Mandalorian warriors; he's earned the right to that armor, by his own prowess. Lord Vader possesses some of the knowledge that belonged to the Mandalorians; I possess more. Believe me, you deal with Boba Fett at your own peril. But in that, he is unique among the bounty hunters. You recommend them to me as tools that I can use against the Rebellion; I say that indicates you are a fool, Xizor. The Bounty Hunters Guild is a joke in which I find no amusement."

Xizor bowed his head. "You anticipate the arguments that I wish to make, my lord."

"I anticipate nothing but more idiotic prattle from you. The bounty hunters with which you display such an obsession are a fading remnant of what they once were. The Bounty Hunters Guild is an organization of senile, aging creatures and incompetent young bumblers. If any of them had the least amount of skills, they would wash their hands of the Guild and go independent like Boba Fett." Deep disgust sounded in the Emperor's voice. "The Guild members band together and cling to each other because they know they would have no chance in the galaxy on their own. That's why Boba Fett has nothing to do with them."

"On that point, my lord, I must respectfully offer a correction." Xizor displayed a thin smile. "The renowned Boba Fett, the most feared bounty hunter in the galaxy, has already applied for membership in the Guild. And I anticipate that Cradossk and the others on the Bounty Hunters Guild council will have no objection to his becoming one of their number."

"That is impossible." Vader's words were flatly emphatic. "I have had enough experience with Boba Fett to know that he would never do such a thing. He values his independence too much, and he has nothing but contempt for the Bounty Hunters Guild. You've gone from unamusing jests, Prince Xizor, to unconvincing lies."

"I neither jest nor lie, Lord Vader." He turned back toward the Emperor on the throne. "Boba Fett has applied for membership in the Bounty Hunters Guild at my instigation. He does not know that it was my idea that he should do so, or that his actions in this matter serve the purposes of the Empire. I used an intermediary to plant the notion in Boba Fett's head, one whose discretion is sufficient for this task." Xizor had no intention of revealing his involvement with the assembler Kud'ar Mub'at; to do so would only heighten Vader's suspicions about his network of shady and outright criminal contacts. "As with everything he does, Boba Fett's actions in this matter are motivated by his own greed." As were Kud'ar Mub'at's; he had gone to the assembler and pitched the scheme to it as the leader of the Black Sun organization, and not as the loyal servant of the Emperor. "His greed matches that of the aged Cradossk and all the rest of the Bounty Hunters

Guild. They all think they have something to gain by this change in their relationship to each other. But it is really you, Emperor Palpatine, that shall reap all the benefits."

"This makes no sense," growled Vader. "How could Boba Fett be convinced that it would be to his advantage to join the Bounty Hunters Guild?"

Xizor turned his knowing half smile in Vader's direction. "It is a rather simpler matter than you think. My intermediary convinced Boba Fett to join the Guild, not to be one of the Guild's members—but to be the agent of its destruction."

The Emperor nodded in appreciation. "I begin to see aspects of your guile, Prince Xizor, of which I had not been aware."

"In your service, my lord. Think of it: You are as knowledgeable as Lord Vader about Boba Fett's nature. His cunning and ruthlessness are legendary throughout the galaxy. Placed in the context of the Bounty Hunters Guild, those elements are bound to be disruptive. Sharp divisions already exist among the Guild's members, between the old leadership of the council members like Cradossk, and the younger bounty hunters such as his son. The Bounty Hunters Guild is in many ways a microcosm of the Republic that your empire has replaced: an aging, bureaucratic conglomerate with its best days far behind it. Where once the Guild was nearly as ruthless and efficient as Boba Fett, it now parcels out assignments to its members, divides up territories and responsibilities, pays off the galaxy's various law-enforcement agencies, shares out the steadily diminishing proceeds to its members, always with more going to the leadership, less to the lower-ranking bounty hunters who are still doing the hard and dangerous work upon which the organization depends. So, naturally, those younger members, if they have any intelligence and self-interest at all, spend more time trying to claw their way up through the Guild's ranks than actually chasing bounties."

Xizor let his own contempt sound in his voice. The fate of the Bounty Hunters Guild was something that he was not going to let happen to Black Sun; in that, he had taken a leaf from Emperor Palpatine's book. Autocracy, even tyranny, was how one kept an organization tough and alive.

"The Republic deserves to die, Prince Xizor." The Emperor raised one hand from the throne's arm. "It sounds as if you have passed a similar judgment upon the Bounty Hunters Guild."

"I did that which I knew you would want me to do, my lord. Your attention is focused upon the weightiest matters of the galaxy, and its transformation from indolence and democracy to a hard, shining instrument of your will. The fate of the Bounty Hunters Guild, while necessary for us to determine to your satisfaction, is but a small part of that process. And easily achieved, given a wisdom that is but a reflection of your own. The Guild is tottering, riven by the antagonistic forces it contains. If the council of the Bounty Hunters Guild had but a fraction of your wisdom, my lord, they would never allow Boba Fett to become a member; they would be able to foresee the doom that he brings into their midst. But their greed blinds them; all they will be able to envision is the possibility of his skills bringing more credits into the Guild's coffers. The younger members of the Guild will see that as well, and their greed will also be stimulated. Each group will try to bring Boba Fett exclusively onto their side, and thus the delicate balance that has kept the Guild in one piece will be destroyed."

"You've put much thought into this, Prince Xizor." The Emperor's bony finger pointed toward him. "If all goes as you believe it will, then there will be rewards for you as well."

"How can it not proceed as I have envisioned?" Xizor raised his head, bringing his eyes straight into the Emperor's intimidating gaze. "My intermediary has convinced Boba Fett of the advantages he will gain by the destruction of the Bounty Hunters Guild; that is why he has gone along with this scheme. The Guild is still an annoyance to him, a hindrance to his own enterprises. Bumblers the Guild's members may be, but they still manage to get in Fett's way from time to time. With the Guild broken up and dispersed, nothing would stand between Boba Fett and complete control of the galaxy's bounty-hunter trade. The fees he charges for his services are already astronomical; with no competition to turn to, clients such as the Hutts would have to pay whatever Fett demands."

"That may be so," said Vader. "But what benefit does the Empire derive from the destruction of the Bounty Hunters Guild? We can already pay Boba Fett anything he asks for, but I see no advantage in being forced to pay him more than he's worth."

"What the Empire gets," replied Xizor, "is a return to the time *before* the creation of the Bounty Hunters Guild. A time when the galaxy's mercenaries were all as independent, hungry, and ruthless as Boba Fett. A time when they were at each other's throats, with no pretense of brotherhood. When the bounty hunters' greed was not limited by the strictures of the bureaucracy they have sealed around themselves. Cradossk and the others of his generation have grown fat and lazy, somnolent within the protective walls of the Guild. Eventually, the Guild and all that remain part of it will wither away and die—but we cannot wait for that time to come. The Rebellion is a threat *now*. The Empire needs many creatures like Boba Fett, hungry and greedy, and independent enough to carry out our dirty work. The younger bounty hunters in the Guild chafe at its weight pressing upon their shoulders, its chains tangled around their feet. To destroy the Bounty Hunters Guild would be to free them—right into the service of the Empire."

"You overvalue these scum—"

"I think not." The Emperor interrupted Vader. "Prince Xizor speaks truly when he says that the forces under my command cannot do that which the bounty hunters are capable of. Or that they *would* be capable of, if the Guild were eliminated. Greed is valuable to me only if it is combined with a capacity for violence—and that capacity is exactly what would be unleashed when the Bounty Hunters Guild is no more. The survivors, whichever ones are left after Boba Fett's presence has shattered the organization, will be forced to adapt to a harsher, less protected existence, one in which they can survive only by placing their boot soles on the throats of those who had been their brothers only a short time before." The Emperor's cruel smile widened. "We will have our choice of them—each savage and driven by their unchecked appetites. The prince is right; these tools will be sharp and murderous, indeed."

"My lord flatters me." Xizor spread his hands, palms outward. "It is only the wisdom I have received from you that has guided both my thoughts and deeds."

"You are the flatterer, Xizor; in that, you do not deceive me. But your value to me has been enhanced by what you have done in this regard." The Emperor's smile faded, replaced by a hard gaze. "You have taken a considerable gamble in proceeding with your little scheme before consulting with me; if you had not been successful in convincing me of its worth, the consequences to you would have been severe."

"I know that, my lord. But time and events press upon us; the Rebellion's forces are not waiting for us to put our affairs in order."

Lord Vader's image shook its head, the points of light from the stars glistening on the black surface of his helmet. "Better that our trust should be put in the Force. Its power is greater than anything that can be derived from all these petty manipulations. The Death Star, Prince Xizor's unleashed bounty hunters—all these distract us from the Empire's real strength." Vader raised a black fist, as though crushing a rebellious world inside it. "Do not let yourself be swayed by the vain schemes of those who have no conception of the power inside you—"

"Advise me not, Lord Vader." The Emperor's anger flared, like fire suddenly revealed beneath gray ashes. "You have some training in the Force's ways; you have even exceeded the training given to you by your vanished Jedi Masters. But do not presume to consider yourself my equal."

Xizor kept his silence, watching the confrontation between Palpatine and the black-garbed figure standing before him. *Let him suffer the Emperor's wrath,* thought Xizor with a measure of satisfaction. The Emperor's seductive powers had created Vader, the call of the Force's dark side turning him into what he now was. The Emperor could destroy Vader as well; Xizor was sure of it. And if that happened— *Then my most powerful enemy would be gone.* And worlds would open before him. The rays of the Black Sun would reach even farther across the galaxy. Perhaps . . . even as far as the shadows of the Emperor's hand.

There would be another reward as well, if Vader's destruction came about. An even more satisfying one, the reward of vengeance accomplished. *That would be my reward,* brooded Xizor, *not that of the Black Sun.* Vader had no idea—yet—of the hatred that was directed toward whatever was left of his heart. The Imperial records had been wiped clean— Xizor's credits and power had seen to that—of any trace of the deaths of his family on the planet Falleen, deaths brought about by Vader's own experiments in developing new forms of biological weaponry for the Empire. Xizor's parents, his brother and sisters, along with a quarter million other innocent Falleens, had been reduced to ashes by the sterilization lasers Vader's orders had turned upon the bacterial outbreak—but those ashes were still hot in Xizor's own heart.

With his face a mask, except for his narrowed gaze, he watched his enemy.

"I mean no presumption, my lord." Darth Vader bowed his head in submission.

"Yet it irks you if I show favor to another of my servants." The Emperor smiled and nodded slowly. "Perhaps that is an indication of the depth of your loyalty to me." His withered hand pointed to Vader and Xizor in turn. "Your animosity toward each other serves my purposes well. There is never a moment when you are not at each other's throats, seeking what advantage you can in your struggle to please me. So be it; it keeps *your* teeth sharp. That is why I think Prince Xizor's scheme has a chance, however slight, of succeeding. The bounty hunters will be to each other what the two of you are: hungry and ruthless. The struggle will end someday, with one of you destroying the other. I'm not sure which one of you will be the victor. And I do not greatly care, either." The Emperor appeared to savor the possibilities. "In the meantime the Empire enjoys the benefits of your little war."

One that I will win, thought Xizor. And after that, it would be time for other plans and schemes. For all his respectful words, the Force and the Emperor's mastery of it meant nothing to him. Of what use was the greatest power in the universe—if it even existed at all, and wasn't just some figment of Vader and Palpatine's imaginations—when it was in the hands of a fool? An aging one, at that, so obsessed with the Rebellion that he would allow a greater danger to him walk the corridors of his palace. *He doesn't know,* thought Xizor, keeping his own face a mask as he gazed at the Emperor. Despite having given himself over to the dark side of the Force, Emperor Palpatine didn't suspect what was still hidden in the shadows surrounding him.

"Go about your self-appointed business, Xizor." The Emperor's hand made a dismissive gesture. "You plot and work to bring about other creatures' destruction; this pleases me. Knowing what I do about Boba Fett and the members of the unfortunate Bounty Hunters Guild, it is a process that I do not anticipate will take long to achieve the desired results. Come and report to me again when these sharper tools are ready to be delivered into my grasp."

"As you wish, my lord." Xizor bowed, then

turned. The edge of his caped robes flared with that motion, the thick rope of his bound hair swinging across the exposed ridges of his vertebrae.

"I also will want to hear of your success." Lord Vader's holo image spoke as Xizor strode from the Emperor's throne room. "Or the lack thereof."

Xizor couldn't help smiling to himself as he left the presence of the Emperor and his chief servant. There would be successes, of that he was confident. But not the kind they expected.

"I must warn you, my lord." The great doors to the throne room had sealed shut once again, leaving Vader in private consultation with the Emperor. "Better you should surround yourself with fools than one with such ambitions."

"Your warning is acknowledged, Lord Vader." Emperor Palpatine gave a knowing smile. "But it is hardly necessary. Prince Xizor likes to keep secrets from me. But I see more deeply into his heart than he realizes."

"Then let me eliminate him for you. And remove the possibility of his treachery."

"And eliminate as well the value he has for me?" The Emperor slowly shook his head. "He is a sharp-edged tool in himself, Vader. He cuts through difficulties with ease. This scheme he has initiated against the bounty hunters—it is a stroke of genius. Even Boba Fett, as smart as he is, will have little conception of what forces have been brought against him." The thin smile showed on the withered face again. "There is a great satisfaction that comes from turning a sentient creature's own strengths against him. Fett and the others like him will soon find out just how that works."

Lord Vader's image was silent for a moment before speaking, words softer than his rasping breath. "And Prince Xizor?"

"His time will come as well," said the Emperor. "When he will learn the same." He gave the same gesture of dismissal with one hand. "Now go." The Emperor turned his throne toward the stars, the vast reaches that extended before him. "I have other things to contemplate."

11

The first quarters they gave him were hung with silken brocades, the richly worked tapestries mirrored in the floors inlaid with precious metals. "I don't think so," said Boba Fett.

He prevailed upon Cradossk's majordomo, an obsequious Twi'lek like the ones so often encountered in high-level service positions, to move him to a more spartan residence in the Guild compound. It didn't take much to convince the nervously smiling and bowing creature to accede to his wishes; merely stating them and turning the threatening visage of his helmet toward the other was enough.

"I hope you'll find this more to your liking." The Twi'lek majordomo's name was Ob Fortuna; his head tails, the bifurcated appendages that curved from his skull and rested on his shoulders like overfed snakes, glistened with a sheen of perspiration. He resembled a distant clan member that Fett had seen in Jabba the Hutt's entourage. The little space, an empty cubicle carved from the planetoid's underlying rock strata, and the corridor through which he'd led Boba Fett, was chill enough to make his breath visible. The sweat was provoked by the bounty hunter's presence. "If there's anything else you require . . ."

"This will do fine." Boba Fett looked away from the Twi'lek and scanned the bare stone walls. "Leave me."

"But of course." Bowing, the majordomo backed away toward the rough-hewn door. "I await Your Fearsomeness's commands."

"Fine. Do it at a distance." Boba Fett kicked the bottom of the door to swing it shut. "That's all I need from you right now."

He could hear the majordomo's steps running down the corridor, the sounds fading away until the space was silent except for a slow drip of water in one corner. A native insect, bristling with antennae and eyestalks—a miniature version of the council member that spoke in nothing but questions—had been aroused by the presence of humanoid body heat. It tried to escape as Boba Fett reached over with his armor-gloved hand, but his forefinger cracked the bug's chitinous shell and left the tiny carcass smeared on the damp rock. Fett watched as a swarm of smaller creatures scurried away. Vermin and cold didn't bother him. He'd been in worse places.

This one had the advantage as well of being easily scoured for other bugs, the kind that would report one's words to Cradossk and his advisers. Fett hadn't even found it necessary to do a scan on the first room to which the Twi'lek had taken him, to know that the wall hangings had been studded with microscopic listening and observation devices. The old Trandoshan's welcoming party, complete with drunk act, hadn't fooled him. *They know something's up,* thought Fett. The Bounty Hunters Guild had been a tougher organization in the past;

Cradossk hadn't become its leader by being a complete idiot.

Fett hadn't survived on his own by being one, either. Cradossk would doubtlessly have expected him to reject the luxury quarters, and have an alternative already prepared. An alternative that would meet Cradossk's requirements. Boba Fett snapped on the scanning sweeps mounted in his helmet; a precisely calibrated grid snapped into view in the narrow visor.

What do we have here? Just as he'd expected: turning slowly on his boot heel, Fett saw the pulsing red spark in the grid that indicated a miniaturized spy module. He completed his scan, finding two more at varying heights on the opposite stone wall. It would have been easy to have extracted them from their niches and crushed them between his fingertips, the way he had the living bug. Instead, he took from one of his belt pouches a trio of audio drones, already set by him to reproduce the nearly subliminal traces of his breath and other homeostatic functions. He tapped the drones into place, directly on top of the bugs. No other sound would get past them; a signal in his gear would switch them off when he left the space, producing perfect silence.

He didn't anticipate spending much time here; he'd really only wanted to give Cradossk a chance to display his hospitality. And subterfuge. Any sleep or meals that Boba Fett required, he would take aboard the *Slave I,* safely docked and secured at the edge of the Guild's main compound. *I've got enough enemies here,* he'd decided. There was no sense in making it any easier for them to get at him.

Though if they wanted to talk with him, face-to-face—this dank little room was sufficient for that.

Just as he'd anticipated, he didn't have long to

wait. A knock sounded on the splintered planks of the door, then the rusting hinges bolted into the stone creaked as a hand with claws and scales pushed it open.

"So we are to be brothers." Bossk stood in the doorway, his slit-pupiled eyes showing both resentment and a primitive guile. "How pleasant that shall be for both of us."

Boba Fett looked over his shoulder at the younger Trandoshan. "That matters little to me. I take my pleasure in my work. And in getting paid for it."

"You're famous for that." Bossk entered the space, his wavering shadow cast ahead by the torches mounted along the corridor. He sat down heavily on the bench carved out of one wall. "I'd find my pleasures the same way—if it weren't for you."

"You speak of the past." Fett stood in the center of the damp stone floor, his arms folded across his chest. "Have you forgotten already what your father said?" The banquet had still been in progress as the Twi'lek majordomo had led Boba Fett to his quarters. "A new time has begun for us. For all bounty hunters."

"Ah, yes; my father." Shaking his head in disgust, Bossk leaned back against the wall. "My father speaks of great and noble things; he always has. It's one of the reasons I despise him. The day will come when I sharpen my teeth on the shards of his bones."

"Family matters don't interest me." Boba Fett shrugged. It had been obvious to him for a long time before this why Trandoshans were not a numerous species. "Deal with the old creature as you feel best. If you think you're capable of it."

A low growl sounded from deep within Bossk's throat. He leaned forward, eyes narrowing into slits as he focused on some personal vision. "Someday . . ." He nodded slowly. "When the Guild is mine . . ."

Fool, thought Boba Fett. The Trandoshan had no idea of the machinery in which he was already caught, the gears grinding out a different future than the one of which he dreamed.

"But that's why you're here, isn't it?" Bossk looked up at him. "Why you've come all this way to join the Bounty Hunters Guild." One clawed hand pulled a small box that had been dangling from one of his chest straps; he flicked open the hinged lid and dug out a wriggling morsel. "Want one?" Bossk held the container out on his scaly palm.

Boba Fett shook his head. The little box's contents were identical to the insect he'd crushed against the stone wall. "What are you talking about?"

"You don't fool me." Bossk grinned as he refastened the box to the strap. "As I said before—you might fool a senile old lizard like my father, but you can't do the same with me. I know exactly why you came here."

"And why would that be?"

"It's simple." Bossk cracked the insect between his front fangs, then swallowed the two oozing pieces. "You're aware of how old Cradossk is. You'd have to know; you had enough encounters with him in the past, before I was even spawned. His time has to come to an end, eventually. And then the leadership of the Guild will pass to me. That's already been decided. There's no one on the council that's any younger than my father; some of them are old enough to have cobwebs growing between their claws. They'll be *glad* to have me take over."

"You might be right about that." Fett had heard of other possibilities. There were other bounty hunt-

ers in the Guild who were as young and hungry as
Bossk. The leadership of the Guild wouldn't be
handed down without some kind of a struggle.

"Of course I'm right." With the point of one
claw, Bossk extracted a fragment of bug shell from
between his fangs. "And you're the proof of it."

"How do you figure that?"

"Come on; let's face it. We've both been around
the galaxy a few times. Maybe I don't have the same
amount of experience that you do, but I'm a fast
learner." Seated on the stone bench, Bossk smiled
with cozy familiarity at Boba Fett. "You'll be glad
you've met up with me like this, rather than both of
us scrabbling over some minor bounty. There's big
credits to be made here; bigger than my father and
his dried-up old cronies ever dreamed of. You know
that, don't you?"

Fett didn't bother to indicate yes or no. "I'm always on the lookout for a profitable arrangement."

"That's what makes you the kind of mean barve
I really like." Bossk's carnivorous grin widened. "My
father was right about one thing: You and I, we
really are like brothers. We should get along just fine,
given the changes that are going to happen around
here." He leaned back against the stone wall. "Like
you said—we have to change with the times. We just
have to make sure the changes go *our* way, huh?"

The assembler knew what it was talking about,
thought Boba Fett. He had to give Kud'ar Mub'at
credit for the accurate assessment of how things
would go here at the Bounty Hunters Guild. Fett had
been here for less than a standard time part, and
already the pieces were falling into place. Better than
that: *leaping* into place. The son of the Guild's leader
was volunteering to take his place in the scheme that
would tear apart the organization.

"You're a clever creature." Boba Fett gave a slow nod of acknowledgment. "Very clever."

"Smart enough to figure out what *you're* up to, pal." The slit-pupiled eyes regarded Fett with satisfaction. "You're famous for a lot of things. One of them is that you've always been a lone operator. You've never worked with a partner, even in the worst situations."

"I've never had to," replied Fett. "I can take care of myself."

"Yeah, and you still can. Like I said—you're not fooling me. All that talk back there in the banquet hall, about the Empire squeezing us out—what a crock of nerf waste. The only reason you got my father and the rest of them to go for that line is because they *wanted* to believe it. They're old and tired, and they're looking for an excuse to roll over and quit. But I'm not buying it. Things don't change like that. I've seen enough of the Empire to know that there's always going to be some use for bounty hunters. There's stuff we can do that nobody else can."

"An astute observation."

"One that you've made as well, I bet." Bossk dug at his fangs again, then inspected the tips of his claws. "If anything, there's going to be *more* business for us with Emperor Palpatine than there ever was under the Republic. There'll be all sorts of creatures that the Emperor wants to get his hands on, who don't want to be found. That's where bounty hunters come in. Plus the Rebellion—they got their needs, too. That's the great thing about being on neither one side nor the other. We can sell our services to anyone who can pay our price. And there's going to be a *lot* of buyers."

This Trandoshan also deserved credit, Boba Fett

had to admit. Bossk might be a fool, and a particularly crass and bloodthirsty one, but he was sharp enough to discern at least one important thing about the nature of evil. Which was that it always bred more of the same. *More business for us,* thought Fett. He felt no emotion about that, one way or the other.

"It's a simple matter, then, isn't it?" Boba Fett spoke his next thoughts aloud. "Of just making sure we get paid the price we want."

"You got that right. And that's why you came walking in here and asked to become a member of the Bounty Hunters Guild, isn't it? Not because things are changing out there"—Bossk waved his clawed and scaled hand, indicating the reaches beyond the mold-encrusted stone ceiling—"*but because the Guild is changing.* Or it's just about to. You've had it pretty easy for a long time, haven't you? Even when my father still had sharp fangs, he was never your equal in the bounty-hunter trade. None of those old creatures were. And as they got older all they really managed to do was get in the way of me and the other young hunters—the ones who would've given you a run for your credits, Fett. So you've really had the field all to yourself, haven't you? Must've been nice."

Fett gave a small shrug. "It hasn't been exactly easy."

"Yeah, but it would've been a lot harder if you'd had to deal with *me.*" Bossk's eyes flashed angry fire as he jabbed the point of one claw into his chest. "If I'd been able to go up against you on some of those jobs, the way I really wanted to. You wouldn't have been raking in those big bounties, the kind that Jabba and the rest of the Hutts put up, if you'd had some real competition for them."

"Yes," said Fett. "If I'd had some *real* competition, it might have been different."

Bossk didn't pick up on the irony concealed in Fett's words. "That's all coming to an end, though, isn't it? That's the real reason you're here. You know that my father and the rest of the Guild council is just about ready to have their bones picked clean. And that somebody else will be taking over. Somebody a lot harder and tougher, who isn't just going to let you walk off with all the easy credits."

"And that someone would be you, I suppose."

"Don't *suppose* with me, Fett. It's time for you and me to work some things out. You didn't come here just because you wanted membership in the Bounty Hunters Guild. You're here because you know it isn't going to be long before I'm running things. I can tell how your mind works."

"Is that so?"

Bossk nodded. " 'Cause it's so much like mine. You and me, we want the same things. Top price, and nobody getting in our way. But we've got to deal with each other." The last of the Trandoshan's smile faded. "As equals."

You idiot. "Negotiations between equals can sometimes be profitable. Or fatal."

"Let's go for a profitable one. Here's the deal, Fett." One claw raised, Bossk leaned forward on the stone bench. "There's no point in us tearing out each other's throats. Even if it would be fun. That just lets the old ones like my father stay in power for a while longer. And they've had their turn long enough. I don't feel like waiting any longer than I have to, just to get my chance."

"What do you want me to do about it?"

"It's not just what I want; it's what *you* want as well. Better you should get on my good side now,

Fett, than have me for an enemy later on." The claw tip pointed to each of them in turn. "Let's be partners, you and me. I *know* that's what you came here for."

"I see that I was correct when I said that you were a clever creature." *Just not clever enough,* thought Fett.

"Flatter me some other time, why don't you? *After* we've taken over the Bounty Hunters Guild." The fanged smile returned to Bossk's face. "When I slice up my father's carcass, I'll save you one of the best pieces."

"Don't bother," said Fett. "I'll be pleased enough knowing that I've accomplished what I came here for." Whether Bossk would be as happy about it remained to be seen.

"I'm glad—*really* glad—that we're in agreement about this." Bossk stood up from the damp stone. He stepped close to Boba Fett, bringing his face to where it almost touched the visor of the helmet. "Because otherwise I would have had to kill you."

"Perhaps." Fett didn't draw away. "Though I think you're actually the lucky one. Look down here."

Bossk's slit-pupiled eyes widened when they glanced down and saw the muzzle of a blaster pressed against his abdomen. Fett rested his thumb on the weapon's firing stud.

"Let's get one thing straight." Boba Fett kept his voice level, stripped of emotion. "We can be partners. But we're not going to be friends. I need those even less."

Bossk regarded the weapon for a moment longer, then lifted his head and barked a raw-edged laugh. "That's good! I like that." All the points of his fangs showed as he glared fiercely into the dark visor.

"You watch out for yourself, and I'll watch out for me. That's *just* the way I like it."

"Good." Fett slipped the blaster back into its holster. "We can do business."

As he stepped out into the corridor Bossk stopped and glanced over his shoulder. "And of course," he said slyly, "this is all a private arrangement, isn't it? Between you and me."

"Of course." Boba Fett hadn't moved from the center of the space. "It'll work better that way."

For me, thought Fett, after the Trandoshan had stridden away, past the flickering torches. *For you, it's another matter.*

The Twi'lek majordomo had other household duties as well. Chief among which was spying.

"Your son has just concluded a long conversation with Boba Fett." All the comings and goings in the Bounty Hunters Guild headquarters were observed by Ob Fortuna. "From what I could tell, your son seemed rather pleased with the results."

"I'm not surprised." Cradossk's blunt claws fumbled with the catches of his ceremonial robes. The heavy fabric, with embroidery that depicted his species' ancient battles and triumphs, was stained with the wine that had been spilled at the banquet. "Bossk gets his eloquence from me." He shrugged off the robes. "Persuasiveness is a specialty of his."

"But aren't you concerned?" The Twi'lek's tapering head tails swung forward as he gathered up the robes. "About what the two of them found to talk about?" He spread the robes out on a lacquered rack at the side of Cradossk's sitting room. "Your son has . . . shall we say"—the Twi'lek's smile was a combination of nerves and obsequiousness—"a bit of a conspiratorial streak."

"Of course he does! He wouldn't be my son, otherwise." Cradossk sat down on the edge of a canopied pallet and stuck his legs out. His claws ached from all the standing he'd had to do, giving toasts and welcoming the famous Boba Fett into the brotherhood of bounty hunters. "I don't expect him to take over the leadership of the Guild someday merely because he has a talent for killing sentient creatures."

The Twi'lek knelt down to unfasten the metal-studded straps laced between Cradossk's claws. "I think," he said softly, "that your son is rather eager to assume that leadership. Perhaps even . . . impatient . . ."

"Good for him. Keeps him hungry." Cradossk leaned back against a mound of pillows. "I know just what my son wants. The same thing I did when I was his age. Blood leaking through my fangs, and a pile of credits in my hand."

"Oh!" Ob Fortuna's eyes glittered at any mention of credits. "But perhaps . . . it would be better for you to be careful."

"Better for me to be smart, you mean. I don't intend to wind up on my son's dinner plate. That's why I'm on *his* side in all this."

The head tails rolled across the Twi'lek's shoulders as he looked up. "I don't understand."

"You wouldn't. You're not a sneaky enough barve. It takes a Trandoshan to understand the subtleties of these kinds of maneuvers. We're born with it, like scales. Do you really think I'm such an idiot that I'd let Boba Fett walk in here and become a member of the Bounty Hunters Guild, and just take everything he has to say on trust?" Cradossk had no anxiety about revealing his thoughts and schemes to his majordomo; Twi'leks were too cowardly to act upon anything they heard. "The man's a scoundrel. Of course, that's nothing I hold against him; he's just not *our* scoundrel. He's still looking out for himself—and why shouldn't he? But in the meantime I'm not fooled by all his talk of some grand alliance between himself and the Bounty Hunters Guild. And if he was taken in by all my rhapsodizing about brotherhood between us, then I really *am* disappointed in the great Boba Fett." He reached down and scratched between the exposed claws of his feet. "That's why I sent my son Bossk in there to talk with him. Bossk may be a bit of a hothead—that's another way he resembles me when I was that age—but he's smart enough to follow through on a good, underhanded plan."

"*You* sent him to talk with Boba Fett?"

"Why not?" Cradossk felt content with the universe, and how things were proceeding in his corner of it. "I told Bossk what to say as well. Probably no more than what Boba Fett was expecting from the impatient young heir to the leadership of the Guild. A partnership between the two of them—and against me."

The Twi'lek gaped at him. "*Against* you?"

"Of course. If I hadn't sent Bossk in there to talk with Fett, and have him propose exactly that, then my son would very likely have done it on his own initiative. Not because Bossk really wants to conspire against me. He's too loyal—*and* too smart for that. Plus he knows I'd have his internal organs for breakfast if he tried anything like that." Cradossk gave a self-satisfied nod of his head. "It's much better this way. Now we have an in with our mysterious visitor and would-be brother, one to whom Boba Fett will confide the true reasons why he's come here to the

Guild. My son gains points with not only his loving father, but also with some of the council members who have voiced some fear about his ambitions. *And* I remain in control of the situation. That's the most important thing."

A puzzled look remained on the Twi'lek's face as he rolled up the leather foot straps and placed them in his employer's ornamentations box. "Could it not be"—the Twi'lek's head tails glistened with the effort of his musing—"that your son has a different idea? Different than the one you put into his head?"

Cradossk folded his claws over the age-yellowed scales of his stomach. "Such as?"

"Perhaps Bossk doesn't want to just *pretend* that he has entered into a conspiracy with Boba Fett. A conspiracy against you and the rest of the Guild council." The Twi'lek rubbed his chin, gazing at some point beyond the sitting room's caparisoned walls, where his infrequently encountered thoughts could be found. "Maybe he would have gone and talked to Boba Fett anyway—whether you had sent him or not. And he would have made just that proposition. For real."

"Now, there's an interesting notion." Cradossk sat up, bringing his heavy-lidded—and unamused—gaze straight into that of his household majordomo. "And one for which I should pull your flopping little head off. Do you realize what you're suggesting?"

The Twi'lek's smile was even more nervous than before. "Now that I think of it . . ."

"You should've done your thinking *before* you opened your mouth." Anger simmered inside Cradossk. The only reason he didn't pull off the Twi'lek's head was that a good majordomo, one that was used to his various ways and preferences, was hard to find. "You're questioning not only my son's intelligence, but his loyalty to me. I realize that members of your species have only an abstract understanding of that concept. But for Trandoshans"—Cradossk thumped his bared chest with his fist—"it is something in our blood. Honor and loyalty, and the faith that exists between family members, even unto the last generations—those are not negotiable substances."

"I beseech your pardon. . . ." Hands clasped together, the Twi'lek bobbed up and down in front of Cradossk, the speed of his genuflections increased by his anxiety. "I meant no disrespect. . . ."

"Very well." Cradossk shooed him away with a quick, contemptuous gesture. "Because you're an idiot, I'll overlook your insulting comments." He wouldn't forget them, though; long, grudge-filled memories were another characteristic of Trandoshans. "Now get out of my sight, before I have reason to be hungry again."

The Twi'lek scurried away, still hunched over and bowing as he retreated toward the sitting room's door.

Maybe I should eat him, brooded Cradossk as he drew on a lounging robe stitched together from the skins of former employees. Standards were becoming deplorably lax among the Guild's hirelings. Staffing had always been a problem over the decades; in that, the Bounty Hunters Guild had the same difficulties that their clients the Hutts did. Not many of the galaxy's sentient creatures were so desperate as to seek employment in establishments where the constant threat of death was one of the working conditions. He wondered if Emperor Palpatine's dismantling of the Republic would improve things in that regard, or just make them worse. The establishment of the Empire promised a net increase in the galaxy's misery quotient—that was good, at least as far as Cradossk was concerned—but also a tighter control over the various worlds' inhabitants. That was probably bad. . . .

Something to think about. Feeling the weight of his age, Cradossk shambled into the memory-bone chamber connected to the sitting room. He lit one of the candles set in a niche filled with years of congealed wax; the guttering flame sent interlaced shadows wavering across the walls and their white treasures.

It had been a long time since he'd had occasion to add another memento to his collection. *My killing days are over,* thought Cradossk, not without regret. He wandered farther into the chamber's ivory-lined recesses, letting memories of vanquished opponents and foolishly recalcitrant captives wash over him.

Until he came to the oldest and tiniest bones. They looked like something that might have been found in a bird's nest, on some planet where all the life-forms had been extinct for centuries. Cradossk let a couple of them rest in his palm as he poked at them with a single claw. Tooth marks showed on the bones' surfaces, from little teeth that had been as sharp and hard as a newborn's. Teeth that hadn't yet been dulled by the coarse flesh of enemies. Those teeth had been his, when he'd just barely been out of his mother's egg sac. The bones were those of his spawn-brothers, hatched just a few seconds later. And too late for them.

Cradossk sighed, mulling over the wisdom he'd been created with, and that which had taken him so long to achieve. He carefully set his brothers' bones back in the hollow of polished rock where he kept them.

This was why lesser entities like that moronic

Twi'lek would never understand. About family loyalty and honor . . .

He pitied creatures like that. They simply had no sense of tradition.

The Twi'lek pushed the door to the sitting room open a crack. Just enough to see what the old Trandoshan was up to.

Cradossk had gone into his chamber of grisly souvenirs. A candle flame showed his silhouette among the stacked and interwoven bones. *Good,* thought the Twi'lek. His boss would usually stay in there for hours, fondling the bones and reminiscing, and sometimes falling asleep, wheezing and dreaming with a splintered femur in his claws.

Plenty of time, then. The Twi'lek slid the door shut without making a sound and strode quickly toward another section of the Bounty Hunters Guild compound. To Bossk's quarters.

"Excellent," said the younger Trandoshan, after listening to the Twi'lek's report. "You're sure of all this?"

"But of course." The Twi'lek made no attempt to conceal the wickedness of his smile. "I have been in your father's service for some time. Longer than any of his previous majordomos. I haven't lasted this long by being blind to his thought processes. I can decipher the old fool like a data readout. And I can tell you this for a fact: He trusts you absolutely. As he told me, that was why he sent you to talk to Boba Fett."

Sitting in a gold-hinged campaign chair, Bossk nodded in approval. "I suppose my father had all sorts of things to say. About loyalty and honor. And all the rest of that nerf dung."

"The usual."

"That must be the hardest part of your job," said Bossk. "Listening to fools talk."

You have no idea, thought the Twi'lek. "I've gotten used to it."

Bossk gave another, slower nod. "The time is coming when you won't have to listen to that particular fool any longer. When I'm running the Bounty Hunters Guild, things will be different."

"I certainly expect so." *More of the same,* the Twi'lek told himself. He was careful to keep his thoughts from showing on his face. "In the meantime . . ."

"In the meantime there will be a nice little transfer of credits to your private account. For all your services." Bossk dismissed him with a simple gesture of his upraised claws. "You can go now."

That fool is right about one thing. The Twi'lek felt a warm glow of satisfaction as he headed back to his own quarters. He was doing a good job—

For himself.

Boba Fett heard the door creak open. He had to work against his own ingrained habits, which had kept him alive in a hard universe, to keep his back turned toward a door. More bounty hunters had lost their lives from a blaster burning into their spines than had ever taken an opponent's shot face-to-face. Fett should know: he had taken out more than his share, just that way.

"Excuse me. . . ." A cautious voice sounded from the doorway.

That was why he'd kept his back toward it. So as to give anyone who came around to this dank chamber, to talk with him, a perceived psychological advantage. Some of the members of the Bounty Hunters Guild were a little short in the courage department. He found it hard to imagine why they might have thought they would have any aptitude for this business. If they had found themselves looking straight into the dark, narrow visor of his helmet, they might have fled before even opening their mouths.

"Yes?" Boba Fett turned around—slowly, as nonthreateningly as possible for someone with his reputation. "What is it?"

"I was wondering"—the short bounty hunter, with the large insectoid eyes and breathing hoses, stood in the doorway—"if I might have a word with you. . . ."

What was this one's name? They all looked alike to Boba Fett. *Zuckuss,* he remembered. The partner of Bossk, at least as recently as that business where he had snatched the accountant Nil Posondum out from under their noses.

"Of course, if you're busy—" Zuckuss clasped his gloved hands together in an obvious show of nervousness. "I can come back some other time—"

"Not at all." Boba Fett had also seen this one at the Guild's banquet hall, close to the reptilian Bossk. So there was undoubtedly still some connection between the two of them. "No time like the present," said Fett. "For talking about important things."

This one didn't take long. Zuckuss was hardly in Fett's quarters for more than a few minutes before he had scuttled back out into the corridor, disappearing before anyone from the Guild could spot him there. *Small fry,* thought Boba Fett. Not one of the major players in the Bounty Hunters Guild that Kud'ar Mub'at had briefed him on. But important enough, with a line straight to the ear of Bossk. Who, as the impatient heir apparent to the Guild leadership, would have a great deal to do with it being torn apart.

The conversation went exactly as Boba Fett had expected, and just as Kud'ar Mub'at would have predicted. Zuckuss was like so many others in the Bounty Hunters Guild, down in the lower ranks: a perfect combination of greed and naïveté. *Just smart enough to kill,* mused Fett after Zuckuss had left. The short bounty hunter had glanced nervously out the doorway, to make sure no one was there to see him as he scurried down the torchlit corridor. *Not smart enough to keep himself from getting killed.* It might not happen this time—Zuckuss might, with the erratic luck of the feckless, survive the breakup of the Guild—but it would eventually.

He supposed that was the big difference between himself and poor Zuckuss, between himself and Bossk and Bossk's vicious, aging father and all the rest of the Guild members. Boba Fett sat down on the stone bench for a moment; the armaments he carried with him, that were as much a part of him as his spine, prevented him from leaning back. He never wasted time thinking about himself, any more than an explosively lethal missile from the rocket launcher strapped to his back would have as it sped toward its doomed and pinpointed target. But he knew that the reason he was alive and that others were dead, or soon would be, was that he possessed the true and essential secret of being a bounty hunter—

As good as he was at catching and, if need be, killing other sentient creatures, he was even better at surviving their attempts to kill him. Everything else was just a matter of superior firepower.

Boba Fett stood up from the stone bench. If he stayed here any longer, there would be others coming to talk to him. Others who thought they could protect themselves the way he did, but who were already fatally enmeshed in the trap spun by Kud'ar Mub'at, so far away that he couldn't be seen or the tugs on the strands of his web even felt. Besides Bossk and Zuckuss, there had also been one of Cradossk's top advisers on the Guild council, and the Twi'lek majordomo, back for a longer talk than when he'd brought Fett to this dank chamber. All of them had been in pure deal-cutting mode, eager to help pull the Bounty Hunters Guild apart so they would get a bigger piece of whatever was left in the wreckage.

Right now he didn't feel like talking to anyone else. Action meant more than words; that was one other thing Boba Fett was sure of. A man was killed by words, and saved by action. Spending so much time talking to other sentient creatures had been like wrapping himself in death. What he wanted to do right now was head back to the *Slave I,* his refuge docked at the edge of the Guild's main compound, lock himself behind its overlapping security layers, all systems primed to fry anyone who tried to breach them, and rest. If not the sleep of the virtuous—Fett had no illusions about that, or regrets—then at least the sleep of someone who had put in a good day's work. In his business, that meant helping others arrange their own destruction.

The presence of those other sentient creatures, carrying their fates around with them, all unaware, laid a cold hand on Boba Fett's heart, or whatever passed for it after all these years of death. It felt like some prophecy of his own death, though he was just as sure that that was a long way off, far from here in both time and space.

Being back inside his own ship would be as much a relief as being out in the emptiness between the stars. He would be alone there, sealed off from all the others, living and dead. . . .

That was what he needed. He pushed the rough wooden door shut behind himself and strode down the corridor, beneath the flickering light of the torches. *Anywhere but here,* thought Boba Fett. The tunnel stretched out before him. Above him, the invisible weight of rock and stone pressed down, like the tomb he hadn't earned yet.

12

"You were saying things." Dengar handed the figure on the pallet a metal cup filled with water. "In your sleep."

Sleep was the wrong word, he knew. *Dying* would have been more accurate. Except that Boba Fett hadn't died, after all. After everything.

"Is that so?" Even unhelmeted, Boba Fett had a gaze that was as cold and exterminating as anything that had looked out from the black, narrow visor. Lying on the improvised bed in the hiding place's smallest subchamber, Fett's lethal potential appeared undiminished, as though his ravaged flesh were only a temporary costume, less real than the ragged battle-gear stacked up in the corner. "What did I say?"

"Nothing important," replied Dengar. He knew better than to have told the truth, if Fett's drugged, unconscious mutterings had amounted to anything. *This barve lives by secrets,* thought Dengar. To get inside any of those secrets would be like stealing something from him. And the consequences of that, Dengar was well aware, would not be pretty. "Something about not liking so many sentient creatures around you. Stuff like that."

"Ah." Boba Fett raised his head and managed to sip the water he'd been given. His smile looked like a blade wound in the abraded skin of his face. "I still don't like it."

"Please do not agitate the patient." The taller of the two medical droids scolded Dengar. The droid and its shorter partner were busily changing the dressings around Boba Fett's torso. Bloodied rags and sterile gel sheets were peeled away from the raw flesh beneath. Wounds such as Fett's took a long time to heal; the Sarlacc's gastric secretions were like acid creeping toward the bone, long after the beast itself was dead. "If I had the authority to do so," continued SHΣ1-B, "I would order you out of this area immediately."

"But you don't." Dengar leaned back against the subchamber's crumbling rock wall. The air inside the hiding place was as hot and desiccating as the interior of one of the ancient burial mounds that studded the farther reaches of the Dune Sea, where Tatooine's double suns turned corpses into withered leather. "Besides," said Dengar, "if you two haven't killed him by now, nothing will."

"Sarcasm." 1e-XE spoke as it readied another combination of opiates and antiseptics. "Nonappreciation."

"There's someone else in this place, isn't there?" Boba Fett had drawn his head back from the metal cup that Dengar had held out to him. The mere effort of his words sent his chest laboring, the dials and readouts on the surrounding equipment blipping into the red. "A female."

Dengar said nothing. He placed the half-empty cup on top of one of the sighing machines that the two medical droids tended. He had other things to take care of, other things to do besides talk with the sinister figure lying on the pallet, a little farther away from death's shores than Fett had been even a couple of days ago. One of the hiding place's power generators had conked out, spewing white sparks and a dense cloud of greasy smoke. That had necessitated shutting down all but the minimum air recyclers, resulting in the hot, thick miasma bound inside the hiding place. Dengar could more profitably take care of the generator, getting it up and back on-line, rather than staying here at Boba Fett's bedside. But the other man's cold gaze held him as tight as the curved hook of a gaffstick.

"There's no need to lie to me about it," said Boba Fett. His words were as cold and unemotional as the gaze from his eyes. "I saw her. She came in here. Yesterday, I suppose. It's still hard for me to tell about these things. But it was dark, and she must have thought I was asleep. Or that I had died, perhaps."

"Please," said SHΣ1-B. It fussed with the tubes running between the machines and Boba Fett's body. "You're making our job considerably more difficult."

Dengar ignored the medical droid. He was about to answer Fett, to tell the bounty hunter who the female was, when the bombs hit. Real bombs.

Dust sifted from the subchamber's ceiling, speckling the lenses of SHΣ1-B's head unit swiveling up toward the sound of thunder. Windstorms infrequently lashed the Dune Sea, floods of sand churning down the stone gulleys and vanishing just as quickly beneath the twin suns. Dengar had always thought that the hiding place he'd dug for himself was too far beneath the planet's surface to take any damage from mere weather. *It'll take something stronger,* he'd decided, *to get in here.*

His own words were still looping around inside

his head when the rocks fell, with even louder thunder from above, onto his face.

He'd looked up, along with the two medical droids. He had a memory flash, of a light sharp as blades against his eyes and brighter than Tatooine's suns combined into one. Then he was spitting out gravel and blood as he felt his arm being tugged by someone unseen.

"Come on!" The voice was Neelah's; her hands gripped tight around his forearm and pulled. Rocks and sand poured off his chest as his scrabbling efforts, feeble at first and then made stronger by sudden desperation, combined with hers to extract him from the remains of the subchamber. "He's still in there!"

She meant Boba Fett, of course. The hiding place's emergency lights flickered as the remaining generator came to life. Dengar could still hear thunder, receding into the distance up on the surface level. The thunder would return, he knew; he was familiar enough with saturation-bombing techniques to be aware that that was what was going on up there. One wave would be succeeded by another, crossing the ground at a right angle from the first sweep. There wouldn't be any stones left, no gulleys or eroded pillars; everything would be hammered into dust. And as for whatever might lie beneath the surface . . .

Neelah was already digging at the rubble that blocked the doorway to the subchamber. Enough of the dust had settled that Dengar could see how the bombs' impact had knocked him back toward the hiding place's main area. If he had been any farther inside, where the medical droids had been taking care of their patient, the rockfall would have come straight down on him, crushing his skull.

"Confusion." Neelah's bleeding fingers had already excavated the smaller of the droids. With its carapace dented, torso readouts cracked and blinking, 1e-XE crawled away from the rocks and righted itself with difficulty. "Noise. Not-goodness."

"What are you waiting for?" Neelah looked back around at him, her eyes blazing through the dust and sweat covering her face. "Help me!"

"Are you crazy?" Dengar reached down and grabbed an arm, pulling Neelah to her feet. "There isn't time for that—whoever's laying down those bombs on the surface will be back in less than a minute. We've got to get out of here!"

"I'm not going without him." Neelah yanked her arm from Dengar's grasp. "Save yourself, if you want to." She turned away and started tugging at one of the larger rocks, nearly as high as herself.

There were tunnels underneath the hiding place, curving and smooth-sided, that ran deep into the planet's bedrock. Dengar had investigated them far enough to know that they connected with the Great Pit of Carkoon; with the Sarlacc beast dead now, they would make a safe refuge from the bombing. But only if they were reached in time, before the next destructive wave collapsed what remained of these spaces.

He hesitated only a moment, before cursing himself as a fool and laying both his hands on the rock, just above Neelah's hands. The stone surface was already slick with her blood; Dengar dug his own fingertips into it and pulled, straining with his weight against the rock's resistance. From far off and above, he could hear the bombing of the surface come to a halt, like a storm that has spent its thunderous fury. *That's only temporary,* he knew. They'd be returning in this direction soon enough.

Dengar put his shoulder against the rock, his hands clawing for a better grip. It struck him, between one gasp for breath and the next, that he didn't even know who it could be that was pounding the Dune Sea above his head into scorched powder. Forces of the Empire, maybe, or the Rebel Alliance, or the Hutts, or the Black Sun organization—at this point it wasn't as important as just surviving the hard, murderous rain. The only thing he knew for certain, down in his gut, was that it had something to do with Boba Fett. Getting involved with this barve was a sure ticket to disaster.

The large rock suddenly shifted, spilling Neelah forward onto the main chamber's rubble-strewn floor. Dengar managed to keep his balance, shifting his hold and thrusting with his bent legs, keeping the stone rolling. Neelah scrambled out of its way as the debris of the subchamber's shattered doorway came tumbling after it.

"You are wasting time," announced SHΣ1-B from within the suddenly revealed space beyond the rocks and settling dust. The medical droid had busied itself by disconnecting the various tubes and monitoring wires that had been hooked up to Boba Fett. "Therapeutic protocols render it imperative that the patient be removed from these unsafe premises at once."

Lying on the pallet, Boba Fett had lapsed back into unconsciousness, either from the crashing impact of the bombing raid or from an anesthetic dose administered by the medical droid. Dengar and Neelah scrambled over the rocks; each took one end of the pallet and lifted, hoisting Fett high enough to carry out into the hiding place's main chamber.

"Wait a second." After they were clear, Neelah set down her end of the pallet and climbed back into what remained of the subchamber space. Cracks spidered across its ceiling, showering down more dust and loose stones as the sharp, percussive hammer strokes from above grew louder. Neelah emerged a second later with Boba Fett's scoured and dented helmet and combat gear; she piled it on top of the unconscious bounty hunter, then grabbed hold of the pallet again. "Okay, let's go."

They both collapsed in exhaustion when they had reached the safety of the lower, Sarlacc-dug tunnels. The two medical droids fretted over their patient as Dengar and Neelah sprawled back against the fused-smooth walls curving around them. From here, the bombing raid sounded as though it were happening on some other, unluckier world.

"What's that smell?" Neelah wrinkled her nose as she turned her gaze toward the darkness and the stench of the tunnel's lower reaches.

Dengar lifted the lantern he had managed to scavenge hastily from the hiding place's equipment. Its feeble glow extended a few meters into the dark before being swallowed up. "Probably the Sarlacc," he said. "Or what's left of it. The part that could be seen in the Great Pit of Carkoon was just its head and mouth; it had tentacles extending all through the rock. Some say as far as the edges of the Dune Sea. When our friend here blew out the Sarlacc's gut"— Dengar pointed with his thumb to Boba Fett on the pallet—"there was a lot of dead beast left rotting down here. You can't expect something like that to smell too good, you know."

The stench of decay grew worse, as though the vibration of the surface bombing had shaken open a buried pustule. Neelah's face paled, then she quickly scrambled to her knees and hurried to a farther bend of the tunnel. The sounds of gagging and retching traveled back to Dengar.

She's not used to this sort of thing, mused Dengar. Or some part of her wasn't; something held in the darkness and hidden memory inside her. That intrigued him. A mere dancing girl, a pretty servant in the court of Jabba the Hutt, would have gotten accustomed to the smell of death quickly enough; it had pervaded the walls of Jabba's palace, seeping up from the rancor pit beneath the throne room. Hutts in general *liked* that smell; it was one of the more loathsome characteristics of their species to revel in a constant olfactory reminder that they were alive and their enemies, and the objects of their lethal amusements, were dead and rotting beneath them. That, among other things, was why Dengar had considered employment with the late Jabba or any of the other members of his clan as a choice of last resort. Especially so after Dengar had found Manaroo—and his love for her. How could one return to that being who represented one's essence, an almost forgotten purity and grace, with the stink of dead, defeated flesh wrapped around oneself? It was impossible.

It seemed impossible for this Neelah to endure as well. She had the temperament of one born to the galaxy's nobility, a bloodline accustomed to command and the obedience of others. Dengar had noted that, just from the way she had faced him down in their first encounter. Anyone else who had gone through the unsavory rigors of Jabba's court, followed by unprotected exposure to the Dune Sea, would have quailed before the obvious superiority of Dengar's strength and weaponry. But some spark of courage inside Neelah had burned even brighter under those conditions, fierce enough to have burned his outstretched hand, if he had dared to touch her.

That aristocratic strain was apparent in the female's face as well, even darkened and toughened as it was by the lash of the double suns and the scouring of the Dune Sea's hot, razorlike winds. *She'll be trouble,* Dengar already knew. He'd had enough on his hands before she had come along, but with her presence added to the equation, the result was increased exponentially.

Neelah returned, face even paler in the glow from the single lantern. "I'm sorry," she said.

"Don't be." Dengar gave a shrug. "I'll be the first to admit that this isn't the most pleasant neighborhood." He got to his feet. "We might as well see what kind of shape we're in."

The two medical droids were stationed on either side of Boba Fett's pallet.

"How's the patient?"

SHΣ1-B glanced back at Dengar. "As well as can be expected," the droid said irritably. "Given the disturbance he's been put through."

"Hey—" Dengar poked himself in the chest. "Did *I* order a bombing raid to start up? Don't blame everything on me."

"That's not a bad question." Standing beside him, Neelah glanced over the unconscious form of the bounty hunter. "Who did order it?"

"Who knows?" Dengar set the lamp on a shoulder-high outcropping. "This guy's got major enemies. It was probably one of them."

"Then that would mean somebody knows that he's alive. Somebody besides us."

That realization snapped together in Dengar's brain, like a pair of wires that had become disconnected during the tumult. *She's right*—somehow the word must've gotten out, to somebody for whom it was an important piece of information, that Boba

Fett hadn't died; that breath, however shallow, was still going in and out of his body. Someone wasn't happy about that. Someone who would send out sufficient explosive force to pulverize an army, just to make sure that there wouldn't be enough left of Boba Fett to take a breath.

"Somebody was spying on us," said Dengar. He had already eliminated himself as the source of the leak, and he had sworn Manaroo to secrecy. Neelah wasn't a likely suspect; there had been no place for her to go, no one for her to talk to while she'd been out in the Dune Sea. And she hadn't left the hiding place since Dengar had taken her in. *Maybe somebody from Jabba's palace,* he thought. There had been plenty of scoundrels there, even after Jabba's death, with the necessary skills for staying unseen while watching the comings and goings out in the wastelands. Especially after losing a lucrative gig with the Hutt, any one of them would be motivated to sell valuable info to the highest bidder. To some agent of the Empire or anybody else who had a big enough grudge against Boba Fett. "That must have been what happened." Dengar nodded slowly. "Somebody saw me taking Fett down into my hiding place."

"Don't be stupid." Neelah shook her head. "If somebody knew exactly *where* Fett had been taken, they wouldn't bother blowing up everything within sight of the Great Pit of Carkoon. One missile, straight down the tunnel entrance, would've done the job. Simple and clean." She pointed toward the silent form on the pallet. "If that's all it took to kill him off, they would have done it the easy way. *And* the quiet way."

She had a point, Dengar admitted to himself. Boba Fett wasn't the only one who lived by secrets;

the kind of clients he'd had, and enemies he'd made, were the same way. A surgical strike would have eliminated Fett without the risk of drawing attention that a bombing raid entailed. Dengar had heard nothing the last time he'd been talking to his own information sources in Mos Eisley about a contract being put out on Boba Fett. So if anybody was actively gunning for him, they were definitely keeping it quiet.

"Unless," said Dengar, "there's some other reason for the raid. . . ."

Neelah gave him a withering look. "Do *you* think there's some other reason?"

He didn't bother to answer. Silence filled the tunnel as he looked upward, listening and waiting. "I think we're all clear now."

"We can go back up?"

"Are you kidding?" Dengar shook his head, then picked up the lantern and directed its light toward the tunnel they had come down. The light picked up the jumbled shapes of the rubble filling the passageway. "We're blocked off. Even if there's anything left of my hiding place—which is a big if, given the pounding that was going on up there—we couldn't get to it now. We'll have to push on, and see if there's some other way of getting out to the surface."

A shiver of disgust ran across Neelah's shoulders. The smell of rot was noticeably stronger toward the tunnel's unlit end.

"Can he travel?" Dengar pointed toward Boba Fett.

"It would be better," said SHΣ1-B, "from a therapeutic standpoint, if he were left undisturbed."

"That's not what I asked."

"I don't know why you bothered to inquire at all." SHΣ1-B's tone was distinctly haughty. "I imagine you'll do whatever you're planning on, no matter what 1e-XE and I tell you."

"Come on." Dengar motioned Neelah over toward the pallet. "These droids don't know how tough this barve really is."

They managed to lift the pallet, with Dengar taking most of the unconscious figure's weight into his arms, until the loose gravel shifted under his feet and he saw how strong Neelah actually was; she braced herself and caught the load from toppling to one side. Dengar instructed one of the medical droids to loop the carrying strap of the pallet around his neck. With the lantern's beam wavering ahead of them, they started downward into the murk and stomach-churning smell.

"How do you know . . ." At the pallet's back end, Neelah gasped for breath. "How do you know we can get out this way?"

"I don't," said Dengar simply. "But there's an air current coming in from somewhere. You can feel it on your face." He glanced over his shoulder at her. The nauseated pallor had diminished slightly; she had gone numb to the smell of the decaying Sarlacc's carcass, buried beneath whatever was left of its nest under the Great Pit of Carkoon. Neelah took a deep breath, nostrils flared, and only gagged slightly. "Even with the stink," continued Dengar, "I can tell it's coming from somewhere outside of these tunnels. If we follow it to its source, we might find someplace where we can either crawl out or dig our way to the surface. Or . . ." He gave a shrug. "We won't. The bombing raid might have collapsed the rest of the tunnels with too much rubble for us to get through. In which case, it's pretty much over for all of us."

"You sound pretty calm about that possibility."

"What's my choices? I volunteered for this gig."
One corner of Dengar's mouth lifted in a grim smile.
"Later on, when I'm actually dying, I might let myself get a little more emotional about it. In the meantime we might as well save our strength for whatever
digging we're going to have to do." He lifted his end
of the pallet higher. "Come on. We might as well find
out what it's going to be."

The two medical droids followed behind. "This
goes against all sound therapeutic protocols."
SHΣ1-B voiced its concern again. "We're not taking
responsibility for whatever happens to our patient."

"Absolution." The shorter one trundled with difficulty over the tunnel's rough terrain. "Lack of
blame."

"Yeah, right. Whatever." Dengar didn't look
back at the complaining droids. "You're off the
hook." The lantern's beam faded away into the darkness ahead of him. "Just don't tell me about it."

"Do you think he'll be okay?" The worry in Neelah's voice was audible. "He's been jostled around
quite a bit. Maybe we should let the droids take a
look at him—"

"That's a good idea." Dengar kept on walking
down the tunnel's slope, his hands gripping the corner of the pallet at his back. "That'll give whoever it
is topside lots of time to take another pass at us."

"Oh." Neelah sounded abashed. "I guess you're
right."

"About this one, I am. We'll all be better off the
sooner we get out of here." He was already thinking
about the next time he would see Manaroo. And *if*
he would ever see her again. A lot of his recent decisions, his plans and schemes, were swiftly metamor-
phosing to regrets. *And this could be the last one,* he
thought as the pallet's weight combined with that of

its unconscious passenger to dig into Dengar's hands. Even his sensory perceptions—the tantalizing hint of fresh air against his sweating face—could have been lies and wishes, rather than the simple truth that he was walking through his own tomb.

His doubts faded a bit when the tunnel's floor leveled beneath his feet; the slope he and Neelah had carried Boba Fett down had extended, through its various twists and turns, at least a hundred yards. That wasn't enough, Dengar knew, to take them out of the territory of another bombing raid. But he was familiar with the rocky outcroppings of the Dune Sea's surface all around what had been his hiding place's entrance; there was a good chance that they had reached a point where the ground's bones hadn't been completely atomized. The bombs' impact might even have created new passages to the oxygen above, untainted by the stench of the rotting Sarlacc. By now, the smell had gotten bad enough that Dengar could taste it, a nauseating film that had crept down the back of his tongue. . . .

"Look!" Neelah called out from behind him.

Dengar glanced over his shoulder, then in the direction in which her upraised hand pointed, as she balanced the corner of the pallet against her thigh. The lantern's beam swept across a slanting heap of broken stone. "I don't see anything. . . ."

"Turn off the lantern," ordered Neelah.

He thumbed off the power switch. The light had been dim enough that his eyes only took a few seconds to adjust to the darkness. Which wasn't complete: a thread of daylight, clouded with dust motes, drew a jag-edged spot only a few inches from the toes of his boots. Dengar tilted his head back and spotted the cleft in the rocks overhead. The hole looked hardly bigger than the width of his hand.

"This'll take a little work." Dengar mulled over the situation. He and Neelah had lowered the pallet between themselves. With the lantern switched back on, he studied the wall of crumbled stone nearest the hole. "I can get up there, all right. And so can you; it doesn't look like that bad a climb." He pointed to Fett. "He's going to be the problem, though."

"You've got a line coil, don't you?" With a nod of her head, Neelah indicated one of the equipment pouches at Dengar's waist. "If you could get up there and pry the gap open wider—or if you could get out to the surface—then I could tie a loop around his chest and under his arms, and you could haul him up."

Nothing had been heard from the medical droids for a while as they had straggled along behind Dengar and Neelah. But now SHΣ1-B spoke up. "The patient," it protested loudly, "is not in any kind of condition for a maneuver as you've described. Very simply, you'll kill him if you try that."

"Yeah, and if we leave him down here, he'll be just as dead." Under the best of circumstances, Dengar would have gotten tired of the droid's officious carping. He took out the line and fastened one end to his belt so his hands would be free for climbing. He gave the rest of the coil to Neelah, then nodded toward Boba Fett. "Pull him back a bit so the both of you will be out of the way of whatever I pull down." There was another possibility that Dengar had left unspoken. Specifically, that in trying to widen the light-spilling gap overhead, he'd bring down the entire roof of this underground space, burying himself and the others under a few tons of rock. The bombing raid had left the area in a state of fragile balance; even removing the smallest stone might trigger a collapse of everything surrounding it.

He left the lantern with Neelah, instructing her to point it toward the area around the bright crevice he'd be working on. As he started to climb, fingertips digging into the loose rock, he could hear her dragging the pallet over to the farthest angle of the space below him.

One stone shifted as he put his hand's weight on it. The stone came free and tumbled away; he would have followed it, crashing hard down the slope he'd traversed so far, if he hadn't managed to loop one arm around a larger outcropping just above and to the side of his head. His feet dangled in air for a moment as more of the dislodged stones rattled and slid out from under his boot soles.

"Are you all right?" Dengar heard Neelah's voice from below as the lantern beam pinned his one hand straining to hold its grip on the outcropping and his other dug in next to it.

"Do I *look* all right?" The hazard annoyed Dengar more than alarmed him. Without turning his head, he shouted down to Neelah. "Move the light . . . over just a bit. . . ."

The beam shifted as he managed to get more of his weight balanced on the outcropping, his chest pressing against its top ridge. He reached up and grasped the edge of the tiny gap he had spotted from the floor of the tunnel. With a push, it gave way; he flung the stone away as he turned his head to shield his eyes from the gravel and dust raining down.

More daylight spilled down from the Dune Sea's surface; Dengar could even see, as he tilted his head back, a patch of cloudless sky. *We can make it,* he thought with relief. Sweat trickled down his neck and across his chest as his free hand yanked out a few more stones jutting into the vertical opening. They fell into darkness, striking the others he had previously torn loose. He was grateful for the fresh air, dry and hot as it was from the suns' pounding temperature, that flooded across his face and into his throat. Anything was better than the stink that filled the caverns and tunnels beneath the surface. . . .

The beam of light suddenly disappeared.

"Hey!" Dengar shouted to Neelah below him. "Swing that light back up here!" The glare of daylight coming down the widened hole wasn't enough for him to make out the details of the space's ceiling; he couldn't see which rock to grab and pull on next. "I still need it—"

"There's something down here!" Neelah's shout echoed off the curved walls of crumbling stone. Her next words were tinged with sudden fear. "Something *big!*"

13

Dengar managed to twist himself around so he could see what she was talking about. A raw laugh burst from his throat as he recognized the mottled surface, rounded and stretching higher than even the tallest humanoid's stature.

"It's the Sarlacc," said Dengar. "Or part of it, at least." From his precarious hold on the rock outcropping, he watched as Neelah played the light across the immense serpentine form, its bulk sealing off the far end of the cavern. There was no sign of the creature's head or tail, as the segment made visible by the lantern lay immobile. "That's why it smells so bad in here, remember? There's probably pieces of it scattered all through these tunnels, or whatever's left of them."

Nose wrinkling in disgust, Neelah stepped a little closer to the giant form. Enough light bounced off its scales, made shinier by patches of decay and the dried ichor of its blood, that the pallet with Boba Fett on it could be seen several meters away. The two medical droids, the readouts on their torsos blinking, regarded Neelah's investigations with only mild curiosity.

Dengar turned back to his work on their escape route. "Get that light beam up here—"

"*It's alive!*"

The force of Neelah's shout came close to knocking Dengar loose from the outcropping. "What're you talking about?" He pulled himself farther up on the stone before looking back down. "You can smell that the thing's deader than—"

"It moved!" With her voice a mixture of fury and alarm, Neelah pointed at the bulk of the Sarlacc segment. "I saw it just now. When I poked at it."

"Nothing to worry about," said Dengar. His arm, where it crossed over the stone's corner ridge, was starting to go numb. "Probably just part of the decomposition process. You must've disturbed some gas bubble inside the tissues. It's probably going to get a lot worse smelling in here real soon—"

His words turned to silence as a visible shiver ran across the towering convex wall of the Sarlacc segment. Dengar could easily see the motion, like a peristaltic wave traveling across the scales and crusted decay patches.

"There!" Neelah kept the lantern beam directed at the glistening bulk. "That's what it did before! I thought you said this thing was dead!"

It'd better be, thought Dengar. A sense of foreboding moved up from the base of his stomach and into his throat. Boba Fett had killed the damn thing; he'd blown his way out of its gut. From trauma like that, the Sarlacc had to have died; there was no other possibility. *None*—the word looped inside Dengar's head with a touch of panic.

That fear rose out of his dark, unbidden wondering. No one had ever seen the Sarlacc entire; it had lain buried in its nest in the Great Pit of Carkoon before there had ever been sentient beings on the planet of Tatooine. The Tusken Raiders, who had ridden their shaggy bantha mounts across the Dune Sea wastes for centuries untold, had ancient legends of the Sarlacc giving birth to itself at this world's center in the days before the twin suns had split apart. Born and growing with the slow persistence of an eternal creature, digging and rooting itself in its tunnels beneath the sand and rocks, until the day would come when it had eaten everything else and would consume itself, continuing an endless cycle of destruction and rebirth.

It was all nonsense, Dengar knew. There was no point in paying attention to Tusken myths. But at the same time nobody on or off Tatooine had ever determined the exact physiology of the Sarlacc. *Maybe it's got more than one stomach,* thought Dengar. *Or it can regenerate itself, like a plant.* Nice possibilities for it; too bad for anybody who might have foolishly wandered into its reach. *Like us—*

His fears proved suddenly correct. The curving wall of the Sarlacc segment reared up, like a giant serpent uncoiling. It reached higher than Dengar's hold on the outcropping, the scales dragging across the roof of the cavern several meters away from him. A shower of rocks and sharp-edged debris rained down as Neelah scrambled to temporary safety near the pallet and the two medical droids.

The interior of the cavern shook with seismic force as the Sarlacc's writhing form crashed down again. Dengar gripped the outcropping tighter, trying to keep from being thrown loose from it. More rubble poured down the widened gap, with hot stones and sand falling across his shoulders and the side of his averted face.

Even before he could see what was happening down below, Dengar had gotten his end of the rope line around the outcropping and had knotted it fast. "Grab the line!" he shouted as the dust started to settle. "I'll pull you up!"

He could feel her tugging at the other end of the line. But when he could see below himself again, the space dimly illumined by a combination of the daylight from above and the beam of the lantern knocked on its side, he saw that Neelah had dragged the unconscious figure of Boba Fett from the pallet and had gotten him upright. Fett's weight was braced against her shoulder as she looped the line around his chest.

"There—" Neelah stepped back and shouted to Dengar. "Take him up! Start pulling!"

Boba Fett's arms dangled at his side, the tautened rope all that kept his limp body from collapsing to the floor of the cavern. His head lolled forward, chin against his chest. The only sign of him still being alive was the slight motion of his ragged breath.

No point in arguing; Dengar knew that it would be a waste of time with the obstinate female. He clambered up onto the outcropping's top surface, then reached down and grabbed the line with both hands. His spine hit the rock wall behind him as he reared back and pulled. The body of the unconscious bounty hunter straightened, feet dangling clear of the ground, as Dengar drew Fett toward himself.

The cavern shook as the Sarlacc segment, either in its death throes or from hunger spurred by its awareness of the humans' presence, convulsively lifted itself and slammed its length against the side of the cavern directly beneath Dengar. Beneath the pounding of his heart, the outcropping trembled and groaned, as though the larger stone it was part of was about to pull free from the upper reaches of the cavern wall. He reached down and grabbed another section of line, hauling Boba Fett higher into the open space; the Sarlacc segment came within inches of the bounty hunter's feet as it doubled upon itself in hissing agony.

Fett was still several meters away from Dengar's grasp as the Sarlacc segment crashed down toward the cavern floor once again. Its head and tail were still unseen, extending into the darkness at either end of the space. The echo of its impact against the ground rolled through the cavern like buried thunder; more sharp bits of rock pelted against Dengar's back. One side of the gap, the escape route to the surface he had been widening, sheered off and fell tumbling, inches away from the suspended figure of Boba Fett. The limp bounty hunter slowly revolved as Dengar strained to pull him higher. That was the only motion Fett showed, as though the loop around his chest had squeezed the last remaining life force from him.

Past Fett, Dengar could see the two medical droids scurrying to safety at the other side of the cavern as the Sarlacc segment twisted onto its side, scales crushing the rocks beneath it to powder. Neelah backed away, the lantern's beam widening against the Sarlacc's flank, then turned and ran as the towering curve gained speed, rolling toward her. As Dengar watched, the stone fragments slid out from beneath her feet, throwing her onto her hands and knees. The lantern clattered to a halt less than a meter away, its beam angling upward onto the bulk of the Sarlacc.

The glowing ellipse of light on the Sarlacc's scales grew larger as the segment continued to twist about, like a hideous tidal wave of rough-edged armor and injured flesh. Neelah gave a cry of mingled pain and fear as the segment rolled onto her foot and lower leg, pinning her to the floor of the cavern. The Sarlacc segment halted its motion, as if some sense within it were aware of the captive it had made. Its convex mass loomed over Neelah as she twisted onto her side and pushed futilely at it with her bare hands. All that it would take to crush her into a lifeless and broken thing would be for the Sarlacc to continue its twisting, rolling motion, the heavy tide of its bulk sweeping through the cavern and obliterating everything in its path.

Dengar tugged the rope line high enough to loop it around the end of the outcropping, leaving the unconscious Boba Fett suspended above the Sarlacc segment. With one hand holding on, he dug with the other into the holster on his belt, caught between his own weight and the rock's surface. He managed to drag out his blaster, leaving abraded skin from the back of his hand across the rough stone. Dengar shifted his position on the outcropping, trying to line up a clear shot, past the dangling figure of Boba Fett and into the mass of the Sarlacc. . . .

That shifting of weight on the stone, plus the damage to the already precarious walls of the cavern caused by the Sarlacc's convulsive thrashing, was enough to break the outcropping free, a hairline crack just past Dengar's elbow splitting open with a puff of dust. The forward edge of the outcropping shot downward as he scrambled to keep hold of it. His teeth rattled in his head as the narrow point of stone jammed itself against the other side of the crevice, a meter below where the outcropping had been positioned before. The knot of the line fastened to Boba Fett slid down the outcropping and caught at the juncture of the stone and the crevice wall.

The sharp, sudden movement had knocked the blaster free from Dengar's grip. Clutching the stone, he watched helplessly, time expanding into slow motion, as the weapon spun in the air and choking dust near the cavern's ceiling, then fell. Grip and muzzle tumbled end over end, beyond any point where Dengar could have caught it, even if he'd been able to take one of his clawing hands away from the stone.

He saw something else then, something that had come to life as unexpectedly as the buried Sarlacc. The sudden drop of the line had snapped Boba Fett's head back, so that his pale, unhelmeted visage was turned toward Dengar and the daylight spilling into the cavern from above. The bounty hunter appeared dead, as though the medical droids' disregarded warnings had proved true, after all; it might as well have been a corpse that Dengar and Neelah had carried through the underground tunnels, and that now dangled unmoving in midair. . . .

Boba Fett's eyes opened, gazing directly into Dengar's. Slow-motion time stopped entirely as Fett's cold regard pierced the other bounty hunter's spirit.

Then time started up again, slamming into microsecond events. One of Boba Fett's hands raised from his side, shot out and caught the falling blaster, as sharply and deftly as an uncoiling serpent striking its prey. The weapon filled his grasp as though it were an extension of his being, a part of him as much as the bones of his spine.

Fett's gaze broke away. As Dengar watched from above, Boba Fett scanned downward to where the great bulk of the Sarlacc segment held Neelah trapped against the cavern's floor. He extended his arm, the blaster's muzzle on the same direct course as his sight, straight into the massive curved flank of the Sarlacc.

The cavern filled with blade-edged shadows as

the blaster erupted into coruscating fire, its explosive touch pulsing at a diagonal across the open space. Its force was enough to deflect the rope line from vertical, like a miniature rocket thrusting Boba Fett away from its flaring burst. Fett kept the blaster's impact pouring into the same spot on the curved surface of the Sarlacc as a burning stench mingled with the thick odor of decay that had already hung in the close, lung-oppressing air.

At the exact same moment the Sarlacc segment reared upward, stung by the blaster's white-hot needle. Bits of broken scales and charred flesh scattered across the cavern; the creature's raw wound, cut deeper by the continuing fire, sizzled beneath an acrid haze of black smoke.

Neelah dug her fingertips into the rubble-strewn cavern floor as more sparks and pieces of blackened tissue rained around her, striking a pool of the Sarlacc's blood with quick, spattering steam. She crawled painfully forward, dragging the leg that had been trapped behind her, as the bright stream from the blaster in Boba Fett's grip continued tearing open a wider and deeper section, like a red doorway being carved into living stone.

A scream of agony, the wordless cry of a wounded beast, sounded from far within the unlit tunnels beyond the cavern space. Louder and shriller, until it was a physical presence, its force shivering the walls and tearing one stone loose from another. Neelah crouched against the side of the cavern, close to the two medical droids, as sections of the cavern's ceiling cracked apart and fell. The broken stones struck the bleeding and charred flank of the Sarlacc segment, then tumbled and rolled to a halt, mounting against the creature.

The cry broke off as a different motion seized

what was left visible of the Sarlacc. The rocks piled against it shifted as the segment retracted into the tunnel opening at the farthest edge of the cavern. From above, Dengar had a momentary glimpse of a ragged terminus, gray and scabbed with the segment that had been torn from its connection with the larger creature. Then it was gone, leaving the stones and churning dust behind.

In Boba Fett's hand, the blaster went silent. He looked back toward the light-filled opening and the outcropping precariously slanting across. Dengar could see in the bounty hunter's face that he was burning up the last of his strength, summoned from a reserve deep within him.

"Lower me. . . ." Fett's voice rasped, like words spoken within an airless tomb. "Now . . ."

Dengar managed to brace his feet against the side of the gap, enough to unfasten the line from the outcropping and pay it out hand over hand, gradually dropping Boba Fett toward the floor of the cavern. When the line slackened, Dengar looped it over his shoulder, using his other hand to climb up the vertical opening. He reached the surface, collapsing onto the hot sands of the Dune Sea. Drawing in an exhausted breath, he sat up and clutched the line tight in his fists.

A tug came on the line. Dengar stood up and pulled, grabbing more of the line as he backed step-by-step away from the opening. He could tell from the weight that there was more than just Boba Fett at the other end of the line now.

More muscle . . . than brain, thought Dengar as he brought the line inch by inch over the rocks and sand. He supposed that was why he had a certain place in the bounty-hunter business, and Boba Fett had a different, and much more famous one. He dug in, the line's tautness keeping him from falling over backward, and finally saw one of Fett's arms reach upward from the hole, his hand sinking into the ground and leveraging his chest into view. Boba Fett had his other arm around Neelah, holding her tight against himself; the hole had been widened just enough, between Dengar's efforts and the crashing of the Sarlacc segment, to allow the two close-pressed bodies to scrape through.

The line went slack, dumping Dengar onto his seat, as Boba Fett got Neelah up onto the sand, then with a final push against the sides of the hole, collapsed beside her.

In all directions, the silence of the Dune Sea extended from them. Wearily, Dengar got to his feet and scanned across the low hills; tilting his head back, he searched the cloudless sky, sun glare almost blinding him. There was no sign of any ships. The bombing raid that had left the desert wasteland cratered and scorched seemed effectively over, its perpetrators having removed themselves beyond the atmosphere of Tatooine. Though by this point, if they had returned, Dengar didn't feel capable of anything other than flopping on the ground and letting the explosive charges finish him off.

He walked over to the other two. Boba Fett lay on his back, eyes closed; the only indication of life was the slow rise and fall of his chest. Whatever strength had been left in him was enough for basic respiratory functions, and nothing else.

"How are you doing?" Dengar's shadow fell across Neelah's face.

She nodded slowly. "I'm okay." With the back of a begrimed hand, Neelah pushed her sweat-damp hair away from her eyes; the motion left a black smear across her face. She sat up and drew her knees toward her breast so she could examine the ankle that had been pinned beneath the weight of the Sarlacc segment. A wince drew her eyes shut for a second as she poked at the bruised flesh. "Nothing's broken, I don't think." Leaning against Dengar for balance, she stood upright and gingerly put her weight on the leg. "Yeah, it's all right."

A voice sounded out of the hole from which they had just escaped. "Given the circumstances I have just observed," called SH∑1-B loudly, "I would anticipate that medical attention is required by all parties in the immediate vicinity. Plus, the patient we had previously been attending is undoubtedly in need of—"

The hectoring comments were cut short when Neelah picked up a rock and tossed it down the hole. It clanked against metal and plastoid, rendering the medical droid silent for a moment.

"I'm not going back down there," announced Neelah. "I've had enough time on that line already."

Dengar gave a weary sigh. As always, he supposed it was up to him. The medical droids still had their uses—for one, SH∑1-B had been obviously right about Boba Fett needing some further attention, especially after what had been drained out of him underneath the Dune Sea's surface. And there were the various supplies—bits and pieces; not much—that he and Neelah had managed to carry with them from the hiding place. Those would undoubtedly come in handy, given their present exposed situation.

"All right," said Dengar. He looked around for the nearest boulder to which to fasten the line. "But when I get done, you're *both* going to owe me. Big time."

"Don't worry about that." Neelah smiled up at

him. "You'll get all the rewards that're coming to you."

He wasn't sure what that meant. Even as he was clambering back down the escape-route hole, the strap of the lantern clenched in his teeth, he was wondering whether those rewards would be a good or bad thing, when they finally got to him.

All that noise had upset the felinx; it trembled in Kuat of Kuat's arms as he stroked its silken fur. "There, there," he soothed the frightened animal. "It's all over now. You have nothing to worry about." That was the difference between creatures such as the felinx and the galaxy's sentient inhabitants. "Go to sleep, and dream whatever you want."

He stood at the great viewport of the Kuat Drive Yards' flagship, watching the mottled sphere of the planet Tatooine dwindle in the distance, a clump of dirt among the hard, cold stars. A good part of that dirt was now in considerably more battered condition than before; the military squadron that had pounded the surface of the Dune Sea to dust was already en route, heading back to Kuat by a circuitous route, jumping in and out of hyperspace to foil any possible attempts at tracking and linking them to the just-concluded bombing raid on Tatooine. All insignia and identification beacons had been carefully stripped from the vessels before they had left on their mission. When word of the raid filtered through the watering holes and back alleys of Mos Eisley, and any corresponding places on other worlds, the speculation would most likely be directed toward the Empire or possibly the Black Sun organization. That notion pleased Kuat of Kuat as he scratched behind the sighing felinx's ears. *We move in secret ways,* mused Kuat. *The better to reach our destination* . . .

The even more pleasing notion was that Boba Fett had reached his final destination. That had been the whole point of the bombing raid. Reports of the bounty hunter's death had already reached Kuat of Kuat; many other sentient creatures, humanoid or not, would have heard of someone going down the gullet of the Sarlacc and would have concluded that was the end of that person. Kuat of Kuat had, however, more experience with the individual in question; Boba Fett had always had an unnerving ability to show up alive, if somewhat battered, long after any ordinary man's death would have been well assured. Attention to detail had made KDY the manufacturing force that it was in the galaxy, supplier of vessels to Emperor Palpatine as well as the shadowy figures that ran Black Sun; the present Kuat of Kuat had inherited the same thoroughness that had characterized his ancestors.

"It's not enough to know that someone is dead," he whispered to the felinx as he held the animal's luxurious fur close to his throat. "You want them buried, or better yet, scattered across the landscape in little pieces—"

"Excuse me, sir."

Kuat of Kuat glanced over his shoulder and saw one of his comm supervisors. "Yes?" Even aboard the corporate flagship, he had no taste for the obsequious formalities that characterized Palpatine's court; KDY was a business, not a theater for monomaniacal self-aggrandizement. "What is it?"

"The damage survey has just come in." The comm supervisor held up a thin, self-contained data readout, with red, glowing numbers arranged in neat rows. "From the monitoring devices we left behind on Tatooine."

He had been expecting those. "What's the analysis?"

"Maximum ground penetration was achieved." The comm supervisor glanced at the readout. "All areas surrounding the Great Pit of Carkoon were effectively saturated by the bombing raid. Probability of anything on the surface of the Dune Sea, or anywhere underground, to a depth of twenty meters, is"—a few quick buttons were punched on the readout's controls—"zero-point-zero-zero-zero-one. The targeted tolerance level we went in with was only two zeroes past the decimal point." A satisfied expression crossed the comm supervisor's face as he lowered the device. "I'd say the chances are pretty good that we achieved our objective."

"Ah." Kuat of Kuat slowly nodded. " 'Pretty good,' you say?"

The comm supervisor's pleased expression vanished; he was one of the younger staff members reporting directly to the heir and owner of the company. "A figure of speech, sir." He still had a lot to learn. "The objective was undoubtedly accomplished."

"That's more like it." The felinx murmured drowsily beneath Kuat of Kuat's hand. "Or as undoubtedly as can be expected in this stubborn universe." He bestowed a smile on his underling. "We have to play the percentages, don't we?"

"Sir?"

"Never mind." A sleepy protest came from the felinx as Kuat bent down and set it on the intricately tessellated floor. "Thanks for the information. You can go now."

The comm supervisor made his exit, and Kuat of

Kuat turned back to his contemplation of Tatooine, now hardly more than a thumbnail-sized blot in the viewport. Its wordless voice louder, the felinx rubbed against his ankles, negotiating to be picked up again.

"A long way to come . . ." Kuat nodded as he murmured his thoughts aloud. "Just for nothing."

He didn't share the comm supervisor's certainty about what had been achieved. Being sure of anything, in this universe, was one of the follies of youth. *Still,* thought Kuat, *it was worth trying.* Just for the sake of thoroughness, and on the off chance that Boba Fett could be killed. There was so much at stake—so many plans and schemes, so deeply laid, and so critical to the survival of KDY—that it was worth any expenditure of time and capital to try to remove Fett from the multileveled game board on which the Empire's pawns advanced. There were other players in the game as well—Black Sun, the Rebellion, smaller and even less savory empires like those of the Hutt clans and their like—but Kuat of Kuat wasn't concerned with those for the moment.

The opponents didn't know, and neither did the pawn, just how important Boba Fett was in this game—Kuat of Kuat found some wry amusement in that datum. If Fett or Emperor Palpatine ever did find out, though, the game would swiftly become more serious. And deadly. There would be no more heirs to Kuat Drive Yards because the corporation itself would cease to exist. The Emperor's scavengers would pick the bones apart like a gem-encrusted corpse. . . .

There were still a great many moves left in the game, though, before that happened. Kuat was determined to play them all.

"I suppose," he told the felinx, "we'll be seeing him again." That had been the main reason that he had canceled any orders for a second bombing run on Tatooine's Dune Sea. The conviction had settled in Kuat of Kuat that it was a pointless endeavor; if Boba Fett was going to be eliminated, it wasn't by any means as relatively crude as that. "He'll take a good deal of killing. Before he's dead enough."

He supposed it hadn't been a complete waste, though. *Perhaps I've slowed him down*—there would be time to shift a few other pieces into position, to contemplate the game board and devise strategies for it.

The felinx had waited long enough; now it impatiently informed its master so.

"Soon enough." Kuat of Kuat cradled the animal in the crook of his arm again and idly scratched the spot behind its ears that it liked the best. "A little time, perhaps. But it won't be long."

It never was, when it came to dealing with Boba Fett. Just as before, on another part of the board, when the pawns had been creatures such as that wretched spidery assembler Kud'ar Mub'at and the Bounty Hunters Guild. That game, Kuat knew, had played out with fatal speed.

"Not long," murmured Kuat of Kuat again. "Not long at all . . ."

14

THEN

"There's something big coming down." Bossk's smile was jagged and ugly. As always. "Something really big."

Boba Fett leaned back against the wall behind the stone bench. Nothing the Trandoshan told him ever came as a surprise; the big reptile just hadn't learned that yet, about how far behind the curve he was always fated to be. *Maybe he will find out,* thought Fett, *before he dies.* "Go on," said Fett. In the meantime there was some value to a pretense of ignorance on his own part. "Tell me about it."

"Wait a second." Bossk turned his scaly head, looking over the bleak contents of Boba Fett's temporary quarters at the Bounty Hunters Guild's main complex. He had already pushed the iron-hinged door shut behind himself with a push from his clawed hand. "This isn't," he growled in a low voice, "something everybody needs to know about." The inspection from his slit-pupiled eyes apparently satisfied him, that there were no obvious listening devices installed in the cracks between the damp stones. "At least, they don't need to for the moment."

"You have a compulsion for secrecy." *Idiot,* thought Boba Fett—a thousand snooping machines could have been hidden in the chamber that a mere visual scan wouldn't have detected. "That's commendable."

"Gotta be careful." Bossk sat down on the bench beside him and leaned in close. "Especially about something like this."

"Which is?"

All around the sparsely furnished, rough-hewn space, the corridors of the Bounty Hunters Guild compound folded and coiled around each other, replicating the devious pathways of the minds contained therein. Those minds, of the bounty hunters themselves, had been getting progressively more devious since Boba Fett's arrival in their midst. He could sense it, like being inside an infinitely replicating maze, branching through fractal progressions of paranoia and deceit. That was fine by him: it was what his plans, and those of the arachnoid assembler Kud'ar Mub'at, called for. The bounty hunters were already getting lost in that maze; some of them wouldn't survive to find their way out.

It's different for me, thought Fett. He was unconcerned about the maze's exponential complexity. It didn't matter whether he had a map, or a thread leading his way out. When the time came, he would break his way through the encircling walls, as though they were made of flimsiplast rather than the stone of other sentient creatures' greed and malice. *Soon enough* . . .

"A big job," said Bossk. His claws tightened reflexively, as though upon either the neck of some merchandise or the credits to be gotten for it. "The kind you like."

Fett kept any trace of emotion out of his voice, words blank as the visor of his helmet. "How big?"

Leaning even closer, Bossk whispered hoarsely into the audio receptor at the side of Fett's helmet. The Trandoshan's fang-lined smile was even bigger when he drew away, the number recited.

"I see." Boba Fett wasn't surprised by the amount of the bounty being offered; he had his own sources of information, so much sharper and beyond those of any Guild member. "That's an enticing sum." He wasn't surprised, either, that Bossk had shaved a quarter million credits off the price. Like most bounty hunters, Bossk had a flexible notion of what constituted a fair division of profits. "Very enticing, indeed."

"Yeah, ain't it?" The contemplation of that kind of credits flow seemed to inspire a new level of glittering-eyed avarice in Bossk. "I knew you'd go for it."

"And what is the exact nature of this merchandise?" Boba Fett already knew, but he had to ask in order to keep up the masquerade; Bossk had to believe that he was revealing the details rather than just confirming them. "Somebody must want it pretty badly to put that kind of price on it."

"You can say that again." Bossk held up one claw. "Here's the scoop. Seems a certain Lyunesi comm handler named Oph Nar Dinnid managed to work himself up a real case of hyper-eros." The toothy smile shifted into a leer. "You know how it goes—the same old story."

Fett knew what the Trandoshan was talking about. The Lyunesi were one of six sentient species on Ryoone, a planet down-spiral from one of the remoter sectors of the Outer Rim Territories. Unusually dismal conditions had been brought about millennia ago by a seemingly permanent suspension of volcanic ash in the upper atmosphere, resulting in a ruthless competition for survival. The other inhabitants of Ryoone would have wiped out the Lyunesi long ago if the fragile creatures hadn't mastered the arts of interspecies communication. Their skills went far beyond mere translation of words and meaning; surrounded by enemies, with the continuation of their own breed dependent upon every nuance of language and gesture, the Lyunesi bought their lives with interpretive skills far beyond even the most highly developed protocol droid. On Ryoone, that meant they made possible all the fluid and rapidly shifting diplomacy between the planet's other species, the madly dissolving and re-forming alliances, the declarations of war and swiftly terminated peace treaties between sentient creatures who didn't even share the same metabolic basis, let alone language. In the galaxy beyond Ryoone, the Lyunesi were found at every communication nexus, sorting out and fine-tuning the messages and negotiations between one wildly dissimilar sector of the Empire and another.

All that expertise at reading other species' intentions and secrets had its downside, though. From time to time various Lyunesi fell prey to their own sensitivity. An all-consuming passion seized them; worse, it was nearly always reciprocated by the object of their desire. Unlike members of the reptilian Falleen species, whose conquests were achieved with a notable coldness and lack of feeling, Lyunesi and their hypererotic targets rapidly found themselves in situations where neither partner was left with a shred of self-preserving intelligence. Given the high-level diplomatic stations where Lyunesi were so often found, the results were usually catastrophic.

And fatal.

"I know the story," said Boba Fett. Both in general and in the specific case of Oph Nar Dinnid, which his own sources had told him about. "Better that a high-ranking female should get involved with someone like Prince Xizor. The experience is reputedly more intense and pleasurable, and after it's over, the female might still be alive. If she keeps her wits about her." Fett supposed that with someone like his sometime employer Xizor, that was what passed as chivalry. "The problem with Lyunesi is that they're not smart enough to be heartless."

"Yeah, well, this Dinnid person managed to get himself into a large-capacity vat of nerf waste." Bossk sneered; he had been born without those wasteful, sentimental emotions. "He was working for one of the major liege-holder clans out in the Narrant system; I won't say which one—"

"You don't have to. They're all alike." Boba Fett was well acquainted with those clans; they were really more loose confederations of genetically linked species, with deep layers of ritual obeisance and internal blood oaths patching over their differences. It didn't work; they needed the ultradiplomatic Lyunesi around just to keep from killing each other off. A good gig for the natives of a backwater world like Ryoone—as long as they didn't screw up.

But they always did.

"Let me guess," said Boba Fett. "Dinnid's employers found him in a, let's say, *compromising* position with a wife or daughter from one of the top clan houses."

"Got that one right." Bossk's eyes glittered as sharp as his fangs. A Trandoshan's enjoyment of another creature's troubles went far beyond the mere anticipation of profit to be gained thereby. "All the way to the top. Right up to the supreme liege-lord himself. And just like these Lyunesi—they've got no sense at all—the revelation of the affair was in public. At one of the formal clan-oath ceremonies, couple thousand sublieges and their retinues all in their lord's great hall. Somebody accidentally struck the curtain behind the dais, it collapses, and there's our Oph Nar Dinnid and the liege-lord's alpha concubine, for all the galaxy to see. Like I said: no sense at all."

Bossk's description of events matched what Fett's sources had told him. "It's remarkable that this Dinnid person got out alive."

"I take it back: the guy had *some* sense." Bossk shrugged. "Not enough to keep himself out of trouble, but at least enough to have already planned his escape route when the nerf droppings hit the ventilation system. There was a lot of confusion in the great hall—you can imagine—and Dinnid hightailed it out to a speeder he'd kept fueled and waiting, with its destination coordinates already programmed in."

"Where could he go? Where he'd be safe, that is." Boba Fett already knew the answer, but continued with his pretense. "The Narrant liege-lords have a sense of honor that doesn't easily accept embarrassment. They'll stop at nothing to get someone who has publicly humiliated them back in their grasp."

"True." Bossk gave a quick nod. "That's why this particular lord has put up such a killer bounty for the merchandise he wants. He can't just take his own troops out and hunt down the little idiot, haul him back, and get whatever satisfaction he can out of Dinnid's hide—at least, not without spreading the story even farther afield. So, naturally, the lord wants the bounty hunters to do his dirty work for him."

Silence was always a desired commodity in the

bounty-hunter trade. Boba Fett had made a specialty of quick, efficient—and quiet—work. "With that kind of credits being put up, I expect every bounty hunter in the Guild will be going after Oph Nar Din-nid."

"It's not that easy," said Bossk. "The sneak not only had his escape means planned, he had the perfect place to hole up figured out as well. He's with the Shell Hutts."

Boba Fett had heard that much as well. Of all the Huttese clans, the Shell Hutts were the least numerous, and the most removed from the various alliances and interconnected dealings that bonded the other Hutts together. The Shell Hutts didn't even look like their distant brethren, except in bulk and physiognomy; they had the same basic body mass and large-eyed, slit-mouthed faces, perfect for greedily stuffing assorted wriggling tidbits into. In that sense, of wanting to control everything on which their immense eyes fastened, they were identical to the rest of the Hutts.

Identical in anatomic toughness as well, with thick leathery skins impervious to blaster shots and acids, and vital organs so deeply buried under layers of blubber that they couldn't be even nicked with a vibroblade—the only physical threat that Hutts feared was specific bands of hard unshielded radiation, the kind whose toxic effects built up in their bodies' shielding fat rather than being dissipated through normal excretion processes. That had kept the Hutts from extending their criminal enterprises to certain areas of the galaxy. Until one of the Huttese clans, sometime in the hazy millennia of the past, had given themselves what their own genetics had failed to: protective armored casings, bolted and welded together from heavy durasteel plates, supported and maneuvered about by built-in repulsor fields. All that showed of the Shell Hutts' soft, gelatinous flesh were their jowly faces, protruding tortoiselike from iris-collared ports at the front of the floating ovoid cases. Even the Shell Hutts' delicate little hands were hidden inside, manipulating the controls for the externally mounted grasping devices. Those seemed to work just as well at grabbing onto and holding big chunks of ill-gotten wealth.

"Why would the Shell Hutts be interested in a comm handler on the run?" Boba Fett had had dealings with various members of the Shell Hutts; he knew they didn't do anything without a credits-related reason, just like the other Huttese. "If they need that level of translation and diplomacy skills, they can just buy whoever's on the market. Someone who doesn't have a price on his head."

"Oph Nar Dinnid made himself valuable to them." A trace of grudging admiration sounded in Bossk's harsh voice. "Seems he had memory augmentors surgically implanted in his cortical areas, and stuffed them full of the Narrant system's top-secret business information, dealings, and records that he had access to from working as the supreme liege-lord's protocol intermediary. There's a lot of data inside Dinnid's head that the Shell Hutts have found to be pretty interesting. And profitable."

"So? That's not something that would keep Dinnid safe for long. The Shell Hutts aren't exactly reticent about stripping data out of somebody's memory and then tossing the remains out like an empty husk."

Bossk leaned closer, close enough that Boba Fett could smell blood and meat through his helmet's air filters. "Dinnid may be an idiot, all right, but he's not *that* kind of idiot. The memory augmentors he had installed inside his skull have a time-based readout function wired into them. All the secret business data from the Narrant system that he's carrying is released a few bits at a time—plus it's under an autodestruct encryption. The Shell Hutts try to crack his head open to get at the data, *everything* gets wiped. But that's not even the best part. They can't even tell how *much* data is inside Dinnid. Basically, he's valuable to the Shell Hutts for an indefinite period of time; it could be *decades* before the information is done spooling out of him."

"That was clever of him." As with the rest of the story that Bossk had just related, Boba Fett feigned hearing it for the first time. "But it also means that the Shell Hutts aren't going to let go of him for a good long time."

"Damn straight," agreed Bossk. He tapped a single claw against Boba Fett's chest. "It's not going to be easy, prying him out of their hands. That's why the bounty hunters aren't going out one by one to try and pull off this job. It's going to take a *team* to nail down this piece of merchandise."

Fett had been expecting this as well. "Are you making me an offer?"

"Maybe." Bossk pulled back, taking another scan around the chamber and toward the rough-hewn door. "Let's face it: things have been pretty tense around here since you showed up." The Trandoshan's slitted eyes bored fiercely into the dark visor of Fett's helmet. "There's a lot of talk going on, from the old guard like my father and the rest of the Guild council, all the way down to the rawest bounty hunter on the membership list."

"What kind of talk?"

"Don't mess with me," growled Bossk. "You're valuable to me right now, but if you start getting funny, I'll eat your brains out of your helmet like a soup bowl. If I'm making you an offer, then it isn't just about catching hold of this Oph Nar Dinnid guy—though that should be reason enough for you to be interested. But it's about the future of the whole Bounty Hunters Guild. There's going to be some big changes coming down here, and people are lining up on one side or another, depending on which way they think it's going to go. Frankly, I'd rather have you on my side than not—but whatever side you're on, I'm still going to win. It'll just be easier with you than without. And it'll be easier if you and I and a couple other handpicked barves pull off this Dinnid job. The bounty we'll get from it will buy us a lot of friends. But more than that, it'll show some of the fence-sitters around here just who's got what it takes to snag the hard merchandise. The ones who can do this job are the ones who *should* be running the Guild."

"You've thought a great deal about this." Boba Fett kept his own voice level and free of emotion. "Again—I'm impressed."

"Cut the flattery." The point of Bossk's claw dug a little deeper into Fett's chest. "All I want to know is, are you with me on this one?"

Bossk's eyes widened in surprise as Boba Fett's hand suddenly grabbed the other's fist, squeezing the bones hard enough to grate them together beneath the overlapping scales. Fett slowly and deliberately moved Bossk's captured hand away from himself, like setting a peculiar and unlovely art object at a distance.

"All right." Fett released his durasteel-hard grip. "I'm with you."

Sulkily, Bossk rubbed the joints of his hand. "Good," he said after a moment. "I'll talk to some of the others. The ones who'll make the kind of team we need." He stood up from the stone bench. "I'll let you know how it's going."

Boba Fett watched the Trandoshan pull the chamber's door shut behind himself, then listened to the sound of his footsteps fading down the corridor outside. *It's almost sad,* thought Fett. The poor barve didn't know just how well things were already going.

But he'd find out. Soon enough . . .

"Your son has just concluded his visit." The major-domo for the Bounty Hunters Guild headquarters bowed his head, an obsequious grin on his face. "And his conversation with the unsavory individual known as Boba Fett proceeded just as you, in your ever-present wisdom, predicted it would."

Cradossk regarded the bobbing figure of the Twi'lek, all crouching curtsies and avarice-brightened eyes. The glistening, bifurcate head tails of his underling reminded him of both Nirellian ground-slugs and uncooked sausages. That notion sparked an automatic twinge of hunger in his gut—but then, most things had that effect upon him.

"Of course it did." In his own luxuriously appointed quarters, Cradossk fidgeted with the heavy straps of his normal business garb, the fabrics a minor-keyed visual symphony in somber yet tasteful grays and blacks. The gaudier robes he'd worn at the banquet welcoming Boba Fett to the Guild had been hung by the majordomo in a vacuum-maintained, humidity-controlled closet. "Things go as I predict them, not because of any wisdom I might possess, but because of a tiresome lack of wisdom on other creatures' parts."

"Your Worshipfulness is entirely too modest."

Ob Fortuna worked his way around Cradossk, pale and clammy hands darting out to make some final adjustments to his employer's everyday outfit. "Would *I* have foreseen such things? Or your illustrious colleagues on the Guild council? Not very likely."

"That's because you and they are fools alike." The thought depressed Cradossk; all the burdens of leadership weighed upon his shoulders. There was no one to help him guide the Bounty Hunters Guild through these perilous shoals, in which conspiratorial enemies thronged like pack sharks. Not even his own son. *Spawn of my seed,* Cradossk mused gloomily. It just showed that true rapacious savvy was derived more from experience than genetics. *I shouldn't have been so easy on him, when he was just a little reptile.*

"Someone else is here to see you." The majordomo made a few more final adjustments to Cradossk's garb. "Did you call for him? Should I grant him admittance?"

"Yes to both questions." The fawning Twi'lek was getting on his nerves. "And it's a private matter. So your presence is not required."

The majordomo ushered in the bounty hunter Zuckuss, then disappeared on the other side of the door he closed behind himself.

Of all the younger, rawer bounty hunters who'd gained admittance to the Guild, Zuckuss had always seemed one of the least suited for the trade. Cradossk gazed at the breathing-masked figure in front of him and wondered why any rational creature would place himself at such risk; it was like a child playing a dangerous adult game, where the wagers were one's own life and the forfeits were measured out in pain and death. His original motivation for pushing

Zuckuss, with that less-than-imposing stature and dangling tubes of breathing-assistance apparatus, onto Bossk had been to give his son an easily disposable partner, someone who could be sacrificed in a tight situation with little regret or loss to the organization. There were more where Zuckuss came from; would-be bounty hunters, with inflated notions about their own skills and toughness, were always lining up at the Guild's doors. This particular situation had changed, though; Cradossk had another use for young Zuckuss.

"I came as quickly as I could." Zuckuss was visibly nervous. And audibly: the breath tubes curving at the bottom of his face mask fluttered. "I hope it isn't anything that—"

"Calm yourself." Cradossk lowered himself into a folding campaign chair made of femurs reinforced with durasteel rods. "If you were in any kind of trouble, believe me, you'd know about it already."

Zuckuss didn't appear reassured. He glanced over his shoulder, as though the door of the chamber had been a trap mechanism snapping shut.

"Actually, there's nothing wrong at all." The bones of the chair were worn smooth beneath Cradossk's palms. "Much of what you've done has met with my approval."

"Really?" Zuckuss turned his gaze back toward the Guild leader.

"Of course," lied Cradossk. "I have had reports concerning you. My son Bossk is not easily impressed—that is, with anyone other than himself. But he spoke quite highly of you. The business with that accountant . . . what was his name?"

"That was Posondum." Zuckuss gave a quick nod. "Nil Posondum. It's really a shame that didn't go better. We nearly had him."

Clawed hands spread wide, Cradossk's shrug was both elaborate and soothing. "One does the best one can. Not everything happens the way it should." To say something like that required genuine acting ability on his part. "Bad luck can happen to anyone." Inside himself, Cradossk still felt like pulling off both his son's and Zuckuss's heads for screwing up that job so badly. Boba Fett had made complete fools out of both of them, and then repeated the ignominy when he'd slipped past them to come sailing into the Bounty Hunters Guild headquarters. "Don't worry about it. There'll be other times, other chances. There's always another piece of merchandise."

"I'm . . . glad you feel that way. . . ."

"You have to take the long view in this business." He had given the exact same lecture to Bossk, and had been sneered at, years ago. "You win some, you lose some. The trick is to win more than you lose. Go for the averages."

"That's true, I guess." Zuckuss's anxiety level now seemed genuinely lowered. "Except for Boba Fett. He always seems to win."

"Even Boba Fett." One of Cradossk's hands made a grand, all-encompassing gesture. "You wouldn't know it just by his reputation, but he and I go back a long way, and I can tell you that he's had his share of times when he's come up empty. Don't let that general aura of invincibility fool you."

"Well . . . it's hard not to be impressed. The things that are said about him . . ."

Cradossk leaned forward in the campaign chair and jabbed a claw into Zuckuss's chest. "I've been in the bounty-hunter trade a long time, boy, and I'm telling you now, you're every bit as tough a barve as the great Boba Fett."

"I am?"

"Sure you are." *In a Gamorrean's eye*, thought Cradossk to himself. He continued with the pitch. "I can tell. There are certain—shall we say?—*ineffable* characteristics of the born bounty hunter. Someone with the appetite and the skills for succeeding in this trade. I can smell 'em. That's why I'm the head of the Bounty Hunters Guild, just because of my being such a keen judge of character." He tapped the side of his snout with one claw. "And my instincts tell me that those are exactly the skills you have."

"Well." Zuckuss slowly shook his head in amazement. "I'm . . . flattered."

It's too easy, thought Cradossk. Telling creatures what they wanted to hear, down in however many hearts they carried around inside themselves, was the quickest and surest way to get them ready for sticking the knife in. Their defenses went down like so many security shields with surge-blown power fuses.

"Don't be." He had this Zuckuss exactly where he wanted him; time to spring the rest of the trap. "The truth in this matter is important to both of us. Because there's something I need you to do for me. Something important."

"Anything," Zuckuss said quickly. He spread his gloved hands apart. "I'd be honored—"

"That's fine." With his own upraised hand, Cradossk cut off the young bounty hunter. "I understand. Loyalty is another one of those characteristics, so important in our trade, that I discern in you." He tilted his head to one side, displaying an uneven, insinuating smile. "But we have to choose our loyalties, don't we?"

"I'm not sure I know what you mean. . . ."

"You've worked with my son Bossk on a couple of jobs. So you're loyal to him, aren't you?"

There was no hesitation before Zuckuss spoke. "Of course. Absolutely."

"Well, get over it." The partial smile disappeared as Cradossk slouched back in the campaign chair. "Your loyalty is to *me*. And that's for a very simple reason. There's some rough times coming around here—as a matter of fact, they've already started. Some creatures aren't going to come out the other end of those times; there'll still be a Bounty Hunters Guild, but it's going to be a lot smaller. You want to be one of those that survive the shakeout, because the alternative is death." He peered closer at Zuckuss, seeing himself reflected and magnified in the other's eyes. "Am I making myself clear?"

Zuckuss gave a rapid nod. "Perfectly clear."

"Good," said Cradossk. "I *like* you—that's why I'm making you this kind of offer." In truth, it was a Trandoshan characteristic to despise all other lifeforms, and he wasn't making any exception in this case. "You stick with me, and there's a good chance you'll make it. I'm not just talking about survival, but really getting somewhere in this organization. Loyalty—to the right creatures, that is—has its rewards."

"What . . . what is it you want me to do?"

"First off, keep your vocal apparatus muted, concerning what we're talking about right now. The first part of loyalty is being able to keep a secret. Any bounty hunter who can't keep his mouth shut isn't long for this galaxy, at least not in any organization that I'm running."

Another fast nod. "I can keep quiet."

"I figured as much." Cradossk let his smile reappear. "We're all scoundrels here, but some of us are better scoundrels than others." He leaned farther forward this time, close enough that the breath from his flared nostrils formed momentary clouds on Zuckuss's eyes. "Here's the deal. You've heard about the Oph Nar Dinnid job?"

"Of course. Everybody in the Guild is talking about it."

"Including my son Bossk, I take it?"

Zuckuss nodded. "He's the one I heard it from."

"I knew he'd jump on it." Cradossk got some satisfaction from that; his spawn was at least ambitious, if not overly smart. "He likes the big jobs, with the big payoffs. This Dinnid job is just the kind of thing to get him salivating. Did he say anything about putting together a team to go for it?"

"Not to me."

"He will," said Cradossk. "I'll see to that personally. My son may show some initial reluctance to having you on the team, but I'll make it worth his while to take you along. There's some equipment to which I can provide access, some inside information sources I'm sure he'd find valuable—that sort of thing. More than enough to make up for whatever share he and the others would have to cut you in on for being part of the operation."

"That's very . . . *kind* of you." Suspicion was discernible behind the curved lenses of Zuckuss's eyes. "But why would you do something like that?"

There was hope for this creature yet; he wasn't a complete idiot. "It's very simple," said Cradossk quietly. "I do something for *you*"—he tapped his claw against the top of the other's face mask—"and you . . . do something . . . for *me*." With the last word, the point of Cradossk's claw tapped against his own chest. "Now, that's not too hard to understand, is it?"

Zuckuss nodded slowly, as though the claw in

front of his face had hypnotized him. "What is it . . . that you want me to do?"

"Now, that's simple as well." Cradossk rested both his hands on the bony arms of the campaign chair. "You're going to go out with the team that my son Bossk is putting together to snag this particular piece of merchandise named Oph Nar Dinnid. The difference between you and Bossk, however, is that you'll be coming back."

It took a few seconds, but illumination finally struck Zuckuss. "Oh . . ." The nod was even slower this time. "I see. . . ."

"I'm glad you do." Cradossk gestured toward the door. "We'll talk some more. Later."

When Zuckuss had scurried out of the chamber, Cradossk allowed himself a few moments of self-satisfied musing. There was lots more to do, strings to pull, words to be whispered in the appropriate ears. But for now, he had to admit to himself that he actually did like this Zuckuss creature. *To a degree,* thought Cradossk. Just smart enough to be useful, but not smart enough to realize how he was being used—at least, until it was too late. He might even feel some regret when it came time to eliminate Zuckuss as well.

But such, Cradossk knew, were the burdens of leadership.

It had taken some doing, plus prying and digging with various tools improvised from stiff, sharp-pointed pieces of wire. But those were the sorts of skills that Twi'lek males were born with. The result, after nearly a year of surreptitious work on the part of the majordomo, was a tiny, undetectable listening hole, up near the ceiling of the anteroom to

Cradossk's private chamber. Better than any electronic snooping device; those could always be detected with a basic security scan-sweep. The majordomo, even as he was listening to the conversation between Cradossk and the young bounty hunter Zuckuss, congratulated himself on his cleverness. One had to be clever to survive working for carnivores like these.

Using a combination of toeholds between the wall's massive stones and an ornamental wall hanging depicting the Guild's past glories, Ob Fortuna clambered down from his eavesdropping post. He had heard Cradossk dismissing Zuckuss, their secretive discussion over for the time being. Past experience enabled the majordomo to calculate precisely how long it would take for someone to turn from in front of the bench in which the Guild leader always sat, and walk the few meters to the chamber door. It was just long enough for the majordomo to get back down and brush the dust and cobweb fragments from himself, as though he had been standing there all along, waiting like a good and faithful—and nonconspiratorial—servant.

"I trust your talk was pleasant?" The majordomo escorted Zuckuss to the next door, leading out of the anteroom to the corridors of the Bounty Hunters Guild headquarters. "And that you found inspiration in it?"

Zuckuss seemed distracted; it took a moment for him to respond. "Yes . . ." He gave a nod as he walked. "Very . . . inspiring. That's the word, all right."

Idiot, thought the majordomo. He had heard every syllable that had passed between this creature and Cradossk. Whether Cradossk was aware of it or not, there were no secrets around here. *Not as far as I'm concerned.*

"Excellent." The majordomo smiled, showing all of his own sharp-pointed teeth. He held open the anteroom door, using his other hand to keep his head tail from falling across his shoulder as he gave a precisely calculated bow. "I trust we will have the pleasure of your company again."

"What?" Standing in the corridor, Zuckuss gazed at him as though puzzled by those simple words. "Oh . . . yes, of course. I imagine you will." He turned and walked away, like one weighted by a new and unforeseen responsibility.

The majordomo watched him go. He was more familiar with the various shades of meaning attached to Cradossk's utterances. Nothing was ever as it seemed on the surface. The poor bounty hunter didn't have a clue as to what kind of lethal mess he was getting into.

But Ob Fortuna did. He glanced behind him, across the length of the anteroom, to make sure that the door to Cradossk's chambers was still closed. Then he hurried down toward the opposite end of the corridor, to where the others who would be interested in this conversation would be waiting. With his hands tucked inside the folds of his long-skirted robes, he was already calculating the profits that would come from another piece of information brokering.

15

"What are we waiting for?" Bossk gnashed his fangs in impatient fury. "We should have been on our way by now!"

"Patience," counseled Boba Fett. "In this case, it is not so much a virtue as a necessity. That is, if you want to pull off this job and live to tell about it."

He watched the Trandoshan resume cursing and muttering under his breath, pacing back and forth in one of the landing docks farthest from the Bounty Hunters Guild complex. It struck Fett that he wouldn't have to do anything at all in order to ensure Bossk's destruction; eventually, the reptilian would explode from the rage bottled up inside him. *Or at the least,* he thought, *that much anger will cause a fatal mistake somewhere along the line.* Boba Fett's own survival was predicated on both violence and the cold, emotionless precision of his strategies and actions. Without the former, all the planning and scheming in the galaxy would be impotent; that was something that the Empire, from Darth Vader's underlings all the way up to Palpatine himself, understood completely. What a creature like Bossk didn't comprehend was that violence, however necessary, was a bomb nestled against one's own heart, in the absence of meticulous calculation. *He'll find out,* thought Fett. *Soon enough.*

The smaller bounty hunter, Zuckuss, glanced nervously from Boba Fett over to Bossk, then back again. "Maybe," he said, "an advance party could head out toward the Shell Hutts. Do some reconnaissance so that when the rest of our team shows up there, we'll be ready to go right in."

"Don't be stupid." Boba Fett shook his head. "The only thing that would accomplish would be to warn the Shell Hutts of our intentions. It's going to be hard enough keeping any element of surprise, without sending them a message like that."

"But the ships are ready to go!" Bossk whirled about on the clawed heel of his foot. "If we wait any longer, the other Guild members will put together teams for taking on this Dinnid job. They'll beat us to it!"

Boba Fett didn't look up from the data readout in his hands; he continued checking the *Slave I*'s armaments list. "It would be no great tragedy if anyone did that. Since they would have no chance of success, our merchandise would still be safely in the hands of the Shell Hutts, waiting for us. And it might actually facilitate our own plans, once we put them into motion. The Shell Hutts would see the difference between us and some crude pack trying to blast their way into the stronghold."

"You keep telling us about these great plans you've made." Bossk aimed a venomous stare at Fett. "When are you going to let us know exactly what they are?"

"As I said before." Unflinchingly, Boba Fett returned the other's hard gaze. "You need to cultivate patience."

Bossk turned away again, his grumbling even louder than before.

The other team member was there with them in the landing dock. IG-88, a droid that had managed to become one of the Bounty Hunters Guild's more respected members—in fact, one of the few that Boba Fett would even consider to be a serious rival—brought his optical scanners around in Fett's direction. "There is patience," said IG-88 in a harshly synthesized voice, "and then there is hesitation. The latter comes from fear and indecision. We decided upon you as the leader of this team's operations because we assumed that such were not your qualities. Our disappointment would be great if we found out otherwise."

"If you think you can pull off this job without me"—Fett lowered the data readout in his hands—"then go ahead."

IG-88 regarded him for a moment longer, then gave a single nod of its head. "You remain our leader. But I warn you: Don't exhaust what patience we do have."

"Mine's already gone." Bossk had obviously continued stewing; the look in his slitted eyes had gone from murderous to annihilating. One hand hovered dangerously close to the blaster slung at his hip. "I've changed my mind. This whole team notion was a stupid idea—"

"Um, Bossk . . ." Zuckuss raised his voice. "It was *your* idea."

"If I started it, then I can put an end to it as well." His gaze slowly moved across the three other bounty hunters. "You lot can do whatever you want. But I'm out of this. I'm going out after Oph Nar Dinnid by myself."

"I'm afraid you don't have that option." Boba

Fett tucked the readout inside one of his armor's storage pouches. His voice seemed even more level and emotionless, compared with Bossk's boiling anger. "You know too much about this operation for you to be on the outside of it. When you come in with me on a job, you stay until it's over. There's really only one way for you to quit."

"Yeah?" Bossk sneered. "What's that?"

IG-88 remained standing as before, his equally cold droid emotions—or the lack of them—observing the confrontation. Zuckuss drew back, ready to duck behind the fuselage of one of the ships in the landing dock as Boba Fett dropped his hand to the curved grip of his own blaster.

"Go ahead," said Boba Fett, "and try walking out on us. And you'll find out."

The atmosphere tensed, as though filling with subphotonic discharge from a battle cruiser's venting ports. In the taut silence, Boba Fett gave a silent command to the heavily armed figure standing in front of him. *Go ahead,* he thought. *It'll save us all a lot of time. . . .*

"There's someone coming!" Zuckuss's voice broke through the adrenaline-frozen moment. He pointed to the distant high arch that formed the entrance to the landing dock; beyond it, a streak of fiery light cut a crescent past the stars. "Another ship—"

Bossk held his gaze tight on Boba Fett's for a moment longer, then glanced over his shoulder. The approaching light had grown brighter, its docking jets flaring into a sudden corona. He looked back at Fett. "Is this who we've been waiting for?"

"It could be." Boba Fett didn't take his hand from the grip of his blaster.

"Lucky for you."

"That's right," said Fett. "If I had killed you, I would have needed to find another person for the team." His hand moved away from the smallest of his weapons. "I find personnel changes to be aggravating."

Zuckuss peered past them at the approaching ship. "I don't recognize this one." It was close enough that its outlines could be seen: a featureless ovoid, barely larger than a TIE fighter, trailing a metallic seine, a stiffly interlinked net, behind its flaring engines. "How did it get clearance—"

"I arranged for that." Boba Fett stepped past Zuckuss and the others, walking toward the pad that the approaching craft had locked upon. "But it wouldn't have made any difference if I had or not."

"What do you mean?" Zuckuss scurried after Fett.

"Believe me—this barve goes where he wants to."

The ovoid could be seen more clearly now as it slid into the landing dock, thrust engines shut down and repulsors on. Its rounded surfaces were pitted and scored with the impact marks of high-intensity armaments, including one large scorch mark where the metal had actually melted and fused back together. As it hovered above the pad its trailing mesh shifted and drew forward, one part curling above like a scorpion's tail, the other forming a reticulated cradle beneath, onto which the craft slowly sank and was still.

"Look at this thing." Fascinated, Zuckuss had walked right up to the ovoid, his boots stepping onto the mesh. He laid a gloved hand on the battered and corrosion-marked surface. "It looks like it's been in every battle since the Clone Wars—"

"Watch out," said Boba Fett. But the warning was already too late.

A microscopic hairline fissure around the top of the ovoid widened, with a hiss of inrushing air. An elliptical section separated from the rest, tilting upward on previously hidden internal hinges. For a moment nothing further showed from inside the craft. . . .

As though released by a high-compression spring, the barrel of a close-range laser cannon rose up, with its power sources and recoil housing mounted directly behind. The gleaming surfaces of black metal shone like the coils of an aroused serpent, intricate and deadly. A faint, shrill electronic whir sounded as the massive weapon's range-sighting devices locked onto Zuckuss, swinging the point of the muzzle down within a meter of the bounty hunter's chest. Another series of sharp, concussive noises sounded within the machinery as the indicator lights' glow shifted from yellow to a hot red, charged and ready to fire. That was followed by silence; Zuckuss froze where he stood, as though hypnotized by the black hole almost within touching distance of his hand, and its lethal potential even closer than that. There would be only a haze of disconnected atoms floating above the scorched remains of his boots after one shot from the weapon.

"Back up," said Boba Fett quietly. "Do it slow, and you probably won't get hurt."

"Hurt?" Beside him, Bossk was gazing in wide-eyed fascination at the laser cannon's darkly gleaming barrel. "He's going to be vaporized!"

Zuckuss was unable to take his own gaze away from the death-bestowing machinery locked upon him. But he did manage to take one cautious step backward, then another; all the while the weapon's tracking systems followed his every move, shifting angle slightly to remain targeted.

A few more steps and Zuckuss was back with the other bounty hunters. "Stay here," Boba Fett told him.

"Don't worry." The stink of panic sweat seeped out of Zuckuss's gear. "I'm not going *anywhere*."

Boba Fett had already stepped past him, leaving Bossk and IG-88 behind as well. He strode without visible apprehension across the landing dock toward the ovoid resting above its glittering mesh. The laser cannon swung and locked onto him as he approached.

"It's been a long time." He stopped and spoke to the weapon itself, as though its charge-primed muzzle were a face masked like his, with the tracking systems as its all-seeing eyes. "A very long time."

The red indicator lights along the weapon's housing cooled from red, through a dull orange, down to a steady-state yellow. The optics and sensors of the tracking systems defocused slightly, as though the hand and mind behind the trigger had relaxed to a state of mere vigilance, rather than instantaneous aggression.

Slowly, the laser cannon rose, as though being lifted on some mechanism inside the ovoid-shaped craft. A cloud of hissing steam surrounded it, obscuring for a moment the outlines of the weapon, as though it were an outcropping of black rock, on a mountain peak wreathed in a sudden, violent storm. The cannon parted the steam as a massive humanoid torso appeared below, its wide shoulders bearing the weapon's crushing weight. From the underside of the barrel, a quarter circle of gear-toothed metal curved down into an anchoring plate set in the creature's chest, with interlocking motors to adjust the muzzle's terminal elevation. Heavy cables, some glistening black, others made of silvery durasteel, looped beneath the arms and around the muscle-sheathed chest and ribs, connecting with the counterbalancing cylinders of power sources flanking the spine. The latter were revealed when the individual climbed out of the ovoid, black-gloved hands and thick-soled boots weighing upon the mesh's strands. From the intricate joins of the weapon's mounting, more steam lashed out, gathered, and dissipated in trailing wisps, indicating the presence of an old-style, liquid-based cooling system, primitive technology dating from the earliest days of the Republic. The laser cannon swung 180 degrees around on its mounting, as though the tracking system optics were actually the eyes in a head made of pure destructive capacity.

A tail section, like a primitive saurian's, but made of segmented black metal and mounted by articulated bolts to the creature's hips, was the last thing to be dragged out of the craft. With its top section hinged back and its pilot standing before it, the resemblance to a giant egg was complete, as though it had just now cracked open to disgorge a new combination of living matter and lethal machinery.

Behind the stranger, the tail curled across the edge of the stiffened mesh. With one hand, the creature unclipped a small keyboard device from the band of metal running from the hip bolts and across his abdomen. His other hand punched in a rapid sequence of ideograms, then thumbed a larger button in the device's corner.

"LONG . . . TIME." The device's speaker crackled as the stranger held it up in front of himself. Underneath the synthesized words, the hissing of the steam from the laser cannon's housing could still be heard. "YOU DO NOT . . . SEEM TO AGE . . . BOBA FETT."

"Should I?" The statement amused him. "Time enough for that when I'm dead."

He could hear the other bounty hunters behind him. Bossk's voice was louder than the rest: "I don't like the looks of this. . . ."

The stranger was instantly transformed; Boba Fett knew that something had triggered a reaction sequence. On the housing of the laser cannon, the indicators flared red again; the tracking systems narrowed their focus, sighting in on a point behind Fett. Steam jetted farther from the housing's apertures as the segmented metal tail stiffened, bracing the stranger into a tripod rigid enough to take the force of the high-powered weapon's recoil.

Boba Fett glanced over his shoulder and saw that Bossk had instinctively dropped his hand to the butt of the blaster slung at his hip; the Trandoshan always did that when something aroused his suspicions.

"Not a good idea," said Fett. With a nod of his helmet, he indicated Bossk's hand, frozen in place by the laser cannon snapping into firing mode. "D'harhan tends to kill first and not bother investigating afterward."

Bossk took his hand away from his blaster.

"Good." Boba Fett looked toward Zuckuss and IG-88 as well. "Now our team is all here."

"D'harhan and I go back a long way." Across the controls of the *Slave I*, Boba Fett's hands moved swiftly, setting the coordinates for dropping back out of hyperspace. "Longer than you can imagine."

"How come I've never heard of him?" The ship's cockpit area was small enough that Zuckuss had to remain standing in the hatchway behind Fett just to exchange a few words with him. "He seems very . . . *impressive.*"

Zuckuss had had a choice of traveling with Bossk and IG-88 in the *Hound's Tooth,* but the Trandoshan's worsening temper had pushed him into the *Slave I* instead. *Let the droid deal with him,* Zuckuss had decided. *Droids don't take all that snarling and muttering personally.*

But heading toward the Shell Hutts' home base, a ring-shaped artificial planetoid called Circumtore, aboard the *Slave I* had proved even more unnerving. The stranger named D'harhan—or friend or mercenary companion, or whatever he might have been at one time to Boba Fett—had found the most secure corner of the ship's belowdecks holding area, and had sat down on the gridded flooring with his back to the angle of the bulkheads. D'harhan had wrapped his flex-shielded arms around his knees, partially resting the weight of the laser cannon mounted on his shoulders on them, the weapon's gleaming barrel thrust slightly forward. When Zuckuss had entered the area, moving as stealthily as possible, he'd suddenly heard a whisper of vented steam; the other's tracking systems had registered his presence, swinging the laser cannon in a horizontal arc toward him. Luckily, the firing indicators on the cannon's housing had remained in their yellow standby mode.

It had taken a few moments for Zuckuss to realize that this intimidating and unfamiliar entity was only partially conscious at that moment. The square, heavily armored box mounted beneath the laser cannon's curved forward support, resembling a thick breastplate with rows of input sockets and flickering LEDs, was the repository of all of D'harhan's cerebral functions, surgically encased and transferred there from the emptied skull, discarded like an empty combat-rations container when the massive weapon's base had been drilled into the collarbones and vertebral column. What Boba Fett had described of the operation had been enough to set Zuckuss's spine crawling. It was one thing to augment oneself with weapons and detection systems—Zuckuss frankly envied Fett's impressive array of sensor and destructive devices; the man was a walking armory— but to go beyond that, to have whole major sections of one's anatomy cut away and replaced with dura-steel and attack-level charge batteries, to actually turn oneself *into* a weapon rather than just a bearer of weapons . . . a sick feeling had moved inside Zuckuss's gut as he'd spied upon the sleeping D'harhan. *That's where it ends up,* he'd thought gloomily. *If you go all the way.* The segmented metal tail, the third leg of the laser cannon's tripod support, curled around D'harhan like a defensive barrier separating him from contact with the universe of living things. . . .

Zuckuss had taken a cautious step closer in the *Slave I*'s hold. He'd known that D'harhan wasn't so much asleep as just partially shut down, conserving energy for the ever-alert weapon above his torso, its glowing lights a simple constellation in the darkness. A residual circuit was triggered by Zuckuss's approach; one of the black-gloved hands turned the illuminated screen of the keyboard voice box outward. DO NOT DISTURB ME, read the screen, its audio function switched off. LEAVE ME BE. Like a sleeping dragon in a cave, the fiery destruction of its breath only smoldering . . .

The silent warning had been enough; Zuckuss had been only too happy to retreat to the ladder leading back to the *Slave I*'s cockpit. The dark, somnolent, yet threatening form of the creature who had turned himself into a weapon aroused mingled dread and nausea inside Zuckuss. Once, before he'd decided to become a bounty hunter himself, he'd caught a fleeting glimpse of Darth Vader, the Dark Lord of the Sith, commanding a punitive sweep of Imperial stormtroopers across the capital city of a world that had been slow to pay obeisance to the distant Emperor Palpatine. The thought had struck him then, as it did again now, that there were some paths one could follow, where even if one wound up powerful beyond one's dreams, one also became somehow diminished, as though the essence hidden inside the armor were progressively stripped away and replaced with unfeeling metal and circuitry.

That was all too deep to think about, especially now, when he had allied himself with creatures like Boba Fett and D'harhan. *Maybe later,* Zuckuss had mused as he'd climbed the ladder to the cockpit. If there was a later.

"I don't get that voice-box device he carries around." Zuckuss nodded toward the ladder and the hold below. "Seems kind of awkward. I would've thought something that left his hands free would be more useful for communicating."

"D'harhan doesn't have a lot of need for communicating." Boba Fett's voice sounded dryly amused. "And before, when there were others like him, they coordinated their actions with their own internal comm network."

"There were others? Like him?" That seemed a dismaying prospect to Zuckuss. "What happened to them?"

Fett made no reply.

Zuckuss tried another question. "What was he

like before?" He didn't even feel like saying the other's name aloud. "Before he became . . . what he is now?"

"That's none of your business." Boba Fett didn't take his eyes away from the *Slave I*'s controls. "He's been as he is for a long time. If you never knew of D'harhan before, it's because he minds his own business, in regions of the galaxy where such as you never travel." Fett glanced over his shoulder at Zuckuss. "For which you should be grateful."

The discussion of the final team member was concluded; Zuckuss knew better than to ask any more prying questions. *I'll be glad when this job is over,* he thought ruefully. Things had been getting increasingly sticky back at the Bounty Hunters Guild, with its rapidly thickening air of conspiracy and stealth, the various backstabbing alliances forming and dissolving and recoalescing with new partners and enemies on a daily, even hourly basis. Going on this Oph Nar Dinnid job, dangerous as the Shell Hutts' defenses were reputed to be, seemed like a piece of baked confectionery by comparison. But even here, in the starless void of hyperspace, Zuckuss knew he was still in the uncomfortable midst of those dangerous spiderwebs; all it would take would be for Bossk or Boba Fett to find out that he was working from Cradossk's agenda, and he'd be pitched out into vacuum from either the *Slave I*'s or the *Hound*'s waste chute, boots first. Agreeing to Cradossk's schemes was beginning to look like less of a good deal now that Zuckuss was out here, with nothing to count on but his own smarts and urge to survive.

"Stop fidgeting." Boba Fett spoke without looking around at Zuckuss. "Brace yourself; we're about to drop into sublight space."

Zuckuss was already familiar with the *Slave I*'s abrupt navigational transitions; Fett's working vessel was stripped of any deceleration buffers that might have impaired its speed or fighting abilities. The ship consequently slammed from one transit mode to another with a gut-wrenching impact. Zuckuss grabbed either side of the hatchway and averted his lidless eyes so he wouldn't have to see the stars blur sickeningly into focus beyond the cockpit's main viewport.

"There's Bossk."

Opening his eyes, Zuckuss saw the *Hound's Tooth* floating before them, engines shut off. A signal light flashed, and Boba Fett reached over and pressed the comm button. "Fett here. Have you made contact with the Circumtore landing authorities?"

"Positive on that." IG-88's flat, expressionless voice sounded from the cockpit speaker. "Approach and landing permission has not—I repeat, *not*—been granted."

"I didn't expect it would be," said Boba Fett dryly. "When people like us show up, hardly anyone puts out a welcome mat."

"At the conclusion of our last exchange, the Shell Hutts indicated they would be sending out a negotiator."

"What level?"

Bossk's voice broke into the discussion. "The fat slugs said it would be an Alpha Point Zero. What's that mean?"

Boba Fett kept his thumb on the comm button. "That's the Shell Hutts' top authority level. They don't go any higher than that. So it means two things: One, we don't have to bother with any small-fry underlings, and two, they're taking our arrival very seriously."

"When this negotiator gets out here, what's our

plan?" Bossk sounded hungry for action, as though the journey out from the Bounty Hunters Guild had been an eternity of chafing inaction. "Kill him?"

Typical, thought Zuckuss, slowly shaking his head. He'd had enough experience with Bossk to know that that was always his Plan A. And there usually wasn't a B.

Fett glanced over his shoulder at Zuckuss. "Don't worry." He turned and pressed the comm button again. "We can be a little more subtle than that. You and IG-88 should transfer over here to the *Slave I* before the Shell Hutts' negotiator arrives. But remember—I do the talking."

Bossk's ship, the heavily armed *Hound's Tooth,* was left in autostandby, its alarm systems set to refuse entry to anyone other than its returning master. Zuckuss was aware of the level of Bossk's paranoia, and the number of lethal booby traps he had installed throughout the *Hound,* all to prevent anyone from invading his base of operations. That was the main reason Zuckuss had gone instead with Boba Fett; his nerves had still been frayed from the last time he had been aboard the *Hound's Tooth,* when he'd constantly had to be on guard against setting off any of the security devices. Better to let the bounty-hunter droid IG-88 take the risk, even if it meant losing track of Bossk—the main reason Zuckuss was on the team for this job—for the duration of the journey.

He went down into the *Slave I*'s holding area to open the transfer hatch between the two ships. The hunched shape of the partially shut-down D'harhan filled one corner of the area; he could feel the laser cannon's standby optics registering his presence, lifting the weapon's barrel slightly and turning it in his direction, as he stepped from the bottom rung of the ladder.

From the small viewport beside the hatch, Zuckuss could see the *Hound's Tooth* being maneuvered into docking position. When it had connected with the *Slave I,* Zuckuss hit the hatch release controls; a sharp hiss sounded as the two ships equalized their internal atmospheric pressures. The hatch irised open, and Bossk and IG-88 stepped aboard. Bossk pressed a button on the remote cockpit control at his waist, and the *Hound* disengaged and drew into a parallel orbit above the surface of Circumtore.

"Where's Fett?" Bossk scanned the *Slave I*'s holding area. Though it was the largest open space aboard the ship, it was already cramped with the three bounty hunters in it. Boba Fett's ship was built for speed and destruction, not comfort.

Zuckuss pointed to the ladder leading to the cockpit. "He's still up there. I think he's getting ready for the arrival of the Shell Hutts' negotiator."

His guess was proved correct when Boba Fett's voice crackled from a speaker mounted on the bulkhead. "We'll need to make room," said Fett over the ship's internal comm system. "I've just been informed that the negotiator is one of the Shell Hutts; they didn't send one of their pet intermediaries. If we're going to get one of those tanks aboard here, we'll need all the space we can get."

"I don't see how . . ." Zuckuss turned, looking around the *Slave I*'s holding area. "The only room down here is in the cages."

"So?" Boba Fett's voice spoke again. "What's the problem?"

Bossk glared at the cages where Boba Fett kept his captured pieces of merchandise, en route to collecting the bounty on them. "I'm not going in there," he growled.

"You're the biggest one here," Zuckuss pointed out helpfully. "Except, of course—" He pointed to D'harhan's massive bulk, the laser cannon's barrel protruding slightly above the drawn-up knees and encircled metal tail. "For *him*."

The three bounty hunters looked over at D'harhan.

"I don't know," said Bossk. Even he seemed intimidated by the presence of a fully charged laser cannon in their midst. "Maybe it's not a good idea to wake him up."

TOO LATE. One of D'harhan's hands tapped out another message on the silenced voice box and turned its glowing screen toward them. I HEAR . . . EVERYTHING YOU SAY.

Zuckuss and the other two bounty hunters stepped back, spines against the bulkhead, as the roused D'harhan slowly stood up, the segmented metal tail drawing around behind him. The housing of the laser cannon mounted onto D'harhan's chest and shoulders reached above even Bossk's head. The massive weapon's tracking systems regarded the bounty hunters in silence for a moment.

"Watch out!" Zuckuss's cry was involuntary, triggered by the sight of the indicator lights on the laser cannon suddenly surging to red. He dived to the floor as Bossk and IG-88 scattered to either side of the cramped holding area.

On the gridded floor, with his arms pulled over his head, Zuckuss heard the quick, sharp sizzle of a laser bolt, then another; their glare lit up the space, stinging his eyes. In the quiet that followed, he could smell ozone and scorched metal.

Lifting his head, Zuckuss saw the lights on the

side of the animate laser cannon dwindling back down to yellow and safety. Flanking the holding area, Bossk and IG-88 looked first toward D'harhan, then toward the target of his ramped-down laser bolts. The impacts had been precisely calculated and aimed, shattering the hinges of the main merchandise cage; fragments of molten durasteel, scattered across the floor, glowed a dull red. Wisps of acrid smoke rose from the edge of the cage door as it fell with a resounding clang.

"THERE," spoke D'harhan's voice box aloud. "NOW YOU SHOULD HAVE . . . NO OBJECTIONS."

"Your point is valid." IG-88's circuitry had recovered completely from the sudden burst of laser fire. The droid stepped over the bars of the fallen door and into what was left of the cage, then turned around.

Bossk regarded D'harhan for a moment longer, his slitted eyes looking up at the cooling laser cannon with something like envy, then followed the other bounty hunter into the area's adjoining space, now incapable of being shut and locked.

That'll take some fixing, thought Zuckuss. Considering the proprietary attitude that Boba Fett naturally took toward the *Slave I* and its fittings, he was more than relieved that D'harhan had blown the holding cage hinges and not him.

At that moment Boba Fett appeared on the ladder coming down from the cockpit. The bounty hunters watched as Fett's visored gaze turned toward the cage in which he transported his merchandise, then down to the barred door lying in front of it.

"That's coming out of your share," Fett told D'harhan.

The black-gloved hand moved across the voice box's keyboard. "NO, IT'S NOT."

For a moment longer they stood facing each other—one masked behind the visored helmet, the other faceless except for the muzzle of the laser cannon—before Boba Fett finally gave a slow nod. "We'll talk."

"There's a ship approaching." Zuckuss pointed to the viewport. "It must be the Shell Hutts' negotiator."

In the viewport, a spherical craft moved closer to the *Slave I;* a simple off-planet shuttle, it displayed tortoise insignia of the Shell Hutts and a diplomatic emblazon showing its unarmed status. The shuttle's forward hatch had already deployed its docking arms, ready to hook up with the *Slave I*'s transfer hatch.

A few moments later, as Zuckuss manned the hatch's controls, a broad face with a slit gash of a mouth appeared floating before the bounty hunters. The elongated, tapering cylinder of the Shell Hutt negotiator moved with ponderous grace into the holding area, its underside repulsor beams pushing invisibly against the floor grids. As the end of the tanklike casing made it through the transfer hatch, Zuckuss hit the button and irised the hatch closed again.

"Ah, Boba Fett!" The casing, studded with rivets and various maintenance ports, swung about in the holding area, past the other bounty hunters and toward the figure standing near the metal ladder. A leering smile formed on the Shell Hutt's face. Tiny mechanical hands dangled beneath a gleaming chromium collar, sealed tight around the wattled gray flesh of its neck; the claws, delicate as a scuttling sea crab's, clicked happily against each other. "How pleasant to see you again."

Fett's response was dry and emotionless. "My

feelings, Gheeta, are the same as the last time we met."

Bossk spoke from the holding cage. "You know this creature?"

"We've had . . . business dealings." Fett didn't look back at the Trandoshan. "A couple times before."

"And very profitable they were, too." The cylinder with the Shell Hutt inside bobbed slightly as it turned toward Bossk. "At least . . . for *some* people." The smile on Gheeta's face soured. "I hope," he said to Boba Fett, "that you're not expecting the same degree of trust that you found previously on Circumtore." The little crablike hands snapped their metal claws together, hard enough to produce sparks. "After that last affair of yours, Fett, you're not going to be greeted with open arms."

"I don't need to be." Boba Fett stood face-to-face with the Shell Hutt. "You're a business creature, Gheeta, and so am I. Warm sentiments have nothing to do with it. If you're ready to do business, then we have something to talk about. If you're not ready, then we don't."

"The same old Boba Fett." The Shell Hutt's head, its jowly neck bound by the floating cylinder's collar, managed an appreciative nod. "It's good to know that some things in this universe never change. Just what business is it you've come to Circumtore to discuss?"

"I think you've got a pretty good idea of that."

Gheeta's expression turned sly, the lids over his large eyes drawing halfway down. "It wouldn't be something to do with a certain Oph Nar Dinnid, would it?"

"Stop wasting time!" Bossk's angry shout broke

in. "You know damn well that's what we're here for!"

An amused glance from the corner of one eye, then Gheeta looked back at Fett. "Your associate has a charming directness about him."

Fett nodded. "Among other virtues."

"The others must be well concealed," said Gheeta dryly. One of the metal hands reached up to scratch between the wattles at the side of his neck. "You realize, of course, that the party under discussion—this Dinnid person—is a guest on Circumtore. You know how all Hutts are about hospitality. The happiness of a guest is a sacred obligation with our species."

Spare me, thought Zuckuss, watching the exchange between Boba Fett and the Shell Hutt. Throughout the galaxy, the treachery and outright malice that Hutts showed toward any who found themselves in one of their windowless palaces was proverbial. Zuckuss had heard things about how the infamous Jabba, the preeminent Huttese crime lord, went through so-called guests and the more disposable type of servants that made his flesh crawl. That was the difference, Zuckuss supposed, between Boba Fett and a creature like this Gheeta. Fett didn't go out of his way to hurt or even kill anyone—if it happened, it happened—whereas Hutts in general took an active delight in other creatures' suffering.

"There are some," said Boba Fett, "who would take an interest in Dinnid's happiness equal to your own."

"Ah, yes." The massive head at the forward end of the repulsor-borne cylinder nodded. "Dinnid's former employers. I take it that you're here on their behalf?"

"I'm here on no one's behalf but my own."

"But of course." Gheeta's smile expanded enough to reveal his wet, flickering tongue. "I really expected nothing else. Altruism is in short supply among the practitioners of your trade. I imagine it's the same for your friends here." One of the little crablike hands raised and gestured at the others in the *Slave I*'s holding area. "Rather an intimidating crew, don't you think, Fett? It makes the heart inside my casing tremble just to look at them." Gheeta peered more closely at Bossk. "Let's see . . . you're Cradossk's son, aren't you?"

Bossk's eyes were two razor slits, his voice a low snarl. "What's that matter to you?"

"You really *are* his son." Gheeta widened his eyes in mock fright. "Give the old reptile my best regards the next time you see him. Which shouldn't be too long from now." The Shell Hutt rotated himself back toward Boba Fett. "Because if you think I'm going to let an obviously vicious bunch like this come sailing down to Circumtore, then you've got a few circuits blown inside that helmet of yours, Fett."

The remark produced no reaction in its target. "We can hardly discuss the matter out here," said Boba Fett. "I make it a rule to talk business only when the merchandise is on the table, so to speak."

"I have to warn you." The claws of the little mechanical hands clicked against each other again. "This is *very* expensive merchandise we're talking about."

"That makes it all the more profitable, then." Fett indicated the other bounty hunters. "And that's why we've come here."

"I can believe that, well enough." Gheeta used one of the claws to scratch the almost boneless flesh of his chin. "I just don't know if you've really changed your ways, my dear Fett, regarding just how you acquire your *profitable* merchandise. I had heard, naturally, about your having joined the Bounty Hunters Guild—and I must admit that all of my clan on Circumtore were surprised by the news. Getting old and tired, are we, Fett?"

"Not tired." Boba Fett gave a slow shake of his head. "Just smart."

"Smart for you, no doubt." The Shell Hutt broadcast his sly, insinuating smile around at the others. "I wonder, though . . . just what your new-found friends here get out of the deal."

Zuckuss found himself gazing straight into the Shell Hutt's eyes as the floating cylinder turned his way. The same sensation came over him as when he had felt the tracking systems of D'harhan's laser cannon locking onto him, calculating the precise angle and force necessary for his destruction. The pupils of Gheeta's eyes were like narrow windows into a realm of avarice, the slow and certain calculus of insatiable appetites. Getting blown away—literally, into disconnected atoms—by a laser bolt would be mercifully quick by comparison.

Another feeling, even more disquieting, moved inside Zuckuss: that the dark pupils regarding him with such amused contempt were not windows, but mirrors into his own heart. *Little creature,* he could hear Gheeta speaking inside his head, *I am what you would like to be. All mouth and gut and hunger.* In this cold galaxy, the commandment of Eat or Be Eaten prevailed, from the throne of Emperor Palpatine all the way down to the smallest carnivore, a Tatooinian womp rat, scuttling across an empty desert.

His heart dwindled within himself, from that moment of recognition in the Shell Hutt's eyes. There had been others who had lived and fought, their struggles guided by a different code; there had been a time when even he had listened to tales of the Jedi Knights defending the old Republic. *But those are just stories now,* Zuckuss told himself. Those days, and the brave creatures that had lived in them, were never coming back. And without them, the Rebels fighting against the Empire were poor, pathetic fools, doomed to failure. Their bones would be picked clean and discarded on the battlefields of worlds without names. The hungry ones, with their greed and lust for dominion, would always win. . . .

Bleak, wordless meditation ended as the Shell Hutt's knowing, judging smile moved away from him. *Pull yourself together,* Zuckuss told himself. He had made his pact with the universe he'd found himself in; he was a bounty hunter now, and had been so long enough to be traveling in league with some of the toughest ones in the galaxy. If he showed any signs of weakness at this point, he knew, he wouldn't have to worry about Emperor Palpatine or any of the Shell Hutts; his own colleagues would tear him apart. A carnivore like Bossk would very likely consume him, in the exact and literal sense of the word. That thought made Zuckuss feel at least a little better about having become part of old Cradossk's intricate scheming. *Better you than me,* he thought, glancing over at Bossk.

"Don't worry about us." That was Bossk's voice, giving a snarling reply to Gheeta. "We can take care of ourselves."

"I'm sure you can." The Shell Hutt didn't stop smiling. "After all . . . you're learning from the master, aren't you? Boba Fett has always done very well for himself."

"I would be doing even better," said Fett, "if we could limit our discussion to that which we came here for. Specifically, that merchandise known as Oph Nar Dinnid."

"But that merchandise isn't on the table right now, is it?" Gheeta's large eyes emitted a spark of anger. "And it's not going to be. Not out here, at least. You want to discuss the fate of our guest, you will indeed have to come down to Circumtore to do it—just as you wish. I'm only here to explain how things are in that regard. I'm giving you the conditions, not cutting the deal."

"Why not?" Zuckuss spoke up. "I don't get it. The other members of your clan wouldn't have sent you out here if you didn't have some kind of authority to speak for them. If they'd just wanted to send us some message, they could've comm'd it out here or sent some flunky of a different species, like a Twi'lek or something. So why mess around? If you're willing to talk about Dinnid at all, why not do it here?"

The smile on the broad, jowly face turned into a sneer. "Your colleague Boba Fett wouldn't ask such a stupid question. A question which has an equally simple answer. We're all aboard the *Slave I* right now, aren't we? The *Slave I* is Boba Fett's ship; he controls it. So as long as we're here, he controls the discussion as well. There have been times when discussions with Boba Fett have gotten . . . a little ugly. Things start out nice and friendly, and then they just . . . *change* somehow." Gheeta feigned mulling over that statement. "Probably because the parties involved couldn't come to an agreement about the value and price of the merchandise being discussed." He glanced over at Fett. "You always like to get things as cheaply as possible, don't you?"

Boba Fett made no reply.

"Cheaply," continued Gheeta, "as far as credits are concerned. When it comes to violence . . . well, that's another story, isn't it?" The floating cylinder turned, bringing the Shell Hutt's face back toward Zuckuss. "That's when your colleague has rather a free hand. Especially when other creatures' skins are involved. And the blood—that can also get a little thick to wade through, when Boba Fett's around." Another shift in angle brought Gheeta's face toward the bounty hunters in general. "So if you think I'm going to remain here, in the heart of Fett's traveling circus of destruction, surrounded by his friends—or if not his friends, then creatures with whom he's come to a certain business arrangement—and talk about the merchandise in question, let alone actually bring that merchandise here . . ." Gheeta's jowls wobbled against the cylinder's gleaming collar as he shook his head. "Then it's not just Boba Fett who's gone a little insane. You're *all* not in sync with reality if you think that's going to happen."

A low growl came from the doorless holding cage. "You've said your piece?" Bossk folded his arms across his chest.

Gheeta looked over at the Trandoshan. "Yes, I have."

"And now you're going to be on your way?"

"As charming as your company is, I see no reason for wasting any more of your time or mine."

"What makes you think we're going to let you leave?"

A weary sigh escaped from the Shell Hutt as he rolled his eyes toward the top of the holding area. "I really expected better from any companions of yours, Fett. Do you want to tell him or should I?"

"He leaves when he wants to," said Boba Fett. He turned the hard gaze of his visored helmet toward the holding cage. "First of all, the merchandise we came here for is still down on Circumtore. Anything

unpleasant we do to the negotiator that the Shell
Hutts sent out will just make it harder to accomplish
anything later, when we actually go on-planet."

Bossk laid his hand on the grip of his blaster.
"Maybe we should just worry about that when we
get down there. I don't see any big difference between taking care of one canned Hutt and a whole
world full of them."

"There's more inside that can than one Hutt. I've
dealt with their negotiators before. They never send
one out that isn't packed with high-thermal explosives."

"You see?" One of the mechanical hands beneath Gheeta's floating cylinder gestured theatrically
toward Boba Fett. "That's why *he's* at the top of the
bounty-hunter profession. It's why he's lasted so
long, while others have met tragically untimely
deaths. Because he's learned that other creatures can
be just as clever . . . and violent, if need be." The
thin metal arm telescoped outward so that the crablike hand could reach up to an access hatch at the
midpoint of the cylinder's tapered length. One claw
pried open the hatch, revealing a ticking mechanism
wired into several flat bricks of a dull gray substance.

From where he stood, Zuckuss could see the emblem and coding symbols of one of the Imperial
Navy's main armaments dumps. The explosive
charges had obviously been stolen, or smuggled out
by some enterprising accomplice—but they were still
more than lethal. Just looking at that much destructive force made Zuckuss's breath catch in the tubes
dangling from his face mask.

IG-88 had also scanned the explosives, from
where it stood next to Bossk. "It would be advis-
able," announced the droid, "if no one made an attempt to forcibly defuse the triggering mechanism. It

has obviously been wired with a detect-and-destruct subsystem to prevent just such an occurrence."

"Of course." Gheeta looked pleased with himself. "As Fett indicated to you, Shell Hutt negotiators don't come into this kind of situation unprepared. If any of you were so foolish as to lay a finger on me, or this little present I came with, then the consequences would be of astronomical significance." His lipless smile broadened. "A glowing cloud of radioactive dust . . . perhaps they'd even be able to see it back at the Bounty Hunters Guild. So at least your friends would know what had become of you."

"I think . . . we can all be reasonable about this." Zuckuss hastened to speak; on the other side of the holding area, Bossk looked furious enough to fling himself at the Shell Hutt and start pulling wires on the explosives, no matter what the consequences might be. "Nobody's going to prevent you from leaving whenever you want."

"Good." Gheeta gave an appreciative nod to Zuckuss. "You, at least, show some intelligence. Keep it up, and someday you might reach the same lofty pinnacle in your trade that Boba Fett has." The crablike hand folded the little hatch back down and sealed it in place. "This thing itches abominably. I'll be glad to be rid of it." The hand scratched at the metal door. "I'll take my departure now. Though I imagine it won't be very long until we all see each other again—down on Circumtore, of course."

The Shell Hutt's tapered casing rotated 180 degrees so that it was facing the transfer hatchway. Without being bidden, Zuckuss hurried to the controls at the side.

As the hatch irised open, Gheeta turned the floating cylinder just enough that he could look back at Boba Fett and the other bounty hunters. "Of course," he said blandly, "that's up to you. About whether we do business or not. Because I have to tell you—we take a very dim view of creatures coming to visit us if they bring along the kind of firepower that you like to carry around."

The cylinder moved through the fully open hatchway. It sealed shut with a hiss; a few seconds later the mechanical noises of the negotiator's ship disengaging were audible. In the small viewport, the craft could be seen as it began traveling back down to Circumtore.

Bossk, looking as angry as before, stepped out of the doorless holding cage. "What was that last bit supposed to mean?"

"It's simple." Boba Fett grasped one of the ladder's rungs. "Like everything with the Shell Hutts." He started up toward the *Slave I*'s cockpit. "We're going to go down and talk business, and we'll do it unarmed. They'll send a shuttle for us to go onworld, and we'll leave all our weapons right here."

"You're joking!" Bossk stared after him in amazement. "I'm not going down there defenseless!"

"That's up to you." At the cockpit hatchway, Boba Fett halted and looked back down at the Trandoshan. "There's an alternative, of course. We can eliminate you from the team right now." He drew his blaster from his hip and aimed it at Bossk. "You decide."

A few seconds passed before Bossk finally gave a slow nod. "All right," he said. "You win. That's how we'll play it." An ugly sneer formed on his face. "But there's a slight problem. What about him?"

Zuckuss and the others turned in the direction to which Bossk's gesture pointed. At the side of the *Slave I*'s holding area, silent and waiting, stood the massive shape of D'harhan. The tracking systems of the laser cannon, bonded inseparably to his torso, looked toward Fett.

"Even him," Fett said quietly. "He's going with us as well."

D'harhan punched a string of words into his voice box and turned the device away from himself. "YOU WOULD HAVE TO KILL ME," it spoke aloud. "TO RENDER ME WEAPONLESS." The voice had sounded like thunder beneath the roiling clouds of steam. The laser cannon's tracking systems gazed hard at Boba Fett as the next words were displayed. THERE IS NO DIFFERENCE . . . BETWEEN ME AND MY WEAPONS.

"Maybe . . ." With growing unease, Zuckuss let his gaze move up the enormous figure. The yellow lights on the side of the laser-cannon housing were darkening, as though they were about to shift to the red of imminent destruction. "Maybe we don't really need to take him with us. I mean . . . if we're just going down to Circumtore to *talk* . . . that's not really his specialty, is it?"

"No one is being left behind," Fett stated with cold finality. "The whole team is going. That's the plan."

"Whose plan?" demanded Bossk.

"Mine." Another simple, flat statement. "That's the only one that matters." Boba Fett turned back toward D'harhan. "I know better than anyone that to remove your weapon would be the same as killing you; I haven't forgotten about these things. I was there when you became as you are now. So I also know other things: that your weapon can be rendered nonfunctional, incapable of firing, by a relatively simple procedure. The removal of the light-mass core alone will do it. And then the Shell Hutts will have no basis for refusing you permission to enter their world."

Zuckuss flattened himself against the holding area's bulkhead as he watched D'harhan rising to his full height, the top of the laser-cannon housing scraping the durasteel ceiling. The light inside the space seemed to dim, as though the creature's expanding form were swallowing it up. D'harhan's chest, the remaining flesh-and-blood part of it, swelled outward, thrusting forward the curved gearing of the weapon mount welded to his breastbone; his shoulders pulled back, arms tensing at his sides, one hand clenching into a fist, the other still holding the muted voice box. Through clouds of hissing steam, the oiled metal of the pistons gleamed like naked sword blades; the indicator lights along the laser cannon's barrel burned a fiery, nebulous red.

Now it's going to happen—fear twisted sickeningly in Zuckuss's gut. *We're all going to die.* Mesmerized, he watched as Boba Fett stepped up in front of D'harhan, the red light blurring through the steam and silhouetting him as though by fire seen through ominous storm clouds.

"YOU'RE WRONG." D'harhan raised the voice box toward Fett. "IT WON'T BE EASY AT ALL."

"I am aware of his meaning." A trace of fear sounded in even the droid IG-88's voice. "The light-mass core is shielded behind a grid of protective interlocks—that is standard for weapons of the class he bears, to prevent just such tampering. Removal is ill-advised, even for a skilled armory technician. You could trigger an overload destruct sequence that would destroy this ship even more thoroughly than the Shell Hutt's explosive charges would have."

"Listen to it," pleaded Bossk. "You're going to kill us all—"

"I know what I'm doing." Boba Fett spoke with

an unnervingly icy calm. "Do not interfere—if you value your lives."

"DO YOU KNOW?" Another cloud of steam hissed from the laser cannon's mounting as the tracking systems narrowed their focus on the man standing in front of them. "THE WEAPON IS MY SPIRIT. WHEN YOU TAKE THAT BY WHICH I KILL OTHERS . . . THEN YOU KILL ME."

"It will only seem that way," said Boba Fett. "There's a difference between this death and true death." Slowly, he reached up toward the glistening machinery whose coils were buried deep in D'harhan's chest. "Trust me."

"Fett . . . don't . . ."

Whether it was his own voice or one of the others, Zuckuss could no longer tell. Flinching from certain doom, he averted his face; the last thing he saw was Boba Fett shrouded in steam, one hand sinking into the coils and wires nested beneath the laser cannon's mounting, as though the bounty hunter were a battlefield surgeon performing a crude, septic heart transplant. With a screech of grinding metal from the geared wheel, the weapon's barrel convulsively angled upward, the tracking systems blindly defocusing, as though a pain voltage beyond the reach of mortal anesthesia had coursed through D'harhan's embedded circuitry. The indicator lights pulsed and flared even brighter than before; Zuckuss could hear someone, probably Bossk, diving to the gridded floor of the holding area, as though there were any chance of hiding from the firepower that would rip the *Slave I* apart.

With all muscles involuntarily tensed, crouching against the bulkhead, Zuckuss awaited the harsh, deafening noise that he knew would be the last thing he would ever hear.

Instead, there was silence, ended by a sighing

emission of steam, as though from a dying machine, the source of its energy shut off by a single valve.

He looked up, bringing his eyes away from his own lowered forearm. The red lights that had burned through the steam mist were gone now; as Zuckuss watched, the inert metal of the laser cannon shifted angle, its dark barrel slowly inching down from its ceiling-high trajectory. The blank voice box swung on a cord from D'harhan's waist as his black-gloved hands trembled open, palms outward. His knees buckled, diminishing the massive form that had reared up inside the ship's holding area, turning him into something weaker and more human than machine. D'harhan collapsed onto the floor, rolling heavily onto one broad shoulder, the muzzle of the laser cannon scraping an arc across the floor, ending at the tip of Boba Fett's boot.

Zuckuss's gaze broke from the silenced weapon and turned toward the other bounty hunter. Boba Fett hadn't moved from where he had been standing, as though the fall of the laser cannon was an ocean tide that he knew would break harmlessly upon the shore, millimeters away from him. In Fett's hand, the one that had reached into the intricate lock and coil of D'harhan's chest, was a dull metal rod, less than half a meter long, thick enough to fill the grip fastened upon it. When Fett dropped it with a leaden clang, the residual heat from the weapon's reactor core brought a final sizzling puff of steam from the water vapor that had collected on the grid's surface.

The barrel of the laser cannon lifted, moving with crippled difficulty. D'harhan's tracking systems focused upon Boba Fett standing above him; one hand grasped the voice box and slowly thumbed in a few words.

YOU OWE ME. D'harhan raised the silent communication device. BIG TIME.

Boba Fett said nothing, but turned away and strode toward the ladder leading to the cockpit. He halted with one boot on the bottom rung and looked over at the others watching him. "They're already waiting for us," he said quietly. "Down on Circumtore."

Then he was gone. Zuckuss looked over at Bossk, just now getting to his feet in the doorless holding cage.

"We're lucky," said Zuckuss, "to be alive."

Bossk glanced up, toward the empty hatchway of the cockpit, then back down. The thin smile he gave Zuckuss contained at least a small particle of admiration.

"I suppose we'll find out"—Bossk slowly nodded, his gaze narrowing—"just how lucky we are. . . ."

16

"What exactly is the history between you and the Shell Hutts?" Zuckuss wasn't asking just to pass the time. Sitting at last on the surface of Circumtore, surrounded by the durasteel-plated Hutts and, even worse, their various guards and mercenaries, he felt no less endangered than before. *It just keeps getting worse,* Zuckuss mused gloomily to himself. Pretty soon he'd be wishing that everyone on this intrepid little team had gotten blown to spiraling, whistling atoms. "I mean . . . the way that the negotiator talked . . ."

Boba Fett stood with his arms crossed, watching the Shell Hutts' customs inspectors poking through the interior of the *Slave I*. They weren't looking for contraband—which was something that the Shell Hutts, like all the members of the species, had no aversion to, as long as they got their piece of the action—but were combing the ship and its passengers for undeclared weaponry. Without his usual panoply of rocket launchers and other means of destruction, Fett looked even more dangerous, oddly enough; as though his simmering anger were some newly aroused lethal force, provoked by the intrusion on his personal domain.

"Hutts say all sorts of things." Boba Fett didn't turn toward Zuckuss as he spoke. "There's a lot of it you can safely ignore. A lot of creatures in the galaxy believe that all the Huttese are efficient businessmen, with nothing but credits on their minds, but they're not. They spend too much time brooding about the past, keeping old scores. Bearing grudges. That kind of emotion always gets in the way of true rationality."

Nobody would ever make that kind of assessment, Zuckuss figured, of Boba Fett. The more time he spent anywhere near Fett, the more he was impressed—and appalled by the cold calculations taking place inside that visored helmet. Even over something like the team disarming itself for its landing on the Shell Hutts' world; if Boba Fett was willing to go along with that, it must mean his intricately worked-out plans included this factor, accounted for it in some way. *We might make it back out of here alive,* thought Zuckuss. *Or at least some of us might.* The plans that he had let himself become part of—Cradossk's plans—called for one death out here, if not more.

"It seemed kind of specific, though. What Gheeta said." Zuckuss tried again. "When he was talking about what happened before. Is there some kind of old score to settle between you and the Shell Hutts?"

The customs inspectors—multilegged droids, bristling with inspection probes and energy-level meters—continued their inspection of the *Slave I*. Their black, spidery forms could be seen through the ship's open hatches and up inside the transparent shielding of the cockpit. One of the inspectors lay crumpled in pieces, a few lights still forlornly blinking, on the thrust-scarred landing dock. That one had been a little too brusque in frisking the Trandoshan Bossk for any concealed weapons, and had paid the price in quick, bolt-snapping disassembly.

"Nothing you have to worry about," said Boba Fett. "It's a personal thing. Actually, between me and Gheeta. There was a time when he wasn't a mere negotiator, being sent out on those kinds of errands to ships seeking permission to land. He was very high up in the Shell Hutt hierarchy. That was why he was in charge of the design and construction of the on-planet terminal and diplomatic reception site—basically, everything you see around you here." Fett gestured with one raised hand; past the landing dock's archways could be seen a complex of inter-linked spires and domes. "His budget allowed for a nearly unlimited expenditure of capital, including the hiring of one of the top freelance architects in the galaxy. A man named Emd Grahvess—"

"I've heard of him." Zuckuss actually had, though he couldn't remember from just where.

"There may be better ones, but if there are, they'd be working for Emperor Palpatine, or someone like Prince Xizor. Exclusively. So Grahvess was the top of the line for the Shell Hutts, and Gheeta knew it; that's why he hired him. The only problem was that Gheeta had other plans for Grahvess, once the project was completed; unfortunately for Gheeta, Grahvess was no fool. He knew how dangerous it can be, working for any kind of Hutt. They don't like paying up, and they like having things that no one else can have. If they can't *buy* exclusivity, they have . . . *other* ways of achieving it. And that's what Grahvess found out: that when this job was done, he wouldn't be taking on any others." Fett glanced over at Zuckuss. "Ever."

"That's kind of cold," said Zuckuss. "Having

somebody killed, right after he's done some great job for you."

"Get used to it. It happens to bounty hunters as well—*if* they're not careful." Boba Fett gave a slow nod. "This galaxy is full of treachery. There's no one you can really trust. . . ."

Words to live by, thought Zuckuss. *Or die.* "So what happened to this architect, this Grahvess person? Did Gheeta manage to have him killed or not?"

"Not." Satisfaction was audible in that single word from Boba Fett. "Because Grahvess was just a little bit smarter than Gheeta. Smart enough to contact me and propose a mutually satisfactory business arrangement."

"Like what?"

"You don't need to know all the details." Boba Fett continued to watch the customs inspectors stalking around inside the *Slave I.* "At least not yet. Let's just say that Grahvess and I had everything worked out well before his work here on Circumtore was completed. So that Gheeta and his hench creatures never had a shot at him. Essentially, Grahvess put out a bounty on *himself.* A nice, fat one, which I was only too happy to collect by making a quick raid here and snatching him away, right out from Gheeta's hands. That's the main reason why the Shell Hutts' security procedures are so tight now; they don't want a repeat of that kind of action. Makes them look foolish. Hutts can't stand that."

"Pretty clever." Zuckuss nodded in appreciation. "The only one that winds up screwed is this Gheeta. The architect gets to keep his life, and you get the credits. Smart."

"I got more than that out of it."

Zuckuss studied the other bounty hunter in puzzlement. "What more would you want out of it than credits?" He couldn't imagine any other incentive for someone like Fett.

"An investment. So to speak." Boba Fett watched the Shell Hutts' customs-inspection droids emerging from the ship. "That pays off later. In a big way."

There wasn't time for Zuckuss to ask what that meant. The inspectors spider-legged their way toward the waiting bounty hunters. A couple of the droids lagged behind and began picking up the scattered wreckage of their forcibly disassembled companion, the broken circuits of its main sensory input/output box still buzzing and moaning.

"Thank you for your cooperation." The lead inspector droid halted in front of Boba Fett. "Our examination of your craft shows no hidden armaments of a force sufficient to disturb the peace and tranquillity of Circumtore."

Zuckuss would have been surprised if the inspector droids had found anything like that. He and IG-88—Bossk had still been unhelpfully sulking over having to lay down his own weapons—had assisted Boba Fett in removing either whole systems or essential parts of them from the *Slave I*'s arsenal, and then packing and sealing them into the coded-access freight container that was now in orbit above the surface of Circumtore, awaiting Fett's return. When that procedure had been completed, the ship had been rendered as defenseless—and more significantly for the Shell Hutts, offenseless—as any unarmed cargo shuttle plodding among the stars.

The bounty hunters' personal weapons had been another matter; those they had brought with them to Circumtore, handing them over directly to the customs-inspection droids. "Here is your receipt for the items we are holding in storage for you." One of the lead inspectors pried open a slender pouch beneath its multilensed eyes and extracted a miniature holoprojector. "If you'd care to check it over and make sure that we haven't forgotten anything . . ."

Boba Fett took the device and thumbed it on. The shimmering visual field winked into existence in front of him and Zuckuss, with a scrolling depiction of the bounty hunters' various weapons. It was a long list. Boba Fett gave it no more than a cursory glance before extinguishing the hologram. "Looks complete."

"Very well." The lead inspector extended one of its optic stalks straight up and swiveled its small lens around to see how the others were coming along with the bits and pieces of the one that Bossk had taken apart. A few last segments were being tucked into an inert-mesh sack, from which the droid's muffled complaints were barely audible. The inspector returned its attention to Boba Fett. "If you'll hold on to that and present it to the landing master when you're ready to leave, all items will be returned to you." A dark oil stain and a couple of glittering, broken transistors were all that were left on the surface of the dock. "It's been a pleasure to serve you."

Canned formalities always sounded even more canned when they came from droids; Zuckuss was glad to see the customs-inspection droids leave, stalking their way delicately across the landing dock, dragging their bagged comrade behind themselves.

As the inspection squadron left the landing dock Bossk came striding over, followed by IG-88. The droid looked as unemotional as ever, but burning resentment showed in Bossk's eyes. "So this is your great plan?" He made a quick, dismissive gesture at the blaster holster hanging empty by his side. "Now we're stuck down here on the Shell Hutts' planet, and if they decide to send their thugs around to kill us, there won't be a thing we'll be able to do about it." He shook his head in disgust. "I don't see why you needed a team to go along with you. If you just wanted to get yourself knocked off, you could have done it on your own just as easily."

Boba Fett regarded the Trandoshan in silence. "You know," he said finally, "I'm going to give you something free. That doesn't happen very often. Even when it's just good advice—I usually let other creatures learn by just suffering the consequences of their actions."

"Yeah?" Bossk sneered at him. "So what's your good advice?"

"Stop whining. Before you really get me irritated." Fett turned toward the other bounty hunters. "Let's get going. Gheeta sent me a message while the ship was being inspected. The Shell Hutts have already prepared a reception for us."

"I just bet they have," grumbled Bossk under his breath. Fett ignored the remark, if he had heard it at all.

IG-88 crossed in front of Zuckuss, following after Boba Fett and toward the open-topped ground shuttle that would take them into the center of Circumtore's administrative complex. Zuckuss drew back even farther as the massive shape of D'harhan trod heavily forward, the barrel of the laser cannon, now rendered inert and harmless, slanting disconsolately, the tip of its muzzle almost scraping against the landing dock's surface. The stilled weapon's tracking systems were switched off, as though the half-humanoid, half-mechanical creature was some slow beast following the voice of the master that had blinded it.

"What do you think's going to happen?"

The voice startled Zuckuss; he snapped his head around and saw Bossk standing next to him, leaning down to speak close to his ear. Zuckuss had been immersed too deep in his thoughts, reflecting on how the altered D'harhan looked like the last survivor of some otherwise extinct saurian species, dragging its age-heavy bones and rusting metal armor to the burial ground of its kin. Bossk had stepped beside him while he was still wondering what had been the point of bringing D'harhan along on this job, if Boba Fett had known all along that the laser cannon's core—D'harhan's spirit, or as much of one as he might have possessed—would need to be extracted. It struck Zuckuss as a needlessly cruel thing to have done to an old comrade; something that he would never have imagined Fett capable of doing.

"Don't ask me." Zuckuss glanced over at Bossk and gave a shrug, lifting his gloved hands to indicate his complete bafflement. "I haven't got a clue about what's going on." Things had seemed a lot simpler back at the Bounty Hunters Guild when he'd agreed to become part of Cradossk's plans—not that those were anything he felt like telling to Bossk. They'd only gotten more complicated since then. And dangerous; the confidence he'd felt at one time, that he'd survive all this just by sticking close to Boba Fett, had been seriously eroded. Fett packing his personal arsenal of blasters and rocket launchers was one thing; a disarmed Fett leading all of the team right into the center of Fett's grudge-bearing enemies was another. *Maybe Bossk is right,* mused Zuckuss. *Maybe Fett is going to get us all killed.* Another thought struck him: Maybe that had been Cradossk's plan all along. The old Trandoshan hadn't been out just to get his own son eliminated, but a couple more of the Guild's young upstarts as well. Zuckuss could see why Cradossk and some of the other Guild elders would want to get rid of the coldly efficient droid IG-88, but he would have been surprised to find that anyone thought that he himself was at that level. And even if that were Cradossk's plan, where would Boba Fett hook up with it? Was Fett just leading Bossk and the other bounty hunters into a prearranged trap—which would mean that somehow Cradossk had gotten the Shell Hutts in on the scheme; how likely was that?—or had the galaxy's smartest and toughest bounty hunter somehow been fooled as well, and Fett was about to get eliminated along with the rest of the team? Or . . .

The brain behind the insectoid eyes started to throb painfully as more and more possibilities swirled within. If he did get killed here on Circumtore, Zuckuss hoped it wouldn't be before he had at least figured out part of what was going on. He was beginning to doubt the wisdom of having even wanted to become a bounty hunter.

"I suppose," growled Bossk, "we'll find out. One way or another."

"Maybe." The others of the team were waiting beside the ground shuttle; Zuckuss nodded toward them. "We better get going." He conquered his reluctance enough to start walking.

Even before the shuttle lifted on its repulsor beams and slid toward the Shell Hutts' spired buildings, Zuckuss had a revelation. He could see his face mask, air tubes dangling, reflected in the dark metal of D'harhan's silent, impotent laser cannon. *It doesn't matter*, realized Zuckuss suddenly. *Whether we have weapons or not*. Whatever was going to happen—which of them would die and which of them would live—would happen whether they were ready for it or not.

There was one of them who might be ready. Zuckuss looked toward Boba Fett, sitting in the front of the shuttle. If anybody was going to survive, it would be him.

That thought, even with all its embodied certainty, didn't make Zuckuss feel any better.

Gheeta came floating up, his welcoming smile nearly wide enough to split his wattled face in two. "At last!" The crablike mechanical hands beneath the rivet-studded cylinder spread expansively. "Now you will have a chance to truly partake of our hospitality."

"We're not here to enjoy ourselves." At the head of the team of bounty hunters, Boba Fett stopped and gazed around the grand reception hall of the Shell Hutts. "This is strictly business for us. I would appreciate it if we could get straight to it."

"All in good time, my dear Fett." The tapering end of the cylinder pointed toward the farther reaches of the hall, its high-vaulted roof interlaced with golden traceries and ornamental center bosses. "You are too dismissive of both pleasure and the past—the pleasures of the flesh, that we can enjoy now, and the memories of that past we share."

IG-88 and the shorter figure of Zuckuss came up on either side of Fett, the droid scanning the space with methodical thoroughness, the other bounty hunter glancing around with nervous apprehension. With a slower and more ponderous tread, D'harhan loomed up behind.

"The past is over," said Boba Fett. The Shell Hutt's wobbling face, protruding from the collar of the repulsor-borne cylinder, evoked a cold revulsion inside him. "If not for you, then it is for me."

"I wonder about that." Gheeta raised one of the cylinder's mechanical hands, using the point of its claw to scratch a deep fold in his chin. "How much do creatures *ever* forget? I hope you'll excuse me for waxing philosophical—I know how impatient you become—but sometimes I feel that *nothing* is forgotten. Everything remains buried, deeply or just beneath the surface, just waiting for its certain resurrection, to be brought out into the light once more."

Boba Fett could decipher the meaning behind the Shell Hutt's words. *What he's saying,* thought Fett, *is that he hasn't forgotten.* The reminder about the past and what it contained, back aboard the *Slave I,* hadn't been enough to indicate how fiercely that humiliation burned in Gheeta's memory. If one looked past all his cloying and ingratiating manners, the show of welcome here on Circumtore, the desire for vengeance could be plainly seen.

And counted on. *He's got his plans,* thought Boba Fett, *and I've got mine.*

For a split second, as Fett gazed back into Gheeta's broad, half-lidded eyes, he wondered if there was another meaning to what the Shell Hutt had spoken. *Resurrection . . . brought out into the light . . .*

When one played a dangerous game, there was always the possibility that the opponent was one move ahead. Fett knew that in this game, that would mean death. *If he found out,* mused Fett as he searched Gheeta's massive face for any clue. *If he's figured out everything that happened here, in the past.* Then the game was already over; there would be no more moves to play, just the sweeping of the broken pieces from the board. Those pieces would include himself and the other bounty hunters that he had brought here with him. And maybe one more . . .

Whatever happens, decided Boba Fett as he gazed unflinching into the dark centers of Gheeta's eyes. *Whatever happens—he's going with me.*

"But enough of all that." The floating cylinder that encased Gheeta rotated slightly, so that one of the mechanical hands could gesture toward the center of the reception hall. "As you have so forcefully reminded me, this is—alas!—more a business occasion than a social one. Let us proceed; there are others here who are more than eager to meet with you and your companions."

"After you," said Boba Fett. "They're your species, not mine."

Years ago he had picked up some profitable merchandise on a backwater world where the dominant form of long-distance transportation had been lighter-than-air freighters—slow and immense, tapered ovoid dirigibles, filled with helium and other buoyant gases. The planet's skies had been filled with the craft, like elongated silvery moons, their crew gondolas and cargo containers slung underneath their curved and shaded bellies. That was what Circumtore's great reception hall reminded Fett of; there were a dozen Shell Hutts besides Gheeta, the riveted cylinders floating on their repulsor beams, turning and bumping into each other with graceless sloth. At the front end of each cylinder protruded another bejowled Huttese face, like a wad of some unpleasant organic substance that had been inserted in the circular metal collar. Some of the Shell Hutt faces appeared younger than Gheeta, their large eyes glittering with avarice, slit nostrils flared by the trace scents on which their constant appetites fastened. The younger ones' encasing cylinders were smaller as well; Boba Fett knew how the Shell Hutts enjoyed throwing lavish parties for themselves, upon the occasion of one's expanding bulk being transferred to a new and larger cylinder.

With their artificial exoskeletons, the cylinders raised by repulsor beams, the size to which Shell Hutts could aspire was no longer restricted by gravity—only by how much they could grab of the galaxy's wealth and stuff into their lipless mouths. Gheeta was only in the middle range when it came to sheer mass; Boba Fett recognized a few of the other Shell Hutts in the great reception hall, elders of the clan that were to Gheeta as an Imperial battle cruiser was to a TIE fighter craft. Those faces protruding from their cylinder's metal collars were so heavily wattled from brow to throat that hooks had been surgically implanted in the blubbery tissue, the sharp metal bits connected to a web of thin, high-tension strands fastened to the top edge of the cylinder. If not for that support, the old Shell Hutts' eyes and nostrils would have been buried beneath avalanches of their own slack flesh.

As Boba Fett and the other bounty hunters approached, the largest of the repulsor-borne cylinders turned majestically, like an interstellar luxury ship being maneuvered into an off-planet berth. A low voice rumbled from the gargantuan Hutt bound by the riveted durasteel plates: "I grow weary, Gheeta." The larger Shell Hutt fastened the irritable gaze of its yellowed eyes upon its clan member. "You keep us waiting . . . and for what? Some of us may still be amused, but I assure you that I am not."

Gheeta bobbed forward, the little crablike hands rising from underneath his cylinder and making fluttery gestures of mollification. "Patience will yet be rewarded, Your Magnitude. Our—ahem—*guests* have arrived at last. The show will begin in a moment."

" 'Show'?" Bossk scowled. "What show are you talking about? We came here on business."

"Of course, of course—just as your leader Boba Fett keeps reminding me." Gheeta turned his wide, wet-edged smile toward the Trandoshan. "*Your* patience will be rewarded as well, I assure you. But you've traveled so far—all of you have." The mechanical hands' gesture took in all of the bounty hunters. "And through some of the emptiest and least rewarding stretches of the galaxy. I'd hate for you to go away from here, after our *business* is concluded, and tell the sentient creatures of all the worlds that the Shell Hutts put out a mean and scanty table for their visitors. We have a reputation for hospitality to maintain, don't we? What would our fellow Hutts, our cousin Jabba for instance, say if he heard that we had not provided for others' famished appetites?"

"We're not hungry," said Boba Fett. "Not for anything that you're likely to serve."

"Ah—I think otherwise, my dear Fett. This meal is one that I've been preparing for a long time; a *very* long time. Since the last time you were here on Circumtore, and things went less than graciously . . . for *some* of us."

"More complaints." The immense Shell Hutt—his name, Fett remembered, was Nullada—rolled his yellow eyes beneath his brow's folded and sagging pouches. "Nothing but complaints," he rumbled oleaginously. "You've been obsessed for too long a time, Gheeta. Perhaps you should be relieved of even those duties that you've retained this far so that you could take a long rest to clear your mind."

A flash of anger showed in Gheeta's face, like a

lightning stroke in storm-heavy clouds. The crablike mechanical hands locked their claws together, as though preventing themselves from slashing a set of parallel bloodied furrows down the older and larger Shell Hutt's face.

"I've had time enough." Gheeta's voice was a snarling whine. "But let's not waste any more of it. Come along, then." Even with just his own jowl-wrapped face protruding from the collar of his floating cylinder, the effort required to regain control was visible. The cylinder turned slightly, angling toward the center of the great reception hall, where more of the Shell Hutts' encased forms jostled around a rect-angular dais, surrounded on all sides by low, concentric steps. "Everything has been placed in readiness for you." The claws unclasped, allowing one of them to make a sweeping gesture toward the dais. "Shall we?"

Boba Fett didn't feel like making any further conversation with their host. He led the way toward the dais, letting the other members of the bounty-hunter team fall in behind. There were enough reflective surfaces scattered throughout the space, beams of polished durasteel supporting the domed roof above, that he could see Bossk and the droid IG-88 following his quick stride, with the Trandoshan glaring with suspicion and enmity at every one of the bobbing and floating Shell Hutts. Behind that pair, the massive shape of D'harhan trod heavily, the inert laser cannon still impressive in its glistening darkness, like an emblem of latent destruction wrapped in trails of hissing steam.

At Fett's elbow, Zuckuss trotted to keep up with him. "I don't like the looks of this," panted the shorter bounty hunter. "I don't like the looks of this one bit—"

He knew just what Zuckuss was talking about. Around the sides of the great reception hall, from alcoves and corridors branching off the central space, other figures had appeared, ones that weren't Shell Hutts. "Mercenaries," said Boba Fett quietly. In black, insignialess uniforms, armed and watching; if he'd wanted to, he could very likely have identified more than a few of them from past encounters. There was always a loose assemblage of thugs and venal murderers, varying in number and quality, depending mainly upon who had been killed recently and to a lesser degree upon who was rotting away in the galaxy's various penal institutions, shifting back and forth among the less civilized worlds, finding employment as enforcers and private hit men. The Shell Hutts' distant species relation, the notorious Jabba on backwater Tatooine, usually paid the highest wages and got the pick of the lot, the quickest with their chosen weapons and the least encumbered by scruples about what kind of jobs they took care of for their employer. "What else," Fett asked Zuckuss, "did you expect?"

"This many?" Still at Boba Fett's side, Zuckuss quickly scanned the perimeter of the great reception hall. "There must be a couple dozen of them. At least." He took another count, looking past the raised dais in the middle of the space. "Maybe fifty of 'em—"

"Gheeta told us that he'd been preparing for this for a long time." Without turning his visored helmet, Boba Fett had taken his own estimate of the forces arrayed along the hall's perimeter. "He's obviously called in a lot of favors." This much firepower didn't come cheap; most of the mercenaries cradled late-model blaster rifles against their chests; Gheeta must have provided the weapons, as they were obviously more expensive than the usual cheap and nasty—if lethally efficient—gear with which mercenaries usually kitted themselves. These types disgusted Fett; they took no real pride in their equipment, the tools of their trade; if they did, they wouldn't spend so much of their ill-gotten pay on their own bad habits. "He couldn't pay for all this himself," continued Boba Fett aloud. "Gheeta must've gone into major hock with his other clan members."

"But what for?" Zuckuss's curved eyes reflected the ominous black-clad figures. "We're unarmed—"

"I know how Gheeta's mind works. Let's just say he's not given to taking chances. Or at least," said Fett, "not after the last time I did business with him."

Bossk had overhead the comment. "I'm ready to do business with him," the Trandoshan growled from behind Boba Fett. "Right now." His clawed hand hung close to the empty blaster holster at his side. Even without a weapon, Bossk looked ready to take on whatever army the Shell Hutts had assembled, as though he could pull each of the mercenaries apart, limb from limb, with nothing but his own brute strength. "Let's get it over with."

"It seems apparent," commented IG-88, "that your desire in that regard is about to be fulfilled."

Pushed along by his riveted casing's repulsor beams, the Shell Hutt Gheeta had floated ahead of the bounty hunters. As they reached the bottom of the steps surrounding the dais, Gheeta had already risen to the top section, where the cylinder bobbed beside a rectangular construction a little over two meters long and a quarter of that dimension in width; its surface was draped with a heavy cloth embroidered with golden thread, the corner tassels loosely knotted and flowing down the steps. On top of the cloth were towering arrangements of exotic, off-planet florals, their brilliant petals thick and heavy as flayed Tatooinian dewback hide; from their stickily wet confluence exuded cloying, opiatelike perfumes. Even through his helmet's filtration units, Boba Fett could taste the acrid molecules collecting on his tongue; they had no effect on the clarity of his own thoughts, but he saw how some of the Shell Hutts gathered closer to the dais, the pupils of their eyes narrowing as their slit nostrils widened, deeply inhaling the laden air. Their lipless mouths curved into all-encompassing pleasure.

Behind him, Boba Fett heard Bossk snort in disgust. He knew that the Trandoshan nervous system lacked any receptor sites for the flowers' narcotic fragrance; any scent less subtle than rotting meat was wasted on him. "Lovely." Bossk sneered. "Looks like you've got the place ready for a funeral."

"How perceptive of you!" Gheeta had perhaps inhaled too deeply, though the scent appeared to have a stimulant rather than a soporific effect on him. "Exactly so!" The floating cylinder spun about, bringing the Shell Hutt's face, luminous with toxic sweat, toward the bounty hunters. Ramping up the strength of the repulsor beams, Gheeta floated above the rank-smelling blossoms, the thick petals quivering with the unseen force. "How often, though, that we fail to understand—" The crablike mechanical hands reached down and scooped through the floral mass, gathering the bright colors and pulpy tissues to the underside of the cylinder. For a moment the crushed blossoms obscured the lower half of Gheeta's face; then his ecstatic expression was revealed again as the gleaming metal appendages flung themselves wide, scattering the flowers across the steps of the dais. "We fail to *appreciate* what a joyous occasion a funeral can be!"

The overripe stench of the flowers filled the inside of Boba Fett's helmet as the petals, bruised and crushed by Gheeta's mechanical arms, fell across the toes of his boots. He looked down at them for a moment, then kicked the flowers away; the heaviest of them left wet, bleeding trails across the inlaid floor of the great reception hall.

"I don't have much of a feeling for funerals," said Fett evenly. He looked up across the dais steps toward Gheeta. "One way or the other."

"Oh, but you should! You *will!*" Gheeta's manner became even more frenetic and excited. The cylinder vibrated as it hovered in place, as though the fever of the creature inside had somehow been transmitted to the enclosing metal. Some of the other Shell Hutts edged away from the central dais, as though fearful of an explosion; Gheeta's agitation had even pierced the stupor of those who had fallen furthest beneath the blooms' heavy fragrance. "I guarantee it!"

"Watch out," said Zuckuss in a low voice. From the corner of his sight, behind the dark visor of his helmet, Boba Fett saw Zuckuss's warning nod toward the edges of the space. But Fett was already conscious of what was happening there: Some of the black-uniformed mercenaries had stepped forward from the alcoves and adjoining corridors where they had first appeared. There were other motions, of weapons being raised, the shoulder straps of the blaster rifles slackening as the barrels were swung up into firing position, the rifle butts braced against the mercenaries' hips. He could see Bossk and IG-88 turning their heads, scanning the details of the trap closing tighter around them. Zuckuss's voice sounded tight with apprehension: "I think they're going to make their move. . . ."

Fett knew that nothing was going to happen, at least not for another few seconds; the cylindrical shapes of the Shell Hutts were still bobbing and floating around, too close to the dais and the team of off-planet bounty hunters. Even as trigger-happy as this bunch of thugs was likely to be, they would still know better than to start shooting while their employers were in the line of fire. And besides, there was one more thing that he was absolutely sure of. Gheeta's little show wasn't over yet. . . .

"You wanted to talk business?" The Shell Hutt's voice had spiraled up into a screech, loud enough to flutter the wattles at his pallid throat. "Fine! Let us do just that! But as you said, there's no point unless the merchandise in question is there on the table, right in front of us!"

"Gheeta . . ." The elder Nullada grabbed hold of the collar of Gheeta's cylinder with a metal-clawed hand. "Don't make more of a fool of yourself than you already have—"

"Silence!" One of Gheeta's crablike hands furiously knocked away the larger Shell Hutt's grasp. "You'll see as well! All of you!" The faces of the other Shell Hutts, protruding from the collars of the floating cylinders, turned toward Gheeta, some with expressions of muddled astonishment, others cruelly relishing the spectacle that was being played out before them. "You were all pleased enough when this scoundrel"—the claw point of one of Gheeta's hands shot out, gesturing toward Boba Fett—"when this *thief* stole from me that which was to be my crowning glory!" Both of the crablike mechanical hands flung upward, indicating the great reception hall's vaulted roof and all that it contained. Gheeta's mad-

dened gaze crossed over Nullada and the other Shell
Hutts. "Don't think I didn't hear your sniggering
jeers and laughter! You were happy to see me fallen
and disgraced, weren't you?"

Boba Fett discerned now that Gheeta's escalating
shrillness was due to more than the intoxicants released by the mounds of flowers and their viscous,
oozing centers. Enough of Gheeta's thick neck had
protruded from his floating cylinder that a thin tube
could be seen, almost buried in the folds of his gray
skin; the tube ended in a surgically implanted IV tap,
a needle plunged and sealed into Gheeta's bloodstream. The tube's other end was concealed inside
the cylinder; Fett could surmise that it was hooked
up to a time-metered dispensary module, leaking
some rage-provoking stimulant through the Shell
Hutt's central nervous system. Just as Boba Fett had
already suspected, the sight of the pharmaceutical
tube confirmed that Gheeta had prepared for this
confrontation by chemically stripping out any sense
of caution that might still have been lingering inside
his brain. Suicidally so; with his having gone this far
out of control, there would be no way that the other
Shell Hutts would let him continue living and operating in their midst. There was a line beyond which
honor and the desire for vengeance interfered with
business, and Gheeta was now obviously well past it.

The others were getting there as well; a sense of
panic tinged the air inside the great reception hall as
the Shell Hutts' floating cylinders collided with each
other, reversing away from the central dais, then
turning and perceiving the armed and ready mercenaries stationed around the perimeter. Some of the
Hutts were obviously fuddled enough by the heavy
opiatelike scent of the scattered florals to have lost
all reasoning ability. That was the main reason that

Boba Fett had programmed the air filters in his helmet to catch and expunge those intoxicating molecules; more than that, he had paid hefty amounts to the galaxy's finest black-market microsurgeons to have the corresponding receptor sites stripped away from the branching ends of his own nervous system. Whatever stimulation to the pleasure centers of his brain that might have been lost thereby was more than compensated for by the control he retained in situations like this; in his business, he couldn't afford the simpleminded hysteria to which the Shell Hutts were already succumbing. From the corners of his vision, as he continued focusing on Gheeta at the top of the dais, he could discern the repulsor-borne cylinders slamming harder into each other, the riveted durasteel plates clanging like an atonal percussion section; the crablike mechanical hands tangled with each other and clawed at the wide-eyed, panting faces of the Shell Hutts as they twisted and spun about, rebounding in fear from the exits, blocked by the blaster-toting mercenaries.

Gheeta was caught up in a spiraling feedback loop, his own overexcited state mounting as it absorbed the frightened, lunatic pulse from the other Shell Hutts. "And you were laughing, too! I know you were!" One of the mechanical hands slung beneath his floating cylinder suddenly jabbed toward Boba Fett, the metal shimmering with the fury of his accusation. "All the way back to whatever hole that scummy architect paid you to hide him in—" Gheeta's lipless mouth had stretched into a frenzied grimace, far enough that a trickle of blood seeped into the milky salivation leaking from its corners. "That was a good joke, Fett! But the best jokes always come with a price attached to them, don't they?"

"Ancient history," said Boba Fett. He could almost feel sorry for the Shell Hutt, locked inside an account that he could never settle to his profit. Almost, but not quite; sympathy was something else that he'd stripped from his nervous system, using the scalpel of his own transforming will. "We came here to talk about other merchandise. We're here for Oph Nar Dinnid."

"Ah, yes!" Gheeta's eyes grew wider and more maniacal as the IV tube pulsed like an artificial vein at the wattles of his neck. "And the merchandise should always be on the table, shouldn't it, before we can start dealing—that's how you want things, isn't it? Then by all means—"

The dangling mechanical hands suddenly shot forward from beneath Gheeta's encasing shell and seized hold of the edge of the dais's central platform. The remaining florals, oozing sap from their broken petals, slid from the top surface and landed wetly across the steps as the thin metal arms tensed, lifting one side of the rectangular shape. From the floating cylinder came a high-pitched whine as the repulsor-beam engines strained against the additional load. That was followed by the grinding, tearing noise of decorative masonry being ripped apart as the rectangular platform came loose from the dais and tilted toward one side. Gheeta gave a final, convulsive push, and the platform tore free and toppled down the dais's encircling steps.

For a moment the panicked motion in the great reception hall ebbed; the crash of the platform at the feet of Boba Fett and the other bounty hunters had been loud enough to distract the fleeing Shell Hutts from their attempts at escape. At the exits, still blocked by the insignialess mercenaries, the floating cylinders turned, their wide-faced occupants looking back toward the figures at the center of the vaulted space.

Plaster dust floated up from the wreckage of the platform; it now looked like a coffin that had been shattered open in a clumsy attempt at excavation, the thin plastoid sides forced apart from each other by the repeated impact of the steps. In the midst of the debris, draped shroudlike by the embroidered cloth, with a single broken-stemmed floral lying on its chest like a bad joke, was a humanoid form, empty eye sockets gazing up at the reception hall's distant ceiling. Without even looking at the man's face, Boba Fett knew who it was.

"There's your Oph Nar Dinnid." Gheeta's voice came from the top of the dais, gloating at the rubble strewn across the floor. "Not such valuable merchandise now, is he?"

From behind Boba Fett, the elder Shell Hutt Nullada pushed forward, hard enough to shove Bossk and IG-88 to one side; the riveted cylinder scraped sparks from the unmoving armor of D'harhan. Fett looked over at the massive figure hovering next to him and saw that Nullada's face was quivering with rage. The silken lines holding up the rolls of fat above the eyes and mouth were shimmering like the bowstrings of an ancient projectile weapon.

"This is madness!" As Nullada shouted at Gheeta he shook one of his mechanical hands, clenched into a compact fist. "Vengeance is one thing—we all desire that—but now . . ." The old Shell Hutt sputtered with incoherent anger. "Now you're interfering with *business!* That creature was valuable to us. He was *credits* . . . and now he's dead *meat.*"

"Calm yourself." Gheeta sneered at the other Shell Hutt. " 'Business' has been taken care of. Perhaps not to your satisfaction, but to mine. And to the satisfaction of the Narrant-system clan whose trade secrets our late guest had stolen and was busily selling to us. I have been in direct communication with the unfortunate victims of Oph Nar Dinnid's larceny, and I encouraged them to set a price on those trade secrets—not on what it would cost to get those secrets back, but on what it would cost to make sure that no one else would be privy to them. In other words, the price of Oph Nar Dinnid's immediate death. The clan made their calculations, named their price, and I accepted on behalf of the Shell Hutts."

"You . . . you had no right to do that. . . ."

"That shows how old and senile you've become." Gheeta's sneer turned even more withering. "You've forgotten that there are no rights, except those that you take unto yourself." The mechanical hands rose, claws curling into sharp-edged fists. "Our treasury is richer now for the dealing that I have done on my own initiative."

"Idiot!" Thick drops of spittle flew from Nullada's mouth. "There's no way that you could have gotten a price from the Narrant system anywhere close to what the information inside Dinnid's head was worth."

"Perhaps not." Gheeta's hands spread apart in a gesture of unconcern. "But the price I got is paid *now,* and not doled out over some twenty years to come. Credits in one's pocket are worth more than the credits that might be sprinkled someday over your grave." An ugly smile welled up on his wide face, like inscribed driftwood surfacing in rubbish-clogged waters. "A grave that I think you'll be in sooner than I will be."

"Silence!" The roar was deafening; it came from Bossk, thrusting himself to the foot of the steps that surrounded the dais. One of his clawed hands shoved aside the floating cylinder of the elder Shell Hutt Nullada. With his other hand, Bossk stepped forward and grabbed the front of the sprawled corpse's jacket, singed with laser fire and stiff with dried blood. "I've heard enough of your endless bickering—" He held the lifeless figure of Oph Nar Dinnid up in front of himself, the corpse's feet dangling inches above the tessellated floor. "*This* is what we came here for?" The corpse danced like a loose-limbed puppet as Bossk angrily shook it. No answer came from Dinnid's slack mouth, the skin of his face turned as pallid and gray as that of the surrounding Hutts. With an inarticulate growl, Bossk flung the corpse back down into the rubble of the dais's broken platform. "That creature's been dead for weeks! I can *smell* his death on him!" Bossk's nostrils flared back, showing his involuntary disgust. Just as with Hutts, Trandoshans were the type of carnivore that preferred its meat fresh. He turned his slit-eyed glare toward Boba Fett. "He was dead before we ever left the Bounty Hunters Guild. This is a fool's errand you've brought us on!" The corner of one scaly lip curled in a sneer. "The great Boba Fett, the *master* of bounty hunters, and he didn't even know that the merchandise was already worthless."

Boba Fett had known that that accusation would come before long, and he had briefly debated with himself about how to answer it. *I could say nothing*—he was not given to explaining his actions and strategies to anyone, let alone a crude, rapacious thug like Bossk. Or he could lie to Bossk, tell him that he hadn't known, or even suspected, that Oph Nar Dinnid had already been killed, long before he'd assembled this team of bounty hunters to come here to Circumtore. Or . . .

"I knew," said Boba Fett quietly. "Why wouldn't I? I've dealt with these creatures before, and I know how their minds work. Especially"—he gestured toward Gheeta, still floating at the top of the dais—"when what's left of one's mind is eaten away with the desire for vengeance."

"Wait a second." At Fett's other side, Zuckuss stared at him, astonishment detectable even through the curved lenses of the smaller bounty hunter's face mask. "You knew all along? But if you knew that Oph Nar Dinnid had already been killed . . . then there was no point in coming here. . . ."

"No point," growled Bossk, "unless Fett wanted to get us all killed as well." He tilted his head toward the perimeter of the great reception hall. The armed mercenaries had stepped farther from the alcoves and exits, herding the other Shell Hutts before them. "Is that it?" Bossk turned his hard gaze back toward Boba Fett. "Maybe you were feeling suicidal—maybe you're tired of being a bounty hunter—so you decided to take some of us with you. That's why you were so willing to hand over our weapons and render us defenseless."

"Don't be an idiot." Fett returned the other's gaze. "Or at least not any more of one than you have to be. You may be without weapons—for the time being—but we were never without defenses. No one walks naked into the midst of creatures like these."

"No one . . . except somebody who's ready to die."

"I'll let you know," said Boba Fett, "when that time comes. But right now I have other *business* to take care of." He raised one arm, turning it so that the inside of his wrist faced him; between that and his elbow was a relay-linked control pad. With the forefinger of his other gloved hand, Fett began punching out a command sequence.

"Calling up your ship, are you?" Gheeta had caught sight of what Boba Fett was doing. "Do you really believe that your precious *Slave I* can get out of our landing docks? It's sealed down tight with tractor beams. And even if it could break away, what good would it do you? It's as stripped of armaments as your pathetic selves."

Boba Fett ignored him. It was a long series of digits to get past the control pad's encryption circuits, and then another one to initiate the program he desired. That one was buried years deep in his memory, but on matters such as this, his memory was infallible. It had to be; in circumstances such as this, he wasn't likely to be given another chance.

"Is it a bluff, then?" The taunting voice of the Shell Hutt came from atop the dais. "How sad for you to think I'd fall for something as simpleminded as that. If you want me to believe that you have some secret plan that will save your skins, you'll have to do a lot better than punching a few meaningless control buttons."

Standing next to Boba Fett, Zuckuss fidgeted and gazed with alarm around the great reception hall. "*Is there a plan?*" His eyes were like curved mirrors, showing the distorted images of the dark-uniformed mercenaries. "You have one, don't you?"

One of the other bounty hunters gave up waiting. With a guttural curse in his native Trandoshan tongue, Bossk reached down and snatched up a long, jagged-ended piece of the wreckage from the dais's top platform. As he lifted it shoulder-high, gripping one end with both his clawed fists, a tiny strip of bloodstained cloth fluttered pennantlike, a scrap from the Dinnid corpse's torn and charred clothing. "They're not taking *me* down without a—"

Bossk's words were lost in the sudden roar of an explosion. Its force struck Boba Fett, a surge of heat and durasteel-hard pressure full against his chest. He remained upright in the storm, his own weight already braced against its impact. The visor of his helmet flashed darker for a microsecond, to protect his sight from the blinding glare. Sharp-edged pieces of debris struck his shoulders, then were swept on by the billows of smoke that poured out from where the dais and its surrounding steps had been.

As the smoke began to thin, restoring visibility to the center of the great reception hall, Boba Fett took his gloved hand away from the control pad on his opposite forearm. The command sequence, keyed to the long-dormant receptor buried in the hall's foundation, had done its job. Perfectly, just as it had been designed and he had expected it to.

The explosion had caught Gheeta unawares— also as Fett had expected—and its force had sent the Shell Hutt's cylinder tumbling and crashing against one of the hall's supporting pillars, hard enough to dent one of the riveted plates and bend the column, its top wrenching loose from the vaulted ceiling above. Gheeta's eyes were dazed, bordering on unconsciousness; a rivulet of blood seeped through the rolls and crevices of his broad face from where the pharmaceutical IV line had been torn out from the vein. The plastoid tube now lay on the rubble-strewn ground like a dead serpent, its single fang weeping drop after drop of a clear liquid.

Some distance behind Boba Fett, the larger cylinder encasing the elder Nullada slowly righted itself, like a planetary oceangoing vessel that had been swamped by a tidal wave. The cylinder rolled from side to side as Nullada groaned in dizzied confusion. The silken lines holding up his face's obscuring rolls of blubbery tissue had all snapped; his repulsive Huttese features, the large yellowed eyes and slavering lipless mouth, appeared and disappeared as gravity shifted the gray wattles back and forth.

"What . . . what was . . ." A gloved hand rose from the tangled, still-smoking rubble directly in front of Boba Fett. The explosion had knocked Zuckuss backward, his breath mask covered with dust and gray flecks of ash. A few broken scraps of construction material, the charred remains of the dais's top platform, tumbled down his chest as he struggled to raise himself up on his elbows. "I can't . . ."

Right now Boba Fett couldn't give the fallen Zuckuss any assistance. The chaos into which the explosion had plunged the great reception hall was still at a peak—past the settling billows of smoke could be heard the cursing and shouts of the armed mercenaries as the frightened Shell Hutts gibbered and collided with each other and their floating cylinders pushed toward the building's exits. That wouldn't last long, Fett knew; even security guards as ill-trained and poorly paid as these would eventually be able to sort things out. He stepped over the struggling body in front of him—one of Zuckuss's gloved hands reached, but failed to catch hold of Fett's boot—and strode quickly into the center of the dais's smoldering wreckage.

As he reached down for the shock-protected container of hardened durasteel that he knew would be there, a bolt from a laser rifle shot a fraction of an inch to one side of Boba Fett's head, then struck and sparked against a pillar farther on. Fett quickly turned, his muscles tensing to dive away from the angle of the following shot—

There wasn't one. The dark-uniformed mercenary that had come sprinting into the hall's center, rifle lifted, was felled by a long section of rubble swung level into his gut. His momentum folded him around the improvised weapon; the mercenary then collapsed onto his face as Bossk's clawed fist struck him with a vertebra-cracking blow to the back of the neck. Bossk threw away the piece of scrap and scooped up the mercenary's blaster rifle. Fett saw a look of fierce delight in the Trandoshan's eyes as Bossk whipped the rifle around, a level arc of bright fire cutting through the smoke and across the other mercenaries who had been foolish enough to move away from the security of the perimeter alcoves.

That'll hold them for a while, thought Boba Fett as he tugged at the end handle of the tube-shaped container, caught tight by the rubble collapsed around it. More laser bolts stitched the air around him with their burning tracery; he glanced over his shoulder and saw Bossk, standing with legs braced wide apart, squeeze the blaster rifle's trigger stud with wild disregard for the counterfire now coming from all directions. IG-88, with the cold rationality typical of droids, had grabbed the weapon of another dark-uniformed figure that had been cut nearly in half by one of Bossk's initial shots; crouching down behind the corpse and a jagged sheet of bent plastoid construction material, IG-88 carefully aimed and picked off its targets.

Another sight had caught Boba Fett's eye even as he wrapped both hands around the durasteel tube's molded grip, braced his boot sole against the singed remnants of one of the platform's side panels, and tugged harder; as he tilted back, arms locked straight down to the tube, a laser shot sizzled through the exact space in which his head had just been. The streak of light temporarily set his helmet visor blind and opaque, so that it was only behind his eyelids that Boba Fett could still see the image of D'harhan, roused from his silent torpor by the sounds of combat echoing inside the great reception hall's spaces. As the mercenaries' fire streaked past D'harhan like a giant spiderweb set aflame, the barrel of the laser cannon, inert and silenced, rose upward, as though it were the neck and head of some primeval beast, taunted to madness by its captors. The optics of the cannon's tracking systems pulsed red through the clouds of hissing steam emitted from the apertures of the black metal housing; as the reptilelike balancing tail thrashed behind him D'harhan's arms spread wide, black-gloved hands clawing into themselves, trembling with their thwarted desire for destruction. A keening, wordless howl sounded from deep within the machinery curving into the creature's heart.

The visor of Boba Fett's helmet cleared as he looked back down at the container trapped in the dais's wreckage. Another tug, putting all of his weight and force into it, and the metal tube finally scraped through the debris, shedding flakes of rust. A dot of green light beside the handle told Fett that the container's seal was still intact, the object inside still as primed and ready to go as it had been when first hidden here, during the construction of the great reception hall.

With a last dragging rasp of metal against metal, the tubular container came free. Boba Fett caught himself from toppling backward, then cradled the heavy object in his arms. As he turned he saw Zuckuss pulling himself upright, a few meters away. The disorienting effects of the explosion had obviously faded from inside the smaller bounty hunter's head; Fett could see the enlightenment behind the other's insectoid eyes, the sudden understanding of all that Zuckuss had been told before. Surrounded by the noise and quick glare of laser bolts, he even managed a slight nod of acknowledgment, to show that he had just now realized what Boba Fett had meant when he had told him those few fragments of the deal that had been struck between a bounty hunter and an architect. *An investment, that pays off later. In a big way . . .*

"Here!" That was Bossk's shout, from a few meters away. Another mercenary, braver or stupider than the rest, had come charging head down toward the Trandoshan, and had actually gotten close enough that Bossk had taken him out with a single blow to the chin, swinging the butt of the blaster rifle around in an upward arc. Another jab of the rifle butt, right between the mercenary's eyes, had made sure he'd be no further trouble. "Get busy!" Bossk had reached down and grabbed a blaster pistol from the holster slung at the fallen mercenary's hip, and now tossed it underhand to Zuckuss. "We could use a little help!"

Zuckuss caught the blaster in both hands and continued holding it that way as he pressed the trigger stud, sending a wild spray of fire across the reception hall as he rolled onto his shoulder, dodging the bolt that dug a molten gash through the floor where he had been kneeling.

The added fire gave Boba Fett enough cover that he could turn with the durasteel tube in his arms and sprint toward D'harhan, still howling in impotent rage at the glaring blaster streaks that laced through the reddened clouds of steam. Before he had taken more than a couple of steps away from the dais wreckage, a pair of thin mechanical arms wrapped themselves around Boba Fett's neck, their crablike claws scrabbling at the visor of his helmet.

Eyes starting from their fat-swaddled sockets, the Shell Hutt Gheeta squealed in maddened rage; blood webbed his broad face as the force of his encasing cylinder's repulsors knocked Boba Fett off balance. Fett managed to remain standing; for a split second he was lifted almost clear of the red-spattered floor as Gheeta dragged him upward by the neck. Then he twisted around in the Shell Hutt's sharp-edged grasp and swung the length of the tube-shaped container around into the side of Gheeta's skull. The impact left a trenchlike dent in the gray, wobbling flesh; Gheeta's eyes went unfocused as the crablike mechanical hands flopped apart, dropping Boba Fett.

There wasn't time, as much as Fett might have wanted, to finish off Gheeta. From the other side of the great reception hall, beyond the erect, howling figure of D'harhan, a volley of blaster fire singed past Fett. With the container tucked under one arm, he grabbed the bolted seams of Gheeta's floating cylinder, gloved fingertips digging a hold on to the metal. Gheeta's dazed eyes rolled as Boba Fett shoved the cylinder ahead of himself as a shield. A frightened scream escaped from the Shell Hutt's mouth as the mercenaries' laser bolts stung and sparked against the cylinder's curved flank.

When he reached D'harhan, he shoved Gheeta aside, with enough force to send him bobbing and twisting into the cross fire that filled the center of the reception hall. The immense form of D'harhan reared above Boba Fett, the inert laser cannon shrouded by hissing steam, the heavy arms crucified against the glare of the mercenaries' rifle fire. Above the cannon's barrel, the optics of D'harhan's tracking systems focused upon the helmeted figure stepping within range of the tearing hands.

Boba Fett halted; with one quick motion, he unscrewed the end cap of the tube-shaped container. The seal hissed, higher-pitched than the steam escaping from the laser cannon's black metal housing, as air rushed into the vacuum. Tilting the container, Fett slid out a fully charged reactor core. He lifted one end of the core in his hands as though he were aiming a rifle, then stepped forward and thrust it into the gaping hole of the receptor site in D'harhan's chest.

When they had been aboard the *Slave I,* D'harhan had howled with the pain of an essence-deep violation as Boba Fett had drawn out a core just like this one. Now a sharp intake of breath sounded inside the throat hidden beneath the laser cannon's barrel; D'harhan's back arched, his segmented tail thrashing convulsively across the broken rubble around him. Every neuron and sinew of D'harhan's frame tensed and surged in sync with his accelerating pulse as the bounty hunter's fist turned inside the exposed chest, locking the reactor core into place.

The pulse of D'harhan's blood seemed to shatter the barrier between flesh and machine as the indicator lights along the laser cannon's housing flashed in a microsecond from yellow to a fiery red. As Boba Fett slammed the locking armature into its socket, then spun and dived for the floor, the cannon barrel swung down from nearly vertical to aiming level. The heat from D'harhan's first shot scorched Fett's spine and shoulder blades as he used the corpse of another dead mercenary to pull himself to a safe distance.

He found the mercenary's blaster rifle and held it to his chest as he rolled onto his back. Pushing himself up with one hand, Fett saw another cannon bolt, a hundred times wider and more destructive than the other shots cutting across the great reception hall's space, enough to rip a hole through the light armor of an Imperial cruiser. And more than enough to reduce one entire wing of the building to charred splinters. Through the rising dust of fractured stone, Boba Fett could hear the screams and shouts of the Shell Hutts and their hired thugs as one pillar and then another toppled into the center of the hall, bringing down a section of roof and exposing the dark sky of Circumtore.

D'harhan turned where he stood, segmented metal tail bracing himself against the recoil of the laser cannon borne by his shoulders and torso. The cannon's barrel rocked back in its housing as another white-hot bolt coursed across the hall, scattering a knot of mercenaries. The screams of the Shell Hutts actually diminished, their panic having increased to the point where all notion of escape had been abandoned. Tortoiselike, each one drew his head back into the safety of his floating cylinder; when the last throat wattle was past the circular metal collar at the front of the cylinder, a ring of crescent blades irised toward the opening's center, sealing off the Shell Hutt inside. The blind cylinders bobbed and collided with each other, pushed and spun by the blaster fire striking their riveted plates.

A few meters away from Boba Fett, a blaster shot went straight toward the reception hall's ceiling; a quick glance to the side showed him that a shot from one of the mercenaries had struck Bossk at one side of his chest, knocking the Trandoshan off his feet and sending him splayed out on the dais's smoldering rubble. Fett swiveled the rifle in his hands and blew away the mercenary, a broken corpse even before he hit the floor.

Another one of the mercenaries had taken command of the remaining dark-uniformed figures; Boba Fett could see the man at the hall's perimeter, signaling to the others and directing their fire. The aim of their blaster rifles turned away from Fett, as well as IG-88 and Zuckuss. A concentrated volley singed the air past the three bounty hunters. Crouching down, Boba Fett turned and saw D'harhan standing in the middle of the fusillade, like a watchtower braced against the onslaught of a storm; the blaster fire sowed hot sparks across the black metal, as though each hit was a lightning strike seen through illuminated clouds.

D'harhan managed to get off one more shot of his own before he was cut down. The laser cannon roared, its massive bolt ripping open another section of the flame-scorched walls and scattering one wing of the mercenaries. Metal could have stood up to their fire even longer, but D'harhan's flesh was weaker than that; the torso beneath the laser cannon's housing was now wrapped in bloodied rags. His knees slowly gave way, and he toppled forward. The cannon's barrel struck the floor as though it had been one of the roof pillars giving way, gouging out a meter-long trench.

He was still alive; Boba Fett could see the laboring of D'harhan's heart and lungs, the rise of the blood-smeared chest forcing itself against the curved mount of the laser-cannon housing. The black-gloved hands rose and tore feebly at the wounds, as though death were something that could be plucked from the torn flesh and exposed fragments of breastbone and rib.

The cannon was alive as well; the indicators

along the barrel showed an unblinking red, bright through the hissing steam. All it needed was a hand on the triggering mechanism, and the will to fire. . . .

Boba Fett threw away the blaster rifle he had taken from one of the dead mercenaries. Ducking beneath the fiery bolts crisscrossing the reception hall, he stepped behind the massive bulk of the fallen D'harhan; with his own adrenaline-charged strength, he gripped the semiconscious figure beneath the arms and half dragged, half lifted him up against the base of a broken pillar. A sudden gasp sounded from within the other's body as Fett grabbed and yanked loose the thick neural-feed cables that had been connected to D'harhan's spine, the hard-spliced socket just between his shoulder blades. The laser cannon's aiming systems automatically went into manual override status; Boba Fett crouched behind the black metal housing as the barrel swung upward.

And into firing position. A small screen tucked underneath the rear of the housing lit up, with a crosshair grid zeroing in on the mercenaries positioned at the far side of the great reception hall. The barrel turned slightly as Boba Fett's hand jabbed at the controls, seeking a specific target; the grid's lines narrowed in and locked on the one dark-uniformed figure who had taken command of the others. Long-range thermal sensors in the laser cannon's tracking systems gave a clear outline of the mercenary behind a shield of bent and torn plastoid construction material. Enough to hide behind . . . but not enough to protect him. Fett hit the cannon's firing stud. The weapon's recoil trembled the black metal housing, its shock traveling all the way up his arms and into his own chest.

The single bolt from the laser cannon took out

most of the remaining mercenaries. When Boba Fett raised his head from behind the housing, he sighted through the clouds of steam, hissing louder now to dissipate the heat from the metal. The far side of the hall was gone now; the violet-tinged light of Circumtore's skies was framed by twisted structural beams, their ends glowing molten. Across the open plaza beyond the reception hall, the bodies of the mercenary commander and the ones who had died with him were scattered like broken toys. Inside the hall, the few that were left alive had ceased firing, pointing the muzzles of their weapons up toward the ceiling; the brutal effectiveness of the laser cannon had set them to reconsidering their ill-paid devotion to the cause for which Gheeta had hired them. A couple of the mercenaries—the smartest of them, Boba Fett figured—made a show of tossing their blaster rifles onto the debris-covered floor in front of them, then raising their hands above their heads.

"Cowards! Traitors!" A hysterical cry came from behind Boba Fett. With his hands still on the controls of the laser cannon, he turned his head and saw the repulsor-borne cylinder of the Shell Hutt Gheeta come darting forward into the center of the reception hall's ruins. "I paid you for results," shouted Gheeta, "not for you to run away and hide!" The crablike mechanical arms shook in impotent fury. "Get him! Now!" The floating cylinder turned as Gheeta jabbed a claw in Boba Fett's direction. "I order you to—"

Gheeta's words broke off as he saw the laser cannon's barrel swiveling toward him. His eyes widened in their fat-heavy sockets as the indicator lights glowed an even brighter red, as though they were points of blood squeezed out by Boba Fett's hands tightening on the black metal.

"No . . ." Gheeta moaned in sudden fright. The crablike arms fluttered in front of him as the cylinder started to back away. "Don't . . ." He pulled his head back inside the cylinder's collar, which then began to iris shut.

But not fast enough. Boba Fett pushed forward on the laser cannon's housing; steam hissed between his gloved fingers as he lowered his shoulder and put his weight into the thrust. Dragging the still-breathing body of D'harhan along, the weapon's barrel lurched forward. The black metal muzzle, shimmering with residual heat, slammed into the vacated collar of Gheeta's floating cylinder just as the curved blades of the seal mechanism locked down tight upon it.

Boba Fett shifted his weight, now pushing down upon the rear of the laser-cannon housing. The barrel angled upward, with the Shell Hutt's cylinder attached like a ripe gourdfruit. When the barrel had reached its maximum elevation, Fett struck the firing stud with his fist.

All eyes in the great reception hall—those of the other bounty hunters, the mercenaries left alive, even the other Shell Hutts who were brave enough to unseal the fronts of their cylinders when the fighting had quieted—turned toward the tapered metal shape that for a moment stood aloft on the black stem of the laser cannon. A few of the observers flinched, but continued watching as the weapon sounded its snarling roar, only slightly muffled by the object clamped onto the barrel's muzzle.

The sound of the laser cannon's bolt echoed through the great reception hall, then faded like the last thunder of a storm broken by daylight. Lightning had flashed, contained with the cylinder caught at the end of the cannon's barrel; it had burst through the seams of the bolted durasteel plates, sending a rain of white-hot rivets arcing across the space and landing like sizzling hail on the rubble left by the battle. When the light of the laser-cannon bolt was gone, as quickly as it had flashed into being, the plates of the Shell Hutt's cylinder were singed around their edges; they rattled dully against each other as the cylinder contracted again, the surge of energy that had forced it larger now only an afterimage burned into the observers' eyes.

Boba Fett lowered the laser cannon's barrel, and the cylinder slid off the end of its muzzle. The cylinder fell to the great reception hall's floor with a lifeless clang. Slowly, a red pool formed around it as Gheeta's liquefied corpse seeped through the joins between the plates and out the empty rivet holes.

"Just as well," wheezed another Shell Hutt's voice. The elder Nullada floated toward the dead cylinder; it looked like a mechanical egg, cracked but not yet peeled of its metal shell. The claws of one of Nullada's crablike arms held back the roll of blubbery tissue over his eyes; with the other he prodded the side of what had been Gheeta's metal casing. Silently, the cylinder rolled back and forth in the red mire. "He had already made more of a nuisance of himself than he had any right to."

That statement, Boba Fett figured, would probably be the extent of Gheeta's obituary. Hutts of any variety were not given to sentimentality. If the late Gheeta had left any estate after having paid off the Narrant-system liege-holder clan and hiring this band of mercenaries—though he had probably gotten them fairly cheap—the remaining assets would be quickly picked apart and swallowed up by the other

Shell Hutts. Nullada himself would no doubt take the largest bite.

At the elder Shell Hutt's direction, a couple of the dark-uniformed mercenaries had come over and dragged Oph Nar Dinnid's body out from under the wreckage of the central dais. "*Most* distressing," said Nullada, with genuine if predacious regret. "This is what happens when someone lets their emotions get in the way of business. We could have gotten a lot more from those parties with an interest in this matter."

Boba Fett wasn't listening to the old Shell Hutt. With Zuckuss and IG-88 watching him, the weapons in their hands lowered, he laid D'harhan's body down upon the floor. The laser-cannon barrel turned and slowly came to rest, its muzzle scraping through the charred debris.

D'harhan's black-gloved hands fumbled for the voice box clipped to his waist. The rise and fall of his chest, pinned by the cannon's curved mount, was quick and labored as a single fingertip punched out a message. Kneeling beside him, Boba Fett looked at the words glowing on the box's screen.

I SHOULD NOT HAVE TRUSTED YOU.

"That's right," said Fett, with a single nod. "That was your mistake."

YOU'RE WRONG. The fingertip moved with agonizing slowness. IT WAS . . . MY DECISION. . . .

Fett said nothing. He waited for the rest of D'harhan's silent words.

I CAN STOP NOW . . . BUT YOU . . . The black-gloved fingertip moved from letter to letter on the voice box's keypad. YOU STILL MUST GO ON. . . .

The hand fell away from the box. D'harhan's forearm struck the ground beside his body. There was no more breath or pulse lifting his chest; after a moment Boba Fett reached over and switched off the last of the laser cannon's red-lit controls.

He stood up and turned toward the other bounty hunters. "We're done here," said Fett. "Now we can go."

17

Zuckuss looked up into the old Trandoshan's eyes, into the black slits of that hard reptilian gaze. And said, "Everything happened the way you wanted it to."

"Good." Cradossk slowly nodded as he turned away. "I expected that."

I bet you did, thought Zuckuss. Being back here in the private quarters of the Bounty Hunters Guild's leader gave him the creeps. This was where Cradossk had sucked him into the distasteful little conspiracy that would result in Bossk's death. It struck Zuckuss, not for the first time, that these Trandoshans were indeed cold-blooded, right down to the marrow of their fenestrated bones. The only thing that could account for their hot tempers was the strength of their carnivorous appetites.

That cold blood had never been more in evidence than just now, when he had told Cradossk the details of what had happened on Circumtore.

"You saw it?" Cradossk had demanded an eye-witness verification of his son's death. "You saw him take the shot?"

"Right in the chest," Zuckuss had answered. "He didn't get up after that." His own blood had chilled when he spotted the little smile on Cradossk's face.

"You came straight here?" Cradossk didn't turn around to look at him again, but continued idly fiddling with a couple of pieces from the bone chamber at the far end of the spacious suite. "As soon as you landed?" The pieces were yellowy white, slender and curved; Zuckuss's own ribs twinged in painful sympathy as he recognized what they were. "You didn't talk to anyone else?"

The tubes of his face mask's breathing apparatus swung back and forth as he shook his head. "No one. Those were your orders. When . . . you know . . . when you gave me the job."

He was still sorry he'd agreed to it. Even though he'd come back from Circumtore with his own skin relatively intact, if somewhat bruised and battered from the action in the Shell Hutts' great reception hall. Going along with someone who'd been making arrangements to get his own son killed—which was what the whole futile journey to acquire an already dead piece of merchandise had been about—still turned him somewhat queasy. *Maybe Boba Fett's right,* he mused bleakly. *Maybe I'm not really cut out for the bounty-hunter trade.*

"I'm glad to see that you can follow orders." Cradossk held the rib bone up close to his aging eyes. The name of the vanquished foe to which it had once belonged was incised along its length, the marks scratched there by one of his own foreclaws. "I'm impressed with your . . . *loyalty.* And your intelligence. Both of those attributes will stand you in good stead in the difficult times before us." He sighed, lowering the memento of past glories, his gaze focusing on some far-off horizon. "How I wish that my son had possessed similar qualities. Or to put it another way—" He turned his head just enough to cast a sidelong glance at the younger bounty hunter. "If only someone such as yourself had been my off-spring."

Sure, thought Zuckuss. He kept himself from showing any other reaction. *And wind up dead, the first time you started feeling paranoid? No thanks.*

"Mark my words." Cradossk's gnarled claws gripped the bone as though it were a club suitable for thrashing miscreants. His voice rumbled lower, matching the heavy scowl on his scaly face. "If the other bounty hunters of your generation were as smart as you—and respectful of their elders' wisdom—then a great deal of trouble could be avoided. But they have . . . *ideas* of their own." He spoke the word with loathing. "Just as my son did. That's why it was so important that he be eliminated, and in a way that would not appear to have been from my conniving at that result. This way . . . to have it happen on a world far from here, and among clever, greedy creatures such as the Shell Hutts . . . it makes his death seem the inevitable consequence of his own stupidity and incompetence. So much for his new ideas." Cradossk sneered. "The old ways are the best ways. Especially when it comes to killing other creatures."

"You'd know," muttered Zuckuss under his breath.

"Did you say something?" Cradossk glanced over at him.

Zuckuss shook his head. "It was a bubble." He pointed to the dangling air tubes. "In my gear."

"Ah." Cradossk resumed his contemplation of his long-dead enemy's rib, letting it evoke deep, mus-ing thoughts. "It's good to remember these things. To be wise. More than wise; *cunning.* Because"—he nodded slowly—"there's going to be a lot more kill-ing before everything's straightened out around here."

"What do you mean?" He already knew what the old Trandoshan meant, but asked anyway. *The creaky old carnivore wants to talk,* Zuckuss told himself, *I should let him talk.* It was only polite, and it didn't cost him anything. Besides—other things were going to happen that Cradossk probably didn't know about. And those things took time to get ready.

He heard a slight noise from the doorway. Glancing over his shoulder, he saw Cradossk's ma-jordomo, the Twi'lek that was always sneaking around the place, on his own and others' shadowy errands. Ob Fortuna held one of his elongated fore-fingers to his lips, signaling Zuckuss to remain silent himself. From the corner of one large eye, Zuckuss looked over at the leader of the Bounty Hunters Guild; the old reptilian was still sunk deep in his brooding meditations. Zuckuss and the Twi'lek ex-changed a quick nod, and the Twi'lek scurried away, down the Guild's dark corridors.

"Now's not the time to start playing stupid." The ancient rib cracked in two, with a splintered fragment in each of Cradossk's tightly squeezed fists. He looked in angry surprise at what he'd just done, then tossed the relic's pieces away. He shot a hard-eyed gaze over his shoulder at Zuckuss. "Don't try telling me you're not smart enough to know what's going on around here."

"Well . . ."

"Bossk was only the first one. The first that had to be eliminated." A bone shard had been left on the back of Cradossk's hand, caught underneath one of his rough-edged scales. He extracted it and used it to pick his fangs, nodding in grim thought all the while. "There will be others; I've got a list."

I bet you do, thought Zuckuss.

"Not all of them young and foolish, either." Cradossk examined a still-wriggling fragment of food on the end of the improvised toothpick, then resumed his meditative work with it. "Some of my oldest and most trusted advisers . . . bounty hunters that I've known and supped blood with for decades . . . so to speak . . ." He ruefully shook his head. "I should've anticipated it—but then again, how could I? I *loved* these killers."

"Anticipated what?" Zuckuss knew that as well, but figured the question would keep Cradossk going awhile longer. By his calculations, the Twi'lek majordomo would need a little while longer to finish up his conspiratorial rounds.

"Traitors . . . backstabbers . . ." Cradossk's voice was a low, muttering growl. "That's what you get in this galaxy for being nice to creatures. Taking them in when they were runny-nosed little scavengers who wouldn't have known how to get their claws on a piece of merchandise if it'd been given to them with a ribbon tied around it. I taught most of these Guild members everything there *is* to know about this business."

"I imagine that's quite a lot."

"You better believe it," Cradossk said fiercely. "There's parts of the bounty-hunter trade that I *invented*. And if these scum think they can get it all away from me . . ." He chomped down on the bone toothpick, grinding it between his back fangs. "They'd better think again."

"What particular scum are you talking about?" Cradossk's mention of a list still had Zuckuss worried. The old Trandoshan might have gone senile, perhaps forgetting just who he was talking to. *Just my luck,* thought Zuckuss glumly, *to find my own name on there.*

"They know who they are. The same as I know. Though maybe . . ." Cradossk gave another slow nod. "Maybe I shouldn't take any chances. Maybe I should just have everyone killed. Wipe clean the whole roster of the Bounty Hunters Guild. Start fresh . . ."

Great, thought Zuckuss. He had been warned about this, by Boba Fett on the way back from Circumtore. Up in the *Slave I*'s cockpit area, Fett had given him another insight into the way Cradossk's mind worked. The Trandoshan had always been paranoid, long before he had clawed to the top of the Bounty Hunters Guild. Arguably, a personality trait like that was what had enabled him to do it, or had at least helped. *Hard on his associates, though,* figured Zuckuss.

"But first," said Cradossk, "we'll get rid of the obvious targets. The ones who have already announced their intentions, to either take over the Guild or split from it and set up a new bounty-hunters organization of their own. As if I'd ever let *that* happen."

Zuckuss and the others returning from Circumtore had already heard about these developments over the *Slave I*'s comm unit. The breakaway faction was eager to get as many Guild members onto its side as possible—especially the great Boba Fett and anyone associated with him. Just having been on the team Fett had assembled for the Oph Nar Dinnid job meant that Zuckuss and IG-88 were now being heavily courted by the bounty hunters who wanted to go out on their own, with an organization that wasn't controlled by the elders such as Cradossk. Always pleasant to be wanted, he supposed—as long as Cradossk and his loyalists didn't get the notion that he had switched allegiances.

"All of them?" It would be better, Zuckuss figured, if he kept the old Trandoshan brooding about creatures who weren't here in his chamber with him. "I mean—like you said—some of them have been with the Bounty Hunters Guild for a long time. Since the beginning; or at least, since you took over."

"Those are the ones I'm going to *enjoy* getting rid of." An ugly smile showed on Cradossk's face, as though he were already relishing the details of that process. "The younger bounty hunters could almost be excused for being stupid. They haven't been around long enough to know any better. But the others, the veteran bounty hunters, who've thrown in their lot with them—they could have predicted how I'd react to their treachery, their assault upon the sanctity of our brotherhood."

Zuckuss rolled his eyes upward; it was just as well that Cradossk couldn't see that reaction. He'd found out that brotherhood with carnivores, at least of the Trandoshan variety, was a negotiable concept.

"There's big changes coming," said Cradossk. "Everybody who's said that has been right—and will continue to be so. The Bounty Hunters Guild will be different from what it was before; this galaxy belongs to Emperor Palpatine now, and we'll just have to deal with that. If this breakaway faction had just bided their time and remained loyal to the Guild, they very likely would have gotten everything they want."

"Except," Zuckuss pointed out, "for getting rid of you."

Cradossk shot him a glance of venomous fury, enough to push him back a step with its intangible force. "That's right," he growled. "That's the one thing that's *not* going to happen. Count on it. The Bounty Hunters Guild is going to be a lot smaller than it was before—a lot of dead wood is going to be cleared away. I admit I should've seen it sooner, myself; that some of the elders in the organization have lost their edge. Well, they'll be gone before very much longer, whether they made the mistake of going with the breakaway faction or whether they're still sucking up to me. There's going to be a lot of blank spaces in the organizational chart; that means room for advancement. Room for someone . . . like *you*." He reached over and tapped a claw against Zuckuss's chest, right below the dangling tubes of the breathing apparatus. "A smart, young bounty hunter such as yourself could do pretty well. *If* you play your cards right."

"I'll . . . try to do my best."

"Ah, don't worry about it." Cradossk pulled the claw back and scratched his scaly chin. "The main thing you have to do is—be careful who you choose to follow, and who you choose as your associates. You've made a good start by letting yourself become a tool of my intentions. Don't screw it all up by thinking you can also be friends with . . . certain other parties."

"Like who?"

Cradossk didn't answer him for a moment. The old Trandoshan's gaze drifted again to some inner point of contemplation. "You know," he said finally, "as inevitable as I suppose this all is, it had to be brought to this crisis by one individual. If it hadn't been for *him*—the Bounty Hunters Guild might have continued as it was for quite a while, Emperor or no Emperor."

Zuckuss knew the individual to whom he referred. "You mean Boba Fett?"

"Who else?" Cradossk gave a slow nod, as though in admiration of that absent other. "It's all because of him. Everything that has happened, and that is going to happen; all the changes, and all the deaths. Well . . . most of them, at any rate. He is the unaccountable factor that has been entered into the equation. It makes you wonder . . . what were his real reasons for journeying here."

"But he told us," said Zuckuss. "When he first arrived. Because of all the changes, with the Empire and everything else—"

"And you believed him?" Cradossk shook his head. "Time for another lesson, child. There is no one you can trust—least of all someone who trades in the deaths and defeats of others. *You* can trust Boba Fett now, if you wish, but I promise you: The day will come when you'll regret it."

A chill ran through Zuckuss's spirit, or whatever was left of it after having become a bounty hunter. Part of him knew that the old Trandoshan had spoken truly; another part hoped that the day he had foretold was still a long way off.

"Well . . . I better be going." Zuckuss gestured toward the door of the private quarters. "There's still a lot I have to take care of." He was pretty sure that the Twi'lek majordomo would have had enough time by now to contact everyone that needed to be. "You know . . . since coming back from the job . . ."

"Of course." Cradossk bent down and picked up the pieces of the shattered rib bone. "I've got to learn to control my temper." Clutching the white splinters in one clawed hand, he smiled at Zuckuss. "Or do you think it's just too late for that?"

Zuckuss had stepped back toward the door. "To

be truthful . . ." He reached behind himself and grasped the door's edge. "It's too late."

"I suppose you're right." Cradossk looked suddenly older, as though weighed down with the burdens of leadership. Carrying the broken trophy from his younger days, he shuffled toward the entrance of the bone chamber, the repository of all his precious memories. "It's *always* too late. . . ."

The door to the private quarters creaked as Zuckuss pulled it farther open, but he didn't step out to the corridor beyond. He stayed where he was so he could watch what he knew was about to happen.

Which took place within seconds: Cradossk found his way blocked by his offspring Bossk. The younger Trandoshan stood with his arms folded across his chest; a wide smile split his face as he gazed down into his father's startled eyes.

"But . . ." Cradossk gaped at his son. "You . . . you're supposed to be dead. . . ."

"I know that was the plan," said Bossk, with feigned mildness. "But I made some changes to it."

Cradossk whirled about, looking back toward the private-quarters door and Zuckuss. "You lied!"

"Not entirely." Zuckuss gave a small shrug. "Just the bit about him not getting up again after he was shot."

With a single foreclaw, Bossk pointed to the sterile bandage running diagonally across his chest, from one shoulder and under the opposite arm. "It really hurt," he said, still smiling. "But it didn't kill me. *You* should know how hard our species is to get rid of. And also—whatever doesn't destroy one of us just makes us that much more pissed off."

A look of panic appeared in Cradossk's yellowed eyes; he took a step backward from the figure looming in front of him. "Now wait a minute. . . ." The bone shards fell on the floor as he raised his scaly hands, palms outward. "I think you might be making some . . . *rash* assumptions here. . . ."

One of Bossk's hands shot out, grabbing his father by the throat. "No, I'm not." The smile was gone from his face. On the other side of the private quarters, Zuckuss could see the red anger tingeing the younger Trandoshan's eyes. "I'm making the same assumption I made a long time ago, before I ever left for Circumtore. And you know what that is? It's that there isn't room in the Bounty Hunters Guild for both you *and* me."

"I . . . I don't know what you're talking about. . . ." Cradossk grabbed the other's wrist, in a futile attempt to ease his hold and get another breath into his own lungs. "The Guild . . . the Guild is for all of us. . . ."

"I'm talking about the same thing you were talking about, just now." With his other hand, Bossk pointed a clawed thumb back toward the unlit depths of the bone chamber behind him. "I was in there the whole time the two of you have been blabbing away. And I heard everything you said. All that stuff about clearing out the undesirables from the Bounty Hunters Guild. And you know what?" Bossk tightened his hold, his fist at Cradossk's throat lifting the older Trandoshan up onto the claws of his toes. "I *agree* with you about all that. You're absolutely right: The Guild is going to be a lot smaller. Real soon."

"Don't . . . don't be an idiot. . . ." Cradossk managed to summon up a reserve of courage. "You can't kill me . . . and get away with it. . . ." His claws dug deeper into Bossk's wrist, enough to let a trickle of blood seep down his son's forearm. "I've got . . . connections . . . friends. . . ." His voice became weaker and more fragmented as the hold at this throat constricted tighter. "All the . . . council of elders . . ."

"Those old fools?" Bossk sneered at his father. "I'm afraid you're a little behind the times; there have been things happening already that you just don't know about. Maybe if you didn't waste so many hours in here, mumbling and fondling your moldy reminders of past glories, these things wouldn't have sneaked up on you quite so fast." Still holding Cradossk upright, he turned and slammed the older reptilian against the table outside the bone chamber's entrance; the impact against his spine visibly dazed Cradossk. "Some of your old friends, your beloved elders, have already seen the light; they've come over to *my* side. In fact, some of them have been on my side for quite a while, just waiting for the right moment to—shall we say?—*force* your retirement. One way or another." The elaborate wording, so much different from Bossk's usual blunt speech, was a cruel way of toying with his father. "Of course, some of the elders weren't so smart; they persisted in their folly. Right up to the end."

"What . . ." Cradossk could barely squeeze any words out at all. "What do you mean . . . ?"

"Oh, come on. What do you *think* I mean?" Bossk looked disgusted. "Let's just say there are going to be some fresh acquisitions in *my* little trophy chamber. The skulls of some of your old friends will look very nice mounted on its walls—"

"Watch out!" Zuckuss shouted a warning to Bossk.

As Cradossk had fallen back against the table one of his hands had reached back and grasped an ornate ceremonial dagger; the gems embedded in its hilt flashed as he swung his arm around, the point of the blade aiming straight for Bossk's throat.

There was no way for Bossk to avoid the blade; if he had leaned back, the movement would only have presented a wider target for the blade to slash across. Instead, he lowered his head, catching the razor-sharp edge with the corner of his brow. The impact of flesh and bone against metal was enough to knock the weapon out of his father's hand and send it spinning off into a far corner of the room.

Taking a hand from his father's throat, Bossk wiped away the blood seeping down through his face scales and into his eyes. "Now that," he said with eerie self-possession, "didn't hurt at all." With a shake of his head, he sent blood spattering across Cradossk's face, as though sealing the bright ideogram of a death sentence there. "But I promise you—this *will*."

From the doorway, Zuckuss could hear shouts and blaster fire coming from somewhere else in the Guild compound. That didn't surprise him; it had been pretty much what he'd been expecting since the Twi'lek majordomo had gone off to notify the others in the breakaway faction.

He turned back toward Cradossk's private quarters and watched the rest of what happened in there. For as long as he could. Then he stepped out into the corridor, shaking his head.

Bossk was certainly right about one thing, he had to admit. It *did* take a lot to kill a Trandoshan.

The sound of the breakaway faction's weapons was heard even farther away.

Not literally; the news was reported secondhand to Kud'ar Mub'at. "Ah," the assembler purred, "that is *most* excellent!" Identifier had relayed all the details to him as they had come in from the listener nodes embedded in the web's fibrous exterior. "Isn't it pleasant," Kud'ar Mub'at asked rhetorically, "when things go *just* the way they're supposed to?" It wrapped several sets of its thin, chitinous legs around itself in a hug of self-satisfaction. "All my planning and scheming, and everything just so. Excellent! *Exceedingly* excellent!"

The assembler's multiple eyes looked around the close space of its throne room, watching how its own pleasure and excitement spread in concentric waves through all the nodes connected to the strands of his nervous system. Even the most developed and relatively independent of them, like Balancesheet, was visibly aglow, with its little claws and arachnoid legs skittering around the tangled walls as though it were the complete embodiment of the assembler's good mood.

Perhaps even a little *too* excited; ostentatiously so, it seemed to Kud'ar Mub'at. Sometimes he detected a certain false note to Balancesheet's displays of enthusiasm. *For a simple number-crunching node,* Kud'ar Mub'at found himself thinking, *that's a bit much.* He made a mental note, one that was carefully shielded from the synaptic connections that would have let the subassembler nodes in on it, to reabsorb this balancesheet and begin growing a new one. Just as soon as this business with Boba Fett and the Bounty Hunters Guild was finished . . .

It didn't seem like that would be much longer, from what the identifier node had just told Kud'ar Mub'at. Ignoring the jabbering of the nodes surrounding itself, the assembler adjusted its soft, globular abdomen into a more comfortable position in the self-generated nest; when it was done making adjustments, it contemplated the news with a calmer, more tranquil attitude. *No sense getting agitated,* it admonished itself, *over something I knew was going to happen.* Empires might rise and fall—they had before—and the galaxy might even collapse upon itself in one dark ball of relentless gravity. But until then, Kud'ar Mub'at, or some creature very much like it, would still be trading in the folly of other sentient creatures. That was its nature, just as it was the nature of those less wise to find themselves enmeshed in the traps spun for them. . . .

"Sometimes," mused Kud'ar Mub'at aloud, "they don't even know until it's too late. And sometimes they *never* know."

"Know what?" Balancesheet, a little calmer after its initial burst of enthusiasm, dangled itself close to the spiky mandibles of its parent's face. "What do you mean?"

That kind of curiosity on a subassembler's part indicated the degree of independence that Kud'ar Mub'at had let develop in the node. There hadn't even been a mention of numbers, and still this tethered offspring wanted to know. A sharp paternal feeling twinged inside Kud'ar Mub'at; it would be a shame, however necessary, to pluck the node's legs one by one and crack its shell to extract the recyclable proteins and cellular matter inside.

Kud'ar Mub'at reached out one thin black leg and stroked the ridges of Balancesheet's small head. "Creatures are dying," said Kud'ar Mub'at, "even as we speak." That had been the gist of the message transmitted through the web by the listener and identifier team of nodes. With the transport engines that had been salvaged decades ago and incorporated into the web's external structure, Kud'ar Mub'at had slowly brought its drifting home-and-body within communication range of the Bounty Hunters Guild. It had wanted to be close to where the action was happening, the pulling shut of the snare he had woven, with no delay in getting word sent out by an encrypted tight-beam signal from his contacts in the Guild compound. "Of course," it said, "there will be other deaths after these; that's all part of the plan." One snare led to another, a universe of entangling strands, as though the contents of Kud'ar Mub'at's web had been turned inside out and transmogrified into something big enough to loop whole planets into its grasp. It spoke matter-of-factly, without sympathy or remorse. "Even the ones who think they're on my side, who believe they are still free—they'll find out the truth soon enough. No one escapes forever."

Balancesheet folded a couple of its own legs across its smaller abdomen. "Not even Boba Fett?"

That question surprised Kud'ar Mub'at. Not that the answer wasn't known to it, but that the question had come from a source such as one of his subassembler nodes. Even from a developed one such as Balancesheet; that indicated a level of strategic thinking that Kud'ar Mub'at hadn't expected.

"Not even Boba Fett," answered Kud'ar Mub'at slowly. It kept a set of eyes on the accountant node, dangling from the intricately woven ceiling of the throne space. It watched for any expression in the narrow-angled face, so much like a miniature version of its own. "How could he? Escape, that is. For him to do so, he would have to be wiser than *I* am." Kud'ar Mub'at peered closer at Balancesheet. "Do you really believe that such a thing is possible?"

The eyes studding Balancesheet's face were like sets of black pearls, darkly shining but revealing no depths beyond their surfaces. "Of course not," said the subassembler. A chorus of other nodes, bobbing or scurrying around the space like the embodiments of Kud'ar Mub'at's own thoughts, echoed the sentiment. "No one is even as wise as you are. Not even Emperor Palpatine."

"True," said Kud'ar Mub'at. Though the assembler had to admit that Palpatine operated on a grander scale. *But that's just megalomania,* brooded Kud'ar Mub'at. For Palpatine to think that he could control the entire galaxy, to lay his cold hand upon the neck of every sentient creature on all the worlds . . . even those who didn't have necks, properly speaking . . . that was madness, sheer madness. And worse, in Kud'ar Mub'at's estimation: it was folly. To become absorbed in the big picture, the sweep of history on a cosmic scale, and overlook the little details, was to risk the complete and utter ruination of one's plans. There were things going on underneath Emperor Palpatine's nose that he knew nothing of; not just the hidden errands of the Rebellion and its sympathizers, but connections between beings that were yet so faint that even it, the wise Kud'ar Mub'at, couldn't trace them out. Bits and pieces of rumors, stories of long-vanquished Jedi Knights, and its own wordless guesses were all that Kud'ar Mub'at had to go on. Something to do with the planet Tatooine, and a few humans who lived thereon, innocent and unaware of exactly how important they were. Or did they know? Perhaps one of them had a notion of these secrets, perhaps that old man living out in the endless wastes of the Dune Sea, that Kud'ar Mub'at had heard of. . . .

Gloom permeated the meditations of Kud'ar Mub'at as the assembler reminded himself of just how much still lay beyond the strands of his web. *Just as well,* it philosophically decided, *that all those things are Palpatine's concerns and not mine.* True wisdom rested in knowing one's limitations.

"Exactly so," chimed in Balancesheet. It had picked up its parent's thought over the spun-silk neural network that both connected and housed them. "That shows how wise you are. Would Emperor Palpatine ever have thought of such a thing?"

For a moment Kud'ar Mub'at was annoyed that the little subassembler node had listened in to these private musings—it thought that it had inhibited the appropriate neurons to prevent just such two-way data flow. Then its mood softened. "Now *you're* the one who's wise," said Kud'ar Mub'at affectionately. It reached over another black, spiky leg and let the accountant node scramble onto its end. "I'll very much regret that day when I'll have to—" Kud'ar Mub'at cut off its words just in time.

"Have to what?" At the end of Kud'ar Mub'at's leg, the accountant node peered back at its progenitor.

"Nothing. Don't worry about it." Kud'ar Mub'at was sure that the little node hadn't picked up on *that* particular thought, the one that had to do with its inevitable—and imminent—death. "Let me do the deep thinking."

"Of course," said Balancesheet. "I would not have it otherwise. The only reason I asked about Boba Fett . . ."

"Yes?"

"I only asked," continued the subassembler node, "because we would have to anticipate the cost of his services to us rising as one of the results of the Bounty Hunters Guild being catastrophically disbanded. Since there would be a considerable diminishment in the number and quality of the competition for such operations. That should be factored into our calculations, regarding any further negotiations involving this individual. Unless of course"—Balancesheet spoke archly—"we were to make *other arrangements* about Boba Fett's future. . . ."

That was a good point; Kud'ar Mub'at realized he should have thought of it himself. Though it was also one of the advantages of having a well-developed, semi-independent node like Balancesheet around. Whatever slipped by Kud'ar Mub'at's attention would be caught by the subassembler's.

"Thank you," said Kud'ar Mub'at to the little creature still tethered to it. "I'll give it some thought."

"Actually," said Balancesheet, "I have suggestions along those lines."

Deep in the heart of the web Kud'ar Mub'at had spun for itself, floating in the cold vacuum between the stars, the assembler listened. Just as though it were listening to its own wise and precise calculations, whispered into its ear from something outside; something almost separate.

From the docking port at the edge of the compound, Boba Fett could hear the shouting and the sound of blaster fire. None of it was aimed his way, so he went on working, recalibrating and tuning *Slave I*'s weapons systems.

There hadn't been time, after he and the rest of the team had lifted off and rendezvoused with the autonomic storage unit in orbit above Circumtore, to get everything fully functional once more. Not if he was going to get Bossk back to the Bounty Hunters Guild in time to lead the breakaway faction's uprising against the elders.

As he bolted down a recoil brace on one of the
ship's exterior laser cannons, Fett supposed that old
Cradossk was already dead by now. That was the
first thing that Bossk had sworn to take care of, once
the Trandoshan had fully comprehended how his father had set him up for getting killed on the Oph Nar
Dinnid job. A few encrypted transmissions from
Slave I, as it had journeyed back toward the Guild
compound, had also arranged for Cradossk's death
to be the start of the coup action.

More blaster fire sounded as Boba Fett's tools
spot-welded the wiring harness's main trunk connections. *Slave I's* armaments were extensive and not
designed for easy removal; some of them had circuitry that reached right down to the innermost bow-
els of the ship. Putting all of that back together was a
long job, and one that had to be done exactly right;
more than once, Fett's life had depended on these
weapons as much as the ones slung across the back
of his uniform and fastened to his wrists and shins.
With his attention thus focused, there was little
chance of his being distracted by the violent internal
politics of the Bounty Hunters Guild.

Besides, thought Boba Fett, *I've already done my
part.* He touched a probe to the bare join, read off
the voltage, then withdrew it and let the replicating
insulation swarm a thin yellow sheath over the wire.
Or at least most of it, he corrected himself. The ship
repair would be completed soon enough, but he
knew there was still more to be taken care of before
the job of destroying the Bounty Hunters Guild was
finished. One great rift, between the old leadership
and the upstarts, wasn't enough. By his calculations,
there would be an even split between the two groups
once the binding agent of Cradossk had been removed. Some of the elders, who had always chafed

under the old Trandoshan's leadership, would throw in their lot with the young, impatient bounty hunters; some of the latter, reluctant to accept Bossk's leading the breakaway faction, would side with whatever was left of the Guild's elder council. But on both sides, Boba Fett would have his ringers and stoolies, feeding him useful information and helping to drive even more wedges of suspicion and greed between one bounty hunter and the next. There were two factions now; soon there would be dozens. *And then,* thought Fett with a cold lack of emotion, *it'll be every bounty hunter for himself.*

That was something he was looking forward to.

He closed the access panel on the *Slave I*'s curved, glistening hull and looked up the craft's length. The muzzle of the laser cannon, a newer and sleeker instrument of destruction than D'harhan had ever carried, could just be seen as it pointed toward the wash of stars overhead. D'harhan was dead, another piece of the past erased as though it had never happened at all; eventually all the past would be gone, consumed as if by the annihilating energy at the heart of the darkest stars. . . .

And that was fine with him as well.

Boba Fett moved over to another panel, close to the ship's anterior maneuvering jets. With the code function embedded in his glove's fingertip, he opened the panel and got to work, tracing and reconfiguring the intricate circuits.

The blaster fire from the compound continued, like the electrical discharge of a distant storm.

Someday, Fett supposed, the destruction of the Bounty Hunters Guild would be nothing but memory. But not his; he had no use for memory.

All remembering was in vain. . . .

18

NOW

She watched him at work. Or getting ready for work. *His kind of work,* though Neelah. That was what was indicated by the weapons, all the various mechanisms of reducing the galaxy's inhabitants to scattered pieces of bleeding or charred tissue. Boba Fett had returned from the land of the dead, from its gray portal in which he'd slept, and was ready to fill his hands again with death.

"Which one's that?" Neelah pointed to the brutally efficient-looking object, all matte-black metal and embedded electronics, in Boba Fett's grasp. An empty lens at the rear of the weapon's metal glittered in a curve of crosshaired glass. "What does it do?"

"Rocket launcher." Boba Fett didn't look up from his painstaking labors. With a tool as delicate as a humanoid hair, improvised from one of the medical droids' IV syringes, he scraped a dried mucuslike substance, a remnant of the weapon's time in the Sarlacc's gut, out of its intricate circuits. "And what it does, if you know how to work it, is kill a lot of creatures. At once. At a nice long distance away."

"Thanks." She felt one corner of her mouth

twisting in an expression that would have been ugly if there had been an audience for it. "But I could figure that much out. Don't think you have to patronize me. I was just trying to pass a little time with something like conversation. But I guess that's not within your range of skills."

He made no answer. The motions of the wire-stiff tool and its sharpened point were reflected in the visor of his helmet as he continued working.

The warhead of the rocket launcher's missile appeared in Neelah's memory as well. She had seen it before, the tapered point rising above Fett's shoulder, on a trajectory parallel to his spine. Now, from where it lay on top of the bounty hunter's crossed legs, it seemed to be aimed at a dusty outcropping of the Dune Sea's fundamental rocks. The oppressive suns glazed the landscape with dry, shimmering heat, still visible in reversed colors when Neelah closed her eyes. Even in the shade of a sloping entrance to Boba Fett's underground cache, the hard radiation of the desert light cracked her dehydrated lips and baked her lungs with each fiery breath.

"You should drink more fluids." The blurry shape of the taller medical droid rolled up in front of her. "To replace the ones constantly being extracted from your body." A jointed appendage held out a canister of water, part of the life-support supplies that Boba Fett had hidden here sometime after starting his short-lived employment with Jabba the Hutt, who hadn't lasted much longer than the job. "The results, physiologically speaking, could be severe otherwise."

Neelah took the container from SHΣ1-B and drained it in one long swallow, head tossed back and thin rivulets leaking down both sides of her throat. She wiped her mouth with the back of her hand and set the can down in the gravel next to where she sat. SH∑1-B trundled over to another part of the shade cast by the overhanging jut of rock, where it consulted with its shorter, less articulate colleague. Another canister stood slowly evaporating next to Boba Fett; he hadn't touched it since it had been brought out to him. Redonning his armor, a set that had been kept under a coded autodestruct lock to foil any thieves who might have stumbled upon their hiding place, had transformed him, from a raw-skinned invalid to the imposing specialist in death that he had been before falling down the Sarlacc's throat. Sealing the restored helmet's edge to the uniform's collar had completed the apotheosis: he didn't drink the water, Neelah realized, because he had become a self-contained unit, sealed against the frailties of mortal creatures. Or at least, that was the impression he tried to give.

She leaned back against the mouth of the cave; the rock's residual heat spread across her shoulder blades. The day was dead time, a matter of waiting until Dengar returned from Mos Eisley. When he made it back here—*if* he did, she reminded herself; she knew enough of the spaceport's notorious reputation to be aware that anything could happen in its various dives and back alleys—then further plans would be finalized among the three of them. All depending, of course, upon what Dengar managed to find out and arrange with his various contacts.

Boba Fett, at least, had something to keep himself busy while the rocks' doubled shadows slid farther across the sands. After they had escaped from the bombing-shattered remnants of Dengar's subterranean hiding place, and the regenerated Sarlacc that had wound its tendrils through the broken stone, only a single night had been spent in the chill open, their bodies huddled against each other to keep from freezing. Even if there had been the means to build a fire, they wouldn't have dared, for fear of attracting the attention of some nocturnal Tusken raiding party, crossing the Dune Sea on bantha mounts, the beasts sniffing out pathways invisible even to daylit eyes. When the morning had finally come, breaking violet across the distant mountains ringing the desert, Boba Fett seemed the strongest of the three humans, as though in the dark he had absorbed some precious segment of the others' dwindling energies. He had led the way, stumbling at first, but then with greater sureness as the landmarks had grown more recognizable. Like the other mercenaries and hard types that had worked for the late Jabba—or at least the smart ones, smart enough not to trust the wily Hutt—Boba Fett had maintained a stash of crucial supplies in the wilderness beyond the squat, iron-doored palace. With that many schemers and back-stabbers all in one place, including Jabba himself, it had always been a possibility, if not a probability, that sooner or later any of the henchmen would find himself on the run, scrabbling for survival. The tools that Fett had hidden away—weapons, replacement armor, comm gear—went a long way to ensure that his surviving would be bought at the price of any pursuers' death.

The bounty hunter's parsimonious streak, though, was apparent to Neelah as she sat in the cache's opening—it had been hollowed out of a sheer rock face, then camouflaged—and watched Boba Fett reassembling himself, piece by piece. None of the weapons or components of his battle armor that had been damaged by the Sarlacc's digestive secretions was discarded until Fett had examined and judged it beyond repair. He had already salvaged

most of the personal armaments with which Neelah
had seen him equipped back at Jabba's palace; a
small blaster pistol had been reduced in the Sarlacc's
gut to a fused lump of metal, and the propulsive
charges for some of the larger ammunition had
leaked away, rendering the shells useless. Those were
replaced with exact duplicates from the sealed containers that Fett had dragged out from the cache's
deep interior.

Like watching a droid, thought Neelah, not for
the first time. Or some piece of Imperial battle machinery, capable of making repairs to itself. She had
wrapped her arms around her knees and continued
to watch as the human elements of Boba Fett had
been progressively submerged and hidden beneath
the layers of armor and weaponry, the hard mechani-
cals seemingly replacing the soft, wounded tissue beneath. The narrow visor of his restored helmet took
away the last vestiges of humanity, the gaze of eyes
like any other man's, caught in acid-ravaged flesh, its
fevered blood seeping through the pores. . . .

"He's pushing himself past all therapeutic limits." SHΣ1-B's high-pitched voice fussed from a
place just outside Neelah's awareness. "Both 1e-XE
and I have tried communicating with him, in an effort to make him aware of the necessity for rest. Otherwise, the potential for a serious physiological
relapse will escalate to a life-threatening status."

Neelah glanced over at the medical droid that
had trundled up next to her. "Really?" The ends of
the droid's jointed appendages clicked against each
other, as though imitating a nervous reaction of living creatures. "That's what you're all in a stew
about?"

"Of course." SHΣ1-B turned the lenses of its di-
agnostician optics toward her. "That is our pro-

grammed function. If there was some way to initiate a change in our basic design, even by means of a complete memory wipe, you can be assured that 1e-XE and I would immediately submit to it, no matter now disorienting it might be. Patching up and mending supposedly sentient creatures, who continually insist upon placing themselves in dangerous situations, is a tiresome and never-ending occupation."

"Eternity," chimed in 1e-XE. The other droid had rolled up behind its companion. "Fatigue."

"Concisely put." SHΣ1-B's head unit gave a nod. "I expect we will be applying sterile bandages and administering anesthetics until the teeth of our gears are worn to nubs."

"Deal with it," said Neelah. "As for our Boba Fett"—she tilted her head toward the bounty hunter, still working at cleaning the rocket launcher's innards—"I wouldn't worry about him. You took care of what was needed at the time. But now . . ." Her nod was one of reluctant but genuine admiration. "Now he's way beyond all your medicine."

"That is a diagnosis to which it is difficult to give credence." The medical droid's tone turned huffy. "The individual being discussed is made of flesh and bone like other creatures—"

"Is he?" Neelah knew that was true, even though, when she looked at Boba Fett, she couldn't help but wonder.

"Of course he is," replied the nettled SHΣ1-B. "And as such, there are limits to his endurance and capabilities."

"That's where you're wrong." Neelah leaned back against the stone of the cache's entrance. She hoped it wouldn't be too much longer before Dengar returned. For a lot of reasons. If the parties responsible for the bombing raid decided to come back and

do a more thorough job on their targets, she was sure
Boba Fett would survive, but her own chances would
be considerably fewer. Fett had plans for getting her
and Dengar, as well as himself, off Tatooine and out
to interstellar space, where they would be safe for at
least a little while. And long enough to set further
plans into motion. The only obstacle lay in getting
the comm equipment that Fett needed. He couldn't
go into Mos Eisley to buy or steal it, not without
raising a general alert that he was still alive; that was
why Dengar had gone into the spaceport instead. *But
if he screws up,* thought Neelah, *then what?* She and
Fett would still be stuck out here, waiting not for
Dengar, but for whatever the next attempt to eliminate them would be.

In the meantime the medical droid persisted in its
arguments. "How could I be wrong? I have been ex-
tensively programmed in the nature of humanoid
physiology—"

"Then you're a slow learner." Neelah closed her
eyes and tilted her head back against a pillow of
rock. "When you're dealing with someone like Boba
Fett, it's not the human parts that make the difference. It's the *other* parts."

The droid fell mercifully silent. It either knew
when it was defeated or when further discussion was
pointless.

He left the swoop bike in the dry, dusty hills outside
Mos Eisley, then walked the rest of the way into the
spaceport. Dengar figured he'd draw less attention to
himself that way. And right now creatures noticing
him—the wrong creatures, at least—was the last
thing he wanted.

Before heading in, along one of the old foot trails

that led to Mos Eisley's back alleys, Dengar uprooted some dead scruff brush and hastily camouflaged the swoop with it. The stripped-down, one-person repulsorlift vehicle belonged to somebody else. Or used to—Big Gizz, the leader of one of Tatooine's toughest swoop gangs, had crashed and burned on this machine. Gizz had been hard and mean enough to have been one of Jabba the Hutt's most valuable employees, but that hadn't been enough to keep his leathery hide intact; creatures who worked for Jabba just naturally seemed to end up with short life expectancies. If the work itself didn't wind up getting them killed, then their own violent natures brought about their fates. Dengar had never thought that the pay scale that Jabba offered was worth the risk. Big Gizz had been luckier than most; there had been enough of him left to scrape up and patch back together. Whatever he was up to these days, he had presumably gotten himself some new transportation to do it with.

The squat, indifferently maintained shapes of Mos Eisley came slowly into view as Dengar worked his way down the last, loose-graveled hillside. His on-foot progress wasn't much slower than the swoop had been, crossing the Dune Sea from where he had left Neelah and Boba Fett. The swoop had been unusable wreckage when Dengar had first found it, the bent and scattered pieces testifying to the way in which Big Gizz had ended that particular run. Dengar had pieced the vehicle back together, even buying and grafting on the bits of the repulsor-engine circuitry that were too burned out to be made functional again, then stashed it away near his main hiding place in the desert. A bounty hunter's life was one in which a working form of transport, no matter how banged up and slow, could be the difference between cashing in on valuable merchandise or winding up as bones being pecked at by the Dune Sea's scavengers.

Tatooine's twin suns were smearing the sky dusky orange as Dengar approached the spaceport's ragged perimeter. Digging the swoop out from the bombing raid's aftermath, the tumbled rocks and displaced sand dunes, had taken a little while longer than he'd expected it to; the swoop had been buried nearly two meters deep, and he found it only because he'd had the foresight to tag it with a short-distance location beacon. *Just my luck*, he had thought sourly, when he'd finally managed to drag the swoop to the surface and start it up. The forward stabilizer blades had been bent almost double by the largest boulder that had crashed onto the minimal vehicle; any movement speedier than a relative crawl sent a spine-jarring shudder through the frame, quickly escalating to a rolling spin that would have crashed him to the ground if he hadn't backed off the throttle. The swoop's damaged condition had necessitated a more circuitous route across the Dune Sea wastes than he would have taken otherwise; he might have been able to outrun a Tusken Raider's bantha mount, but not a shot from one of their ancient but effective rifles.

"Looking for anything . . . *special*?" A hood-shrouded figure, with a distinctive crescent-shaped proboscis, sidled up to Dengar as soon as he'd made his way between the first of the low, featureless buildings. "There are creatures in this district . . . who can accommodate . . . *all* interests."

"Yeah, I bet." Dengar brushed past the meddlesome creature. "Look, just take a hike, why don't you? I know my way around."

"My apologies." The hem of the creature's

rough-cloth robe swept across the alley dust as it made a small bow. "I mistakenly thought . . . that you were a . . . *newcomer* here."

Dengar kept walking, quickening his strides. That had been an unfortunate encounter; he had been hoping to make it to the cantina at the center of Mos Eisley without being noticed. The spaceport abounded with snitches and informers, creatures who made a living selling out others either to the Empire's security forces or to whichever criminals and assorted marginal dealers might have a financial interest in someone else's comings and goings. That was what had always made Mos Eisley, an otherwise dilapidated port on a backwater planet, one of the galaxy's prime hangouts for those practicing the bounty-hunter trade. If you stuck around long enough, you eventually heard something that could be turned to profit. The downside, as Dengar was well aware, was that it was hard to keep one's business a secret around here. A couple of whispers in the right ear holes, and *you* wound up becoming someone else's merchandise.

Right now he wasn't aware of anyone looking for him; he wasn't that important. Though that might change all too rapidly, when word got out of his being hooked up with Boba Fett. An alliance with the galaxy's top bounty hunter brought a lot of less-than-desirable baggage with it: other creatures' schemes and grudges, all of which they might figure could be advanced by either going through or eliminating anyone as close to Fett as Dengar had become. The bombing raid had proved that Boba Fett had some determined enemies. If those parties found out that a minor-rank bounty hunter had made himself useful to the object of their furious wrath, they might eliminate the individual in question just on general principle.

Those and other disquieting speculations scurried around inside Dengar's skull as he made his way through Mos Eisley's less pleasant—and less frequented—byways. A pack of sleek, glittering-eyed garbage rats scurried at his approach, diving into their warrens among the alley's noisome strata of decaying rubbish, then chattering shrill abuse and brandishing their primitive, sharp-edged digging tools at his back. The rats, at least, wouldn't report his presence in the spaceport to anyone; they kept to themselves for the most part, with a supercilious attitude toward larger creatures' affairs.

Dengar halted his steps, in order to peer around a corner. From this point, he had a clear view of Mos Eisley's central open space. He saw nothing more ominous than a couple of Imperial stormtroopers on low-level security patrol, prodding the muzzles of their blaster rifles through an incensed Jawa's merchandise bales. Bits of salvaged droids—disconnected limbs and head units with optical sensors still blinking and vocal units moaning from the shock of disconnected circuits—bounced out of the cart and clattered on the ground as the Jawa shook its fist, hidden in the bulky sleeve of its robe, and yammered its grievances against the white-helmeted figures.

No one crossing or idling in the plaza regarded the confrontation with more than mild curiosity, except for a pair of empty-saddled dewbacks tethered nearby; they grizzled and snarled, drawing away from the noisy Jawa with instinctive aversion. The stormtroopers caused no concern for Dengar, either. He was more worried about those who might be on the other side of the law, the various scoundrels and sharpies who would be more likely to have heard the latest scuttlebutt and be looking to profit from it.

Dengar drew his head back from the building's corner. There was a fine line between being too paranoid and being just paranoid enough. *Too paranoid* slowed you down, but *not enough* got you killed. He'd already decided to err, if necessary, on the side of caution.

Keeping close to the building's crumbling white walls, Dengar found the rear entrance to the cantina. With a quick glance over his shoulder, he slid into the familiar darkness and threaded his way among the establishment's patrons. A few eyes and other sensory organs turned in his direction, then swung back to discreetly murmured business conversations.

He rested both elbows on the bar. "I'm looking for Codeq Santhananan. He been in lately?"

The same ugly bartender, familiar from all of Dengar's previous visits, shook his head. "That barve got drilled a coupla months ago. Right outside the door. I had a pair of rehab droids scrubbing the burn mark for two whole standard time periods, and it still didn't come out." The bartender remembered Dengar's usual, a tall water-and-isothane, heavy on the water, and set it down in front of him. The scars on the bartender's face shifted formation as one eye narrowed, peering at Dengar. "He owe you credits?"

Dengar let himself take a sip; he had gotten seriously dehydrated, riding the damaged swoop across the Dune Sea. "He might."

"Well, he owed *me*," growled the bartender. "I don't appreciate it when my customers get themselves killed and I'm the one that gets stiffed." He furiously swabbed out a glass with a stained towel. "Creatures in these parts oughta think of somebody besides themselves for a change."

Listening to the bartender's complaints wasn't accomplishing anything. Dengar drained half the glass and pushed it away. "Put it on my tab."

He worked his way into the shadow-filled center of the cantina's space, gazing around as best he could without making direct eye contact with anyone. Some of the more hot-tempered cantina habitués were known to take violent offense over such indiscretions; even if he didn't wind up being the one laid out on the damp floor, Dengar didn't want to draw that kind of attention to himself.

"Excuse the lamentable discourtesy"—a hand with bifurcate talons tugged at Dengar's sleeve— "but I couldn't help overhearing. . . ."

Glancing to his side, Dengar found himself looking into the black bead eyes, no more than a couple of centimeters in diameter, of a Q'nithian aeropteryx. One of the beads swelled larger as the creature's other set of claws held a magnifying lens on a jeweled handle in front of it. Dengar had been expecting something like this; one's business didn't stay secret for very long in the cantina, if spoken in anything louder than a whisper.

"Let's go over to one of the booths," said Dengar. Those were far enough away from the cantina's crowded main area for a measure of privacy. "Come on."

The Q'nithian flopped after him on the flattened tips of its shabby gray wings, useless for any kind of flight. It struggled into the seat on the booth's opposite side, then settled down as though wrapped in a feathered cloak. "I heard you mention poor Santhananan's name." The taloned hand protruded from under the wings so that the Q'nithian could scratch itself with the magnifying-lens handle. "He met a sad demise, I'm afraid."

"Yeah, I'm sure it was tragic." Dengar set his arms on the table and leaned forward. He wanted to wrap up his errand here before the bartender had a chance to pressure him into settling his account. "What I want to know is, did anybody pick up on his business?"

The lens shifted to the other beady eye. "The late Santhananan had various enterprises." The Q'nithian's voice was a grating squawk. "A creature of many interests, some of them even legal. To which of them do you refer?"

"Keep it down. You know what I'm talking about." Dengar glanced across the cantina, then turned back to the Q'nithian. "The message service he used to run. That's what I'm interested in."

"Ah." The Q'nithian made a few thoughtful clacking noises with its rudimentary beak. "What great good fortune for you. It just so happens that that is an enterprise . . . over which *I* now exercise control."

Great good fortune—that was one way of putting it. Dengar wondered for a moment just how the late Santhananan had met his end, and how much this Q'nithian had had to do with it. But that was none of his business.

"Whatever communication you require," continued the Q'nithian, words and voice all mild blandness, "I think I can assist you with it."

"I bet you can." Dengar looked hard into the magnifiying lens and the mercenary intelligence behind it. "Here's the deal. I need to send a hyperspace messenger pod—"

"Really?" The feathers above one beady eye rose in apparent surprise. "That's an expensive proposition. I'm not saying it can't be done. Just that—since

I haven't done business with you before—it would have to be done on a strictly credits-up-front basis."

Dengar reached inside his jacket and pulled out a small pouch. He loosened its drawstring and poured the contents out on the table. "Will that do?"

Even without the magnifying lens, the Q'nithian's eyes grew larger. "I think"—the bifurcate talons reached out for the little hoard of hard credits—"we may be in business here. . . ."

"Not so fast." Dengar grabbed the other creature's thin, light-boned wrist and pinned it to the tabletop. "You get half now, half when I hear that the message reached its destination."

"Very well." The Q'nithian watched as Dengar divided the credits into two piles, one of which went back into the pouch, and then inside Dengar's jacket again. "That's a regrettably standard arrangement. But I can live with it." The talons picked up the rest of the credits and drew it someplace under the cloak-like wings. "So—what's the message you want to send?"

Dengar hesitated. He'd known how far he could trust Codeq Santhananan—he'd dealt with him before—but this Q'nithian was an unknown quantity. Still . . . right now there was no alternative. And if the Q'nithian wanted the other half of the payment for his services, there was a limit to any double-dealing he might be contemplating.

"All right." Dengar leaned even farther across the table, until he could see himself reflected in the Q'nithian's darkly shining eyes. "Just four words."

"Which are?"

" 'Boba Fett,' " said Dengar, " 'is alive.' "

Both of the Q'nithian's feathered brows rose. "That's the message? That's it?" The wings lifted and fell in a rudimentary shrug. "Seems to me . . .

that you're spending an awful lot of credits . . . on some odd kind of hoax." The Q'nithian studied Dengar through the lens. "Not that anyone is going to believe it, anyway. Everybody knows . . . that Boba Fett got eaten by the Sarlacc. Some of Jabba the Hutt's ex-employees . . . came right here into the cantina . . . and told all about it."

"Good for them. I hope somebody bought 'em a drink."

"You appear to be . . . a serious person. And you're paying . . . serious credits." The eye behind the magnifying lens blinked. "Are you telling me . . . that the renowned Boba Fett *is* alive?"

"That's none of your business," said Dengar. "I'm just paying you to get the message to where it needs to go."

"As you wish," replied the Q'nithian. "And just where is that?"

"The planet Kuat. I want Kuat of Kuat to receive it."

"Well, well." The Q'nithian's feathers rustled as he shifted position on the seat opposite Dengar. "Now, that is interesting. What makes you think a creature as important as the CEO of Kuat Drive Yards . . . would be interested . . . in hearing something like that? Whether it's true or not."

"I told you already." Dengar spoke between gritted teeth. He was about ready to reach over and crush the magnifying lens in his fist. "That's not your business."

"Ah. But I think . . . it *is*." The beak opened in a crude simulation of a humanoid smile. "We are something like partners now . . . you and I. If Boba Fett is alive . . . there are others who would be interested in knowing that . . . rather intriguing fact."

Dengar glared at the Q'nithian. "When Santhananan ran this business, he knew that his customers weren't just buying a message being transmitted. They were also buying him keeping his mouth shut."

"You're not dealing . . . with Santhananan now." The bright gaze behind the magnifying lens was unperturbed. "You're dealing with *me*. And my backers; I'm not a completely independent agent the way Santhananan was . . . but then, that may be why he's dead and I'm not. Let's just say . . . that I have certain additional expenses . . . that I need to cover." The tip of the lens pointed toward Dengar. "For which you should be grateful."

"Yeah, I'm grateful, all right." Dengar shook his head in disgust. That was the problem with doing business in Mos Eisley; there were always payoffs that had to be made, bribes in either the form of credits or information. And disregarding what he was holding back for the on-delivery payment for the message, he was effectively tapped out of credits. That left only one thing to barter. "You want to know why Kuat would be interested? I'll tell you. It's because he just made one hell of an effort to make sure that Boba Fett was dead. Did word of that bombing raid out on the Dune Sea reach here?"

"Of course it did," said the Q'nithian. "The seismic shocks had structural beams cracking . . . all over Mos Eisley. Really—the Imperial Navy cannot engage in a routine practice operation such as that . . . and not have sentient creatures notice it."

"It wasn't the Imperial Navy. It was a private operation."

"Oh? And what proof do you have of that?"

Dengar reached inside his jacket, past the drawstring pouch with the rest of the credits and to the larger, heavier object he'd found when digging up the damaged swoop. Back there, he'd brushed the sand off the device, a dully gleaming sphere that had filled his hand with its weight and potentiality, and had read the words and serial numbers incised upon its thick, armored shell. Reading those words, and realizing what they meant, had changed all his plans in an instant; they were why he was here in the Mos Eisley cantina, talking to a message expediter like this Q'nithian. That hadn't been part of Boba Fett's plans for this little errand into the spaceport. Dengar was operating on his own now.

He handed the sphere, with its two off-center cylindrical protrusions, to the Q'nithian. "Take a look."

The sphere was cradled in the taloned hand before the Q'nithian realized what it was. He almost dropped it, then his twin claws gripped it desperately tighter and kept it from bouncing on the tabletop. A dismayed, wordless squawk sounded from deep within the feather-wrapped body as he thrust it back toward Dengar.

"What's the matter?" Dengar let his own smile turn cruel, savoring the other creature's discomfiture. "Something frighten you?"

"Are you mad?" The Q'nithian gaped at him without benefit of the magnifying lens. "Do you know what this is?"

"Sure," answered Dengar easily. "It's an atmospheric phase-change detonator for an Imperial-class M-12 sweep bomb. If it's the same as the others I've come across, it'd be set to ignite an attached charge at a perceived twenty-millibar differential." His smile widened. "Good thing it's not hooked up to one, huh?"

"You idiot!" The sphere trembled in the

Q'nithian's talons. "There's still enough explosive in this fuse to take out half of Mos Eisley!"

"Relax." Dengar took the sphere back from the Q'nithian. "It's cold. Safely inert. Look—" He turned the object so a thumbnail-sized data readout showed. "Do you see those three illuminated red LEDs?"

The Q'nithian shook his head. "No." He raised the magnifying lens and peered closer. "I don't see any lights at all."

"Exactly." Dengar set the sphere down between them. "This one's a dud. These particular detonation devices have a failure rate in the field approaching almost ten percent. That's why the Imperial Navy doesn't use them anymore; they've upgraded to a more reliable gravity-wave system that's integrated into the main explosive's casing. It's not removable like this thing. That should've been your first clue that it wasn't the Empire doing a practice bombing run out there in the desert."

"Hmm." The Q'nithian's ruffled feathers smoothed back down. "You seem to possess . . . an unusual degree of expertise in these matters."

"I've worked at other things besides bounty hunting."

"I admire your versatility," said the Q'nithian. "That's a useful trait in a sentient creature." He gingerly prodded the sphere with the tip of the magnifying lens. "I'll grant you . . . for the sake of your exposition . . . that this is not an Imperial device. But I fail to see the connection between it and Kuat of Kuat."

"Check it out." Dengar held the sphere up to the lens. "Serial numbers. All these devices were manufactured at one armory subcontractor, which has ties to the Kuat Drive Yards engineering facilities on the planet Kuat. The devices were numbered sequentially, in production runs of a quarter million. All the ones numbered *below* the twelve-million mark were reserved for KDY's own use, for designing and testing the munitions storage chambers aboard the heavy cruisers and destroyers that were being built for the Imperial fleet." Dengar tapped the tiny incised number with his fingertip. "This is one of those devices. Obviously, KDY decided there would be a use someday for some major bombing action—the company didn't get to be the leading shipbuilder for the Empire by just underbidding its competition, you know. So it held some bombs and fuses back, after all the testing on the Imperial ships was finished. If this one had gone off like the others, nobody would have known who had made that bombing run out on the Dune Sea."

"Interesting." The Q'nithian's beady gaze flicked from the sphere to Dengar's face. "Perhaps there is reason to believe that Kuat of Kuat wishes Boba Fett dead—if Fett is alive at all. But that leaves many other questions unanswered."

"They'll have to remain unasked, too. For the time being." Dengar leaned back on his side of the booth, tucking the metal sphere back inside his jacket. "I don't have time to give you a full rundown on everything that's happened out there. Some things you're just going to have to take on trust."

"Trust?" The gray feathers rose again in a shrug. "That . . . is a variable commodity, my friend. Like so many other things. And it has its price."

"Which I've already paid," said Dengar. "With more to come into your pocket. If everything goes as planned. You can puzzle over the answers to your unasked questions later, if you'd rather do that than count your credits."

"Counting my credits," said the Q'nithian, "is a favorite avocation of mine. But there's one question that I still must ask now. You wish to inform the rich and powerful Kuat of Kuat that, despite all his efforts to the contrary, Boba Fett yet lives. When Kuat comes and finds you, as he undoubtedly will . . . and as I presume is your intention that he should . . . then what?"

Dengar remained silent. *That's a good question,* he thought to himself. One that he'd been working on during the whole long ride from the Dune Sea into Mos Eisley. A dangerous question as well, since he was now sneaking around behind the back of one of the deadliest individuals in the galaxy. If Boba Fett were to find out that he was being two-timed—which was what contacting Kuat of Kuat amounted to— then Dengar's life wasn't worth the smallest coin in the pouch inside his jacket. *Still,* mused Dengar, *I've got to look out for myself.* If not for his own sake, then for that of Manaroo as well; he was still betrothed to her. His decision to send her away, to keep her at a safe distance from this unsavory business into which he had fallen, was something that still produced mixed feelings in his heart. Dengar missed her terribly, as though a living part of himself had been excised without the benefit of anesthesia, a wound that could never heal. *But I had to do it,* Dengar told himself again. Getting involved with the fate of Boba Fett in any way was too dangerous— and the life expectancy of those who had put their trust in him was on the short side. Fett's offer of a partnership between the two of them still worried Dengar. Now that Boba Fett had just about recovered completely from his time in the Sarlacc's gut— and had gotten nearly all of his old strength and skills back—how long would he have any use for another bounty hunter cutting in on his action? *He's always been a lone operator*—the suspicion that that hadn't changed for Boba Fett was sharp and nettlesome in Dengar's mind. Fett could be playing him for a fool, the way he had done to others; a lot of those had survived only long enough to regret trusting a barve like that, and then they'd been the merchandise that Boba Fett dealt in. Or ashes, or even less.

None of those were fates that Dengar wanted for himself. *So it's all a matter,* he told himself again, *of who sells out the other first.* And as a purchaser, somebody as rich and powerful as Kuat of Kuat had some definite advantages. Not only in terms of the price that could be paid, but also in the protection he could give. It had only been a fluke that the bombing raid hadn't reduced Boba Fett to dust and disconnected atoms; the next effort that Kuat made would be even more severe. *I could get the credits,* thought Dengar, *and there would be nothing that Boba Fett could do about it. Because he'd be dead.*

The shining bead eyes of the Q'nithian seemed to have read his thoughts. "It's a dangerous game you're playing," the Q'nithian remarked.

"I know that." Dengar slowly nodded his head. "But it's the only one I've got."

There were a few more details to settle, and he and the Q'nithian took care of them. Dengar knew that Boba Fett was planning on getting off Tatooine; that would make it difficult, if not impossible, for Kuat of Kuat to get back in touch with the sender of the message about Fett's still being alive. So the Q'nithian would also act as the contact point; that meant he would also get a cut of whatever payment Kuat made for the necessary information of Boba Fett's whereabouts.

"So when will you be sending off the messenger pod?" Dengar worked at securing the fastenings of his gear. Even from inside the windowless cantina, he knew that night had settled in on the Dune Sea. It would be a long cold journey on the exposed saddle of the swoop to get back to where he had left Boba Fett and the girl Neelah. "The sooner you send it, the better."

"Don't worry," soothed the Q'nithian. He folded his bifurcate talons on top of each other, with the magnifying lens laid flat on the table. "It will be on its way to Kuat, both the planet and the man himself, within a matter of hours."

"Great." Dengar slid out from the booth. "I'll be checking to make sure that it gets there."

He stopped inside the same arched doorway by which he had entered the cantina. The place was packed now; it had taken some effort to squeeze his way among the various off-planet anatomies that frequented this dive. At the side of the cantina's central area, the jizz-wailer band had set up on the little stage they always used; their clattering, wailing racket had already added another layer of noise above the mingled conversations. Nobody ever actually listened to the music, but it provided a useful acoustic cover for the various business dealings that the cantina's patrons wished to keep private.

Dengar moved up the short flight of steps that led to the street level outside. From the doorway's arch, he could see across the heads of the crowd, all the way back to the booth where he had left the Q'nithian. Even if he hadn't been in shadow, the Q'nithian's weak eyesight would have ruled out his being spotted as he watched and waited. Several minutes passed, and he didn't see the Q'nithian get up from the booth, and none of the other creatures in the cantina joined him there, either. Dengar figured that was a good sign; if the Q'nithian was going to sell him out, stab him in the back by passing on the information about Boba Fett to some other interested party in the cantina, the creature would have done so immediately. That way, some bunch of thugs could have jumped him before he'd had a chance to get out of Mos Eisley, then painfully extracted the other bounty hunter's location from him.

He was jostled a few times by other creatures entering the cantina before he finally decided that the Q'nithian was staying on the up-and-up with him— or at least as much as he could reasonably expect from one of Mos Eisley's shadier denizens. Dengar turned and headed up the rest of the steps. A few seconds later he was threading his way through the spaceport's dark alleys. He had one more errand to take care of—the one on which Boba Fett had sent him here—before he could return to the hills on Mos Eisley's outskirts, where he had left the damaged swoop.

What Dengar hadn't seen was the little creature that inched its way down the metal support pillar of the booth's table, then started a slow, laborious crawl across the cantina's floor. Still no bigger in diameter than Dengar's hand, it had been thin as paper when it had surreptitiously emerged from the cloak of the Q'nithian's feathers; by the time the mimbrane organism had finished listening to the conversation between the two larger creatures in the booth, it had swollen pillowlike, to the thickness of a humanoid finger joint.

Its milkily translucent tissues shimmered with the acoustic energy stored within as the tiny, rudimentary legs around its edges helped it slither past the feet of the cantina's paying customers. A row of primitive sensory organs on its top surface gave the mimbrane just enough ability to distinguish between light and shadow; it navigated mainly by ingrained memory, taking the route it had been taught between the Q'nithian and the other creatures who were waiting for it.

High above the mimbrane's creeping progress, one of the Tonnika sisters, her face all avaricious delicacy framed between intricate braids, laughed at the joke her identical-twin companion had just told her; the punch line had something to do with a crude comparison between Wookiee mating practices and the sour, pinched faces of the Imperial Navy's top admirals. The gray trail rising from the smoking wand in Senni Tonnika's fine-boned hand drew a wavering line in the cantina's muggy air as she took a step backward, too quickly for the mimbrane to scurry away from the sharp point of her boot heel. It caught the mimbrane at one corner of its amorphous body, with just enough force to squeeze out the last thing it had absorbed while clinging to the underside of the booth's table.

"Did you hear something?" Senni stopped laughing and looked around herself in puzzlement.

"I hear a lot of things." Her sister, Brea, smiled and leaned closer, drawing deep the smoke the other had just exhaled. "All the time . . ."

"No—" She frowned and looked down toward the floor, slick with spilled drinks and littered with the discarded wrappings of small, unmarked packages. "I mean from down *there*." She gave a shake of her head. "I very distinctly heard a little voice, and it said, 'I'll be checking to make sure that it gets there.' "

"You're imagining things."

The mimbrane had already crept away, hurrying as best it could toward its destination. When it reached the booth on the farthest side of the cantina, it didn't need to climb up to the table. A greasy, black-nailed hand reached down and picked it up.

"Fat little thing, ain't it?" Vol Hamame had once been a member of Big Gizz's swoop gang. They had had a parting of the ways, and not an amicable one. Since then, Hamame had found other employment, equally criminal. But a little more profitable. In a lot of ways, life had improved since he had been able to get away from Spiker, Gizz's obnoxious second in command. "Looks like the Q'nithian sent it over here, all stuffed with information."

"What else?" Hamame's partner was equally villainous-looking; the mucus-lined pleats of his nasopharynx fluttered wetly with each breath. "That's what these things are for." The mimbrane's tiny legs wriggled futilely as Phedroi flipped it onto its glistening back. "Let's see what it's got for us."

Only one of the Q'nithian system's moons had its own atmosphere; it was there, on deeply creviced fault lines, grinding constantly against each other from the tidal pull of the moon's captor planet, that the thick clusters of the mimbrane creatures grew and multiplied like the shelf fungi found on arboreal worlds. They lived on acoustic energy, absorbing sound vibrations and incorporating them layer by layer into their own simple bodies. Millennia of seismic shifts and groans were recorded in the oldest mimbranes, buried beneath the weight of their overlapping offspring and grown into undulating masses big enough to wrap around an Imperial cruiser like a shining blanket.

Small, fresh mimbranes had more practical uses.

They were the perfect eavesdropping device, record-ing into their gelatinous fibers any sounds that struck the tympanic cells in which the creatures were sheathed. Being totally organic, they couldn't be de-tected by the usual antibugging sweep devices.

Hamame's jag-edged fingertip pressed down on the bulging center of the mimbrane. The stored en-ergy converted back into sound.

"I heard you mention poor Santhananan's name." The Q'nithian's familiar squawk spoke the words. *"He met a sad demise, I'm afraid."*

"That's right." Phedroi gave a smirking nod. "You had us murder him for you."

"Shut up," said Hamame. "Let's hear the rest." He prodded the mimbrane again.

"Yeah, I'm sure it was tragic." The mimbrane emitted Dengar's recorded voice. *"What I want to know is, did anybody pick up on his business?"*

The two thugs listened to all of the deal that had gone down between Dengar and the Q'nithian. "Now, that's interesting." Hamame leaned back on his side of the booth. "That Q'nithian is a sneaky type, but he's earned his keep with this bit." On the table between him and Phedroi, the mimbrane was now perfectly flat, all the stored acoustic energy drained from its cells. "So Boba Fett's still alive."

"That's one tough barve." Phedroi gave an ad-miring shake of his head, the coarse and dirty ring-lets of his beard scraping across his tunic collar. "You just can't kill him. If falling down a Sarlacc won't do the trick, then what will?"

Hamame reached inside his jacket and pulled out his blaster. He pointed the muzzle up toward the cantina's ceiling. *"This* will."

19

It had taken a long time for him to come into his own. To receive, to possess all that should have been his from the beginning. To be known as the toughest, hardest, most feared bounty hunter in the entire galaxy . . .

Bossk leaned back in the pilot's chair of the *Hound's Tooth,* savoring the pleasures that came with success. Mingled with a simmering anger that never completely ebbed from the essence of a Trandoshan; he folded the claws of both hands across the scales of his chest and gazed slit-eyed at the stars visible through the viewport. *Too long,* he brooded; *too long a time.* If all the creatures on all those worlds had had any sense, they would have recognized him as the best. The absolute best.

Instead—and this brought the fire inside him to a hotter pitch—he'd had to wait until Boba Fett was dead. And that had been *much* too long in coming.

A thread of regret mingled with the other emotions. He would have liked to have killed Fett himself, torn out his competitor's throat with one roundhouse sweep of his claws. Or to have focused the crosshairs of a blaster rifle's sight upon that narrow-visored helmet, then pressed the firing stud and seen Boba Fett's masked visage replaced by a quick explosion of blood and bone splinters . . .

Bossk slowly nodded. Now, *that* would have been a real pleasure. And one that he would have deserved to savor, just like the taste of Fett's blood leaking between his fangs, after having suffered so many humiliations at the hands of that sneaking, underhanded barve.

Some of the anger was replaced with self-pity. There were so many things of which he had been cheated in this life. The leadership of the Bounty Hunters Guild—that should have been his as well. Now it could hardly be said that the Guild existed at all. Granted, a lot of *personal* satisfaction had come with killing old Cradossk, his father—that was the sort of thing that really defined the relationship between Trandoshan generations—but he hadn't gotten much material benefit out of the act. Instead of becoming the head of a galaxy-wide organization of predators, skimming a cut off the bounties collected on all the hard merchandise changing hands on any inhabited world, he'd wound up on his own, a scrabbling independent agent like all the other bounty hunters. That had all been Boba Fett's doing; the breakup of the Bounty Hunters Guild had been a long time ago, before Bossk had learned one of the most important lessons in this business—

Don't trust your competition. Kill them.

That's true wisdom, Bossk assured himself. *For a lot of reasons.* There had been other sources of anger, other humiliations he had suffered at Boba Fett's hands. They had just kept piling up, one after another. When Bossk had stood within striking distance of Fett, back when Darth Vader had been giving the job to all the best bounty hunters in the galaxy, to track down and find Han Solo's *Millen-*

nium Falcon, it had taken all of his self-control not to leap over and rip out Fett's throat. And then that last infuriating maneuver, when Fett had outsmarted both him and his partner, Zuckuss, delivering the carbonite-encased form of Han Solo to Jabba's palace right beneath Bossk's outstretched claws—that had driven him almost insane with rage.

So when the word had reached him that Boba Fett was dead, dissolved in the digestive secretions of the Sarlacc beast, a combination of elation and frustration had welled up inside him. If the universe was going to be so obliging as to just give him that which he'd most fervently longed for, he'd just have to accept that as philosophically as he could. The fact that he was now forever frustrated in taking care of the job himself, of reaping the intense pleasure of personally separating Boba Fett from the realm of the living—that just showed that the universe wasn't really fair and just, after all. But Bossk had set the *Hound's Tooth* at maximum speed for the too-familiar planet of Tatooine, just to bask in the atmosphere that had been the last to fill his enemy's lungs.

He didn't get that far, though; Tatooine hung like a dusky smudge in the aft viewport screen. Before he'd had time to set landing coordinates for the Mos Eisley spaceport, Bossk had found something just as familiar—and even more intriguing—in autonomic orbit outside Tatooine's atmosphere. When he'd first spotted the *Slave I* in the cockpit's forward viewport, and recognized it as Boba Fett's ship, his hands had immediately darted to the targeting and firing controls of the *Hound's* blaster cannons. The only thing that had kept him from blowing *Slave I* into atoms floating in empty space was the realization that the other ship hadn't trained any of its weapons onto his own. That, and remembering Boba

Fett was already dead. A simple hailing call had returned the information that *Slave I* was empty, but still under the protection of its internal guard circuitry.

This is too good, Bossk had decided. It was one thing to inherit—by default—the mantle of top bounty hunter in the galaxy. But to also stumble upon the late Boba Fett's personal ship, the repository of all his weaponry and databases, all the painstakingly acquired secrets and strategies that had put him at the top of this dangerous trade—Bossk couldn't resist an opportunity like that.

He was smart enough to avoid trying to crack *Slave I*'s security measures himself. Other creatures had gotten killed trying to do just that. Boba Fett had wired the ship with enough traps and self-aiming firepower to wipe out a small army, if it had attempted to enter without the appropriate password authorization. But with Fett being dead, there was no time pressure about getting past the ship's circuits; Bossk had the credits and the leisure that allowed for calling in professional assistance.

That was one advantage to being this close to Tatooine; services of that kind were exactly the sort available in Mos Eisley. If one could afford to pay the price.

A harsh electronic buzz sounded from the *Hound*'s comm unit. A message had been received; undoubtedly, the one for which Bossk had been waiting. He pulled himself closer to the cockpit's control panel and saw something that puzzled him for a moment.

There were *two* messages waiting for him.

The first was from *Slave I,* just as he had expected. The other had arrived almost simultaneously: a messenger pod, sent straight from the surface of

Tatooine; the small, self-propelled device was now sitting in the receptor bay of the *Hound's Tooth.* Bossk prodded a few more buttons with his foreclaw and got a readout from it.

The coded message unit was from a Q'nithian message expediter down in Mos Eisley with whom Bossk had a long-standing working arrangement. A business relationship: the Q'nithian had a general knowledge of the kinds of things that Bossk was interested in. Any message that the Q'nithian was hired to send across the galaxy, that fit those criteria, would get routed first to Bossk before continuing on the rest of its journey.

Bossk read the destination info off the unit. It was headed to the distant engineering center of Kuat, to the head of Kuat Drive Yards, Kuat of Kuat. Bossk nodded to himself as he read the address data. The Q'nithian had been correct in figuring that he would want to see this. *Anything,* thought Bossk, *that's being sent to someone as rich and powerful as Kuat is something that I'm interested in.* A successful bounty hunter always had to have his info sources open wideband so he could filter through all the galaxy's secrets and rumors for the bits that might turn out profitable.

He had already decided, though, to read the encoded message unit later—after he had taken care of the other business, for which he had been waiting so long. The tip of his claw hit the next button on the cockpit's comm controls.

"I'm all finished over here." The recorded voice, dry and emotionless, was that of the lead technician for D/Crypt Information Services, one of the many semilegitimate businesses that abounded in Mos Eisley. "The security codes have been sieved out, and you now have full access to the ship designated as *Slave I*. After you pay me, of course."

That detail was already taken care of. Bossk transmitted an account transfer order to Mos Eisley's black-market escrow exchange, then fired up the primary navigation engines. In the time it would take for him to maneuver the *Hound's Tooth* over to the other ship, the D/Crypt tech would already have received the payment confirmation.

"Good thing you didn't keep me waiting." The D/Crypt technician was a wizened little humanoid, the top of his bald head barely coming up to Bossk's chest. "I don't like to be kept waiting. If you had kept me waiting, I would have charged you triple overtime."

"Don't sweat it." Bossk let the transfer connection, between his own *Hound* and the *Slave I*, seal shut behind him. "I would've paid." He glanced around the bleakly functional confines of *Slave I*'s cargo hold; the bars of the merchandise cages were uncomfortably familiar to him from the last time he had been aboard the ship. The hinges of the main cage's door had been repaired, but still showed signs of the laser bolt that D'harhan had unleashed upon them. That had been a long time ago, when Boba Fett had still been alive and busily engaged upon breaking up the old Bounty Hunters Guild. "Everything's clear?"

"As far as I can determine, it is." With his high-power trifocals slid up onto his pink, unsunned brow, the D/Crypt tech busily packed up his equipment cases.

"What's that mean?"

The tech blinked myopically at Bossk. "Nothing's perfect. Not in this galaxy, at least." He gave a shrug with his thin shoulders. "Ninety-nine percent, though; I can guarantee you that much. A less than one-percent chance that there's any security device aboard this ship that I wasn't able to locate and deactivate."

"Yeah?" Bossk looked back at him sourly. "And what's the payoff on the guarantee? Some booby trap takes my head off—you're going to refund my credits?"

"I'll put a flower on your grave." The D/Crypt tech clicked shut the last of the case latches and straightened up. "If there's enough of you left to put in one."

When the technician had boarded his minuscule shuttlecraft, then disconnected it from *Slave I* and headed back down to Tatooine, Bossk turned from the transfer port and drew his blaster from its holster. Even a one-percent chance of something going wrong was enough to make him nervous. Warily, he stepped forward into the ship's cargo hold. He doubted if there would be anything of value to be found here. Grasping one of the rungs with his free hand, he climbed up into the cockpit.

From the forward viewport, Bossk could see his own ship and the landing claw tethering it to *Slave I*. The urge to abandon his investigation and return to that known safety was almost overwhelming; every particle of this craft, including the recycled air seeping into his lungs, was imbued with its departed owner's invisible presence. Boba Fett might be dead, but the memory of him was still intimidating. The grip of the blaster sweated in Bossk's hand; he half expected to glance over his shoulder and see that narrow-visored gaze watching him from the hatchway.

He didn't sit down in the pilot's chair. Instead, he leaned over it and punched out a few quick commands on the ship's computer. *Those were credits well spent,* decided Bossk, when he saw the file directory appear on the screen in front of him. The D/Crypt technician had cracked and stripped out the password protection; all of Boba Fett's secrets lay there exposed, ready for his careful examination.

Some of the nervousness drained from Bossk's spine and muscles. If there had been a trap remaining, he would have instinctively expected it to be here, guarding all that was most precious to Fett, the essence of his devious mind and hard-won experience. Bossk reached out and blanked the computer screen; going through all those files would take a long time. He'd have to bring over a mem device from the *Hound's Tooth* so he could do a core dump and take everything back to his own ship, to be sorted out at his leisure. It might take years. *But then*—Bossk smiled to himself—*I've got the time. And Boba Fett doesn't. Not anymore.*

The blaster went back into its holster. Bossk turned away from the cockpit controls, feeling genuinely relaxed. The barve was dead. In a business where sheer survival was the biggest part of winning, Boba Fett had finally come up a loser. The warm glow of victory, like a blood-rich meal slowly dissolving in his gut, filled Bossk and radiated through every fiber of his being.

Just outside the cockpit hatchway, Bossk saw a door partly ajar, one that he didn't remember from his previous time aboard *Slave I*. He saw now that it was cleverly constructed, the hinges concealed and the door's edges the same dimensions as the surrounding bulkhead panel; anyone who hadn't known of it would have had a hard time locating it. When the D/Crypt technician had scoured out the security systems, Bossk figured, the door's powered lock must have sprung it open.

Or—Bossk's hand froze on the door as he started to pull it open. *Or maybe this is the trap.*

He pulled his hand back, automatically reaching for the blaster slung at his hip. The space he could see on the other side of the door was unlit. But only for a moment longer; a quick shot from the blaster lit up everything inside.

The door now dangled loose; Bossk kicked it farther open. Light from the cockpit spilled past him and through the doorway. There was only one object in the enclosed space; a featureless, almost cubical shape, it stood nearly as tall as Bossk. For a moment he thought it was some kind of storage locker, until he spotted the pair of short, stubby legs upon which it balanced. A droid, an inert-screen load shifter; Bossk recognized the variety as one used in engineering facilities and interstellar shipyards. The large shape was essentially a shielded container for transporting quantities of lethal fissionable materials. This droid showed signs of use—its metal sides were dented and scraped—but it had obviously been decontaminated; the radiation detector that Bossk kept clipped to his belt would have gone off otherwise.

None of the droid's sensor circuits lit up as Bossk stepped closer to it. The simple electronic brain had been removed as well. Bossk wondered why Boba Fett would have bothered to do something like that—or why a droid of this dull, uninteresting type was even here aboard the *Slave I*.

The access hatch on the side of the droid was unlatched; Bossk pulled it open, bending his head to see inside. He unclipped a small electric torch from his belt and shone it around the container's interior.

Something was wrong. Bossk could tell that immediately; there was no shielding material lining the droid's cargo space. Not much room for fissionables, either; the interior was crowded with various pieces of linked equipment. Spy equipment; discreet surveillance gear was a familiar category in the bounty-hunter trade. Some of the stuff inside the droid was pretty sophisticated; Bossk recognized a full array of optical and auditory pickups, wired to micropinhole elements studding the droid's battered carcass.

Or supposedly battered. Working from a hunch, Bossk scraped a claw across the droid's exterior rust streaks; the orangish-red color came right off. *This was faked,* decided Bossk. Somebody had worked on this droid to make it look decrepit and falling apart.

He spotted another fake. Wiring from a remote-signal receiver led to a tiny radiation emitter mounted at the edge of the droid's cargo hatch. An old trick: when the emitter was activated—at a distance, with somebody's thumb on a transmitter button—there would be just enough radiation to trigger the alarms on any detection devices nearby. That would usually be enough to get even hard-core scavengers like the Jawas to abandon the machinery, for fear of contamination.

Bossk poked around some more, inside the deactivated droid. If Boba Fett had been doing the same a while back—maybe before he'd gone down to Tatooine and hired on at Jabba the Hutt's palace—he must have been interrupted before he'd gotten very far. Most of the seals were still in place on the various bits of enclosed gear. When Bossk snapped one and peeled it off a circuit module, he made an interesting discovery: the corporate emblem of Kuat Drive Yards was embossed on the silvery metal ribbon dangling in his hands.

There's a coincidence, mused Bossk. He knew it

was more than that. The messenger pod that the Q'nithian in Mos Eisley had routed his way had an intended destination at the planet Kuat, the headquarters of Kuat Drive Yards; it was supposed to go right into Kuat of Kuat's hands. Bossk's mercenary instincts were aroused by these overlapping signs of interest on the part of one of the galaxy's richest and most powerful creatures.

The big question right now was what Kuat had been using this pseudo-dilapidated droid to spy on. Bossk poked some more in the droid's innards and found at last what he was looking for, what he had known would be there. He pulled his head back out of the droid's hollow space, holding in one hand the multitrack recording unit that had been connected to the various sensors.

That must have been what Boba Fett had been looking for as well, before he'd been called away, leaving this investigation unfinished. The only other object in the concealed chamber was a tripod-mounted holographic playback unit with a full assortment of auto-adaptive connectors and data channels. Bossk sorted through the connectors until he found the one that matched up with the recorder. Both units lit up; after a few seconds of format scanning, a miniaturized, fuzzy-edged landscape formed in front of Bossk.

Someplace on Tatooine; Bossk could tell that much just from the quality of light, the mingled shadows that came with the planet's twin suns. Bossk leaned in closer to the holo image, trying to make out the details. It looked like one of those miserable, dreary moisture farms that eked out a low-profit existence on the edges of the Dune Sea.

Parallel lines from the segmented treads of a ground transport were embedded in the gravelly terrain. Even at the holo image's low resolution, Bossk could tell that they dated from at least a day before the recording had been made; the tracks were blurred by windblown sand. He figured they were from the sandcrawler of the Jawas who had dumped off this droid when they had been tricked into believing that it was contaminated with lethal radiation. Probably some farther distance away from the moisture farm so its autonomic spy circuits could kick in and it could find a surreptitious vantage point by which it could observe and record whatever happened.

And whatever happened hadn't been good. Bossk could see ugly black smoke rising to the top of the holo image as the shot's point of view moved in closer. The spy circuits in the droid must have felt it was all right to come out in the open—since every creature at the moisture farm was obviously dead. With clinical detachment, Bossk studied the charred, skeletal remains strewn in front of what was left of the farm's low, rounded structures. *Looks like a standard stormtrooper hit,* he judged. All the markings, unsubtle even by Bossk's standards, were there. The Empire's white-uniformed killers always left a clear signature on their grisly work, to intimidate anyone who stumbled upon it later.

The silence of the recorded image was broken by the rising whir of a speeder approaching from somewhere in the distance. For a moment the image's point of view tilted and bounced; obviously, the spying droid had scrambled back to someplace in the surrounding dunes where it wouldn't have been spotted.

The shot steadied at long distance, then zoomed forward as the spy circuits switched to a powerful telephoto lens. That enabled Bossk to recognize at least the figure that had scrambled out of the speeder when it had come to a bobbing halt. *That's Luke Skywalker,* he thought; there was no mistaking that youthful human face and tousled blond hair.

He leaned closer to the image, suddenly fascinated by it. *This must be the stormtrooper raid—* Bossk slowly nodded. *On that moisture farm, where Skywalker grew up.* He knew more about it than most creatures in the galaxy did; in a spaceport watering hole considerably grungier and more disreputable than even the Mos Eisley cantina, Bossk had bought drinks for and pried information out of a twitching human wreck, a former stormtrooper cashiered from the Imperial Navy for various psychological problems. Guilt, Bossk had supposed at the time; it wasn't an emotion he'd ever personally experienced. The ex-stormtrooper hadn't been involved in any action on Tatooine, but had heard grisly bits and pieces from some of his barracks mates. In typical bounty-hunter fashion, Bossk had filed away the data—and the Luke Skywalker connection—inside his head, against the day when it might prove useful. Now he wondered if that time might have come at last.

Bossk drew back from the floating image, watching as the image of Skywalker discovered the charred skeletons of the aunt and uncle who had raised him from childhood. He knew how much tighter those bonds of sentiment were for other species. He also knew about Luke Skywalker's ties to the Rebel Alliance; rumors and stories had already spread throughout the galaxy, along with ID holos and other tracking data. This mere youngster, from an obscure backwater planet, had somehow become overwhelmingly important to Emperor Palpatine and—perhaps even more so—to Lord Vader, the Empire's black-gloved fist. Vader's creatures, his personal legions of spies and informers, were still scouring all the inhabited worlds for leads on Skywalker. Why, though, was still a carefully guarded secret.

The deactivated droid and its contents were now even more intriguing to Bossk. It might not provide Skywalker's current location—which would've been worth credits; Vader would pay for that kind of data—but there might be some kind of clue as to just why both the Emperor and the Dark Lord of the Sith were so interested in him. And to a smart barve like Bossk, that could be worth even more.

Others might pay even more than Vader or Palpatine. Bossk mulled over the possibilities. After all, the droid with its carefully concealed surveillance equipment had all the appearances of having been put together by Kuat Drive Yards. Why would Kuat of Kuat have been interested in Skywalker? That would be something worth finding out as well.

In front of Bossk, the holographic image froze, having reached the end of the recording. The black smoke from the stormtroopers' raid on the moisture farm hung motionless in the small segment of the past, like the scrawled emblem of the dark forces that controlled the universe. . . .

Part of Bossk's brain, the most evolved and cautious part, told him that this was nothing with which he should get involved. The closer one got to those circles of intrigue and deceit, with Darth Vader at their center, the closer drew one's own death. *Look at what happened to Boba Fett,* he reminded himself. Fett might have suffered his final, terminal defeat because of Luke Skywalker, but he wouldn't have even been there on Jabba's sail barge, up above the Great Pit of Carkoon, if it hadn't been for Vader's endless manipulations of other sentient creatures.

The cautions voiced inside Bossk's head fell silent, consumed by the other, hungrier elements that made up a Trandoshan's nature. Boba Fett had died because he was a fool; his death proved that he was a fool. That was all the logic that Bossk needed. *He's dead and I'm alive*—that also proved he was smarter than Fett had ever been. So what was there to be afraid of?

It's this ship, Bossk thought. *I can't get any work done here.* He'd have a better chance of figuring out what the holographic recording meant if he took it back over to the *Hound's Tooth* and puzzled over it. The holographic image blinked out of existence as he reached inside the droid's cargo space and started disconnecting the circuits.

One of the data leads surprised him. It was hooked up to an olfactory sensor on the droid's exterior. He could understand wanting to get a high-resolution visual and auditory record of the event, but why collect scent molecules in the air? Corpses and stormtroopers smelled like death, if anything.

The data cable was routed to an analyzer unit rather than the recording device. The small readout panel on its angled top showed that it was set to detect organic anomalies, anything of a biological nature that shouldn't have been at the scene that the droid had spied upon. Bossk pulled out the analyzer and peered closer at the screen. It had picked up something from the recording; numbers and symbols flickered by as the device sorted out the possibilities.

After a moment the numbers slowed, then turned to letters, then words. PHEROMONES DETECTED. Another second passed before the rest appeared. SUBTYPE SEXUAL, GENDER MALE. Then the last: SPECIES MATCH—FALLEEN. The words remained until Bossk blanked the screen with a press of his clawed thumb.

That was even more interesting. Bossk nodded slowly to himself, the analyzer device resting silent in his hands. Falleens didn't serve in the Imperial stormtroopers; the whole species was too congenitally arrogant to submit to military discipline. They were fearsome enemies, but strictly solo fighters. And schemers, given to intrigues matched only by those of Emperor Palpatine himself.

And there was one Falleen in particular, who had risen almost to the top in Palpatine's court. Prince Xizor had been perhaps the only one there who could get away with defying Lord Vader's commands, and Xizor was dead now. There had been even more to Xizor's defiance than the Emperor had been aware of, though rumors told of Vader having suspected the truth. That Prince Xizor had been in fact the secret head of the infamous Black Sun, the criminal organization that spanned the galaxy, an empire in its own right.

Speculations raced inside Bossk's skull. Had Prince Xizor also been there on Tatooine when Vader's stormtroopers had raided the moisture farm at the edge of the Dune Sea? When Luke Skywalker's aunt and uncle had been killed? That was what the olfactory record in the droid's spy circuits would indicate. But it didn't tell why Xizor would have been there—or why Kuat of Kuat would have planted a surveillance system that would detect the evidence of Xizor's involvement. Or how Boba Fett had come to possess the spy recording . . .

That many questions without answers made Bossk's head hurt, as though it might explode from the pressure building within. *This is going to take some time,* he thought grimly, *to figure out.* He extracted the rest of the recording devices from the droid, stacked the metal boxes up in his hands, and turned back toward the secret chamber's doorway.

Back aboard the *Hound's Tooth*, Bossk set the spy devices down beside a corner of the cockpit's main control panel. His head ached, the scales of his brow almost visibly flexing from the pounding of his thoughts. He decided it would be better if he waited awhile—maybe even slept a bit, in the lowered respiration and nearly stilled heartbeat mode of the cold-blooded Trandoshans—before tackling the mysteries of the recorded hit on the moisture farm. *Go at it fresh,* Bossk told himself.

In the meantime there was the other matter to check out, the encoded message unit that the Q'nithian down in Mos Eisley had routed his way. Bossk was already wondering if there might be some connection between it and what he had just discovered aboard Boba Fett's *Slave I* ship. The name of Kuat was popping up in a suspicious number of connections right now—the encoded message unit was addressed to Kuat of Kuat, and the deactivated spy droid was an obvious Kuat Drive Yards construction.

He sat down at the cockpit controls of his own *Hound's Tooth* and pulled the encoded message unit over to himself. The Q'nithian had provided him with a simple bypass key and decryption protocol, with which he'd be able to read the enclosed information, then seal up the message unit and send it on its way without the eventual recipient being able to tell that its security had been breached.

Bossk extracted a single slip of paper from the unit. *That's it?* he thought, feeling slightly disappointed. When this much attempted secrecy was involved, there were usually items of obvious significance to be found—entire Imperial code manuals, battle plans, that sort of thing. As he turned the slip over he couldn't imagine that he'd find anything important on it. . . .

A moment later Bossk came to; he found himself lying on the floor, a befuddled consciousness slowly seeping back into his brain. The pilot's chair was tilted backward, from where he had toppled from it.

With trembling claws, he plucked the slip of paper from his chest. He held it up in front of his unwilling gaze. The same four words were still there. Words that changed everything, that turned the universe inside out, expelling Bossk from its bright center—

BOBA FETT IS ALIVE.

He couldn't believe it. But at the same time . . . he knew it was true.

It was always true.

20

"There they are." Phedroi used the muzzle of his blaster rifle to point over the top of the dune. "We could probably take 'em all out, right now."

Beside him, lying belly-down in the sand, Hamame shook his head. "Naw—" His rifle lay parallel to his partner's, aimed toward the three distant figures. Five, if the two medical droids were counted. "They're worth more alive than dead. Or at least Boba Fett is."

"Are you kidding?" Phedroi looked over at him in amazement. "You're going to try and take Boba Fett *alive*? That's crazy. The barve's too dangerous for that. Why push our luck? We should just be glad to get the chance to kill him."

Heat radiated up from the dune, though Tatooine's suns had set long ago. But it was more than the temperature differential between the ground and the star-swept night that kept both men sweating. One thing, Hamame knew now, to have followed the other bounty hunter Dengar all the way from Mos Eisley to here, keeping a safe distance so they wouldn't be detected; it was something entirely different to have ditched their swoops and crept within firing distance of a tough customer like this.

There was a history of bad things happening to creatures who thought they had the drop on Boba Fett.

Hamame kept watching what was going on at the mouth of the tunnel slanting beneath a low crest of hills. "There's Dengar to take care of as well," he said, voice barely more than a whisper. "Plus there's some female there—I suppose you want to off her, too."

"Well, sure." That was how Phedroi's mind worked. It probably seemed obvious enough to him. Dengar had never had much of a reputation, but if he and this woman were hanging around with Boba Fett, it would be better to err on the side of caution. And he didn't know of any safer way of handling things, other than just wiping out everyone as long as there was the chance to do so. "Isn't that what you were planning on doing?"

"Not until I've had a chance to find out some more." Hamame nodded toward Fett and his companions. "Dengar picked up a sublight relay modulator back in Mos Eisley; that's what Fett's working on right now, getting it sync'd in with his comm equipment. So, obviously, he's going to be making some kind of contact just outside the planet's atmosphere. The question is, who with?"

"How should I know?"

"Exactly," said Hamame. "You don't know. And you're going to off Boba Fett without discovering who it is he wants to talk to? Maybe there's someone out there that wants to keep him alive. Who would pay big credits if we had him and *didn't* kill him."

Phedroi thought it over. "I suppose that could be the case."

"Yeah, well, you suppose and I *know*." Hamame squinted at the scene in question, lit by Dengar holding up a small portable worklight. His and the female's shadows stretched away and merged with the surrounding darkness as they watched Boba Fett applying the sizzling point of a miniature torch to exposed circuitry. "There's a lot more going on here than what it looks like. I can tell that right down in my gut."

"I'm getting a bad feeling about this. . . ." Phedroi shook his head. "Maybe we should go back and get some more people in on this action. You know, like safety in numbers." If he could have arranged for a whole Imperial battalion to help them out, his nervousness would have been only slightly diminished. "I mean, especially if we're going to take on Boba Fett . . ."

"What, and wind up splitting the profits with every scrabbling little thief in Mos Eisley?" Hamame looked over at him in disgust. "Look. From what we can get for Boba Fett—from *somebody*—we'll be able to retire from this game. One big score, and we're golden."

Of course, he had laid that kind of talk before on his partner. That was how they had both wound up on a forsaken dump of a planet like Tatooine. *But this time*, vowed Hamame, *it'll be different*. They just had to see it through.

"All right." Phedroi looked along his blaster rifle's barrel at the other figures in the night, then back to his partner. "So just what is it you're going to do?"

Hamame stood up, his boots digging into the slope of the dune. "Simple." He smiled as he slung his blaster rifle's leather strap across his shoulder. "I'm going to go down there and talk to them."

"That does it," muttered Phedroi aloud as he watched his partner go striding toward the distant pool of light. "This is *definitely* the hardest merchandise you've ever gotten me mixed up with."

She watched him tighten and seal the last connectors. "Is that thing ready to go?" Neelah pointed to the comm unit on the pebble-strewn ground, its interior filled with the hard shadows cast by the worklight in Dengar's upraised hand.

"It has to run through its logic checks," said Boba Fett, "before it can sync up with the database of transmission codes." He set down the handheld servodriver he had been using, then picked up a circuit probe; he tapped its point against the side of his helmet. "We were real lucky—none of the onboard memory in here got corrupted, in spite of all the banging around it's gone through. If I'd had to build the comm protocols up from scratch, it would've taken a couple of days. At least."

For a moment she thought he had been talking about the contents of his head, the brain tissue encased in bone, and all its memories and hard, unfeeling personality. *The true Boba Fett,* thought Neelah. *Back from the dead.* Then she realized he was talking about the elaborate circuits inside the helmet itself, the comlink between him and his ship orbiting above the planet's atmosphere. What was it called? He'd told her; something sinister and cold, stripped of even the minimal affection that could exist between a sentient creature and his tools. *Slave,* Neelah remembered. *Slave I; that was it.* Something to be used and discarded, when its pure functionality was at an end. She supposed that human beings and all other sentient creatures were that way for him as well. That was how things had been in the palace of Jabba the Hutt as well; when there had been more amusement to be gained from tossing poor Oola into the rancor pit, nothing else mattered to the master holding the other end of the chain.

She had been there, and she had been lucky to escape. Not just luck; she had fought and schemed her way out of the palace and the inevitable death it had held. Better to die out in the wastes of the Dune Sea, bones cracked by the desert's scavengers, than be the victim of a fat slug's idle boredom. *But where did I wind up instead?* That was the question that circled in Neelah's mind as she watched the two bounty hunters. It had been one thing to get hooked up with a mercenary creature like Boba Fett when he had represented nothing more than a mystery to her, the black hole of her own hidden past. It was another thing entirely now that he had recovered from his wounds and was pursuing his own agenda again. Revenge and credits, supposed Neelah, in varying proportions; that was all that any bounty hunter was concerned with. Even this Dengar, though he had given some indication of a human nature developed beyond those two fundamental desires. She knew that she could trust either one of them just about as far as she pitch them both across the dunes with one hand. Creatures who trusted *any* bounty hunter usually wound up as merchandise or corpses, depending upon what was best for business.

The questions inside her head were going to be answered soon. Neelah didn't know yet what those answers were going to be, but she had already started preparing herself for them. *Whatever happens,* she told herself again, *I'm not going to be left behind.* The bigger questions were all tied up with Boba Fett; if she was going to uncover both her past and her fate, she couldn't let the bounty hunter slip away from her. Even if it meant risking her life to follow after him. Or losing her life, to find out those things.

Neelah turned and walked away from the pool of light toward the desert's surrounding darkness. The answers might not be anywhere on this planet, but the night provided enough emptiness to hold her thoughts.

"Stay right there." A man's voice. "Don't move."

She found herself gazing into a scruff-bearded face, pockmarks and scars underneath the grime of hard, exposed traveling. One corner of his mouth lifted in a smile, exposing yellow teeth. Before she could react, the man had raised the muzzle of a blaster rifle, slung by a leather strap from his shoulder. At waist height, the weapon pointed straight at her.

"Nothing to worry about," said the man. "This is just to show you that I'm serious. You be serious, too—no messing around—and nothing bad is gonna happen."

"What do you want?" Neelah kept her voice low. She wasn't sure which would be worse, alarming this person or the two bounty hunters somewhere behind her. Any one of them might start firing, just to quickly settle matters. If she was standing between the blasters and their targets, that would be just too bad. For her.

"Not you. At least, not right now." The other corner of the man's mouth lifted, slowly, as though dragged upward by an invisible hook. "Later maybe we can discuss some off-time interests. But right now I gotta go talk to your friends."

Both Boba Fett and Dengar glanced over as Neelah walked back into the worklight's circle. When they saw the man close behind her, Fett stood up, leaving the comm unit's last bolt untightened. Dengar reached for the blaster pistol in his holster, then stayed his hand without drawing the weapon.

"Well, here's a happy little gathering." The man lowered the barrel of his blaster rifle from where it had been pressing into the small of Neelah's back. "Old friends like us really oughta try to get together more often."

"Vol Hamame," said Dengar with a sour grimace and a nod. "I thought I spotted you back there in Mos Eisley."

"You should've said hello. Then I wouldn't have had to come all the way out to this place. Not that it doesn't have its charms." The man looked around at the sloping hillsides, barely visible at the edge of the worklight's glow. Then he turned back to the two bounty hunters. "But I'm more of a city kind of guy, if you know what I mean."

"Then that's where you should stay." Boba Fett spoke up, his voice level and emotionless. "So you can mind your own business, instead of interfering with anyone else's."

Looking over her shoulder, Neelah saw the man called Hamame shake his head, feigning regret.

"Actually, this *is* my business." Hamame used his free hand to point toward the bounty hunters. "That's why I followed Dengar out here. Pretty easy, actually, what with that frapped-out swoop bike he was on. Just about fell asleep, it went so slow. But it was worth it, just to get here and find out that you really are alive, after all."

Boba Fett looked over at Dengar. "Seems as though you didn't do a very good job of keeping things secret."

"Don't blame him," said Hamame. "Let's just say I've got my contacts pretty well lined up in Mos

Eisley. There isn't much that I *don't* hear about. I get the news on all the little stuff, so it wouldn't have been very likely that I'd miss out on something big like this. There's a whole galaxy out there that's heard you're dead; most creatures would figure you'd be just about digested inside the Sarlacc by now. Some creatures—I don't know who—might be happy to hear you made it out. There's a whole bunch of others who would probably be a lot *less* than happy when they find that you're walking around again."

"That's their problem." Fett gave a slight shrug. "And it might be a while before they find out, anyway. Especially since you won't be telling them."

"Hold it right there." With one quick motion, Hamame pushed Neelah aside as his other hand swung the blaster rifle up into firing position. The shove was hard enough to send her sprawling onto her knees, the sand and gravel scraping her palms raw. "Get your hands up." He gestured with the rifle's muzzle. "Step away from that box."

"This?" Boba Fett's gloved hands were already level with his helmet. With the toe of his boot, he gave the comm unit a kick. "It's not even operational."

"I don't care if it's as dead as you're supposed to be." A few lights had blinked on the control panel of the comm unit. Hamame raised the muzzle of the blaster rifle higher, aiming from his hip straight toward Boba Fett's helmet. "Just get away from it. You know what kind of reputation you've got, being a tricky barve and all. I don't want any surprises."

Fett moved toward where Dengar was standing with his hands raised. "Careful," said Fett. "Trust me—you won't get nearly as much for a corpse as you will for living merchandise."

"I'll take what I can get," said Hamame. "Especially since you don't have any choice about talking right now." He smiled as he kept the blaster rifle trained toward Dengar and Boba Fett. "Amazing how persuasive something as simple as this can be when you're looking down its barrel. There's a bunch of questions I'd like some answers to. *Profitable* answers."

"Don't be an idiot." Dengar spoke up. "If you want credits, there are easier ways of getting them than this. And less dangerous. Just let us go, and we'll make it worth your while."

"Oh, *sure;* I'll trust you to send the credits. You can send it care of the Mos Eisley cantina." Hamame shook his head with a grimace of disgust. "Get real. Whatever you two could pay for your hides isn't anything compared to what some others would be willing to." He looked straight toward the other bounty hunter. "There are some *big* players interested in Boba Fett's welfare, and I mean to make sure that they're gonna have to make me happy before they get to do whatever it is they want with you."

Neelah lay on the ground where she had landed, keeping still as she listened to the exchange going on above. The man's choice of words tipped her off. *Whatever you two could pay for your hides.* He was exactly the sort who'd forget all about a female's presence, whenever he didn't have any specific use for her. Just as if she didn't exist . . . or couldn't do something about the situation.

"You forgot something."

Her voice actually surprised him, as though it had suddenly come from nowhere. The man's startled gaze swung around and then down to her; that slight movement was echoed in his torso, turning it toward her. That opened up just enough of an angle for Neelah to dig the points of her elbows into the ground, plant one boot sole flat with her leg bent, and straighten the other leg into a kick straight to the man's crotch. The look in his eyes showed that he was fully aware of her now.

The man went down, falling heavily on his side, but managing to keep some semblance of control. He jammed the butt of the blaster rifle hard against his ribs as his knees drew up in an instinctive fetal position. His fist squeezed tight on the trigger, getting off a line of fire that coursed within inches of Neelah's head as she scrambled to her feet and ran toward the others. She had to take another dive to get out of the way as Boba Fett snatched up his own blaster from the pile of equipment he had stacked up while working on the comm unit. Without taking time to aim, Fett laid down a quick series of shots that stitched the ground close to the other figure, now rolling shoulder-first into a sandy hollow. His return fire, desperate and inaccurate, was still enough to drive Fett back toward the rocky hillside.

"In here!" Dengar grabbed Neelah's forearm and pulled her into the safety of the shallow cave. He pushed her behind himself, then grabbed the blaster rifle that had been propped against the side of the opening. He braced the weapon against himself and started firing. The covering barrage lit up the night, sending hard-edged shadows jittering across the rocks and sand dunes. The shots forced the other man's head below the lip of his shelter, giving Boba Fett enough time to break off his own fire and sprint, back hunched low, to his companions.

From inside the cave, Neelah and the two bounty hunters heard the raised voice of the man outside. "Phedroi!" He wasn't shouting to them, but to some other figure, unseen in the surrounding darkness. "Get in on this! Now!"

The command was hardly necessary; his partner, who must have been watching everything all along, now directed a hot fusillade their way from an angle that gave him a clear shot into the cave's mouth. Boba Fett fired back as all three of them retreated farther inside.

"Now what?" Neelah looked around the rough-hewn rock as the barrage of blaster fire lit up the space. All the other weapons in Boba Fett's carefully hidden stash had already been dragged outside with the other gear. Both Fett and Dengar had their spines planted against opposite walls of the cave, leaning forward just enough to get off a few quick shots before snapping their heads back from the bolts that sizzled past them. "We're stuck here—this hole doesn't go anywhere!"

"It wasn't meant to." Boba Fett didn't look back around at her. "You don't get anywhere by running away from creatures like these."

"Good theory." Across the cave, Dengar held his blaster rifle close against his chest, watching the shifting shadows in the darkness outside, waiting for another chance at a well-aimed shot. "Gets a little tight when you try to put it into practice."

Boba Fett gave a small shrug, his shoulders scraping against the rock behind him. "Don't worry about it." His voice remained as calm and drained of apparent emotion as before. "Everything's under control."

"What are you talking about?" From the back of the cave, Neelah stared at the bounty hunter in dismay. She had already come to the limit of the space, no more than a few meters from the opening in the hillside's rocky slope. "There's no way out of here!

They've got us pinned down—they can either wait us out, till your blasters are exhausted, or they can call in more of their friends." A couple more shots blazed through the middle of the cave, striking the roof above her and showering down a rain of scorched rock shards. "Either way, they've got us!"

"As I said, don't worry."

The bounty hunter's calm response infuriated Neelah. The thought of dying in this hole—or worse, being dragged out of it after the pair outside had finished off Boba Fett and Dengar—infuriated her. *I didn't escape from Jabba's palace to wind up like this.* There were still too many things she didn't know, too many questions without answers—her real name, where she had come from, how she had gotten here—to let bleed away into the sand. If there had been any chance of pulling it off, she would have grabbed one of the blasters out of the others' hands and made a break, firing and charging headlong at the two-man siege force outside. Anything would be better than waiting here for the inevitable.

Dengar turned his face away from the cave opening. "If you've got some kind of plan—" The blaster rifle's muzzle touched his chin as he held the weapon in a diagonal line across his chest. "I'd appreciate being let in on it, too."

"If there was anything you could do about it, one way or the other, I might tell you." Boba Fett fired a quick couple of bursts outside, before glancing over at Dengar. "But there isn't. All you have to do is wait. And you'll see."

"That's great," said Neelah sourly. She had to raise her voice over the noise of another fusillade streaking through the dark and carving the back of the cave out in sparks. Her disgust had reached the point where nothing, not even laser bolts, could make her flinch. "All this time I thought you were recovering from what happened to you—only it turns out that your brains are still fried."

Boba Fett made no reply. "Hold your fire," he instructed Dengar.

"But they've come in closer." Dengar used the rifle muzzle to point outside. "The one that was out in the dunes—he's moved up. He's got an even better angle now."

"That's all right. I want the two of them together. Or close enough."

"Why?" Dengar looked puzzled. "You think you can take both of them out? I can cover you if you want to take a shot at it."

"That won't be necessary."

The flashes from the weapons outside were enough for Neelah to tell that Dengar was correct; the two besiegers were now within a couple of meters of each other, crouching down behind a shallow lip of rock. From there, they would be able to fire straight into the cave.

"Don't bother trying to talk to him." Neelah nodded toward Boba Fett. "He's so far gone he can't tell when there's no way—"

A sudden noise interrupted her. From above, as though the night itself had split open; the sound grew from a distant shriek to a roar that spanned the audible frequencies. The cave itself vibrated, as had the one containing the Sarlacc's still-living segment; dust sifted from cracks spidering overhead, then pebbles and finally broken rocks large enough to cut Neelah's arm as she shielded her brow. From underneath her forearm, she could see Dengar leaning forward, blaster rifle lowered, gazing outside in wonderment.

His shadow leaped toward her, as did that of Boba Fett; both bounty hunters were silhouetted by the fiery glare that had banished what was left of the night. The encircled sand dunes were lit up as though by the fall of Tatooine's twin suns. Beyond the cave's mouth, the two other figures were visible, turning onto their sides and raising their outspread hands, trying to ward off the weight rushing down toward them.

All that happened in a few seconds, from the first whisper and bare glow, to the half-rounded shape that appeared just above the desert floor, balanced on the fiery column of its landing engines. One of the two men was able to scramble to his feet and run, making a final dive headlong that took him beyond the quickly braked impact of the ship. The other managed only to get to his knees, blaster rifle pressed into the sand beneath his palm; then the tail of the craft, nozzles blackened and still hot, crushed him flat.

"Oh." Dengar's voice broke the silence, the thrusting roar replaced by the glassy crackle of the molten sand cooling. "It's your ship. It's the *Slave I*."

Neelah realized what had happened. *He got through,* she thought. *On the comm unit.* The link between the gear inside his helmet, the small transceiver antenna mounted at the side, and the equipment that Dengar had fetched back from the Mos Eisley spaceport—Boba Fett must have gotten that up and running just before the other two men had shown up. And all the time that the one named Hamame had been talking, and then when he had swung the blaster rifle up onto his hip, Fett had been sending a signal straight to his ship, outside Tatooine's atmosphere. Giving *Slave I*, as Dengar had called the craft, the exact coordinates of this location—exact enough to bring it right down on the heads of the two men. One of them was still partly visible underneath the ship, a leg and an arm showing, his weapon lying on the sand just a few inches away from his fingers. He wouldn't be making any deals anytime soon.

"Come on." Boba Fett moved toward the cave's opening. "Let's get going. There's no reason to hang around here."

She didn't know whether he had been speaking to both of them or just to Dengar. But she wasn't taking any chances. Neelah let the two men go before, at a quick sprint toward the *Slave I* ship. From the darkness of the surrounding dunes, a volley of laser bolts scorched the sand at their feet; the other besieger hadn't given up yet. Neelah didn't let that stop her from following after Boba Fett and Dengar, and quickly scooping up the dead man's blaster rifle as she ran.

"Hold it." At the hatchway of the ship, Neelah raised the weapon, her thumb at its firing stud. "Stop right there."

Dengar was already inside; with one gloved hand grasping the side of the hatch, Boba Fett turned and looked over his shoulder, his visored gaze meeting that of the blaster rifle's muzzle.

"You're not going anywhere without me," said Neelah coldly.

Boba Fett's hand shot out before she could react, the motion faster than her eye could perceive. His fist locked onto the rifle barrel; with a quick twist of his arm, he had wrenched it out of her grasp. The weapon went spinning through the air as he flung it away, landing within inches of the corpse's unmoving arm.

They stood looking at each other for a moment. Then Boba Fett reached down and grabbed Neelah's wrist, and pulled her up toward the hatchway.

"Don't be stupid." Fett's grasp tightened, squeezing the bones together. "I'm the one who decides who goes and who stays. And right now you're too valuable a piece of merchandise to leave behind."

A second later she was inside the ship, with the hatchway door sliding shut behind herself. "Brace yourself," said Fett as he headed for a metal ladder at the side of the space. "We're leaving now."

Neelah rubbed her aching wrist. As she looked about herself, at the bleak metal bars of the cages, she realized—though she didn't know when, in what part of her shrouded past—that she had been here before.

"That is just so *entirely* typical." SHΣ1-B tilted his head unit back, watching the ship ascend swiftly into the night sky. "You go to all that trouble fixing them up, putting them back together, and they don't even bother to thank you."

"Ingratitude." 1e-XE stood next to the taller medical droid. They had both come creeping out of their hiding places when the shooting had finally stopped. By now, even the human out in the dunes had presumably left, heading back to whatever den of iniquity he had come from; at least, there was no longer any indication of his presence. That was a further disappointment to both droids; after an encounter with Boba Fett, the man might have had some interesting wounds to take care of. "Thoughtlessness."

"But of course, what else can you expect?" The ship's glowing trail had already dwindled to a speck of light among the stars. The hope had formed inside SHΣ1-B's circuits—to the degree that a droid *could* hope—that it and 1e-XE would have been taken along with the humans, particularly the one they had nursed back to health, the one named Boba Fett. They would have certainly been able to earn their energy sources, what with the considerable amount of tissue damage he had the knack for creating. "It's their nature, I suppose. All flesh thinks it's immortal." SHΣ1-B brought its gaze down from the sky to the surrounding empty desert. "Now what?"

"Unemployment," squeaked 1e-XE's voice. "Needlessness."

SHΣ1-B looked at its companion for a moment. Then it extruded one of its scalpel-tipped arms and scraped a spot of rust from 1e-XE's dented carapace. "You know"—SHΣ1-B's voice spoke with measured consideration—"you could use a little maintenance. . . ."

21

He hated to do it. But Bossk knew he had to.

The greed impulses in his Trandoshan brain, as hardwired as any droid's circuits, almost overruled all the others. He could hear the words inside his head, ancient bounty-hunter wisdom, told to him by his own father: *The live ones are worth more than the dead ones.* Old Cradossk had known what he was talking about, at least about that; whenever Bossk ran his clawed hands along the picked-clean bones he'd kept as mementos, he had a renewed sense of legacy and tradition. But even so, another truth remained, equally hard and obdurate. Things were different when you were dealing with a creature like Boba Fett.

On the screen of the *Hound's Tooth*'s long-distance scanner, in the cramped cockpit, Bossk could see the tiny speck of light that represented Fett's ship. The *Slave I* had already left the surface of Tatooine, as Bossk had known it would. Soon— within seconds—it would be beyond the planet's atmosphere, and then it would be within his own sighting and tracking range. That was how little time Bossk had remaining to him to press the button beneath his clawed thumb and accomplish all that was necessary. No time for rethinking his decisions or regretting lost profits.

He had been back aboard *Slave I*, extracting a few more interesting files from its data bank, when the comm controls had lit up like the bright sparks of a disintegrating asteroid. That could mean only one thing: that the message about Boba Fett being alive was true, and that he had just reinitiated contact with the ship that he had left in orbit above Tatooine. Bossk had also known what was to follow. *Slave I* would obediently follow Boba Fett's remote-transmitted commands, switch on and prime its engines, and head down to Tatooine to rendezvous with its master. And then Boba Fett would not only be alive, but free and active in the galaxy once again. Free and active—and the top, number-one bounty hunter on all the galaxy's scattered worlds.

Bossk could still feel the rage and fear that had come boiling up inside him. Rage was a familiar emotion—Trandoshans woke up angry—but fear was something new. And powerful: it had pushed him into action, quick and efficient.

He hadn't wasted any thought on the mysteries that had been so tantalizingly uncovered to him. If the rich and powerful Kuat of Kuat was interested in Boba Fett being alive or dead, so be it; Bossk might still be able to cash in by confirming it to the owner of Kuat Drive Yards. And if there was some connection between Prince Xizor, the Black Sun's hidden ruler, and the raid on the moisture farm at the Dune Sea's edge . . . the answers about that weren't going to come from Boba Fett. Bossk would make sure of that.

There had been just enough time to haul a sufficient quantity of high-thermal explosives over from the *Hound's Tooth*, conceal them in the holding cages of Fett's ship, and rig the remote triggering device. Then Bossk had sealed the entrance hatchway of *Slave I*, disconnected his own ship, and watched from his cockpit viewport as the other craft had sped planet-ward.

Now that ship was heading back into space, bearing its helmeted master. The speck of light had grown larger; another second, and Bossk would have waited too long. All regret was expunged from his heart. He pressed the button on the cockpit's control panel. Instantaneously, the ominous light was transformed into a ball of churning flame, surrounded by extinguishing vacuum. Radiant sparks, bits of heated metal no bigger than a human's hand, drifted away from the core of the explosion, the dust and atoms of the other ship.

Bossk leaned back in the pilot's chair, feeling exhausted as the tension began to drain from his coiled muscles. *That does it,* he thought with relief. *Boba Fett's dead now. For good . . .*

No regrets; he knew it had to be done.

But one thing still puzzled Bossk as he gazed out at the emptiness between the stars.

Why did he still feel afraid?

About the Author

K. W. JETER is one of the most respected sf writers working today. His first novel, *Dr. Adder,* was described by Philip K. Dick as "a stunning novel . . . it destroys once and for all your conception of the limitations of science fiction." *The Edge of Human* resolves many discrepancies between the movie *Blade Runner* and the novel upon which it was based, Dick's *Do Androids Dream of Electric Sheep?* Jeter's other books have been described as having a "brain-burning intensity" (*The Village Voice*), as being "hard-edged and believable" (*Locus*) and "a joy from first word to last" (*San Francisco Chronicle*). He is the author of over twenty novels, including *Farewell Horizontal* and *Wolf Flow.* His new novel, *Noir,* will be published shortly.

The World of
STAR WARS Novels

In May 1991, *Star Wars* caused a sensation in the publishing industry with the Bantam Spectra release of Timothy Zahn's novel *Heir to the Empire*. For the first time, Lucasfilm Ltd. had authorized new novels that *continued* the famous story told in George Lucas's three block-buster motion pictures: *Star Wars*, *The Empire Strikes Back*, and *Return of the Jedi*. Reader reaction was immediate and tumultuous: *Heir* reached #1 on the *New York Times* bestseller list and demonstrated that *Star Wars* lovers were eager for exciting new stories set in this universe, written by leading science fiction authors who shared their passion. Since then, each Bantam *Star Wars* novel has been an instant national bestseller.

Lucasfilm and Bantam decided that future novels in the series would be interconnected: that is, events in one novel would have consequences in the others. You might say that each Bantam *Star Wars* novel, enjoyable on its own, is also part of a much larger tale.

Here is a special look at Bantam's *Star Wars* books, along with excerpts from the more recent novels. Each one is available now wherever Bantam Books are sold.

The Han Solo Trilogy:
THE PARADISE SNARE
THE HUTT GAMBIT
REBEL DAWN
by A. C. Crispin
Setting: Before *Star Wars: A New Hope*

What was Han Solo like before we met him in the first STAR WARS movie? This trilogy answers that tantalizing question, filling in lots of historical lore about our favorite swashbuckling hero and thrilling us with adventures of the brash young pilot that we never knew he'd experienced. As the trilogy begins, the young Han makes a life-changing decision: to escape from the clutches of Garris Shrike, head of the trading "clan" who has brutalized Han while taking advantage of his piloting abilities. Here's a tense early scene from The Paradise Snare *featuring Han, Shrike, and Dewlanna, a Wookiee who is Han's only friend in this horrible situation:*

"I've had it with you, Solo. I've been lenient with you so far, because you're a blasted good swoop pilot and all that prize money came in handy, but my patience is ended." Shrike ceremoniously pushed up the sleeves of his bedizened uniform, then balled his hands into fists. The galley's artificial lighting made the blood-jewel ring glitter dull silver. "Let's see what a few days of fighting off Devaronian blood-poisoning does for your attitude—along with maybe a few broken bones. I'm doing this for your own good, boy. Someday you'll thank me."

Han gulped with terror as Shrike started toward him. He'd lashed out at the trader captain once before, two years ago, when he'd been feeling cocky after winning the gladiatorial Free-For-All on Jubilar—and had been instantly sorry. The speed and strength of Garris's returning blow had snapped his head back and split both lips so thoroughly that Dewlanna had had to feed him mush for a week until they healed.

With a snarl, Dewlanna stepped forward. Shrike's hand dropped to his blaster. "You stay out of this, old Wookiee," he snapped in a voice nearly as harsh as Dewlanna's. "Your cooking isn't *that* good."

Han had already grabbed his friend's furry arm and was forcibly holding her back. "Dewlanna, no!"

She shook off his hold as easily as she would have waved off an annoying insect and roared at Shrike. The captain drew his blaster, and chaos erupted.

"Noooo!" Han screamed, and leaped forward, his foot lashing out in an old street-fighting technique. His instep impacted solidly with Shrike's breastbone. The captain's breath went out in a great *houf!* and he went over backward. Han hit the deck and rolled. A tingler bolt sizzled past his ear.

"Larrad!" wheezed the captain as Dewlanna started toward him.

Shrike's brother drew his blaster and pointed it at the Wookiee. "Stop, Dewlanna!"

His words had no more effect than Han's. Dewlanna's blood was up—she was in full Wookiee battle rage. With a roar that deafened the combatants, she grabbed Larrad's wrist and yanked, spinning him around and snapping him in a terrible parody of a child's "snap the whip" game. Han heard a *crunch,* mixed with several *pops* as tendons and ligaments gave way. Larrad Shrike shrieked, a high, shrill noise that carried such pain that the Corellian youth's arm ached in sympathy.

Grabbing the blaster from his belt, Han snapped off a shot at the Elomin who was leaping forward, tingler ready and aimed at Dewlanna's midsection. Brafid howled, dropping his weapon. Han was amazed that he'd managed to hit him, but he didn't have long to wonder about the accuracy of his aim.

Shrike was staggering to his feet, blaster in hand, aimed squarely at Han's head. "Larrad?" he yelled at the writhing heap of agony that was his brother. Larrad did not reply.

Shrike cocked the blaster and stepped even closer to Han. "Stop it, Dewlanna!" the captain snarled at the Wookiee. "Or your buddy Solo dies!"

Han dropped his blaster and put his hands up in a gesture of surrender.

Dewlanna stopped in her tracks, growling softly.

Shrike leveled the blaster, and his finger tightened on the trigger. Pure malevolent hatred was etched upon his features, and then he smiled, pale blue eyes glittering with ruthless joy. "For insubordination and striking your captain," he announced, "I sentence you to death, Solo. May you rot in all the hells there ever were."

SHADOWS OF THE EMPIRE
by Steve Perry
Setting: Between *The Empire Strikes Back* and *Return of the Jedi*

Here is a very special STAR WARS story dealing with Black Sun, a galaxy-spanning criminal organization that is masterminded by one of the most interesting villains in the STAR WARS universe: Xizor, dark prince of the Falleen. Xizor's chief rival for the favor of Emperor Palpatine is none other than Darth Vader himself—alive and well, and a major character in this story, since it is set during the events of the STAR WARS film trilogy.

In the opening prologue, we revisit a familiar scene from The Empire Strikes Back, *and are introduced to our marvelous new bad guy:*

He looks like a walking corpse, Xizor thought. *Like a mummified body dead a thousand years. Amazing he is still alive, much less the most powerful man in the galaxy. He isn't even that old; it is more as if something is slowly eating him.*

Xizor stood four meters away from the Emperor, watching as the man who had long ago been Senator Palpatine moved to stand in the holocam field. He imagined he could smell the decay in the Emperor's worn body. Likely that was just some trick of the recycled air, run through dozens of filters to ensure that there was no chance of any poison gas being introduced into it. Filtered the life out of it, perhaps, giving it that dead smell.

The viewer on the other end of the holo-link would see a close-up of the Emperor's head and shoulders, of an age-ravaged face shrouded in the cowl of his dark zeyd-cloth robe. The man on the other end of the transmission, light-years away, would not see Xizor, though Xizor would be able to see him. It was a measure of the Emperor's trust that Xizor was allowed to be here while the conversation took place.

The man on the other end of the transmission—if he could still be called that—

The air swirled inside the Imperial chamber in front of the Emperor, coalesced, and blossomed into the image of a figure down on one knee. A caped humanoid biped dressed in jet black, face hidden under a full helmet and breathing mask:

Darth Vader.

Vader spoke: "What is thy bidding, my master?"

If Xizor could have hurled a power bolt through time and space to strike Vader dead, he would have done it without blinking. Wishful thinking: Vader was too powerful to attack directly.

"There is a great disturbance in the Force," the Emperor said.

"I have felt it," Vader said.

"We have a new enemy. Luke Skywalker."

Skywalker? That had been Vader's name, a long time ago. Who was this person with the same name, someone so powerful as to be worth a conversation between the Emperor and his most loathsome creation? More importantly, why had Xizor's agents not uncovered this before now? Xizor's ire was instant—but cold. No sign of his surprise or anger would show on his imperturbable features. The Falleen did not allow their emotions to burst forth as did many of the inferior species; no, the Falleen ancestry was not fur but scales, not mammalian but reptilian. Not wild but coolly calculating. Such was much better. Much safer.

"Yes, my master," Vader continued.

"He could destroy us," the Emperor said.

Xizor's attention was riveted upon the Emperor and the holographic image of Vader kneeling on the deck of a ship far away. Here was interesting news indeed. Something the Emperor perceived as a danger to himself? Something the Emperor feared?

"He's just a boy," Vader said. "Obi-Wan can no longer help him."

Obi-Wan. That name Xizor knew. He was among the last of the Jedi Knights, a general. But he'd been dead for decades, hadn't he?

Apparently Xizor's information was wrong if Obi-Wan had been helping someone who was still a boy. His agents were going to be sorry.

The Bounty Hunter Wars
Book 1: THE MANDALORIAN ARMOR
by K. W. Jeter
Setting: During *Return of the Jedi*

The most cunning and dangerous bounty hunter in the universe, Boba Fett, struggles to fight Prince Xizor and defeat his evil plan to smash the power of the bounty hunters' guild.

THE TRUCE AT BAKURA
by Kathy Tyers
Setting: Immediately after *Return of the Jedi*

The day after his climactic battle with Emperor Palpatine and the sacrifice of his father, Darth Vader, who died saving his life, Luke Skywalker helps recover an Imperial drone ship bearing a startling message intended for the Emperor. It is a distress signal from the far-off Imperial outpost of Bakura, which is under attack by an alien invasion force, the Ssi-ruuk. Leia sees a rescue mission as an opportunity to achieve a diplomatic victory for the Rebel Alliance, even if it means fighting alongside former Imperials. But Luke receives a vision from Obi-Wan Kenobi revealing that the stakes are even higher: the invasion at Bakura threatens everything the Rebels have won at such great cost.

Star Wars: X-Wing:
by Michael A. Stackpole
ROGUE SQUADRON
WEDGE'S GAMBLE
THE KRYTOS TRAP
THE BACTA WAR

WRAITH SQUADRON
IRON FIST
by Aaron Allston
Setting: Three years after *Return of the Jedi*

Inspired by X-wing, the bestselling computer game from LucasArts Entertainment Co., this exciting series chronicles the further adventures of the most feared and fearless fighting force in the galaxy. A new generation of X-wing pilots, led by Commander Wedge Antilles, is combating the remnants of the Empire still left after the events of the STAR WARS movies. Here are novels full of explosive space action, nonstop adventure, and the special brand of wonder known as STAR WARS.

In this scene from the opening of Wraith Squadron, *Wedge Antilles must enter into a devil's bargain in order to create a controversial new unit:*

"You'll remember when I reorganized Rogue Squadron a few years back, I took the best pilots I could transfer or steal . . . but when it came down to choosing between pilots of equal skill, I always chose the one who had useful ground-based skills as well."

"Yes. You wanted pilots who could also be commandos."

"I got them. And they got quite a workout as commandos, especially in the liberation of Coruscant from the Empire and then of Thyferra from Ysanne Isard."

Ackbar managed to smile again. "You have certainly justified our faith in your experiment. Rogue Squadron performed magnificently."

"Thank you. Speaking for my men and women, I have to agree. But I'd originally thought that Rogue Squadron would be used opportunistically: a strike mission would reveal a ground-based weakness, and we'd have the training and supplies to go down and perform the necessary ground mission. The way it turned out, we keep landing full-fledged commando missions. So I think we need another commando X-wing squadron, one where we choose pilots so as to have a full range of intrusion and subversion skills. Rogue Squadron was designed as a fighter unit first, commando unit second; this time, I want to go the other way around."

Admiral Ackbar's expression, so far as Wedge could read was dubious. "Historically, we've had few problems coordinating the efforts of commandos on the ground and fighter pilots for aerial support."

"I don't agree. Commandos can communicate strike locations to the pilots, but the pilots still won't have the familiarity with these locations that the intrusion team will. Commandos who've had their extraction plans busted might want to seize enemy spacecraft to escape; the way things stand, they can't count on having enough pilots to make that escape, while commando-trained pilots could. Normal pilots follow orders and conform themselves to standard tactics—and should! But a commando X-wing unit might develop new tactics. New ways of mounting even ordinary raids and pursuits. New ways of anticipating assaults and ambushes."

Ackbar abruptly leaned back from him, his eyes half closing; it looked to Wedge like a frown of concentration. "What made you say that?"

"Thinking about the subject on the long flight home, and during the time we were garrisoned on Thyferra before that," Wedge said. "Even though the garrison assignment was cut short from the two months originally planned, it still gave me plenty of time to think."

"You haven't heard any news?"

"No, sir. About what?"

Ackbar shook his head. "Please go on."

"Well, that's actually about it. I can dress it up in a formal report for you. But one other thing I think is important—I can give you a unit like this for free."

Ackbar snorted, the sound emerging as a series of rubbery pops. "Can you, now?"

"Yes, sir. First, the replacement Rogue Squadron is being disbanded, its pilots and X-wings being returned to their original units. Correct?"

"Correct."

"So you'll be issuing a dozen new X-wings to us, won't you? To the original Rogue Squadron."

"Why would we? Your X-wings are in functional shape, are they not?"

"Well, yes, but they're not New Republic property any longer. They were sold to my second-in-command, Tycho Celchu, at the start of our operation against Thyferra. They're his personal property, held in trust for all of us, until and unless he decides to vest ownership in their pilots."

"How uncharitable of you. You could donate their use to the New Republic. I believe one of your pilots has been using his personal X-wing all along."

"Yes, sir. Lieutenant Horn. And Tycho would be glad to loan his snubfighters to the New Republic, for the use of Rogue Squadron, if . . ."

"If the next dozen X-wings out of the factories are assigned to your new commando squadron."

"Yes, sir."

"That's blackmail. It's unbecoming."

"Most unconventional tactics are unbecoming until they succeed, Admiral. I direct your attention to the planet Thyferra . . ."

"Be quiet. There's still the matter of pilots. Fresh out of the Academy, their training costing hundreds of thousand of credits apiece. That is not 'free.' "

'No, sir. I don't want new pilots. I want experienced ones."

"Which is an even more significant expense."

"No, sir, not with these pilots. I want pilots no one else wants. Washouts. Pilots staring court-martials in the face. Troublemakers and screwups."

Ackbar stared as if he couldn't believe his tympanic membranes. "In the name of the Force, Commander, *why*?"

"Well, some of them, of course, will be irredeemable. I'll wash them out, too. Some of them will be good men and women who've screwed up one time too many, who know their careers are dead but would give anything for one more chance . . ."

"You're more likely to get a proton torpedo up your engines than you are to get a functional squadron out of such pilots. The torpedo might be launched accidentally . . . but that's no comfort to a widow."

Wedge spread his hands, palms up, and smiled. "Problem solved. I'm not married."

"I know you're not. You know what I mean."

"Yes, sir."

"What would become of Rogue Squadron?"

"I'd be happy to remain in charge officially, but for all squadron activities, Captain Celchu is more than qualified to lead . . . and now that he's been cleared of the formal charge of Corran Horn's murder and the informal charge of being a brainwashed double agent, there shouldn't be any responsible objection to his full return to duties. I'd return Lieutenant Hobbie Klivan to Rogue Squadron as second-in-command and take Lieutenant Wes Janson as my own second-in-command. Once the new squadron is established, of course, I'd hope to return to direct command of Rogue Squadron."

"You're committed to this idea, aren't you?"

"Yes, sir." Wedge considered what he was about to say. "Since the battle at Endor, the military's public relations groups have represented Rogue Squadron as if we were the lightsaber of the New Republic. A bright, shiny weapon to cut down any dark Imperial holdovers who still stand against us. But, sir, not all battles call for lightsabers. Some of them are fought with vibroblades in back alleys. The New Republic needs those vibroblades too, and doesn't have them."

"I understand." Ackbar nodded agreeably. "Request refused."

Wedge couldn't speak; suddenly all the air seemed to leave his chest. He'd thought he was so close, thought he had convinced the admiral.

"Unless . . ."

Wedge found his voice again. "Unless?"

"I'll make a bet with you, Commander. You get your chance at forming this squadron. If, three months after it goes operational, it has proven its worth—in *my sole estimation*—you can do as you please.

Continue with the new squadron, go back to command Rogue Squadron, whichever you choose.''

''And if I lose?''

''You accept promotion to the rank of general and join my advisory staff.''

Wedge kept his dismay from his face. ''I would seem to win either way, sir.''

''Stop it. You're not fooling anyone. If you had your way, you'd continue flying snubfighters and commanding fighter squadrons until your were a century old. How many promotions have you turned down? Two? Three?''

''Two.''

''Well, if you lose your bet, you accept his one.''

Wedge sighed and thought it over. He needed to keep flying; he wouldn't be happy in any other way of life. But the New Republic military needed this new tactic, needed many new ways of doing things, before they became as tactically fossilized as the Empire had been. ''I accept, sir.''

THE COURTSHIP OF PRINCESS LEIA
by Dave Wolverton
Setting: Four years after *Return of the Jedi*

One of the most interesting developments in Bantam's STAR WARS novels is that in their storyline, Han Solo and Princess Leia start a family. This tale reveals how the couple originally got together. Wishing to strengthen the fledgling New Republic by bringing in powerful allies, Leia opens talks with the Hapes consortium of more than sixty worlds. But the consortium is ruled by the Queen Mother, who, to Han's dismay, wants Leia to marry her son, Prince Isolder. Before this action-packed story is over, Luke will join forces with Isolder against a group of Force-trained ''witches'' and face a deadly foe.

The Empire Trilogy:
HEIR TO THE EMPIRE
DARK FORCE RISING
THE LAST COMMAND
by Timothy Zahn
Setting: Five years after *Return of the Jedi*

This #1 bestselling trilogy introduces two legendary forces of evil into the STAR WARS literary pantheon. Grand Admiral Thrawn has taken control of the Imperial fleet in the years since the destruction of the

Death Star, and the mysterious Joruus C'baoth is a fearsome Jedi Master who has been seduced by the dark side. Han and Leia have now been married for about a year, and as the story begins, she is pregnant with twins. Thrawn's plan is to crush the Rebellion and resurrect the Empire's New Order with C'baoth's help—and in return, the Dark Master will get Han and Leia's Jedi children to mold as he wishes. For as readers of this magnificent trilogy will see, Luke Skywalker is not the last of the old Jedi. He is the first of the new.

The Jedi Academy Trilogy:
JEDI SEARCH
DARK APPRENTICE
CHAMPIONS OF THE FORCE
by Kevin J. Anderson
Setting: Seven years after *Return of the Jedi*

In order to assure the continuation of the Jedi Knights, Luke Skywalker has decided to start a training facility: a Jedi Academy. He will gather Force-sensitive students who show potential as prospective Jedi and serve as their mentor, as Jedi Masters Obi-Wan Kenobi and Yoda did for him. Han and Leia's twins are now toddlers, and there is a third Jedi child: the infant Anakin, named after Luke and Leia's father. In this trilogy, we discover the existence of a powerful Imperial doomsday weapon, the horrifying Sun Crusher—which will soon become the centerpiece of a titanic struggle between Luke Skywalker and his most brilliant Jedi Academy student, who is delving dangerously into the dark side.

CHILDREN OF THE JEDI
by Barbara Hambly
Setting: Eight years after *Return of the Jedi*

The STAR WARS characters face a menace from the glory days of the Empire when a thirty-year-old automated Imperial Dreadnaught comes to life and begins its grim mission: to gather forces and annihilate a long-forgotten stronghold of Jedi children. When Luke is whisked onboard, he begins to communicate with the brave Jedi Knight who paralyzed the ship decades ago, and gave her life in the process. Now she is part of the vessel, existing in its artificial intelligence core, and guiding Luke through one of the most unusual adventures he has ever had.

DARKSABER by Kevin J. Anderson
Setting: Immediately thereafter

Not long after Children of the Jedi, *Luke and Han learn that evil Hutts are building a reconstruction of the original Death Star—and that the Empire is still alive, in the form of Daala, who has joined forces with Pellaeon, former second in command to the feared Grand Admiral Thrawn.*

PLANET OF TWILIGHT
by Barbara Hambly
Setting: Nine years after *Return of the Jedi*

Concluding the epic tale begun in her own novel Children of the Jedi *and continued by Kevin Anderson in* Darksaber, *Barbara Hambly tells the story of a ruthless enemy of the New Republic operating out of a backwater world with vast mineral deposits. The first step in his campaign is to kidnap Princess Leia. Meanwhile, as Luke Skywalker searches the planet for his long-lost love Callista, the planet begins to reveal its unspeakable secret—a secret that threatens the New Republic, the Empire, and the entire galaxy.*

The first to die was a midshipman named Koth Barak. One of his fellow crewmembers on the New Republic escort cruiser *Adamantine* found him slumped across the table in the deck-nine break room where he'd repaired half an hour previously for a cup of coffeine. Twenty minutes after Barak should have been back to post, Gunnery Sergeant Gallie Wover went looking for him.

When she entered the deck-nine break room, Sergeant Wover's first sight was of the palely flickering blue on blue of the infolog screen. "Blast it, Koth, I told you . . ."

Then she saw the young man stretched unmoving on the far side of the screen, head on the break table, eyes shut. Even at a distance of three meters Wover didn't like the way he was breathing.

"Koth!" She rounded the table in two strides, sending the other chairs clattering into a corner. She thought his eyelids moved a little when she yelled his name. "Koth!"

Wover hit the emergency call almost without conscious decision. In the few minutes before the med droids arrived she sniffed the coffeine in the gray plastene cup a few minutes from his limp fingers. It wasn't even cold.

Behind her the break room door *swoshed* open. She glanced over her shoulder to see a couple of Two-Onebees enter with a table, which was already unfurling scanners and life-support lines like a monster in a bad holovid. They shifted Barak onto the table and hooked him up. Every line of the readouts plunged, and soft, tinny alarms began to sound.

Barak's face had gone a waxen gray. The table was already pumping stimulants and antishock into the boy's veins. Wover could see the initial diagnostic lines on the screen that ringed the antigrav personnel transport unit's sides.

No virus. No bacteria. No Poison.

No foreign material in Koth Barak's body at all.

The lines dipped steadily towards zero, then went flat.

THE CRYSTAL STAR
by Vonda N. McIntyre
Setting: Ten years after *Return of the Jedi*

Leia's three children have been kidnapped. That horrible fact is made worse by Leia's realization that she can no longer sense her children through the Force! While she, Artoo-Detoo, and Chewbacca trail the kidnappers, Luke and Han discover a planet that is suffering strange quantum effects from a nearby star. Slowly freezing into a perfect crystal and disrupting the Force, the star is blunting Luke's power and crippling the Millennium Falcon. *These strands converge in an apocalyptic threat not only to the fate of the New Republic, but to the universe itself.*

The Black Fleet Crisis Trilogy:
BEFORE THE STORM
SHIELD OF LIES
TYRANT'S TEST
by Michael P. Kube-McDowell
Setting: Twelve years after *Return of the Jedi*

Long after setting up the hard-won New Republic, yesterday's Rebels have become today's administrators and diplomats. But the peace is not to last for long. A restless Luke must journey to his mother's homeworld in a desperate quest to find her people; Lando seizes a mysterious spacecraft with unimaginable weapons of destruction; and waiting in the wings is a horrific battle fleet under the control of a ruthless leader bent on a genocidal war.

THE NEW REBELLION
by Kristine Kathryn Rusch
Setting: Thirteen years after *Return of the Jedi*

Victorious though the New Republic may be, there is still no end to the threats to its continuing existence—this novel explores the price of keeping the peace. First, somewhere in the galaxy, millions suddenly perish in a blinding instant of pain. Then, as Leia prepares to address the Senate on Coruscant, a horrifying event changes the governmental equation in a flash.

Here is that latter calamity, in an early scene from The New Rebellion:

An explosion rocked the Chamber, flinging Leia into the air. She flew backward and slammed onto a desk, her entire body shuddering with the power of her hit. Blood and shrapnel rained around her. Smoke and dust rose, filling the room with a grainy darkness. She could hear nothing. With a shaking hand, she touched the side of her face. Warmth stained her cheeks and her earlobes. The ringing would start soon. The explosion was loud enough to affect her eardrums.

Emergency glow panels seared the gloom. She could feel rather than hear pieces of the crystal ceiling fall to the ground. A guard had landed beside her, his head tilted at an unnatural angle. She grabbed his blaster. She had to get out. She wasn't certain if the attack had come from within or from without. Wherever it had come from, she had to make certain no other bombs would go off.

The force of the explosion had affected her balance. She crawled over bodies, some still moving, as she made her way to the stairs. The slightest movement made her dizzy and nauseous, but she ignored the feelings. She had to.

A face loomed before hers. Streaked with dirt and blood, helmet askew, she recognized him as one of the guards who had been with her since Alderaan. *Your Highness*, he mouthed, and she couldn't read the rest. She shook her head at him, gasping at the increased dizziness, and kept going.

Finally she reached the stairs. She used the remains of a desk to get to her feet. Her gown was soaked in blood, sticky, and clinging to her legs. She held the blaster in front of her, wishing that she could hear. If she could hear, she could defend herself.

A hand reached out of the rubble beside her. She whirled, faced it, watched as Meido pulled himself out. His slender features were covered with dirt, but he appeared unharmed. He saw her blaster and cringed. She nodded once to acknowledge him, and kept moving. The guard was flanking her.

More rubble dropped from the ceiling. She crouched, hands over her head to protect herself. Small pebbles pelted her, and the floor shivered as large chunks of tile fell. Dust rose, choking her. She coughed, feeling it, but not able to hear it. Within an instant, the Hall had gone from a place of ceremonial comfort to a place of death.

The image of the death's-head mask rose in front of her again, this time from memory. She had known this was going to happen. Somewhere, from some part of her Force-sensitive brain, she had seen this. Luke said that Jedi were sometimes able to see the future. But she had never completed her training. She wasn't a Jedi.

But she was close enough.

The Corellian Trilogy:
AMBUSH AT CORELLIA
ASSAULT AT SELONIA
SHOWDOWN AT CENTERPOINT
by Roger MacBride Allen
Setting: Fourteen years after *Return of the Jedi*

This trilogy takes us to Corellia, Han Solo's homeworld, which Han has not visited in quite some time. A trade summit brings Han, Leia, and the children—now developing their own clear personalities and instinctively learning more about their innate skills in the Force—into the middle of a situation that most closely resembles a burning fuse. The Corellian system is on the brink of civil war, there are New Republic intelligence agents on a mysterious mission which even Han does not understand, and worst of all, a fanatical rebel leader has his hands on a superweapon of unimaginable power—and just wait until you find out who that leader is!

SPECTER OF THE PAST
and coming soon,
VISION OF THE FUTURE
by Timothy Zahn
Setting: Nineteen years after *Star Wars: A New Hope*

The new, two-book series by the undisputed master of the STAR WARS novel. Once the supreme master of countless star systems, the Empire is tottering on the brink of total collapse. Day by day, neutral systems are rushing to join the New Republic coalition. But with the end of the war in sight, the New Republic has fallen victim to it own success. An unwieldy alliance of races and traditions, the confederation now finds itself riven by age-old animosities. Princess Leia struggles against all odds to hold the New Republic together. But she has powerful enemies. An ambitious Moff Disra leads a conspiracy to divide the uneasy coalition with an ingenious plot to blame the Bothans for a heinous crime that could lead to genocide and civil war. At the same time, Luke Skywalker, along with Lando Calrissian and Talon Karrde, pursues a mysterious group of pirate ships whose crew consists of clones. And then comes the worst news of all: the most cunning and ruthless warlord in Imperial history has returned to lead the Empire to triumph. Here's an exciting scene from Timothy Zahn's spectacular new STAR WARS novel:

"I don't think you fully understand the political situation the New Republic finds itself in these days. A flash point like Caamas—especially with Bothan involvement—will bring the whole thing to a boil. Particularly if we can give it the proper nudge."

"The situation among the Rebels is not the issue," Tierce countered coldly. "It's the state of the Empire *you* don't seem to understand. Simply tearing the Rebellion apart isn't going to rebuild the Emperor's New Order. We need a focal point, a leader around whom the Imperial forces can rally."

Disra said, "Suppose I could provide such a leader. Would you be willing to join us?"

Tierce eyed him. "Who is this 'us' you refer to?"

"If you join, there would be three of us," Disra said. "Three who would share the secret I'm prepared to offer you. A secret that will bring the entire Fleet onto our side."

Tierce smiled cynically. "You'll forgive me, Your Excellency, if I suggest you couldn't inspire blind loyalty in a drugged bantha."

Disra felt a flash of anger. How dare this common soldier—?

"No," he agreed, practically choking out the word from between clenched teeth. Tierce was hardly a common soldier, after all. More importantly, Disra desperately needed a man of his skills and training. "I would merely be the political power behind the throne. Plus the supplier of military men and matériel, of course."

"From the Braxant Sector Fleet?"

"And other sources," Disra said. "You, should you choose to join us, would serve as the architect of our overall strategy."

"I see." If Tierce was bothered by the word "serve," he didn't show it. "And the third person?"

"Are you with us?"

Tierce studied him. "First tell me more."

"I'll do better than tell you." Disra pushed his chair back and stood up. "I'll show you."

Disra led the way down the rightmost corridor. It ended in a dusty metal door with a wheel set into its center. Gripping the edges of the wheel, Disra turned; and with a creak that echoed eerily in the confined space the door swung open.

The previous owner would hardly have recognized his onetime torture chamber. The instruments of pain and terror had been taken out, the walls and floor cleaned and carpet-insulated, and the furnishings of a fully functional modern apartment installed.

But for the moment Disra had no interest in the chamber itself. All his attention was on Tierce as the former Guardsman stepped into the room.

Stepped into the room . . . and caught sight of the room's single occupant, seated in the center in a duplicate of a Star Destroyer's captain's chair.

Tierce froze, his eyes widening with shock, his entire body stiffening as if a power current had jolted through him. His eyes darted to Disra, back to the captain's chair, flicked around the room as if seeking evidence of a trap or hallucination or perhaps his own insanity, back again to the chair. Disra held his breath . . .